THE ETERNAL CHAMPION

BY MICHAEL MOORCOCK

Published by:

White Wolf Inc.
4598 Stonegate Industrial Boulevard
Stone Mountain, Georgia 30083

White Wolf Fiction

Editor: Stewart Wieck
Assistant Editor: Staley Krause
Sales: Michael Krause
Marketing: Wes Harris
Art Director: Richard Thomas
Graphic Designer: Michelle Prahler

ISBN: 1-56504-176-3

Printed in the United States.

First hardcover edition September 1994

For further information about Michael Moorcock and his work,
please send a stamped, self-addressed envelope to
Nomads of the Time Streams, P.O. Box 5201 Pinehurst, NC 28374.

THE ETERNAL CHAMPION

By Michael Moorcock

I found in dreams a place of wind and flowers,
  Full of sweet trees and colour of glad grass,
  In midst whereof there was
A lady clothed like summer with sweet hours.
Her beauty, fervent as a fiery moon,
  Made my blood burn and swoon
        Like a flame rained upon.
Sorrow had filled her shaken eyelids' blue
And her mouth's sad red heavy rose all through
  Seemed sad with glad things gone.

She held a little cithern by the strings,
  Shaped heartwise, strung with subtle-coloured
hair
  Of some dead lute player
That in dead years had done delicious things.
The seven strings were named accordingly;
  The first string charity,
        The second tenderness,
The rest were pleasure, sorrow, sleep, and sin,
And loving kindness, that is pity's kin
  And is most pitiless.

Ernest Wheldrake, "A Ballad of Life,"
from *Tanalorn, an Elegy*, 1868

CONTENTS

INTRODUCTION

Dear Reader,

Most writers of imaginative fiction are occasionally asked where they get their ideas. Terry Pratchett claimed that his came from a warehouse in Croydon, England, while Harlan Ellison would tell people that his arrived every month from a mysterious mail-order place in Peoria, Illinois.

The truth is, of course, that a writer's ideas come from a whole variety of sources, not all of them conscious, including, if the writer is lucky, from some consistent inner vision.

Writers are sometimes tempted to claim illustrious antecedents — at least one best-selling tolkienoid claims Henry James as a model — and forget early inspiration like comic books, movies, tv series and pulp fiction. One's influences can also include, perfectly legitimately and coherently, the plays of Shakespeare, the novels of Dickens and Balzac, the films of Bergman and Kurosawa and the cartoons of Walt Disney. Human beings are influenced by all experience and one's writing has as much to do with environment as reading.

I have always been glad to celebrate the many writers who inspired me as I was growing up. I wrote the first version of *The Eternal Champion* when I was seventeen. The second version appeared as a novella in SCIENCE FANTASY magazine, 1962, and the book version was first published in the U.S. in 1970. Since then I have revised the story twice, for the new U.S. edition of 1978 and for the British omnibus sequence in 1992. This is the third, and almost certainly last, version, which I hope will be definitive. Like Tanelorn and like the multiverse (created in *The Sundered Worlds*) and the Realms of Law and Chaos (acknowledgments to John Milton, Poul Anderson & c,) the Tale of the Eternal Champion is constantly malleable, constantly subject to change,

THE ETERNAL CHAMPION

constantly open to fresh interpretation. This new edition of the sequence (consisting of 15 omnibus volumes) attempts to put some sort of linear form on a sequence that is fundamentally non-linear. The order was arrived at after much discussion with John Davey, who has been invaluable in preparing this project.

The Eternal Champion was inspired by Sir Walter Scott, H. Rider Haggard, Robert E. Howard, W.B. Yeats and Edgar Rice Burroughs. It was inspired by the Hollywood and London epics of De Mille, Korda and Curtiz, by an intense reading of 19th century Romantic poetry, especially Shelley and Swinburne, of Gothic fiction by Maturin, Lewis or Radcliffe.

Amongst my non-literary inspirations for the refinements of the Cosmic Balance, the ideas of Law and Chaos and the rest of the cosmology associated with *The Eternal Champion* (which I continue to explore and develop) I've been most recently indebted to Benoit Mandelbrot's *Fractal Geometry of Nature*, but I suspect my original inspiration came from the writings of that gentle philosopher Rudolf Steiner. From the age of seven, until I was expelled, I attended Michael Hall school in Sussex. The school was run on Steiner's "anthroposophical" Christian principles. (I was expelled, ironically, for running away.) While by no means an anthroposophist, I have continued to be guided by the ideals and moral principles which Michael Hall and Steiner's visionary writings inspired in me, though I have had little exposure to more orthodox Christianity.

That is not to say that these particular stories should be mined for extra meanings or profound moral statements. Their first purpose is to entertain on as varied a level as possible. In the course of a fairly long career I have had the chance to develop my ideas of the multiverse and the Eternal Champion. I have been able to make use of the symbols and storytelling techniques these ideas provided. But finally a story must be about human beings, no matter how strange their environment, and moral abstractions must take physical shape if they are to have a legitimate place in fiction.

The moral point of *The Eternal Champion* is pretty simple but I think it is worth mentioning. Recently, in a radio interview, I was asked if my use of the forces of Law and Chaos was not, after all, merely another version of Tolkien's or Howard's Good and Evil. I replied emphatically — I use the ideas of Law and Chaos precisely because I am suspicious of simplistic notions of good and evil. In my multiverse, Law and Chaos are both legitimate ways of interpreting and defining experience. Ideally, the Cosmic Balance keeps both sides in equilibrium. By playing "the Game of Time" (or the Blood-Red Game as Asquiol calls it) the various participants maintain that equilibrium. When the scales tip too far towards Law we move toward rigid orthodoxy and social sterility, a form of decadence. When Chaos is uppermost we move too far towards undisciplined and destructive creativity. The Elizabethan ideal of social Moderation, of Harmony in Nature and so on, which I discussed in *Gloriana; or, The Unfulfilled Queen*, is that perfect balance between these two great forces.

Milton, said William Blake, was "of Satan's party but did not know it" because Milton showed evil as attractive and convincing, explaining why a significant portion of the Heavenly Host was willing to lose God's grace by joining Satan in his rebellion. I'm also of that old-fashioned persuasion which believes evil can't be addressed unless it is understood and can't be credible unless it's described. In my view society only ever does itself harm by refusing to address issues and by demonising those it fails to understand. The drug economy and culture will never, for instance, be properly understood until it is examined as the complex and sophisticated phenomenon it is. The simplistic follies of recent governments have done enormous harm to our societies and are characteristic of any formulaic politics, whether from left or right. If the people at the top think that reaching for a gun will solve the problem, why shouldn't the people at the bottom think the same?

My work has, I'll admit, always been fired by a degree of anger at society's follies. I must confess to a taste for the great ranting English visionaries, in particular John Bunyan, whose *Pilgrim's Progress* had an enormous effect on me as a child, and was the first book I bought with my own money, but that element has never I hope interfered with my storytelling.

The Eternal Champion was the first book I ever planned to write. It is the cornerstone of my heroic fantasy sequence and in some ways a key to my other, more ambitious, novels.

Stylistically this romance is one of my least complex. As a story it is one of my simplest. However, since it is the starting point for so many other stories, these qualities are probably virtues. It is the "first" book in the Eternal Champion cycle which includes eight Elric books, seven Hawkmoon books, six Corum books, three Michael Kane books, the von Bek books, the stories of Jack Karaquazian and his associates, several science fiction novels and record albums and, more or less directly, almost all my other books, where the idea is often used as metaphor. Together with the idea of the multiverse and Tanelorn, it forms the chief rationale and central symbol to my fiction. In recent years, of course, with the Cornelius books, the Oswald Bastable books, the Dancers at the End of Time and others, these ideas have also provided a kind of ironic counterpoint.

The "multiverse" (the Ghost Worlds of the first romance) is a multitude of alternative universes intersecting sometimes with our own and to which, of course, our own belongs — an infinite number of slightly different versions of reality in which one is likely to come across a slightly different version of oneself. In its more sophisticated use this enables me to deal in non-linear terms with varieties of perception, to make, in the few didactic books I've written, simplified models of ideal worlds to show, I hope, by what particular injustices and hypocrisies those worlds might be maintained.

By using these devices to connect one book with another, I hope to look at a number of different aspects of the same theme while firmly linking the most outrageous fables with experience of the world we all share. Thanks to these ideas, I have characters who can move easily between this world and all the others without any sense of discrepancy or incoherence.

The Eternal Champion is not one of my ambitious books, but it is central to my work for the reasons I have described. It contains in simplistic form many of the themes of more complicated novels and a fair amount of their atmosphere. *The Eternal Champion* is in one sense the shout of a young man who finds the world a more complicated place than he imagined and feels, therefore, betrayed. Betrayal is certainly one of its primary themes, as in so many of my fantasy romances, from the Elric stories onwards, but the simple message has always been the same: We are not betrayed by others — we betray ourselves by too readily accepting orthodoxy, whether it comes from politicians or CNN. Jerry Cornelius, that most ambitious of all the Champion's aspects, is forever brought low by his own ego, by his willingness to live according to the formulae of his society's myths and fantasies. In this sense, most of my books are anti-romantic.

The Eternal Champion has proved a useful jumping off point not only for a number of books, but also for a rock stage-show with Hawkwind (parts of which are on the record *Warrior on the Edge of Time*), a film script (so far unshot), posters and cards, various games, comics and stories by different writers and a set of toy soldiers! The Champion is a kind of romantic Everyman (or, often, Everywoman) whose struggles and confusions reflect, very broadly, those which most of us experience. I am making no claims here for this particular sequence, which is essentially an escapist romance, written in more innocent days, but I am glad of the opportunity to publish a new edition, with an introduction which gives me the chance to answer a few of the questions asked by readers, many of whom are sometimes puzzled by the apparent disparity between the different forms in which I work.

To Rescue Tanelorn... is included here because it is the first time that I introduced that mysterious, malleable city of peace. For me Tanelorn represents one's coherent inner self, that core of silence and understanding most of us eventually find, a place to which we can return when we need to, and take stock of ourselves and our world — a place, if you like, where the soul can rest and recover. It is one of the few stories I ever wrote under the influence of William Morris (another of my heroes) and Lord Dunsany.

This will be the first time a U.S. edition of *The Sundered Worlds* will have been copy-edited and proofread before publication and it will be the first time I read it since I was 21, when I wrote it as a two-parter for E.J. Carnell's SCIENCE FICTION ADVENTURES, meant to be the last of the British pulps but which kept slipping from its lowly intentions by publishing stories such as "The Drowned World" by J.G. Ballard. I believe my story brought the standards of the magazine back to a level more appropriate to its title. I wrote it in thirty-six hours and have a feeling that the best bits were inspired by my friend Barrington Bayley. It is a space opera in the tradition of the fiction I always preferred to the more respectable stuff found in my boyhood's interminable introductory anthologies which sought to broaden the popularity and literary acceptability of science fiction. I liked PLANET STORIES best, then STARTLING STORIES and then THRILLING WONDER STORIES. Not for me the carefully tailored stories of THE MAGAZINE OF FANTASY AND SCIENCE FICTION. I wanted *Queen of the Martian Catacombs* and moody men riding oddly shaped beasts across the achingly beautiful desolation of the Martian landscape where always awaiting them was a mysterious sorceress drawing her powers from an ancient, pre-human science.

Donald A. Wollheim, who enthusiastically published so much of that stuff (including mine) used to accuse me of being a pseudo-intellectual bent on killing the tree of science fiction at its roots. He could never reconcile my enthusiasm for his favorite authors with my policies in *New Worlds*, the avante garde magazine with which I'm still associated.

What he didn't understand was that I was trying, in common with Judith Merril, Cele Goldsmith, Harlan Ellison, Samuel R. Delany, Roger Zelazny and others in the U.S., to get some of that sense of wonder back into a genre which, we thought, had grown moribund and prone to a kind of literary Uncle Tomism for which I — welcoming the pulps in the same way that, in common with so many others of my generation, I embraced rock and roll — had no patience. I didn't want sf to become respectable. The previous generation of writers was a bit like middle-class jazz-men chuckling at the antics of Elvis Presley and smugly confident that the public would eventually come back to The Original Dixieland Stompers. Again in common with what would be called "the

Alternative Society," we rejected what we saw as the bland conventions of the genre and took our inspiration from those romantic queens of the space opera, Catherine L. Moore and Leigh Brackett who, with the likes of Jack Williamson, Edmond Hamilton, Charles Harness, Alfred Bester and Philip K. Dick, ruled the pulps I grew up reading. This was pretty much the only kind of science fiction I ever enjoyed.

I was perfectly happy to write some myself when Carnell suggested it (as he had suggested I write the Elric stories). It was how I learned that the form was harder to write well than I had guessed and that it didn't really lend itself to many of my literary aspirations. But, like *The Eternal Champion*, which I wrote around the same time, it gave me the frame for later, more sophisticated ideas.

I've been told by people well-educated in these matters that I had predicted in *The Sundered Worlds* such marvelous discoveries and inventions as black holes, quasars, Chaos Theory, VR, RPGs, cyberpunk and other monumental developments of late-20th century science and society. My vanity was hugely flattered by this (which, of course, is why I retail it) but in justice I could only claim that consciously I had invented only one thing in *The Sundered Worlds*, a neologism, viz: The Multiverse, to describe the idea of the near infinity of co-existing space-time continua each fractionally different, in which certain struggles and stories are played out through eternity, on a vast number of planes of existence.

Unfortunately, I now know that I didn't invent the term either. According to the current *SF Encyclopedia*, John Cowper Powys came up with it in, I believe, 1957. For this discovery I am indebted to the critic, editor and novelist John Clute.

It would also have been nice, too, to have claimed a wonderful prescience derived from an assiduous reading of advanced scientific theory, or even that I was the first freak on Ladbroke Grove to drop the acid that inspired the visions. But I must thank David Britton of Savoy Editions, a fellow migraine sufferer, who reminded me that videos of Julia and Mandelbrot sets resembled exactly the hallucinations you get during a bad attack. The videos have all the gain and none of the pain.

Shortly after *The Sundered Worlds* was published I was at a science fiction convention where I learned that the guests of honor, Leigh Brackett and her husband Edmond Hamilton, were asking to meet me. Delighted, I was introduced to those great stylists of the pulp magazines, who brought the highest standards of craftsmanship and talent to their romances. Leigh told me how much she had enjoyed the story and Ed pumped me warmly by the hand. "I just wanted," he said, "to congratulate the man who beat me at my own game. They called me 'the galaxy smasher,' but you, Michael, you destroyed *the entire universe*!" I have never had more welcome praise.

I have dedicated other books to Leigh and Ed, who became good friends, so I dedicate this one (originally dedicated to Barrington J. Bayley who remains our greatest living writer of metaphysical "hard" sf since Olaf Stapleton) to John Clute.

My special thanks must go to the people who made this edition a reality: to Ed Kramer (the broker); to Stewart Wieck (the publisher at White Wolf); to John Davey, whose editing work has been significant; and to my wife Linda, who spent far more time in the multiverse than, I suspect, she ever meant to. And, as always, my thanks to the readers, whose comments are always listened to and whose suggestions have helped me prepare this new edition.

Yours,
Michael Moorcock
Lost Pines,
Texas.
May 1994

THE ETERNAL CHAMPION

THE ETERNAL CHAMPION

To the memory of Douglas Fairbanks, the greatest hero of them all.

PROLOGUE

THEY CALLED FOR ME.

That is all I really know.

They called for me and I went to them. I could not do otherwise. The will of the whole of humanity was a strong thing. It smashed through the ties of time and the chains of space and dragged me to hell.

Why was I chosen? I still do not know, though they believed they had told me. Now it is done and I am here. I shall always be here. And if, as wise men tell me, time is cyclic, then I shall one day return to part of the cycle I knew as the twentieth century, for (it was no wish of mine) I am immortal.

O N E

A CALL ACROSS TIME

Between wakefulness and sleeping we have most of us had the illusion of hearing voices, scraps of conversation, phrases spoken in unfamiliar tones. Sometimes we attempt to attune our minds so that we can hear more, but we are rarely successful. These illusions are called "hypnagogic hallucinations" — the beginning of the dreams we shall later experience as we sleep.

There was a woman. A child. A city. An occupation. A name: John Daker. A sense of frustration. A need for fulfillment. Though I loved them. I know I loved them.

It was in the winter. I lay miserably in a cold bed and I stared through the window at the moon. I do not remember my exact thoughts. Something to do with morality and the futility of human existence, no doubt. Then, between wakefulness and sleeping, I began every night to hear voices...

At first I dismissed them, expecting to fall immediately asleep, but they continued and I began trying to listen to them, thinking, perhaps, to receive some message from my unconscious. But the most commonly repeated word was gibberish to me:

Erekosë... Erekosë... Erekosë...

I could not recognize the language, though it had a peculiar familiarity. The closest language I could place it with was the language of Sioux Indians, but I knew only a few words of Sioux.

Erekosë... Erekosë... Erekosë...

Each night I redoubled my efforts to concentrate on the voices and gradually I began to experience much stronger hypnagogic hallucinations, until one night it seemed that I broke free from my body altogether.

Had I hung for an eternity in limbo? Was I alive — dead? Was there a memory of a world that lay in the far past or the distant future? Of another world which seemed closer? And the names? Was I John Daker or Erekosë? Was I either of these? Many other names — Corum Jhaelen Irsei, Aubec, Sexton Begg, Elric, Rackhir, Iliam, Oona, Simon, Bastable, Cornelius, the Rose, von Bek, Asquiol, Hawkmoon — fled away down the ghostly rivers of my memory. I hung in darkness, bodiless. A man spoke. Where was he? I tried to look but had no eyes with which to see...

"Erekosë the Champion, where are you?"
Another voice: "Father... it is only a legend..."
"No, Iolinda. I feel he is listening. Erekosë..."

I tried to answer, but I had no tongue with which to speak.

Then there were swirling half-dreams of a house in a great city of miracles; a swollen, grimy city of miracles, crammed with dull-colored machines, many of which bore human passengers. There were buildings, beautiful beneath their coatings of dust, and there were other, brighter buildings not so beautiful, with austere lines and many windows. There were screams and loud noises.

There was a troop of riders galloping over undulating countryside, flamboyant in armour of lacquered gold, coloured pennants draped around their blood-encrusted lances. Their faces were heavy with weariness.

Then there were more faces, many faces. Some of them I half-recognized. Others were completely unfamiliar. Many of these were dressed in strange clothes. I saw a white-haired man in middle age. He wore a tall, spiked crown of iron and diamonds upon his head. His mouth moved. He was speaking...

"Erekosë. It is I—King Rigenos, Defender of Humanity...
"You are needed again, Erekosë. The Hounds of Evil rule a third of the world and humankind is weary with the war against them. Come to us, Erekosë. Lead us to victory. From the Plains of Melting Ice to the Mountains of Sorrow they have set up their corrupt standard and I fear they will advance yet farther into our territories.
"Come to us, Erekosë: Lead us to victory. Come to us Erekosë. Lead us..."
The woman's voice:

THE ETERNAL CHAMPION

"Father. This is only an empty tomb. Not even the mummy of Erekosë remains. It became drifting dust long ago. Let us leave and return to Necranal to marshal the living peers!"

I felt like a fainting man who strives to fight against dizzy oblivion but, however much he tries, cannot take control of his own brain. Again I tried to answer, but could not.

It was as if I wavered backwards through Time, while every atom of me wanted to go forward. I had the sensation of vast size, as if I were made of stone with eyelids of granite that measured miles across—eyelids which I could not open.

And then I was tiny: the most minute grain in the universe. And yet I felt I belonged to the whole far more than did the stone giant.

Memories came and went.

The panorama of the twentieth century, its discoveries and its deceits, its beauties and its bitterness, its satisfactions, its strife, its self-delusion, its superstitious fancies to which it gave the name of Science, rushed into my mind like air into a vacuum.

But it was only momentary, for the next second my entire being was flung elsewhere — to a world which was Earth, but not the Earth of John Daker, not quite the world of dead Erekosë...

There were three great continents. Two close together were divided from the third by a vast sea containing many islands, large and small.

I saw an ocean of ice which I knew to be slowly shrinking — the Plains of Melting Ice.

I saw the third continent, which bore lush flora, mighty forests, blue lakes and which was bound along its northern coasts by a towering chain of mountains — the Mountains of Sorrow. This I knew to be the domain of the Eldren, whom King Rigenos had called the Hounds of Evil.

Now, on the other two continents, I saw the wheatlands of the West on the continent of Zavara, with their tall cities of multicoloured rock, their rich cities — Stalaco, Calodemia, Mooros, Ninadoon and Dratarda.

There were the great seaports — Shilaal, Wedmah, Sinana, Tarkar — and Noonos with her towers cobbled in precious stones.

Then I saw the fortress cities of the continent of Necralala, with the capital city Necranal chief among them, built on, into and about a mighty mountain, peaked by the spreading palace of its warrior kings.

Now I began to remember as, in the background of my awareness, I heard a voice calling, *"Erekosë, Erekosë, Erekosë…"*

The warrior kings of Necranal, kings for two thousand years of a humanity united, at war, and united again. The warrior kings of whom King Rigenos was the last living — and aging now, with only a daughter, Iolinda, to carry on his line. Old and weary with hate — but still hating. Hating the unhuman folk whom he called the Hounds of Evil, mankind's age-old enemies, reckless and wild; linked, it was said, by a thin line of blood to the human race — an outcome of a union between an ancient queen and the Evil One, Azmobaana. Hated by King Rigenos as soulless immortals, slaves of Azmobaana's machinations.

And, hating, he called upon John Daker, whom he named Erekosë, to aid him with his war against them.

"Erekosë, I beg thee answer me. Are you ready to come?" His voice was loud and echoing, and when, after a struggle, I could reply, my own voice seemed to echo, also.

"I am ready," I replied, "but seem to be chained."

"Chained?" There was consternation in his voice. *"Are you, then, a prisoner of Azmobaana's frightful minions? Are you trapped upon the Ghost Worlds?"*

"Perhaps," I said. "But I do not think so. It is Space and Time which chain me. I am separated from you by a gulf without form or dimension."

"How may we bridge that gulf and bring you to us?"

"The united wills of Humanity may serve the purpose."

"Already we pray that you may come to us."

"Then continue," I said.

I was falling away again. I thought I remembered laughter, sadness, pride. Then, suddenly, more faces. I felt as if I witnessed the passing of everyone I had known, down the ages, and then one face superimposed itself over the others — the head and shoulders of an amazingly beautiful woman, with blonde hair piled beneath a diadem of precious stones which seemed to light the sweetness of her oval face. "Iolinda," I said.

I saw her more solidly now. She was clinging to the arm of the tall, gaunt man who wore the crown of iron and diamonds: King Rigenos.

They stood before an empty platform of quartz and gold and resting on a cushion of dust was a straight sword which they dared not touch. Neither did they dare step too close to it, for it gave off a radiation which might slay them.

It was a tomb in which they stood.

The tomb of Erekosë. My tomb.

I moved toward the platform, hanging over it.

Ages before, my body had been placed there. I stared at the sword, which held no dangers for me, but I was unable, in my captivity, to pick it up. It was my spirit only which inhabited that dark place — but the whole of my spirit now, not the fragment which had inhabited the tomb for thousands of years. That fragment had heard King Rigenos and had enabled John Daker to hear it, to come to it, to be united with it.

"Erekosë!" called the king, straining his eyes through the gloom as if he had seen me. "Erekosë! We pray."

Then I experienced the dreadful pain which I supposed must be like that of a woman experiencing childbirth, a pain that seemed eternal and yet was intrinsically its own vanquisher. I was screaming, writhing in the air above them. Great spasms of agony — but an agony complete with purpose — the purpose of creation.

I shrieked. But there was joy in my cry.

I groaned. But there was triumph there.

I grew heavy and I reeled. I grew heavier and heavier and I gasped, stretching out my arms to balance myself.

I had flesh and I had muscle and I had blood and I had strength. The strength coursed through me and I took a huge breath and touched my body. It was a powerful body, tall and fit.

I looked up. I stood before them in the flesh. I was their god and I had returned.

"I have come," I said. "I am here, King Rigenos. I have left nothing worthwhile behind me, but do not let me regret that leaving."

"You will not regret it, Champion." He was pale, exhilarated, smiling. I looked at Iolinda, who dropped her eyes modestly and then, as if against her will, raised them again to regard me. I turned to the dais on my right.

"My sword," I said, reaching for it.

I heard King Rigenos sigh with satisfaction.

"They are doomed now, the dogs," he said.

"THE CHAMPION HAS COME!"

They had a sheath for the sword. It had been made days before. King Rigenos left to get it, leaving me alone with his daughter.

Now that I was here, I did not think to question how I came and why it should have been possible. Neither, it seemed, did she question the fact. I was there. It seemed inevitable.

We regarded one another silently until the king returned with the scabbard.

"This will protect us against your sword's poison," he said.

He held it out to me. For a moment I hesitated before stretching my own hand toward it and accepting it.

The king frowned and looked at the ground. Then he folded his arms across his chest.

I held the scabbard in my two hands. It was opaque, like old glass, but the metal was unfamiliar to me — or rather to John Daker. It was light, flexible and strong.

I turned and picked up the sword. The handle was bound in gold thread and was vibrant to my touch. The pommel was a globe of deep red onyx and the hilt was worked in strips of silver and black onyx. The blade was long and straight and sharp, but it did not shine like steel. Instead, in color, it resembled lead. The sword was beautifully balanced and I swung it through the air and laughed aloud, and it seemed to laugh with me.

"Erekosë! Sheathe it!" cried King Rigenos in alarm. "Sheathe it! The radiation is death to all but yourself!"

I was reluctant now to put the sword away. The feel of it awakened a dim remembrance.

"Erekosë! Please! I beg you!" Iolinda's voice echoed her father's. "Sheathe the sword!"

Reluctantly I slid the sword into its scabbard. Why was I the only one who could wear the sword without being affected by its radiation?

Was it because, in that transition from my own age to this, I had become constitutionally different in some way? Was it that the ancient Erekosë and the unborn John Daker (or was it vice versa?) had metabolisms which had adapted to protect themselves against the power which flowed from the sword?

I shrugged. It did not matter. The fact itself was enough. I was unconcerned. It was as if I was aware that my fate had been taken almost entirely out of my own hands. I had become a tool.

If only I had known then to what use the tool would be put, then I might have fought against the pull and remained the harmless intellectual, John Daker. But perhaps I could not have fought and won. The power that drew me to this age was very great.

At any rate, I was prepared at that moment to do whatever Fate demanded of me. I stood where I had materialized, in the tomb of Erekosë, and I reveled in my strength and in my sword.

Later, things were to change.

"I will need clothes," I said, for I was naked. "And armour. And a steed. I am Erekosë."

"Clothes have been prepared," said King Rigenos. He clapped his hands. "Here."

The slaves entered. One carried a robe, another a cloak, another a white cloth which I gathered had to serve for underwear. They wrapped the cloth around my lower quarters and slipped the robe over my head. It was loose and cool and felt pleasant on my skin. It was deep blue, with complicated designs stitched into it in gold, silver and scarlet thread. The cloak was scarlet, with designs of gold, silver and blue. They gave me soft boots of doeskin to put on my feet, and a wide belt of light brown leather with an iron buckle in which were set rubies and sapphires, and I hung my scabbard on this. Then I gripped the sword with my left fist.

"I am ready," I said.

Iolinda shuddered. "Then let us leave this gloomy place," she murmured.

With one last look back at the dais on which the heap of dust still lay, I walked with the king and the Princess of Necranal out of my own tomb and into a calm day that, while warm, had a light breeze blowing. We were standing on a small hill. Behind us the tomb, apparently built of black quartz, looked time-worn and ancient, pitted by the passing of many storms and many winds. On its roof was the corroded statue of a warrior mounted on a great battle charger. The face had been smoothed by dust and rain, but I knew it. It was my face.

I looked away.

Below us a caravan was waiting. There were the richly caparisoned horses and a guard of men dressed in that same golden armour I had seen in my dreams. These warriors, however, were fresher-looking than the others. Their armour was fluted, embellished with raised designs, ornate and beautiful but, according to my sparse reading on the subject of armour, coupled with Erekosë's stirring memory, totally unsuitable for war. The fluting and embossing acted as a trap to catch the point of a spear or sword, whereas armour should be made to turn a point. This armour, for all its beauty, acted more as an extra danger than a protection.

The guards were mounted on heavy war horses, but the beasts that knelt awaiting us resembled a kind of camel from which all the camel's lumpen ugliness had been bred. These beasts were beautiful. On their high backs were cabins of ebony, ivory and mother-of-pearl, curtained in scintillating silks.

We walked down the hill and, as we walked, I noticed that I still had on my finger the ring that I had worn as John Daker, a ring of woven silver that my wife had given me. My wife — I could not recall her face. I felt I should have left the ring behind me, on that other body. But perhaps there is no body left behind.

We reached the kneeling beasts and the guards stiffened their backs to acknowledge our arrival. I saw curiosity in many of the eyes that looked at me.

King Rigenos gestured toward one of the beasts. "Would you care to take your cabin, Champion?" Though he himself had summoned me, he seemed to be slightly wary of me.

"Thank you." I climbed the little ladder of plaited silk and entered the cabin. It was completely lined with deep cushions of a variety of hues.

The camels climbed to their feet and we began to move swiftly through a narrow valley whose sides were lined with evergreen trees which I could not name — something like spreading monkey-puzzle trees, but with more branches and broader leaves.

I had laid my sword across my knees. I inspected it. It was a plain soldier's sword, having no markings on the blade. The hilt fitted perfectly into my right hand as I gripped it. It was a good sword. But why it was poisonous to others I did not know. Presumably it was also lethal to those whom King Rigenos called the Hounds of Evil — the Eldren.

As we traveled through the soft day I drowsed on my cushions, feeling strangely weary, until I heard a cry and pushed back the curtains of my cabin to look ahead.

There was Necranal, the city which I had seen in my dreams.

Far away still, it towered upwards so that the entire mountain upon which it was built was hidden by its wondrous architecture. Minarets, steeples, domes and battlements shone in the sun and above them all loomed the huge palace of the warrior kings, a noble structure, many-towered, the Palace of Ten Thousand Windows. I remembered the name.

I saw King Rigenos peer from his own cabin and cry: "Katorn! Ride ahead and tell the people that Erekosë the Champion has come to drive the Evil Ones back to the Mountains of Sorrow!"

The man he addressed was a sullen-faced individual, doubtless the Captain of the Imperial Guard. "Aye, sire," he growled.

He drew his horse out of line and galloped speedily along the road of white dust which wound now down an incline. I could see the road stretching for many miles into the distance toward Necranal. I watched the rider for a while but wearied of this eventually and instead strained my eyes to make out details in that great city structure.

The cities of London, New York or Tokyo were probably bigger in area, but not much. Necranal was spread around the base of the mountain for many miles. Surrounding the city was a high wall upon which turrets were mounted at intervals.

So, at last, we came to the great main gate of Necranal and our caravan halted.

A musical instrument sounded and the gates began to swing open. We passed through into streets packed with jostling, cheering people who shouted so loudly I was forced, at times, to cover my ears for fear they would rupture.

T H R E E

THE ELDREN THREAT

Now the cheering gradually fell away as the little caravan ascended the winding road to the Palace of Ten Thousand Windows. A silence settled and I heard only the creak of the howdah in which I sat, the occasional jingle of harness or the clatter of a horse's hoof. I began to feel discomfited. There was something about the mood of the city that was not altogether sane and which could not be explained away in conventional terms. Certainly the people were afraid of enemy attack; certainly they were weary with fighting. But it seemed to me that this mood held something morbid — a mixture of hysterical elation and melancholic depression that I had sensed only once before in my previous life, during my single visit to a mental hospital.

Or perhaps I was merely imposing my own mood on my surroundings. After all, it could be argued that I was experiencing classic paranoid-schizophrenic symptoms! A man with two or more well-defined identities, who also happened to be considered, in this world, the potential saviour of mankind! For a moment I wondered if in fact I had not gone completely insane, if this were not some monstrous delusion, if I were not *actually* at this moment in the very madhouse I had once visited!

I touched the draperies, my scabbarded sword; I peered out at the vast city now stretched out below me; I stared at the huge bulk of the Palace of Ten Thousand Windows above me. I attempted to see beyond them, deliberately assuming that they were an illusion, expecting to see the walls of a hospital room, or even the familiar walls of my own apartment. But the Palace of Ten Thousand Windows remained as solid as ever. The city of Necranal had none of the qualities of a mirage. I sank back in my cushions. I had to assume that this was real, that I had been transported somehow across the ages and through space to this Earth of which there were no records in any history book I had ever read (and I had read many) and of which there were only echoes in myths and legends.

I was no longer John Daker. I was Erekosë — the Eternal Champion.

A legend myself, come to life.

I laughed then. If I were mad, then it was a glorious madness, a madness of which I would never have considered myself capable of inventing!

At length our caravan arrived at the summit of the mountain and the jeweled gates of the palace opened for us and we passed inside a splendid courtyard in which trees grew and fountains played, feeding little rivers spanned by ornamental bridges. Fish swam in the rivers and birds sang in the trees as pages came forward to make our beasts kneel down and we stepped out into the evening light.

King Rigenos smiled with pride as he gestured around the great courtyard. "You like this, Erekosë? I had it built myself, shortly after I came to the throne. The courtyard was a gloomy sort of place until then — it did not fit with the rest of the palace."

"It is very beautiful," I said. I turned to look at Iolinda, who had joined us. "And not the only beautiful thing you have helped create — for here is the most beautiful adornment to your palace!"

King Rigenos chuckled. "You are a courtier as well as a warrior, I see." He took my arm and Iolinda's and guided us across the courtyard. "Of course, I have little time these days to consider the creation of beauty. It is weapons we must create now. Instead of plans for gardens, I must concern myself with battle plans." He sighed. "Perhaps you will drive the Eldren away forever, Erekosë. Perhaps, when they are destroyed, we shall be able to enjoy the peaceful things of life again.

I felt sorry for him at that moment. He only wanted what every man wanted — freedom from fear, a chance to raise children with a reasonable certainty that they would be allowed to do the same, a chance to look forward to the future without the knowledge that any plans made might be wrecked forever by some sudden act of violence. His world, after all, was not so different from the one I had so recently left.

I put my hand on the king's shoulder. "Let us hope so, King Rigenos," I said. "I will do what I can."

He cleared his throat. "And that will be a great deal, Champion. I know it will be a great deal. We shall soon rid ourselves of the Eldren menace!"

We entered a cool hall whose walls were lined with beaten silver over which tapestries were draped. It was a pleasant hall, though very large. Off the hall led a wide staircase and down the staircase now descended a whole army of slaves, servants and retainers of all kinds. They drew themselves up in ranks at the bottom and knelt to greet the king.

"This is Lord Erekosë," King Rigenos told them. "He is a great warrior and my honoured guest. Treat him as you would treat me — obey him as you would obey me. All that he wishes shall be his."

To my embarrassment, the assemblage fell to its knees again and chorused: "Greetings, Lord Erekosë."

I spread my hands. They rose. I was beginning to take this sort of behaviour for granted. There was no doubt that part of me was used to it.

"I shall not burden you with ceremony for tonight," Rigenos said. "If you would like to refresh yourself in the apartments we have set aside for your use, we shall visit you later."

"Very well," I said. I turned to Iolinda and put out my hand to take hers. She extended it after a moment's hesitation and I kissed it. "I look forward to seeing you both again in a little time," I murmured, looking deep into her marvelous eyes. She dropped her gaze and withdrew her hand, and I allowed the servants to escort me upstairs to my apartments.

Twenty large rooms had been set aside for my use. These contained quarters for a staff of some ten personal slaves and servants and they were most of them extravagantly furnished with an eye to luxury that, it seemed to me, the people of the twentieth century had lost. "Opulent" was the word that sprang to mind. I could not move but a slave would come forward and take my surcoat or help me pour a glass of water or arrange the cushions of a divan. Yet I was still somewhat uneasy and it was a relief, on exploring the apartments, to come upon more austere rooms. These were weapon-lined warriors' rooms, without cushions or silks or furs, but with solid benches and blades and maces of iron and steel, brass-shod lances and razor-sharp arrows.

I spent some time in the weapons rooms and then returned to eat. My slaves brought me food and wine and I ate and drank heartily.

When I had finished, I felt as if I had been asleep for a long time and had awakened invigorated. Again I paced the rooms, exploring them further, taking more interest in the weapons than in the furnishings, which would have delighted even the most jaded sybarite. I stepped out onto one of the several covered balconies and surveyed the great city of Necranal as the sun set over it and deep shadows began to flow through the streets.

THE ETERNAL CHAMPION

The faraway sky was full of smoky colour. There were purples, oranges, yellows and blues and these colours were reflected in the domes and steeples of Necranal so that the entire city seemed to take on a softer texture, like a pastel drawing.

The shadows grew blacker. The sun set and stained the topmost domes scarlet and then night fell and fire flared suddenly all around the distant walls of Necranal, the yellow and red flames leaping upward at intervals of a few yards and illuminating much of the city within the walls. Lights appeared in windows and I heard the calls of nightbirds and insects. I turned to go in and saw that my servants had lit lamps for me. It had grown colder, but I hesitated on the balcony and decided to stay where I was, thinking deeply about my strange situation and trying to gauge the exact nature of the perils which Humanity faced.

There came a sound behind me. I looked back into the apartments and saw King Rigenos entering. Moody Katorn, Captain of the Imperial Guard, was with him. Instead of a helmet, he now wore a platinum circlet on his head and, instead of a breastplate, a leather jerkin stamped with a design in gold, but the absence of armour did not seem to soften his general demeanour. King Rigenos was wrapped in a white fur cloak and still wore his spiked crown of iron and diamonds. The two men joined me on the balcony.

"You feel rested, I hope, Erekosë?" King Rigenos inquired almost nervously, as if he had expected me to fade into air while he was away.

"I feel very well, thank you, King Rigenos."

"Good." He hesitated.

"Time is valuable," Katorn grunted.

"Yes, Katorn. Yes, I know." King Rigenos looked at me as if he hoped I already knew what he wished to say, but I did not and could only stare back, waiting for him to speak.

"You will forgive us, Erekosë," said Katorn, "if we come immediately to the matter of the Human Kingdoms. The king would outline to you our position and what we require of you."

"Of course," I said. "I am ready." I was in fact very anxious to learn the position.

"We have maps," said King Rigenos. "Where are the maps, Katorn?"

"Within, sire."

"Shall we...?"

I nodded and we entered my apartments. We passed through two chambers until we came to the main living room, in which was a large oak table. Here stood several of King Rigenos's slaves with rolls of parchment under their arms. Katorn selected several of the rolls and spread them, one on top of the other, on the table. He drew his heavy dagger to weight one side and picked up a metal vase studded with rubies and emeralds to hold the other side.

I looked at the maps with interest. I already recognized them. I had seen something similar in my dreams before I had been called here by King Rigenos's incantations.

Now the king bent over the maps and his long, pale index finger traced over the territories shown.

"As I told you in your — your tomb, Erekosë, the Eldren now dominate the entire southern continent. They call this continent Mernadin. There." His finger now hovered over a coastal region of the continent. "Five years ago they recaptured the only real outpost we had on Mernadin. Here. Their ancient seaport of Paphanaal. There was little fighting."

"Your forces fled?" I asked.

Katorn came in again. "I admit that we had grown complacent. When they suddenly swept out of the Mountains of Sorrow, we were unprepared. They must have been building their damned armies for years and we were unaware of it. We could not be expected to know their plans — they're aided by sorcery and we are not!"

"You were able to evacuate most of your colonies, I take it?" I put in.

Katorn shrugged. "There was little evacuation necessary. Mernadin was virtually uninhabited since human beings would not live in a land which had been polluted by the presence of the Hounds of Evil. The continent is cursed. Inhabited by fiends from Hell."

I rubbed my chin and asked innocently: "Then why did you drive the Eldren back to the mountains in the first place if you had no need of their territories?"

"Because, while they had the land under their control, they were a constant threat to Humanity!"

"I see." I made a tiny gesture with my right hand. "Forgive me for interrupting you. Please continue."

"A constant threat—" began Katorn.

"That threat is once again imminent," the king's voice broke in. It was thick and trembling. His eyes were suddenly full of fear and hatred. "We expect them at any moment to launch an attack upon the Two Continents — upon Zavara and Necralala!"

"Do you know when they plan this invasion?" I asked. "How long have we to ready ourselves?"

"They'll attack!" Katorn's bleak eyes came to life. The thin beard framing his pale face seemed to bristle.

"They'll attack," agreed King Rigenos. "They would have overrun us now if we did not constantly war against them."

"We have to keep them back," added Katorn. "Once a breach is made, they will engulf us!"

King Rigenos sighed. "Humanity, though, is battle weary. We needed one of two things — though ideally both — fresh warriors to drive the Eldren back or a leader to give the warriors we have new hope."

"And you can train no fresh warriors?" I asked.

Katorn made a short, guttural sound in his throat. I took this to be a laugh. "Impossible! All mankind fights the Eldren menace!"

The king nodded. "So I called you, Erekosë — though believing myself to be a desperate fool willing to think a mirage reality."

Katorn turned away at this. It seemed to me that this had been his private theory — that the king had gone mad in his desperation. My materialization seemed to have destroyed this theory and made him in some way resentful of me, though I did not think I could be blamed for the king's decision.

The king straightened his shoulders. "I called you. And I hold you to your vow."

I knew of no vow. I was surprised. "What vow?" I said.

Now the king looked astonished. "Why, the vow that, if ever the Eldren dominated Mernadin again, you would come to decide the struggle between them and Humanity."

"I see." I signed to a slave to bring me a cup of wine and I sipped it and stared at the map. As John Daker, I saw a meaningless war between two ferocious, blindly hating factions, both of whom seemed to be conducting a racial jehad, one against the other. Yet my loyalties were clear. I belonged to the human race and should use all my powers to help defend my kind. Humanity had to be saved.

"The Eldren?" I looked up at King Rigenos. "What do they say?"

"What do you mean?" Katorn growled. "Say? You speak as if you do not believe our king."

"I am not questioning the truth of your statements," I told him. "I wish to know the exact terms in which the Eldren justify their war against us. It would help if I had a clearer idea of their ambitions."

Katorn shrugged. "They would wipe us out," he said. "Is that not enough to know?"

"No," I said. "You must have taken prisoners. What do the prisoners tell you?" I spread my hands. "How have the Eldren leaders justified their war against Humanity?"

King Rigenos smiled patronizingly. "You have forgotten a great deal, Erekosë, if you have forgotten the Eldren. They are not human. They are clever. They are cold and they have smooth, deceitful tongues with which they would lull a man into a false sense of tranquillity before tearing his heart from his body with their bare fangs. They are brave, though, I'll give them that. Under torture they die, refusing to tell us their true plans. They are cunning. They try to make us believe their talk of peace, of mutual trust and mutual help, hoping that we will drop our defenses long enough so that they may turn and destroy us, or get us to look them full in the face so that they can work the evil eye upon us. Do not be naive, Erekosë. Do not attempt to deal with an Eldren as you would deal with a human being, for if you did so, you would be doomed. They have no souls, as we understand souls. They have no love, save a cold loyalty to their cause and to their master Azmobaana. Realize this, Erekosë — the Eldren are demons. They are fiends to whom Azmobaana in his dreadful blasphemy has granted something like a human form. But you must not be blinded by the form. That which is inside an Eldren is *not* human — it is everything, in fact, that is inhuman."

Katorn's face twisted.

"You cannot trust an Eldren wolf. They are treacherous, immoral and evil. We shall not be safe until their whole race is destroyed. Utterly destroyed — so that not a fragment of their flesh, not a droplet of their blood, not a splinter of their bone, not a strand of their hair is left to taint the Earth. And I speak literally, Erekosë, for whilst one finger clipping of an Eldren survives upon our world, then there is the chance that Azmobaana can re-create his servants and attack us again. That demon brood must be burned to the finest ash — every man, every female and every youngling. Burned — then cast to the winds, the clean winds. That is our mission, Erekosë, the mission of Humanity. And we have the Good One's blessing for that mission."

Then I heard another voice, a sweeter voice, and I glanced toward the door. It was Iolinda.

"You must lead us to victory, Erekosë," she said candidly. "What Katorn says is true — no matter how fiercely he declaims it. The facts are as he tells you. You must lead us to victory."

I looked again into her eyes. I drew a deep breath and my face felt hard and cold.

"I will lead you," I said.

F O U R

I O L I N D A

The next morning I awoke to the sounds of the slaves preparing my breakfast. Or was it the slaves? Was it not my wife moving about the room, getting ready to wake up the boy as she did every morning?

I opened my eyes expecting to see her.

I did not see her. Nor did I see my room in my apartment where I had lived as John Daker.

Nor did I see slaves.

Instead, I saw Iolinda. She was smiling down at me as she prepared the breakfast with her own hands.

I felt guilty for a moment, as if I had betrayed my wife in some obscure way. Then I realized that there was nothing I could be ashamed of. I was the victim of Fate — of forces which I could not hope to understand. I was not John Daker. I was Erekosë. I realized that it would be the best for me if I were to insist on that. A man divided between two identities is a sick man. I resolved to forget John Daker as soon as possible. Since I was Erekosë now, I should concentrate on being Erekosë only. In that I was a fatalist.

Iolinda brought a bowl of fruit toward me. "Would you eat, Lord Erekosë?"

I selected a strange, soft fruit with a reddish-yellow skin. She handed me a small knife. I tried to peel it, but since the fruit was new to me, I was not sure how to begin. She gently took it from me and began to peel it for me, sitting on the edge of my low bed and concentrating rather excessively, in my opinion, on the fruit she held.

At last the fruit was peeled and she quartered it and placed it on a plate and handed the plate to me, still avoiding my direct gaze, but smiling a little mysteriously as she looked about her. I picked up a piece of the fruit and bit it. It was sharp and sweet at the same time and very refreshing.

"Thank you," I said. "It is good. I have never had this fruit before."

"Have you not?" She was genuinely surprised. "But the ecrex is the commonest fruit in Necralala."

"You forget I am a stranger to Necralala," I pointed out.

She put her head on one side and looked at me with a slight frown. She pushed back the flimsy blue cloth that covered her golden hair and made a great play of arranging her matching blue gown. She really did seem to be puzzled. "A stranger.. ." she murmured.

"A stranger," I agreed.

"But" — she paused — "but you are the great hero of Humanity, Lord Erekosë. You knew Necranal as it was in its greatest glory — when you ruled here as the Champion. You knew Earth in ancient times, when you set it free from the chains the Eldren had bound around it. You know more of this world than I do, Erekosë."

I shrugged. "I admit that much of it is familiar — and growing increasingly familiar. But until yesterday my name was John Daker and I lived in a city very different from Necranal and my occupation was not that of warrior or, indeed, anything like it. I do not deny that I am Erekosë — the name is familiar and I am comfortable with it. But I do not know *who* Erekosë was, any more than do you. He was a great hero of ancient times who, before he died, swore that he would return to decide the issue between Eldren and Humanity if he were needed. He was placed in a rather gloomy tomb on a hillside along with his sword, which only he could wield."

"The sword Kanajana," murmured Iolinda.

"It has a name, then?"

"Aye — Kanajana. It — it is more than a name, I believe. It is some sort of mystic description — a description of its exact nature — of the powers it contains."

"And is there any legend that explains why only I can bear that blade?" I asked her.

"There are several," she said.

"Which do you prefer?" I smiled.

Then, for the first time that morning, she looked directly at me and her voice lowered and she said: "I prefer the one that says that you are the chosen

THE ETERNAL CHAMPION

son of the Good One, the Great One — that your sword is a sword of the gods and that you can handle it because you are a god — an Immortal."

I laughed. "You do not believe that?"

She dropped her gaze. "If you tell me that it is not true, then I must believe you," she said. "Of course."

"I admit that I feel extremely healthy," I told her. "But that is a long way from feeling as a god must feel! Besides, I think I would know if I were a god. I would know other gods. I would dwell in some plane where the gods dwell. I would count goddesses amongst my friends." I stopped. She seemed disturbed.

I reached out and touched her and said softly: "But then perhaps you are right. Perhaps I am a god — for I am certainly privileged to know a Goddess."

She shrugged off my hand. "You are making mock of me, my lord."

"No. I swear it."

She got up. "I must appear foolish to such a great lord as yourself. I apologize for wasting your time with my chatter."

"You have not wasted my time," I said. "You have helped me, in fact."

Her lips parted. "Helped you?"

"Yes. You have filled in part of my somewhat peculiar background. I still do not remember my past as Erekosë, but at least I know as much about that past as anyone here. Which is not a disadvantage!"

"Perhaps your centuries-long sleep has washed your mind free of memory," she said.

"Perhaps," I agreed. "Or perhaps there have been so many other memories during that sleep — new experiences, other lives."

"What do you mean?"

"Well, it seems to me that I have been more people than just John Daker and Erekosë. Other names spring to mind — strange names in unfamiliar tongues. I have a vague — and perhaps stupid — notion that while I slept as Erekosë, my spirit took on other shapes and names. Some in the future, some in the past, some — elsewhere…" I could not explain, but added lamely: "Perhaps that spirit cannot sleep, but must forever be active." I stopped. I was getting deep into the realms of metaphysics — and I had never possessed any great predilection for metaphysics. I considered myself a pragmatist, in fact. Such notions as reincarnation I had always scoffed at — still scoffed at, really, in spite of the evidence, such as it was.

But Iolinda pressed me to continue what I considered to be pointless speculation. "Go on," she said. "Please continue, Lord Erekosë."

If only to keep the beautiful girl beside me for a short while longer, I did as she asked.

"Well," I said, "while you and your father were attempting to bring me here, I thought I remembered other lives than this one as Erekosë or the other one, as John Daker. I remembered, very dimly, other civilizations — though I could not tell you whether they existed in the past or in the future. In fact, the idea of past and future seems meaningless to me now. I have no idea, for instance, whether this civilization lies in the "future" that I know as John Daker or in the "past." It is here. I am here. Perhaps there is only ever "the present"? There are certain things that I will have to do. That is all I can say."

"But these other incarnations," she said. "What do you know of them?"

I shrugged. "Nothing. I am attempting to describe a dim feeling, not an exact impression. A few names which I have now forgotten. A few images which have almost completely faded away as dreams fade. And perhaps that is all they ever were — just dreams. Perhaps my life as John Daker, which in its turn is beginning to fade in my memory, was merely that, a dream. Certainly I know nothing of any supernatural agencies of whom your father and Katorn have spoken. I know of no "Azmobaana," no Good and Great One, no demons or, indeed, angels. I know only that I am a man and that I exist."

Her face was grave. "That is true. You are a man. You exist. I saw you materialize."

"But from where did I come?"

"From the Other Regions," she said. "From the place where all great warriors go when they die, and where their women go to join them, to live in eternal happiness."

Again I smiled, but then smothered the smile for I did not wish to offend her beliefs. "I remember no such place," I said. "I remember only strife. If I have been away from here, it was not in some land of eternal happiness — it was in many lands, lands of eternal warfare."

Suddenly I felt depressed and weary. "Eternal warfare," I repeated and I sighed.

Her look became sympathetic. "Do you think that this is your fate — to war forever against the enemies of Humanity?"

I frowned. "Not quite, for I seem to remember times when I was not human as you would understand the word. If I have a spirit, as I said, that inhabits many forms, then there have been times when it has inhabited forms that were — different." I rejected the thought. It was too difficult to grasp, too frightening to tolerate.

It disturbed Iolinda. She rose and darted a look of incomprehension at me. "Not — not as an . . ."

I smiled. "An Eldren? I do not know. But I do not think so, for the name is not familiar to me in that respect."

She was relieved. "It is so hard to trust..." she said sadly.

"To trust what? Words?"

"To trust anything," she said. "I once thought I understood the world. Perhaps I was too young. Now I understand nothing. I do not know whether I shall even be alive next year."

"I think that may be described as a common fear to all we mortals," I said gently.

"'We mortals'?" Her smile was without humour. "You are not mortal, Erekosë!"

I had not up to now considered it. After all, I had been summoned into existence in thin air! I laughed. "We shall soon know whether I am or not," I said, "when we have joined battle with the Eldren!"

A little moan escaped her lips then. "Oh!" she cried. "Do not consider it!" She moved toward the door. "You *are* immortal, Erekosë! You *are* invulnerable! You *are* — eternal! You are the only thing of which I can be sure, the only person I can trust! Do not joke so! Do not joke so, I beg you!"

I was astonished at this outburst. I would have risen from the bed to hold her and comfort her, but I was naked. Admittedly she had seen me naked once before, when I had originally materialized in Erekosë's tomb, but I did not know enough of the customs of these people to guess whether it would shock her or not.

"Forgive me, Iolinda," I said. "I did not realize..."

What had I not realized? The extent of the poor girl's insecurity? Or something deeper than that?

"Do not go," I begged.

She stopped by the door and turned, and there were tears in her huge, wide eyes. "You are eternal, Erekosë. You are immortal. You can never die!"

I could not reply.

For all I knew I would be dead in the first encounter with the Eldren.

Suddenly I became aware of the responsibility I had tacitly agreed to assume — a responsibility not just to this beautiful woman but to the whole human race. I swallowed hard and fell back on my pillows as Iolinda rushed from the room.

Could I possibly bear such a burden?

Did I wish to bear such a burden?

I did not. I had no great faith in my own powers and there was no reason to believe that those powers were any more potent than, say, Katorn's. Katorn was, after all, far more experienced in warfare than I. He had a right to be resentful of me. I had taken over his role, robbed him of his power and of a responsibility which he had been prepared to shoulder — and I was unproven. Suddenly I saw Katorn's point of view and sympathized with it.

What right had I to lead Humanity in a war that could decide its very existence?

None.

And then another thought came to me — a more self-pitying thought.

What right had Humanity to expect so much of me?

They had, let us say, awakened me from a slumber which I had earned, leading the quiet, decent life of John Daker. And now they were imposing their will upon me, demanding that I give back to them the self-confidence and — yes — self-righteousness that they were losing.

I lay there in the bed and for a while I hated King Rigenos, Katorn and the rest of the human race — including the fair Iolinda, who had been the one to bring this question to my mind.

Erekosë the Champion, Defender of Humanity, Greatest of Warriors, lay wretched and sniveling in his bed and felt very sorry for himself indeed.

FIVE

KATORN

I arose at last and dressed myself in a simple tunic, having been washed and shaved — much to my embarrassment — by my slaves. I went by myself into the weapons rooms and there took down my sword from where it hung in its scabbard on a peg.

I unsheathed the blade and again a sort of exultation filled me. Immediately I forgot my qualms and scruples and laughed as the sword whistled around my head and my muscles flexed with the weight of it.

I feinted with the sword and it seemed that it was part of my very body, that it was another limb whose presence I had been unaware of until now. I thrust it out at full reach, pulled it back, swung it down. It filled me with joy to wield it!

It made me into something greater than I had ever felt I was before. It made me into a man. A warrior. A champion.

And yet, as John Daker, I had handled swords perhaps twice in my life — and handled them most clumsily, according to those friends of mine who had considered themselves experts.

At last I reluctantly sheathed the sword as I saw a slave hovering some distance away. I remembered that only I, Erekosë, could hold the sword and live.

"What is it?" I said.

"The Lord Katorn, master. He would speak with you." I put my sword back on its peg. "Bid him enter," I told the slave.

Katorn came in rapidly. He appeared to have been waiting some time and was in no better a mood than when I had first encountered him. His boots, which seemed to be shod with metal, clattered on the flagstones of the weapons room.

"Good morning to you, Lord Erekosë," he said.

I bowed. "Good morning, Lord Katorn. I apologize if you were made to wait. I was trying out that sword."

"The sword Kanajana." Katorn looked at it speculatively.

"The sword Kanajana," I said. "Would you have some refreshment, Lord Katorn?" I was making a great effort to please him, not only because it would not do to have so experienced a warrior as an enemy when plans of battle were being prepared, but because I had, as I said, come to sympathize with his situation.

But Katorn refused to be mollified. "I broke my fast at dawn," he said. "I have come to discuss more pressing matters than eating, Lord Erekosë."

"And what are those?" Manfully I restrained my own temper.

"Matters of war, Lord Erekosë. What else?"

"Indeed. And what specific matters would you wish to discuss with me, Lord Katorn?"

"It seems to me that we should attack the Eldren before they come against us."

"Attack being the best form of defense, eh?"

He looked surprised at this. He had plainly not heard the phrase before. "Eloquently put, my lord. One would think you an Eldren yourself, with such a way with words." He was deliberately trying my temper. But I swallowed the insinuation.

"So," I said, "we attack them. Where?"

"That is what we shall have to discuss with all those concerned in planning this war. But it seems there is one obvious point."

"And that is?"

He wheeled and strode into another chamber, returning with a map which he spread on a bench. It was a map of Mernadin, the third continent, the one entirely controlled by the Eldren. With his dagger he stabbed at a spot I had seen indicated the night before.

"Paphanaal," I said.

"While it is the logical point of an initial attack in a campaign of the sort we plan, it seems to me unlikely that the Eldren will expect us to make so bold a move, knowing that we are weary and under strength."

"But if we are weary and weak," I said, "would it not seem a good idea to attack some less important city first?"

"You are forgetting, my lord, that our warriors have been heartened by your coming," Katorn said dryly.

I could not help grinning at this cut. But Katorn scowled, angry that I had not taken offence.

I said quietly: "We must learn to work together, my lord Katorn. I bow to your great experience as a warrior leader. I acknowledge that you have had much more recent knowledge of the Eldren than have I. I need your help surely as much as King Rigenos believes he needs mine."

Katorn seemed slightly comforted by this. He cleared his throat and continued.

"Once Paphanaal, province and city, are taken, we shall have a beachhead from which other attacks inland can be made. With Paphanaal again in our hands, we can decide our own strategy — initiate action rather than react to the Eldren's strategy. Only once we have pushed them back into the mountains will we have the wearying task of clearing them all out. It will take years. But it is what we should have done in the first place. That, however, will be a matter for ordinary military administration and will not concern us directly."

"And what kind of defenses has Paphanaal?" I asked.

Katorn smiled. "She relies almost entirely on her warships. If we can destroy her fleet, then Paphanaal is as good as taken." He bared his teeth in what I gathered was a grin. And he looked at me, his expression changing to one of sudden suspicion, as if he had revealed too much to me.

I could not ignore the expression. "What is on your mind, Lord Katorn?" I asked. "Do you not trust me?"

He controlled his features. "I must trust you," he said flatly. "We all must trust you, Lord Erekosë. Have you not returned to fulfill your ancient promise?"

I gazed searchingly into his face. "Do you believe that?"

"I must believe it."

"Do you believe that I am Erekosë the Champion returned?"

"I must believe that also."

"You believe it because you surmise that, if I am not Erekosë — the Erekosë of the legends — then Humanity is doomed?"

He lowered his head as if in assent.

"And what if I am not Erekosë, my lord?"

Katorn looked up. "You must be Erekosë — my lord. If it were not for one thing, I would suspect…"

"What would you suspect?"

"Nothing."

"You would suspect that I were an Eldren in disguise. Is that it, Lord Katorn? Some cunning unhuman who had assumed the outer appearance of a man? Do I read your thoughts correctly, my lord?"

"Too correctly." Katorn's thick brows came together and his mouth was thin and white. "The Eldren are said to have the power to probe minds. But human beings do not possess that power."

"And are you, then, afraid, Lord Katorn?"

"Of an Eldren? By the Good One, I'll show you..." and Katorn's heavy hand rushed to the hilt of his sword.

I raised my own hand and then pointed at the sword that hung sheathed on the peg on the wall. "But that is the one fact that does not fit your theory, isn't it? If I am not Erekosë, then how is it that I can handle Erekosë's blade?"

He did not draw his sword, but his grip remained on the hilt.

"It is true, is it not, that no living creature — human or Eldren — can touch that blade and live?" I said quietly.

"That is the legend," he agreed.

"Legend?"

"I have never seen an Eldren try to handle the sword Kanajana."

"But you must assume that it is true. Otherwise..."

"Otherwise, there is little hope for Humanity." The words were dragged from his lips.

"Very well, Lord Katorn. You will assume that I am Erekosë, summoned by King Rigenos to lead Humanity to victory."

"I have no choice but to assume that."

"Good. And there is something that I, too, must assume, for my part, Lord Katorn."

"You? What?"

"I must assume that you will work *with* me in this enterprise. That there will be no plots behind my back, that there will be no information withheld from me that might prove vital, that you will not seek to make allies against me within our own ranks. You see, Lord Katorn, it could be your suspicions that might wreck our plans. A man jealous and resentful of his leader is capable of doing more harm than any enemy.

He nodded his head and straightened his shoulders, the hand falling away from his sword. "I had considered that question, my lord. I am not a fool."

"I know you are not a fool, Lord Katorn. If you were a fool, I should not have bothered to have had this conversation."

His tongue bulged in his cheek as he mulled over this statement. Eventually he said: "And you are not a fool, Lord Erekosë."

"Thank you. I did not suspect that you judge me that."

"Hmph." He removed his helmet and ran his fingers through his thick hair. He was still thinking.

I waited for him to say something further, but then he replaced his helmet firmly on his head, dug his thumb into the side of his mouth and picked at a tooth with the nail. He withdrew the thumb and stared at it intently for a moment. Then he looked at the map and murmured, "Well, at least we have an understanding. With that, it will be easier to fight this stinking war."

I nodded. "Much easier, I think."

He sniffed.

"How good is our own fleet?" I asked him.

"It's a fine fleet still. Not as large as it was, but we are remedying that, too. Our shipyards work night and day to build more and larger men-o'-war. And in our ironworks up and down the land we forge powerful guns with which to arm those ships."

"And what of men to crew them?"

"We are recruiting all we can. Even women are used in certain tasks — and boys. You were told that, Lord Erekosë, and it was true — the *whole* of Humanity fights the Eldren warriors."

I said nothing, but I had begun to admire the spirit of this people. I was less divided in my mind concerning the rights or wrongs of what I did. The folk of this strange time and place in which I found myself were fighting for nothing more nor less than the survival of their species.

But then another thought came to me. Could not the same be said of the Eldren?

I dismissed the thought.

At least Katorn and I had that in common. We refused to concern ourselves with speculation on moral and sentimental issues. We had a task to perform. We had assumed the responsibility for that task. We should do it to the best of our ability.

S I X

PREPARING FOR WAR

And so I talked with generals and with admirals. We pored over maps and discussed tactics, logistics, available men, animals and ships, while the fleets massed and the Two Continents were scoured for warriors, from boys of ten years old to men of fifty or older, from girls of twelve to women of sixty. All were marshalled beneath the double banner of Humanity which bore the arms of Zavara and Necralala and the standards of their king, Rigenos, and their war champion, Erekosë.

As the days passed, we planned the great land-sea invasion of Mernadin's chief harbour, Paphanaal, and the surrounding province, which was also called Paphanaal.

When not conferring with the commanders of the armies and navies, I practiced weaponry, riding, until I became skilled in those arts.

It was not a question of *learning* so much as *remembering*. Just as the feel of my strange sword had been familiar, so was the sensation of a horse between my legs. Just as I had always known my name was Erekosë (which, I had been told, meant "The One Who Is Always There" in some ancient tongue of Humanity which was no longer used) so I had always known how to pull an arrow on a bowstring and let it fly at a target as I galloped past on horseback.

But Iolinda — she was not familiar to me. Though there was some part of me that seemed able to travel through time and space and assume many incarnations, they were plainly not the same incarnations. I was not living an episode of my life over again, I had merely become the same person again, going through a different series of actions, or so it seemed. I had a sense of free will, within those terms. I did not feel that my fate was preordained. But perhaps it was. Perhaps I am too much of an optimist. Perhaps I am, after all, a fool and Katorn was wrong in his assessment of me. The Eternal Fool.

Certainly I was willing to make a fool of myself where Iolinda was concerned. Her beauty was almost unbearable. But with her I could not be a fool. She wanted a hero, an Immortal — and nothing less. So I must play the hero for her, to comfort her, though it went ill with my preferred manner, which has always been pretty casual. Sometimes, in fact, I felt more like her father than her would-be lover and, with my pat twentieth-century notions of human motivation, wondered if I were really nothing more than a substitute for the strong father she expected in Rigenos.

I think that she secretly despised Rigenos for not being more heroic, but I sympathized with the older man (older? I think it is I who am older, infinitely older — but enough of that) for Rigenos bore a great responsibility and bore it pretty well as far as I could make out. After all, he was a man who would rather plan pleasant gardens than battles. It was not his fault that he had been born a king without a close male successor to whom he could have, if he had been luckier, transferred responsibility. And I had heard that he bore himself well in battle and never backed away from any responsibility. King Rigenos was meant for a gentler life, maybe — though he could be fierce enough when it came to hating the Eldren. I was to be the hero that he felt incapable of being. I accepted that. But I was much more reluctant to be the father that he could not be. I wanted to enjoy a much healthier relationship with Iolinda or, so I told myself, I would not enjoy one at all!

I am not sure I had a choice. I was mesmerized by her. I would probably have accepted her on any terms.

We spent whatever time we could together, whenever I could get away from the military men and my own martial training. We would wander arm in arm along the closed balconies which covered the Palace of Ten Thousand Windows like a creeping plant, winding from top to bottom of the great palace and containing a superb variety of flowers, shrubs and caged and uncaged birds that fluttered through the foliage of these spiraling passages and perched amongst the branches of the vines and the small trees and sang to us as we wandered. I learned that this, too, had been King Rigenos's idea, to make the balconies more pleasant.

But that had been before the coming of the Eldren.

Slowly the day approached when the fleet would gather together and sail for the distant continent where the Eldren ruled. I had begun by being impatient to get to grips with the Eldren, but now I was becoming more and more reluctant to leave — for it would mean leaving Iolinda and my lust for her was growing quite as strongly as my love.

Although I gathered that day by day the society of humankind was becoming less and less open, more and more bound by unpleasant and unnecessary restrictions, it was still not considered wrong for unwed lovers to sleep together, so long as they were of an equal social standing. I was much relieved when I discovered this. It seemed to me that an Immortal — as I was assumed to be — and a princess were quite decently matched. But it was not the social conventions that hampered my ambition — it was Iolinda herself. And that is one thing that no amount of freedom or "licence" or "permissiveness" or whatever the old fogies call it can cope with. That is the odd assumption found in the twentieth century (I wonder if you who read this will know what those two stupid words mean?): — that, if the laws that man makes concerning "morality" — particularly sexual morality — are done away with, then one huge orgy will begin. It forgets that people are, generally speaking, only attracted to a few other people and only fall in love with one or two in their whole lives. And there may be many other reasons why they may not be able to make love, even if their love is confirmed.

Where Iolinda was concerned, I hesitated because, as I have said, I did not wish to be merely a substitute for her father — and she hesitated because she needed to be absolutely sure she could "trust" me. John Daker would have called this a neurotic attitude. Perhaps it was, but on the other hand, was it neurotic for a relatively normal girl to feel a bit peculiar about someone she had only lately seen materialize from thin air?

But enough of this. All I should say is that, although we were both deeply in love at this point, we did not sleep together — we did not even discuss the matter, though it was often on the tip of my tongue.

What, in fact, began to happen was, oddly, that my lust began to wane. My love for Iolinda remained as strong as ever — if not stronger — but I did not feel any great need to express it in physical terms. It was not like me. Or perhaps I should say that it was not like John Daker!

However, as the day of departure came closer, I began to feel a need to express my love in some way and, one evening as we wandered through the balconies, I paused and put my hand under her hair and stroked the back of her neck and gently turned her to face me.

She looked sweetly up at me and smiled. Her red lips parted slightly and she did not move her head as I bent my own lips to hers and kissed her softly. My heart leaped. I held her close against me, feeling her breasts rise and fall against my chest. I lifted her hand and held it against my face as I looked down at her beauty. I thrust my hand deep into her hair and tasted her warm, sweet breath as we kissed again. She curled her fingers in mine and opened her eyes and her eyes were happy — truly happy for the first time. We drew apart.

Her breathing was now much less regular and she began to murmur something, but I cut her off short. She smiled at me expectantly, with a mixture of pride and tenderness.

"When I return," I said softly, "we shall be married."

She looked surprised for a moment and then she realized what I had said — the significance of what I had said. I was trying to tell her that she could trust me. It was the only way I could think of to do it. Perhaps a John Daker reflex, I don't know.

She nodded her head, drawing off her hand a wonderfully worked ring of gold, pearls and rose-coloured diamonds. This she placed on my little finger.

"A token of my love," she said. "An acceptance of your proposal. A charm, perhaps, to bring you luck in your battles. Something to remind you of me when you are tempted by those unhuman Eldren beauties." She smiled when she made this last retort.

"It has many functions," I said, "this ring."

"As many as you wish," she replied.

"Thank you."

"I love you, Erekosë," she said simply.

"I love you, Iolinda." I paused, then added, "But I am a crude sort of lover, am I not? I have no token to give you. I feel embarrassed and a bit inadequate."

"Your word is enough," she said. "Swear that you will return to me."

I looked at her nonplussed for a second. Naturally I would return to her.

"Swear it," she said.

"I'll swear it. There is no question."

"Swear it again."

"I'll swear it a thousand times if once is not enough. I swear it. I swear that I will return to you, Iolinda, my love, my delight."

"Good." She seemed satisfied.

There came the sound of hurried footsteps along the balcony and we saw a slave I recognized as one of my own rushing toward us.

"Ah, master, there you are. King Rigenos has asked me to bring you to him."

It was late. "And what does King Rigenos want?" I asked.

"He did not say, master."

I smiled down at Iolinda and tucked her arm in mine. "Very well. We shall come."

S E V E N

THE ARMOUR OF EREKOSË

The slave led us to my own apartments. They were empty of anyone save my retinue.

"But where is King Rigenos?" I asked.

"He said to wait here, master."

I smiled at Iolinda again. She smiled back. "Very well," I said. "We shall wait."

We did not wait long. Presently slaves began to arrive at my apartments. They were carrying bulky pieces of metal wrapped in oiled parchment and they began to pile it in the weapons room. I watched them with as little expression as possible, though I was greatly puzzled.

Then at last King Rigenos entered. He seemed much more excited than usual and Katorn was not, this time, with him.

"Greetings, Father," said Iolinda. "I..."

But King Rigenos raised a hand and turned to address the slaves. "Strip off the coverings," he said. "Hurry."

"King Rigenos," I said. "I would like to tell you that..."

"Forgive me, Lord Erekosë. First, look at what I have brought. It has lain for centuries in the vaults of the palace. Waiting, Erekosë — waiting for you!"

"Waiting?"

Then the oiled parchment was torn away and lay in curling heaps on the flagstones, revealing what was to me a magnificent sight.

"This," said the king, "is the armour of Erekosë. Broken from its tomb of rock deep beneath the palace's lowest dungeons so that Erekosë can wear it again."

The armour was black and it shone. It was as if it had been forged that day and forged by the greatest smith in history, for it was of exquisite workmanship.

I picked up the breastplate and ran my hand over it.

Unlike the armour worn by the Imperial Guard, this was smooth, without any kind of raised embellishment. The shoulder pieces were grooved, fanning high and away from the head, to channel a blow of sword, axe or lance from the wearer. The helmet, breastplates, greaves and the rest were all grooved in the same manner.

The metal was light, but very strong, like that of the sword. But the black lacquer shone. It shone brightly — almost blindingly. In its simplicity, the armour *was* beautiful — as beautiful as only really fine craftsmanship can be. Its sole ornament was a thick plume of scarlet horsehair which sprang from the crest of the helmet and cascaded down the smooth sides. I touched the armour with the reverence one has for fine art. In this case it was fine art designed to protect my life and my reverence was, if anything, that much greater!

"Thank you, King Rigenos," I said, and I was honestly grateful. "I will wear it on the day we set sail against the Eldren."

"That day is tomorrow," said King Rigenos quietly.

"What?"

"The last of our ships has come in. The last member of the crew is on board. The last cannon has been fitted. It will be a good tide tomorrow and we cannot miss it."

I glanced at him. Had I been misled in some way? Had Katorn prevailed upon the king not to let me know the exact time of sailing? But the king's expression showed no sign of a plot. I dismissed the idea and accepted what he said. I turned my gaze to Iolinda. She looked stricken.

"Tomorrow," she said.

"Tomorrow," confirmed King Rigenos.

I bit my lower lip. "Then I must prepare."

She said: "Father…"

He looked at her. "Yes, Iolinda?"

I began to speak and then paused. She glanced at me and was also silent. There was no easy way of telling him and suddenly it was as if we should keep our love, our pact, a secret. Neither of us knew why.

Tactfully the king withdrew. "I will discuss last-minute matters with you later, Lord Erekosë."

I bowed. He left.

Somewhat stunned, Iolinda and I stared at each other and then we moved into each other's arms and we wept.

John Daker would not have written this. He would have laughed at the sentiments, just as he would have scoffed at anyone who considered the arts of war important. John Daker would not have written this, but I must:

I began to feel a rising sense of excitement for the coming war. The old exultant mood started to sweep through me again. Overlaying my excitement was my love for Iolinda. This love seemed to be a calmer, purer love, so much more satisfying than casual, carnal love. It was a thing apart. Perhaps this was the chivalrous love which the peers of Christendom are said to have held above all other.

John Daker would have spoken of sexual repression and of swordplay as a substitute for sexual intercourse.

Perhaps John Daker would have been right. But it did not seem to me that he was right, though I was well aware of all the rationalist arguments that supported such a view. There is a great tendency for the human race to see all other times in its own terms. The terms of this society were subtly different — I was only dimly aware of many of the differences. I was responding to Iolinda in those terms. It is all I can say. And later events, I suppose, were also played out in those terms.

I took Iolinda's face in my two hands and I bent and I kissed her forehead and she kissed my lips and then she left.

"Shall I see you before I leave?" I asked as she reached the door.

"Yes," she said. "Yes, my love, if it is possible."

When she had gone, I did not feel sad. I inspected the armour once again and then I went down to the main hall, where King Rigenos stood with many of his greatest captains, studying a large map of Mernadin and the waters between it and Necralala.

"We start here in the morning," Rigenos told me, indicating the harbour area of Necranal. The River Droonaa flowed through Necranal to the sea and the port of Noonos, where the fleet was assembled. "There must be a certain amount of ceremony, I fear, Erekosë. Various rituals to perform. I have already sketched them to you, I believe."

"You have," I said. "The ceremony seems more arduous than the warfare."

The captains laughed. Though somewhat distant and a trifle wary of me, they liked me well enough, for I had proved (to my own astonishment) to have a natural grasp of tactics and the warlike arts.

"But the ceremony is necessary," Rigenos said, "for the people. It makes a reality for them, you see. They can experience something of what we shall be doing."

"We?" I said. "Am I wrong? I thought you implied that you were sailing, too."

"I am," Rigenos said quietly. "I decided that it was necessary."

"Necessary?"

"Yes." He would say no more, particularly in front of his marshals. "Now, let us continue. We must all of us rise very early tomorrow morning."

As we discussed these final matters of order and tactics and logistics, I studied the king's face as best I could.

No one expected him to sail with his armies. He would lose no face at all by remaining behind in his capital. Yet he had made a decision which would put him in a position of extreme danger and cause him to take actions for which he had no palate.

Why had he made the decision? To prove to himself that he could fight, perhaps? Yet he had proved it already. Because he was jealous of me? Because he did not altogether trust me? I glanced at Katorn, but saw nothing in Katorn's face to indicate satisfaction. Katorn was merely his usual surly self.

Mentally I shrugged. Speculation at this point would get me nowhere. The fact was that the king, not an altogether robust man now, was coming with us. It might give extra inspiration to our warriors, at least. It might also help control Katorn's particular tendencies.

Eventually we dispersed and went our ways. I went straight to my bed and, before I slept, lay there peacefully, thinking of Iolinda, thinking of the battle plans I had helped hatch, wondering what the Eldren would be like to fight — I still had no completely clear idea of how they fought (save "treacherously and ferociously") or even what they looked like (save that they resembled "demons from the deepest pits").

I knew I would soon have some of the answers, at any rate. Soon I was asleep.

My dreams were strange dreams on that night before we sailed for Mernadin.

I saw towers and marshes and lakes and armies and lances that shot flames and metallic flying machines whose wings flapped like those of gigantic birds. I saw monstrously large flamingoes, strange mask-like helmets resembling the faces of beasts.

I saw dragons — huge reptiles with fiery venom, flapping across dark, moody skies. I saw a beautiful city tumbling in flames. I saw unhuman creatures that I knew to be gods. I saw a woman whom I could not name, a small redheaded man who seemed to be my friend. A sword — a great, black sword more powerful than the one I now owned — a sword that perhaps, oddly, was myself!

I saw a world of ice across which strange, great ships with billowing sails ran and black beasts like whales propelled themselves over endless plateaux of white.

I saw a world — or was it a universe? — that had no horizon and was filled with a rich, jeweled mosaic atmosphere which changed all the time and from which people and objects emerged only to disappear again. It was somewhere beyond the Earth, I was sure. Yes — I was aboard a spaceship — but a ship that traveled through no universe conceived of by Man.

I saw a desert through which I stumbled weeping and I was alone — lonelier than any man had ever been.

I saw a jungle — a jungle of primitive trees and gigantic ferns. And through the ferns I saw huge, bizarre buildings and there was a weapon in my hand that was not a sword and was not a gun, but it was more powerful than either.

I rode strange beasts and encountered stranger people. I moved through landscapes that were beautiful and terrifying. I piloted flying machines and spaceships and I drove chariots. I hated. I fell in love. I built empires and caused the collapse of nations and I slew many and was slain many times. I triumphed and was humiliated. And I had many names. The names roared in my skull. Too many names. Too many...

And there was no peace. There was only strife.

E I G H T
T H E   S A I L I N G

Next morning I awoke and my dreams went away and I was left in an introspective mood and there was only one thing that I desired.

That thing was an Upmann's Coronas Major cigar.

I kept trying to push the name from my mind. To my knowledge John Daker had never smoked an Upmann's. He would not have known one cigar from another! Where had the name come from? Another name came into my head — Jeremiah. And that, too, was vaguely familiar.

I sat up in bed and I recognized my surroundings and the two names merged with the other names I had dreamed of and I got up and entered the next chamber where slaves were finishing preparing my bath. With relief I got into the bath and, as I washed my body, I began to concentrate once again on the problem at hand. Yet a sense of depression remained with me and again for a moment I wondered if I were mad and involved in some complicated schizophrenic fantasy.

When the slaves brought in my armour I began to feel much better. Again I marveled at its beauty and its craftsmanship.

And now the time had come to put it on. First I donned my underclothes, then a sort of quilted overall and then I began to strap the armour about me. Again it was easy to find the appropriate straps and buckles. It was as if I had clad myself in this armour every morning of my life. It fitted perfectly. It was comfortable and no weight at all, though it completely covered my body.

Next, I strode to the weapons room and took down the great sword that hung there and I drew the belt of metal links around my waist and settled the poisonous sword in its protecting scabbard against my left hip, tossed back the scarlet plume on my helmet, lifted the visor and was ready.

Slaves escorted me down to the Great Hall, where the peers of Humanity had assembled to make their final leave taking with Necranal.

The tapestries which had earlier hung on the walls of beaten silver had now been removed and in their place were hundreds of bright banners. These were the banners of the marshals, the captains and the knights, who were gathered there in splendid array, assembled according to rank.

On a specially erected dais the throne of the king had been placed. The dais was hung with a cloth of emerald green and behind it were the twin banners of the Two Continents. I took my place before the dais and we waited tensely for the arrival of the king. I had already been coached concerning the responses I was to make in the forthcoming ceremony.

At last there came a great yelling of trumpets and beating of martial drums from the gallery above us and through a door came the king.

King Rigenos had gained stature, it seemed, for he wore a suit of gilded armour over which was hung a surcoat of white and red. Set into his helmet was his crown of iron and diamonds. He walked proudly to the dais and ascended it, seating himself in his throne with both arms stretched along the arms of the seat.

We raised our hands in salute:

"Hail, King Rigenos!" we roared.

And then we kneeled. I kneeled first. Behind me kneeled the little group of marshals. Behind them were a hundred captains, behind them were five thousand knights, all kneeling. And surrounding us, along the walls, were the old nobles, the ladies of the court, men-at-arms at attention, slaves and squires, the mayors of the various quarters of the city and from the various provinces of the Two Continents.

And all watched Rigenos and his champion, Erekosë.

King Rigenos rose from his throne. I looked up at him and his face was grave and stern. I had never before seen him look so much a king.

Now I felt that the attention of the watchers was on myself alone. I, Erekosë, Champion of Humanity, was to be their saviour. They knew It.

In my confidence and pride, I knew it, also.

King Rigenos raised his hands and spread them out and began to speak:

"Erekosë the Champion, Marshals, Captains and Knights of Humanity — we go to wage war against unhuman evil. We go to fight something that is more than an enemy bent on conquest. We go to fight a menace that would destroy our entire race. We go to save our two fair continents from total annihilation. The victor will rule the entire Earth. The defeated will become dust and will be forgotten — it will be as if he had never existed.

"This expedition upon which we are about to embark will be decisive. With Erekosë to lead us, we shall win the port of Paphanaal and its surrounding province. But that will only be the first stage in our campaigns."

King Rigenos paused and then spoke again into the almost absolute silence that had fallen in the Great Hall.

"More battle must follow fast upon the first so that the hated Hounds of Evil will, once and for all, be destroyed. Men and women — even children — must perish. We drove them to their holes in the Mountains of Sorrow once, but this time we must not let their race survive. Let only their memory remain for a little while — to remind us what evil is!"

Still kneeling, I raised both my hands above my head and clenched my fists.

"Erekosë," said King Rigenos. "You who by the power of your eternal will made yourself into flesh again and came to us at this time of need, you will be the power with which we shall destroy the Eldren. You will be Humanity's scythe to sweep this way and that and cut the Eldren down as weeds. You will be Humanity's spade to dig up the roots wherever they have grown. You will be Humanity's fire to burn the waste to the finest ash. You, Erekosë, will be the wind that will blow those ashes away as if they had never existed! You will destroy the Eldren!"

"I will destroy the Eldren!" I cried and my voice echoed through the Great Hall like the voice of a god. "I will destroy the enemies of Humanity! With the sword Kanajana I will ride upon them with vengeance and hatred and cruelty in my heart and I will vanquish the Eldren!"

From behind me now came a mighty shout:

"WE SHALL VANQUISH THE ELDREN!"

Now the king raised his head and his eyes glittered and his mouth was hard.

"Swear it!" he said.

We were intoxicated by the atmosphere of hate and rage in the Great Hall.

"We so swear!" we roared. *"We will destroy the Eldren!"*

Hatred seared from the king's eyes, trembled in his voice:

"Go now, Paladins of Mankind. Go — *destroy the Eldren offal. Clean our planet of the Eldren filth!*"

As one man, we rose to our feet and yelled our battle cries, turned in precision and marched from the Great Hall, out of the Palace of Ten Thousand Windows and into a day noisy with the swelling cheers of the people.

But as we marched, one thought preyed on my mind. Where was Iolinda? Why had she not come to me? There had been so little time before the ceremony and yet I would have thought she would have sent a message at least.

Down the winding streets of Necranal we marched in glorious procession. Through the cheering day with the bright sun shining on our weapons and our armour and our flags of a thousand rich colours waving in the wind.

And I led them. I, Erekosë, the Eternal, the Champion, the Vengeance Bringer — I led them. My arms were raised as if I were already celebrating my victory. Pride filled me. I knew what glory was and I relished it. This was the way to live — as a warrior, a leader of great armies, a wielder of weapons.

On we marched, down toward the waiting ships which were ready on the river. And a song came to my lips — a song that was in an archaic version of the language I now spoke. I sang the song and it was taken up by all the warriors who marched behind me. Drums began to beat and trumpets to shout, and we cried aloud for blood and death and the great red reaping that would come to Mernadin.

That is how we marched. That is how we felt.

Do not judge me until I have told you more.

We reached the wide part of the river where the harbour was and there were the ships. There were fifty ships stretched along both quays on either side of the river. Fifty ships bearing the fifty standards of fifty proud paladins.

And these were only fifty. The fleet itself waited for us to join it at the port of Noonos. Noonos of the Jeweled Towers.

The people of Necranal lined the banks of the river. They were cheering, cheering — so that we became used to their voices as men become used to the sounds of the sea, scarcely hearing them.

I regarded the ships. Richly decorated cabins were built on the decks and the ships of the paladins had several masts bearing furled sails of painted canvas. Already oars were being slipped through the ports and dipped into the placid river waters. Strong men, three to a sweep, sat upon the rowing benches. These men were not, as far as I could see, slaves, but free warriors.

At the head of this squadron of ships lay the king's huge battle barge — a magnificent man-o'-war. It had eighty pairs of oars and eight tall masts. Its rails were painted in red, gold and black, its decks were polished crimson, its sails were yellow, dark blue and orange and its huge carved figurehead, representing a goddess holding a sword in her two outstretched hands, was predominantly scarlet and silver. Ornate and splendid, the deck cabins shone with fresh varnish which had been laid over pictures of ancient human heroes (I was among them, though the likenesses were poor) and ancient human victories, of mythical beasts and demons and gods.

Detaching myself from the main force that had drawn itself up on the quayside, I walked to the tapestry-covered gangway and strode up it and boarded the ship. Sailors rushed forward to greet me.

One said: "The Princess Iolinda awaits you in the Grand Cabin, excellency."

I turned and then paused, looking at the splendid structure of the cabin, smiling slightly at the representations of myself painted upon It. Then I moved toward it and entered a comparatively low door into a room which was covered, floor, walls and ceiling, with thick tapestries in deep reds and blacks and golds. Lanterns hung in the room, and in the shadows, clad in a simple dress and a thin, dark cloak, stood my Iolinda.

"I did not wish to interrupt the preparations this morning," she said. "My father said that they were important — that there was little time to spare. So I thought you would not want to see me."

I smiled. "You still do not believe what I say, do you, Iolinda? You still do not trust me when I proclaim my love for you, when I tell you that I would do anything for you." I went toward her and held her in my arms. "I love you, Iolinda. I shall always love you."

"And I shall always love you, Erekosë. You will live forever, but…"

"There is no proof of that," I said gently. "And I am by no means invulnerable, Iolinda. I sustained enough cuts and bruises in my weapons practice to realize that!"

"You will not die, Erekosë."

"I would be happier if I shared your conviction!"

"Do not laugh at me, Erekosë. I will not be patronized!"

"I am not laughing at you, Iolinda. I am not condescending to you. I only speak the truth. You must face that truth. You must."

"Very well," she said. "I will face it. But I feel that you will not die. Yet, I have such strange premonitions — I feel that something worse than death could befall us."

"Your fears are natural, but they are baseless. There is no need for gloom, my dear. Look at the fine armour I wear, the powerful sword I bear, the mighty force I command."

"Kiss me, Erekosë."

I kissed her. I kissed her for a long time and then she broke from my arms and ran to the door and was gone.

I stared at the door, half thinking of running after her, of reassuring her. But I knew that I could not reassure her. Her fears were not really rational — they reflected her constant sense of insecurity. I promised myself that later I would give her proof of security. I would bring constants into her life — things she could trust.

Trumpets sounded. King Rigenos was coming aboard.

A few moments later the king entered the cabin, tugging off his crowned helm. Katorn was behind him, as sullen as ever.

"The people seem enthusiastic," I said. "The ceremony seemed to have the effect you desired, King Rigenos."

Rigenos nodded wearily. "Aye." The ritual had plainly taken much from him and he slumped into a hanging chair in the corner and called for wine. "We'll be sailing soon. When, Katorn?"

"Within the quarter-hour, my lord king." Katorn took the jug of wine from the slave who brought it and poured Rigenos a cup without offering one to me.

King Rigenos waved his hand. "Would you have some wine, Lord Erekosë?"

I declined. "You spoke well in the hall, King Rigenos," I said. "You fired us with a fine bloodlust."

Katorn sniffed. "Let us hope it lasts until we get to the enemy," he said. "We have some raw soldiers sailing on this expedition. Half our warriors have never fought before — and half of those are boys. There are even women in some detachments, I've heard."

"You seem pessimistic, Lord Katorn," I said.

He grunted. "It is as well to be. This finery and grandeur is all right for cheering up the civilians, but it's best you don't believe it yourself. You should know, Erekosë. You should know what real war is all about — pain, fear, death. There's nothing else to it."

"You forget," I said. "My memory of my own past is clouded."

Katorn sniffed and gobbled down his wine., He replaced the cup with a clatter and left. "I'll see to the casting off.

The king cleared his throat. "You and Katorn…" he began, but broke off. "You…"

"We are not friends," I said. "I dislike his surly, mistrustful manner — and he suspects me of being a fraud, a traitor, a spy of some sort."

King Rigenos nodded. "He has hinted as much to me." He sipped his wine. "I told him that I saw you materialize with my own eyes, that there is no question you are Erekosë, that there is no reason not to trust you — but he persists. Why, do you think? He is a sane, sensible soldier."

"He is jealous," I said. "I have taken over his power."

"But he was as agreed as any of us that we needed a new leader who would inspire our people in the fight against the Eldren!"

"In principle, perhaps," I said. I shrugged. "It does not matter, King Rigenos. I think we have worked out a compromise."

King Rigenos was lost in his own thoughts. "There again," he murmured, "it could have nothing to do with war, at all."

"What do you mean?"

He gave me a candid look. "It might concern matters of love, Erekosë. Katorn has always been pleased by Iolinda's manner."

"You could be right. But again there is nothing I can do. Iolinda seems to prefer my company."

"Katorn might see it as mere infatuation with an ideal rather than a real person."

"Do you see it as that?"

"I do not know. I have not talked to Iolinda about it."

"Well," I said, "perhaps we shall see when we return."

"If we return," said King Rigenos. "In that, I must admit, I'm in agreement with Katorn. Overconfidence has often been the main cause of many defeats."

I nodded. "Perhaps you are right."

There came shouts and cries from outside and the ship lurched suddenly as the ropes were cast off and the anchors hauled in.

"Come," said King Rigenos. "Let us go out on deck. It will be expected of us." Hastily he finished his wine and placed his crowned helmet upon his head. We left the cabin together and, as we came out, the cheering on the quayside swelled louder and louder.

We stood there waving to the people as the drums began to pound out the slow rowing rhythm. I saw Iolinda seated in her carriage, her body half-turned to watch as we left. I waved to her and she raised her own arm in a final salute.

"Goodbye, Iolinda," I murmured.

Katorn darted me a cynical look from the corner of his eye as he passed to supervise the rowing.

Goodbye, Iolinda.

The wind had dropped. I was sweating in my war gear, for the day was oppressed by a great flaming sun, blazing in a cloudless sky.

I continued to wave from the stern of the swaying vessel, keeping my gaze on Iolinda as she sat there erect in her carriage, and then we had rounded a bend in the river and saw only the rearing towers of Necranal above and behind us, heard only the distant cheering.

We beat down the Droonaa River, moving fast with the current toward Noonos of the Jeweled Towers — and the fleets.

N I N E

A T   N O O N O S

Oh these blind and bloody wars…

"Really, Bishop, you fail to understand that human affairs are resolved in terms of action."

Brittle arguments, pointless causes, cynicism disguised as pragmatism.

"Would you not rest, my son?"

"I cannot rest, Father, while the Paynim horde is already on the banks of the Danube."

"Peace…"

"Will they be content with peace?"

"Perhaps."

"They won't be satisfied with Vietnam. They won't be content until the whole of Asia is theirs… And after that, the world."

"We are not beasts.

"We must act as beasts. They act as beasts."

"But if we tried…"

"We have tried."

"Have we?"

"Fire must be fought with fire."

"Is there no other way?"

"There is no other way."

"The children…"

"There is no other way."

A gun. A sword. A bomb. A bow. A vibrapistol. A flamelance. An axe. A club.

"There is no other way."

On board the flagship that night, as the oars rose and fell and the drum continued its steady beat and the timbers creaked and the waves lapped at the hull, I slept poorly. Fragments of conversations. Phrases. Images. They tumbled in my tired brain and refused to leave me in peace. A thousand different periods of history. A million different faces. But the situation was always the same. The argument — made in myriad tongues — did not change.

Only when I rose from my bunk did my head clear and at length I resolved to go on deck.

What sort of creature was I? Why did it seem that I was forever doomed to drift from era to era and act out the same role wherever I went? What trick — what cosmic joke had been played upon me?

The night air was cool on my face and the moonlight struck through the light clouds at regular intervals so that the beams looked like the spokes of some gigantic wheel. It was as if the chariot of a god had sunk through the low cloud and become imbedded in the coarser air beneath.

I stared at the water and saw the clouds reflected in it, saw them break to reveal the moon. It was the same moon I had known as John Daker. The same bland face could be made out staring down in contentment at the antics of the creatures of the planet it circled. How many disasters had that moon witnessed? How many foolish crusades? How many wars and battles and murders?

The clouds moved together again and the waters of the river grew black as if to say that I would never find the revelation I sought.

I looked to the banks. We were passing through a thick forest. The tops of the trees were silhouetted against the slightly lighter darkness of the night. A few night animals voiced their cries from time to time and it seemed to me that they were lonely cries, lost cries, pitiful cries. I sighed and leaned against the rail and watched the water creamed gray by the slashing oars.

I had better accept that I must fight again. Again? Where had I fought before? What did my vague memories mean? What significance had my dreams? The simple answer — the pragmatic answer (or certainly one that John Daker could have best understood) — was that I was mad. My imagination was overwrought. Perhaps I had never been John Daker. Perhaps he, too, was another crazed invention.

I must fight again.

That was all there was to it. I had accepted the role and I must play it to the finish.

My brain began to clear as the moon set and dawn lightly touched the horizon.

THE ETERNAL CHAMPION

I watched the sun rise, a huge scarlet disc moving with steady grandeur into the sky, as if curious to discover the sounds that disturbed the world — the beat of the drum, the crack of the oars.

"You are not sleeping, Lord Erekosë. You are eager, I see, to do battle."

I felt I did not need Katorn's banter added to the burden. "I thought I would enjoy watching the sun rise," I said.

"And the moon set?" Katorn's voice implied something that I could not quite grasp. "You seem to like the night, Lord Erekosë."

"Sometimes," I said. "It is peaceful," I added as significantly as I could. "There is little to disturb a man's thoughts in the night."

"True. You have something in common with our enemies, then."

I turned impatiently, regarding his dark features with anger. "What do you mean?"

"I meant only that the Eldren, too, are said to prefer the night to the day."

"If it is true of me, my lord, "I said, "then it will be a great asset to us in our war with them if I can fight them by night as well as by day."

"I hope so, my lord."

"Why do you mistrust me so, Lord Katorn?"

He shrugged. "Did I say that I did? We struck a bargain, remember?"

"And I have kept my part of it."

"And I, mine. I will follow you, do not doubt that. Whatever I suspect, I will still follow you."

"Then I would ask you to discontinue these little jibes of yours. They are naive. They serve no purpose."

"They serve a purpose for me, Lord Erekosë. They ease my temper — they channel it into a suitable area."

"I have sworn my oath to Humanity," I told him. "I will serve King Rigenos's cause. I have my own burdens to bear, Lord Katorn."

"I am deeply sympathetic."

I turned away. I had come close to making a fool of myself — appealing to Katorn for mercy, almost, by claiming my own problems as an excuse.

"Thank you, Lord Katorn," I said coldly. The ship began to turn a bend in the river and I thought I could see the sea ahead. "I am grateful for your understanding." I slapped at my face. The ship was passing through a cloud of midges hovering over the river. "These insects are irritating, are they not?"

"Perhaps it would be best if you did not allow yourself to be subjected to their intentions, my lord," Katorn replied.

"Indeed, I think you are right, Lord Katorn. I will go below."

"Good morrow, my lord."

"Good morrow, Lord Katorn."

I left him standing on the deck and staring moodily ahead.

In other circumstances, I thought, I would slay that man.

As it was, there seemed a growing chance that he would do his utmost to slay me. I wondered if Rigenos were correct and Katorn was doubly jealous of me — jealous of my reputation as a warrior, jealous of Iolinda's love for me.

I washed and dressed myself in my war gear and refused to bother myself with all these pointless thoughts. A little later I heard the helmsman shout and went on deck to see what his call signified.

Noonos was in sight. We all crowded the rails to get a glimpse of this fabulous city. We were half blinded by the glare from the towers for they were truly jeweled. The city flared with light — a great white aura speckled with a hundred other colours, green and violet and pink and mauve and ochre and red, all dancing in the brighter glow created by a million gems.

And beyond Noonos lay the sea — a calm sea gleaming in the sunshine.

As Noonos came closer, the river widened until it was clear that this was where it opened into the ocean. The banks became more and more distant and we kept closer to the starboard bank, for that was the bank on which Noonos was built. There were other towns and villages dotted amongst the wooded hills overlooking the river mouth. Some of them were picturesque, but they were all dominated by the port we were approaching.

Now seabirds began to squeal around our topmast and, with a great flapping of wings, settle in the yards and squabble, it appeared, for the best spot in the rigging.

The rhythm of the oars became slower and we began to backwater as we approached the harbour itself. Behind us the squadron of proud ships dropped anchor. They would join us later when the pilot had come out to give them their mooring order.

Leaving our sister ships behind, we rowed slowly into Noonos, flying the standard of King Rigenos and the standard of Erekosë — a black field supporting a silver sword.

And the cheering began again. Held back by soldiers in armour of quilted leather, the crowds craned their necks to see us as we disembarked. And then, as I walked down the gangplank and appeared on the quayside, a huge chanting began that startled me at first when I realized what the word was that they were chanting.

"*EREKOSË! EREKOSË! EREKOSË! EREKOSË!*"

I raised my right arm in salute and almost staggered as the noise increased until it was literally deafening. I could barely refrain from covering my ears!

Prince Bladagh, Overlord of Noonos, greeted us with due ceremony and read out a speech that could not be heard for the shouting and then we were escorted through the streets toward the quarters we were to use while making our brief stay in the city.

The jeweled towers were not disappointing, though I noticed that the houses built closer to the ground made a great contrast. Many of them were little better than hovels. It was quite plain where the money came from to encrust the towers with rubies, pearls and emeralds.

I had not noticed this great disparity between the rich and the poor in Necranal. Either I had been too impressed by the newness of the sights or the royal city took pains to disguise any areas of poverty, if they indeed existed.

And there were ragged people here, to go with the hovels, though they cheered as loudly as the rest, if not louder. Perhaps they blamed the Eldren for their misery.

Prince Bladagh was a sallow-featured man of about forty-five. He had a long, drooping moustache, pale, watery eyes and his gestures were those of an irritable but fastidious vulture. It emerged, and I was not surprised, that he would not be joining us in our expedition but would remain behind "to protect the city" — or his own gold most likely, I thought.

"Ah, now, my liege," he muttered as we reached his palace and the jeweled gates swung back to admit us (I noticed that they would have shone better if they had been cleaned). "Ah, now — my palace is yours, King Rigenos. And yours, too, Lord Erekosë, of course. Anything you need."

"A hot meal — and a simple one," King Rigenos said, echoing my own sentiments. "No banquets. I warned you not to make a large ceremony of this, Bladagh."

"And I have not, my liege." Bladagh looked relieved. He did not seem to me to be a man who enjoyed spending money. "I have not."

The meal *was* simple, though not particularly well-prepared. We ate it with Prince Bladagh, his plump, stupid wife, Princess Ionante, and their two scrawny children. Privately I was amused at the contrast between the city seen from a distance and the appearance and way of life of its ruler.

A short while later the various commanders who had been assembling in Noonos for the past several weeks arrived to confer with Rigenos and myself.

Katorn was among them and was able to outline very succinctly and graphically the battle plans we had worked out between us in Necranal.

Among the commanders were several famous heroes of the Two Continents — Count Roldero, a burly aristocrat whose armour was as workmanlike and free from decoration as my own; also there was Prince Malihar and his brother, Duke Ezak, both of whom had been through many campaigns; Earl Shanura of Karakoa, one of the farthest provinces and one of the most barbaric. Shanura wore his hair long, in three plaits that hung down his back. His pale features were gaunt and crisscrossed with scars. He spoke seldom and usually to ask specific questions. The variety of the faces and the costumes surprised me at first. At least, I thought ironically, Humanity was united on this world, which was more than could be said for the world John Daker had left. But perhaps they were only united for the moment, to defeat the common enemy. After that, I thought, their unity might well suffer a setback. Earl Shanura, for instance, did not seem too happy about taking orders from King Rigenos, whom he probably considered soft.

I hoped that I could keep so disparate a group of officers together in the battles that were to follow.

At last we were finished with our discussions and I had spoken a word or two with every commander there. King Rigenos glanced at the bronze clock that stood on the table and which was marked with sixteen divisions. "It will be time to put to sea soon," he said. "Are all ships ready?"

"Mine have been ready for months," Earl Shanura said gruffly. "I was beginning to feel they would rot before they saw action."

The others agreed that their ships would be able to sail with little more than an hour's notice.

Rigenos and I thanked Bladagh and his family for their hospitality and they seemed rather more cheerful now that we were leaving.

Instead of marching from the palace, we now hurried in coaches to the quayside and rapidly boarded our ships. The king's flagship was called the *Iolinda*, a fact which I had not noticed before, my thoughts being full of the woman who bore that name. Our other ships from Necranal were now in port and their sailors were refreshing themselves in the short time they had, while slaves took on board the last provisions and armaments that were needed.

There was still a mood of slight depression hanging over me from my strange half-dreams of the previous night, but it was beginning to disperse as my excitement grew. It was still a month's sailing to Mernadin, but already I was beginning to relish the chance of action. At least action would help me forget the other problems. I was reminded of something that Pierre told Andrei in *War and Peace* — something about all men finding their own ways of forgetting the fact of death. Some womanized, some gambled, some drank and some, paradoxically, made war. Well, it was not the fact of death that obsessed me — indeed, it seemed that it was the fact of eternal existence that was preying on my mind. An eternal life involving eternal warfare.

Would I at some stage discover the truth? I was not sure that I wanted to know the truth. The thought frightened me. Perhaps a god could have accepted it. But I was not a god. I was a man. I knew I was a man. My problems, my ambitions, my emotions were on a human scale, save for the one abiding problem — the question of how I came to exist in this form, of how I had become what I was. Or was I truly eternal? Was there no beginning and no end to my existence? The very nature of Time was held in question. I could no longer regard Time as being linear, as I had once done as John Daker. Time could not be conceived of any longer in spatial terms.

I needed a philosopher, a magician, a scientist to help me on that problem. Or else I could forget it. But could I forget it? I would have to try.

The seabirds squawked and circled as the sails smacked down and swelled in the sultry wind that had started to blow. The timbers creaked as the anchors were weighed and the mooring ropes cast off from the capstans and the great flagship, *Iolinda*, heaved herself from the port, her oars still rising and falling, but making faster speed now as she sailed toward the open sea.

T E N

FIRST SIGHT OF THE ELDREN

The fleet was huge and contained great fighting ships of many kinds, some resembling what John Daker would have called nineteenth-century tea clippers, some that looked like junks, some with the lateen rig of Mediterranean craft, some that were very like Elizabethan caravels. Sailing in their separate formations, according to their province of origin, they symbolized the differences and the unity of mankind. I was proud of them.

Excited, tense, alert and confident of victory, we sailed for Paphanaal, gateway to Mernadin and conquest.

Yet I still felt the need to know more of the Eldren. My cloudy memory of the life of an earlier Erekosë could only conjure an impression of confused battles against them and also, perhaps, somewhere a feeling of emotional pain. That was all. I had heard that they had no orbs to their eyes and that this was their chief distinguishing nonhuman characteristic. They were said to be inhumanly beautiful, inhumanly merciless, and with inhuman sexual appetites. They were slightly taller than the average man, had long heads with high cheekbones and slightly slanting eyes. But this was not really enough for me. There were no pictures of Eldren anywhere on the Two Continents. Pictures were supposed to bring bad luck, particularly if the evil eyes of the Eldren were depicted.

As we sailed, there was a great deal of ship-to-ship communication, with commanders being rowed or hauled in slings to and from the flagship, depending on the weather. We had worked out our basic strategy and had contingency plans in case it should prove impossible to exercise. The idea had been mine and seemed a new one to the others, but they soon grasped it and the details had now all been decided upon. Each day the warriors of every ship were drilled in what they were to do when the Eldren fleet was sighted, if it was sighted. If it was not, we should dispatch part of the fleet straight to Paphanaal and begin the attack on the city. However, we expected the Eldren to send out their defense fleet to meet us before we reached Paphanaal and it was on this probability that we based our main plan.

Katorn and I avoided each other as much as possible. There were, in those first few days of sailing, none of the verbal duels of the sort we had had in Necranal and on the Droonaa River. I was polite to Katorn when we had need to communicate and he, in his surly way, was polite to me. King Rigenos seemed to be relieved and told me that he was glad we had settled our differences. We had not, of course, settled anything. We had merely waived those differences until such time as we could decide them once and for all. I knew eventually that I must fight Katorn or that he would try to murder me.

I took a liking to Count Roldero of Stalaco, though he was perhaps the most bloodthirsty of all when it came to discussing the Eldren. John Daker would have called him a reactionary, but he would have liked him. He was a staunch, stoical, honest man who spoke his mind and allowed others to speak theirs, expecting the same tolerance from them as he gave. When I had once suggested to him that he saw things too plainly in black and white, he smiled wearily and replied:

"Erekosë, my friend, when you have seen what I have of the events that have taken place in my lifetime on this planet of ours, then you will see things quite as clearly in black and white as I do. You can only judge people by their actions, not by their protestations. People act for good or they act for ill and those who do great ill are bad and those who do great good — they are good."

"But people may do great good accidentally, though with evil intentions — and conversely people may do great evil though having the best of intentions," I said, amused by his assumption that he had lived longer and seen more than I had — though I think his assumption was meant in jest.

"Exactly!" Count Roldero replied. "You have only repeated my point. I do not care, as I said, what people protest their intentions to be. I judge them by the results they achieve. Take the Eldren…"

I raised my hand, laughing. "I know how wicked they are. Everyone has told me of their cunning, their treachery, their black powers."

"Ah, you seem to think I hate Eldren individuals. I do not. For all I know they may be kind to their own children, love their wives and treat their animals well. I do not say that they are, as individuals, monsters. It is as a force that they must be considered. It is what they do that must be judged. It is on the threat of their own ambitions that we must base our attitude toward them."

"And how do you consider that force?" I asked.

"It is not human, therefore its interests are not human. Therefore, in terms of its own self-interest, it needs to destroy us. In this case, because the Eldren are not human, they threaten us merely by existing. And, by the same token, we threaten them. They understand this and would wipe us out. We understand this and would wipe them out before they have the chance to destroy us. You understand?"

The argument seemed convincing enough to the pragmatist that I considered myself to be. But a thought came to mind and I voiced it.

"Are you not forgetting one thing, Count Roldero? You have said it yourself — the Eldren are *not* human. You are assuming that they have human interests."

"They are flesh and blood," he said. "They are beasts, as we are beasts. They have those impulses, just as we have them."

"But many species of beast seem to live together in basic harmony," I reminded him. "The lion does not constantly war with the leopard; the horse does not war with the cow; even among themselves they rarely kill each other, no matter how important the issue to them."

"But they would," said Count Roldero, undaunted. "They would if they could anticipate events. They would if they could work out the rate at which the rival animal is consuming food, breeding, expanding its territory."

I gave up. I felt we were both on shaky ground now. We were seated in my cabin, looking out at a beautiful evening and a calm sea through the open porthole. I poured Count Roldero more wine from my dwindling store (I had taken to drinking a good deal of wine shortly before I went to bed, to insure myself of a rest not broken by visions and memories).

Count Roldero quaffed the wine and stood up. "It's getting late. I must return to my ship or my men will think I've drowned and be celebrating. I see you're running short of wine. I'll bring a skin or two on my next visit. Farewell, friend Erekosë. Your heart's in the right place, I'm sure. But you're a sentimentalist, for all you say to the contrary.

I grinned. "Good night, Roldero." I raised my half-full wine cup. "Let's drink to peace when this business is over!"

Roldero snorted. "Aye, peace — like the cows and the horses! Good night, my friend." He left laughing.

Rather drunkenly, I removed my clothes and fell into my bunk, chuckling foolishly at Roldero's parting remark. "Like the cows and the horses. He's right.

Who wants to lead a life like that? Here's to war!" And I flung the wine cup through the open porthole and fell to snoring almost before my eyes had closed.

And I dreamed.

But this time I dreamed of the wine cup I had hurled through the porthole. I imagined I saw it bobbing on the waves, its gold and jewels glittering. I imagined I saw it caught by a current and borne far away from the fleet — out to a lonely place where ships never sailed and land was never in sight, tossed forever on a bleak sea.

For the whole month of our sailing, the sea was calm, the wind good and the weather, on the whole, fine.

Our spirits rose higher. We took this to be a sign of good luck. All of us were cheerful. All, that is, save Katorn, who grumbled that this could well be the calm before the storm, that we must expect the worst of the Eldren when we eventually engaged.

"They are tricky," he would say. "Those filth are tricky. Even now they could know of our coming and have planned some maneuver we are not expecting. They might even be responsible for the weather."

I could not help laughing openly at this and he stalked off up the deck in anger. "You will see, Lord Erekosë," he called back. "You will see!"

And the next day the opportunity came.

According to our charts, we were nearing the coasts of Mernadin. We posted more lookouts, arranged the fleets of Humanity in battle order, checked our armament and cut our speed.

The morning passed slowly as we waited, the flagship in the forefront rocking on the waves, its sails reefed, its oars raised.

And then, around noon, the lookout in our topmast yelled through his megaphone:

"Ships for'ard! Five sails!"

King Rigenos, Katorn and I stood on the foredeck, staring ahead. I looked at King Rigenos and frowned. "Five ships? Five ships only?"

King Rigenos shook his head. "Perhaps they are not Eldren ships."

"They'll be Eldren craft," Katorn grunted. "What else could they be in these waters? No human merchants would trade with the creatures!"

And then the cry of the lookout reached us again.

"Ten sails now! Twenty! It's the fleet — the Eldren fleet! They are sailing fast upon us!"

And now I thought I glimpsed a flash of white on the horizon. Had it been the crest of a wave? No. It was the sail of a ship, I was sure.

"Look," I said. "There." And I pointed.

Rigenos screwed up his eyes and shielded them with his hand. "I see nothing. It is your imagination. They could not be coming in so fast."

Katorn, too, peered ahead. "Yes! I see it, too. A sail! They are that swift! By the Sea God's scales — slimy sorcery aids them! It is the only explanation."

King Rigenos seemed skeptical. "They are lighter craft than ours," he reminded Katorn, "and the wind is in their favour."

Katorn, in turn, was not convinced. "Maybe," he growled. "Perhaps you are right, sire."

"Have they used sorcery before?" I asked him. I was willing to believe anything. I had to if I was to believe what had happened to me!

"Aye!" spat Katorn. "Many times. All kinds! Ooph! I can smell sorcery on the very air!"

"When?" I asked him. "What kind? I wish to know so that I can take countermeasures."

"They can make themselves invisible sometimes. That's how they took Paphanaal, so it's said. They can walk on water, sail through the air."

"You have seen them do this?"

"Not myself. But I've heard many tales, tales I can believe from men who do not lie."

"And these men have experienced this sorcery?"

"Not themselves. But they have known men who did."

"So their use of sorcery remains a rumour," I said.

"Ach! Say what you like!" Katorn roared. "Do not believe me — you who are the very essence of sorcery, who owes his existence to an incantation. Why do you think I supported the notion to bring you back, Erekosë? Because I felt we needed sorcery that would be stronger than theirs! What else is that sword at your side but a sorcerous blade?"

I shrugged. "Let us wait, then," I said, "and see their sorcery."

King Rigenos called up at the lookout. "How big's the fleet you see?"

"About half our size, my liege!" he shouted back, his words distorted by the megaphone. "Certainly no larger. And I think it is their whole fleet. I see no more coming."

"They do not seem to be drawing any closer at this moment," I murmured to King Rigenos. "Ask him if they're moving."

"Has the Eldren fleet hove to, master lookout?" called King Rigenos.

"Aye, my liege. It no longer speeds hither and they seem to be furling their sails."

"They are waiting for us," Katorn muttered. "They want us to attack them. Well, we shall wait, too."

I nodded. "That is the strategy we agreed."

And we waited.

We waited as the sun set and night fell and far away on the horizon we caught the occasional glimpse of silver that could have been a wave or a ship. Hasty messages were sent by swimmers back and forth among the vessels of the fleet.

And we continued to wait, sleeping as best we could, wondering when, if at all, the Eldren would attack.

Katorn's footsteps could be heard pacing the deck as I lay awake in my cabin, trying to do the sensible thing and preserve my energy for the next day. Of all of us, Katorn was the most impatient to engage the enemy. I felt that, if it had been up to him, we should even now be sailing on the Eldren, having thrown our carefully worked-out battle plans overboard.

But luckily it was up to me. Even King Rigenos did not have the authority, except under exceptional circumstances, to countermand any of my orders.

I rested, but I could not sleep. I had had my first glimpse of an Eldren craft, yet I still did not know what the ships really looked like or what my impression of their crews would be.

I lay there, praying that our battle should soon begin. A fleet of only half our size! I smiled without humour. I smiled because I knew we should be victorious.

When would the Eldren attack?

It might even be tonight. Katorn had said that they loved the night.

I would not care if it was at night. I wanted to fight. A huge battle lust was building within me. I wanted to fight!

E L E V E N

THE FLEETS ENGAGE

A whole day passed and another night and still the Eldren remained on the horizon.

Were they deliberately hoping to tire us, make us nervous? Or were they afraid of the size of our fleet? Perhaps, I thought, their own strategy depended on our attacking them.

On the second night I did sleep, but not the drink-sodden slumber I had trained myself to. There was no drink left. Count Roldero had never had a chance to bring his wineskins on board.

And the dreams, if anything, were worse than ever.

I saw entire worlds at war, destroying themselves in senseless battles.

I saw Earth, but this was an Earth without a moon, an Earth which did not rotate, which was half in sunlight, half in a darkness relieved only by the stars. And there was strife here, too, and a morbid quest that as good as destroyed me. A name — Clarvis? Something of the sort. I grasped at these names, but they almost always eluded me and, I suppose, they were really the least important parts of the dreams.

I saw Earth — a different Earth again, an Earth which was so old that even the seas had begun to dry up. And I rode across a murky landscape, beneath a tiny sun, and I thought about Time.

I tried to hang on to this dream, this hallucination, this memory, whatever it was. I thought there might be a clue here to what I was, what had begun it all.

Another name — the Chronarch. Then it faded. There seemed to be no extra significance to this dream than to the rest.

Then this dream had faded and I stood in a city beside a large car and I was laughing and there was a strange sort of gun in my hand and bombs were raining from planes and destroying the city. I tasted an Upmann cigar.

I woke up, but was almost at once dragged back into my dreams.

I walked, insane and lonely, through corridors of steel and beyond the walls of the corridors was empty space. Earth was far behind. The steel machine in which I paced was heading for another star. I was tormented. I was obsessed with thoughts of my family. John Daker? No — John.

And then, as if to confuse me further, the names began. I saw them. I heard them. They were spelled in many different forms of hieroglyphics, chanted in many tongues.

Aubec. Byzantium. Cornelius. Colvin. Bradbury. London. Melniboné. Hawkmoon. Lanjis Liho. Powys. Marca. Elric. Muldoon. Dietrich. Arflane. Simon. Kane. Begg. Corum. Persson. Ryan. Asquiol. Pepin. Sewart. Mennell. Tallow. Hallner. Koln. Carnelian. Bastable. von Bek...

The names went on and on and on.

I awoke screaming.

And it was morning.

Sweating, I got out of my bunk and splashed cold water all over my body. Why did it not begin? Why?

I knew that, once the fighting started, the dreams would go away. I was sure of it.

And then the door of my cabin burst open and a slave entered.

"Master—"

A trumpet voiced a brazen bellow. There were the sounds of running men all over the ship.

"Master, the enemy ships are moving."

With a great sigh of relief I dressed myself, buckling on my armour as quickly as I could and strapping my sword about me.

Then I ran up on deck and climbed to the forecastle where King Rigenos stood, clad in his own armour, his face grim.

Everywhere in the fleet the war signals were being flown and voices called from ship to ship, trumpets snarled like metallic beasts and drums began to beat.

Now I could see for certain that the Eldren ships were on the move.

"Our commanders are all prepared," Rigenos murmured tensely. "See, our ships are already taking their positions."

I looked with pleasure as the fleet began to form itself according to our much rehearsed battle plan. Now, if only the Eldren would behave as we had anticipated, we should be the victors.

I looked forward again and gasped as the Eldren ships drew closer, marveled at their rare grace as they leaped lightly over the water like dolphins.

But they were not dolphins, I thought. They would rend us all if they could. Now I understood something of Katorn's suspicion of everything Eldren. If I had not known that these were our enemies, that they intended to destroy us, I would have stood there entranced at their beauty.

They were not galleons, as most of our craft were. They were ships of sail only — and the sails were diaphanous on slim masts. White hulls broke the darker white of the surf as they surged wildly, without faltering, toward us.

I studied their armament intently.

They mounted some cannon, but not as many as ours. Their cannon, however, were slender and silver and, when I saw them, I feared their power.

Katorn joined us. He was snarling with pleasure. "Ah, now," he growled. "Now. Now. See their guns, Erekosë? Beware of them. There is sorcery, if you do not believe me!"

"Sorcery? What do you mean?"

But he was off again, shouting at the men in the rigging to hurry their work.

I began to make out tiny figures on the decks of the Eldren ships. I caught glimpses of eldritch faces, but still could not, at that distance, discern any special characteristics. They moved swiftly about their ships as they swam speedily toward us.

Now our own fleet's maneuvers were almost complete and the flagship began to move into position.

I myself gave the orders to heave to and we rocked in the sea, awaiting the Eldren ships rushing toward us.

As planned, we had maneuvered to form a square that was strong on three sides, but weak on the side facing the Eldren fleet.

Some hundred ships were at the far end of the square, set stem to stern with cannon bristling. The two other strong sides also had about a hundred ships each and were at a far enough distance from each other so that their cannon could not accidentally sink one of their own craft. We had placed a thinner wall of ships — about twenty-five — at the side of the square where the Eldren were drawing in. We hoped to give the impression of a tightly closed square formation, with a few ships in the middle flying the royal colors, to give the impression that this was the flagship and its escorts. These ships were bait. The true flagship — the one on which I stood — had temporarily taken down its colors and lay roughly in the middle of the starboard side of the square.

Closer and closer now the Eldren ships approached. It was almost true what Katorn had said. They did seem to fly through the air rather than through the waves.

My hands began to sweat. Would they take the bait? The plan had struck the commanders as original, which meant that it was not the classical maneuver it had been in some periods of Earth's history. If it did not work, I would lose Katorn's confidence still further and it would not make my position any better with the king, whose daughter I hoped to marry.

But there was no point in worrying about that. I watched.

And the Eldren took the bait.

Cannon roaring, the Eldren craft smashed in a delta formation into the thin wall and, under their own impetus, sailed on to find themselves thickly surrounded on three sides.

"Raise our colours!" I shouted to Katorn. "Raise the colours! Let them see the originator of their defeat!"

Katorn gave the orders. My own banner went up first — the black field with the silver sword — and then the king's. We moved to tighten the trap, to crush the Eldren as they realized they had been tricked.

I had never seen such highly maneuverable sailing craft as the slender ships used by the Eldren. Slightly smaller than our men-o'-war, they darted about seeking an opening in the wall of ships. But there was no opening. I had seen to that.

Now their cannon bellowed fiercely, gouting balls of flame. Was this what Katorn had meant by "sorcery"? The Eldren ammunition was fire bombs rather than solid shot of the sort we used. Like comets, the fireballs hurtled through the noonday air. Many of our ships were fired. They blazed, crackling and groaning as the flames consumed them.

Like comets they were and the ships were like flashing sharks.

But they were sharks caught in a net that could not be broken. Inexorably we tightened the trap, our own guns booming heavy iron that tore into those white hulls and left black, gaping wounds; that ripped through those slim masts and brought the yards splintering down, the diaphanous sails flapping and fading like the wings of dying moths.

Our own monstrous men-o'-war, their heavy timbers clothed in brass, their huge oars churning the water, their dark, painted sails bulging, drew in to crush the Eldren.

Then the Eldren fleet divided into two roughly equal parts and dashed for the far corners of the net of ships — its weakest points. Many Eldren craft broke through, but we were prepared for this and with monumental precision our ships closed around them.

The Eldren fleet was now divided into several groups and it made our work easier. Implacably we sailed in to crush them.

The skies were filled with smoke and the seas with flaming wreckage and the air was populated by screams, yells and war shouts, the whine of the Eldren fireballs, the roar of our own shot, the shattering bellowings of the cannon. My face was covered by a film of grease and ash from the smoke and I sweated in the heat from the flames.

From time to time I caught a glimpse of a tense Eldren face and I wondered at their beauty and feared that perhaps we had been overconfident in our assumption of our victory. They were clad in light armour and moved about their ships as gracefully as trained dancers and their silver cannon did not once pause in their bombardment of our craft. Wherever the fireballs landed, the decks or rigging became instantly alight with a shrieking, all-consuming flame that burned green and blue and seemed to devour metal as easily as it did wood.

I gripped the rail of the foredeck and leaned forward, trying to peer through the stinging smoke. All at once I saw an Eldren ship side-on immediately ahead of us.

"Prepare to ram!" I yelled. "Prepare to ram!"

Like many of our ships, the *Iolinda* possessed an iron-shod ram lying just below the waterline. Now was our chance to use it. I saw the Eldren commander on his poop deck shout orders to his men to turn the ship. But it was too late even for the speedy Eldren. We bore down on the smaller craft and, our whole ship reverberating with the mighty roar, we drove into its side. Iron and timber screamed and ruptured, and foam lashed skyward. I was thrown back against the mast, losing my footing, and, as I clambered to my feet, I saw that we had broken the Eldren craft completely in two. I looked on the sight with a mixture of horror and exultation. I had not guessed the brutal power of the *Iolinda*.

On either side of our flagship I saw the two halves of the enemy ship rear in the water and begin to go down. The horror on my own face seemed matched by that on the Eldren commander's as he fiercely strove to hold himself erect on his sloping poop deck while his men threw up their arms and leaped into the dark, surging sea that was already full of smashed timbers and drifting corpses.

Swiftly now the sea swallowed the slim ship and I heard King Rigenos laughing behind me as the Eldren drowned.

I turned. His face was smeared by soot and his red-rimmed eyes stared wildly out of his haggard skull. The helmet-crown of iron and diamonds was askew on his head as he continued to laugh in his morbid triumph.

"Good work, Erekosë! The most satisfying method of all when dealing with these creatures. Break them open. Send them to the depths of the ocean so that they can be that much closer to their master, the Lord of Hell!"

Katorn climbed up. His face, too, was exultant. "I'll give you that, Lord Erekosë. You have proved you know how to kill Eldren."

"I know how to kill many kinds of men," I said quietly. I was disgusted by their response. I had admired the way in which the Eldren commander had died. "I merely took an opportunity," I said. "There is nothing clever in a ship of this size crushing lighter craft."

But there was no time to dispute the issue. Our ship was moving through the wreckage it had created, surrounded by orange tongues of flame, shrieks and yells, thick smoke which obscured vision in all directions so that it was impossible to tell how the fleets of Humanity fared.

"We must get out of this," I said. "Into clearer sea. We must let our own ships know that we are unharmed. Will you give the orders, Katorn?"

"Aye." Katorn went back to his duties.

My head was beginning to throb with the din of the battle. It became one great wall of noise, one huge wave of smoke and flame and the stench of death.

And yet — it was all familiar to me.

Up to now my battle tactics had been somewhat notional — intellectual rather than instinctive. But now it did seem that old instincts came into play and I gave orders without working them out first.

And I was confident that the orders were good. Even Katorn trusted them.

Thus it had been with the order to ram the Eldren craft. I had not stopped to think. It was probably just as well.

Its oars pulling strongly, the Iolinda cleared the worst of the smoke and her trumpets and drums announced her presence to the rest of the fleet. A cheering went up from some of the nearby ships as we emerged into an area relatively free of smoke, wreckage and other ships.

A few of our craft had begun to single out individual Eldren vessels and were hurling out their grappling irons toward the shark-ships. The savage barbs cut into the white rails, ripped through the shining sails, bit into flesh and tore off arms and legs. The great men-o'-war dragged the Eldren craft toward them, as whalers haul in their half-dead prey.

Arrows began to fly from deck to deck as archers, their legs twisted in the rigging, shot at enemy archers. Javelins rattled on the decks or pierced the armour of the warriors, Eldren and human, and threw them prone. The sound of cannon could still be heard, but it was not the steady pounding it had been. The shots became more intermittent and were replaced by the clash of swords, the shouts of warriors fighting hand to hand.

Smoke still formed acrid blossoms in the air above that watery battlefield. And when I could see through the murk to the green, wreckage-strewn ocean itself, I saw that the foam was no longer white. It was red. The sea was covered by a slick of blood.

As our ship beat on to join battle once again, I saw upturned faces staring at me from the sea. They were the faces of the dead, both Eldren and human, and they seemed to share a common expression — an expression of astonished accusation.

After a while, I tried to ignore the sight of those faces.

T W E L V E

THE BROKEN TRUCE

Two more ships fell to our ram and we sustained hardly any damage at all. The *Iolinda* moved through the battle like a dignified juggernaut, as if assured of her own invulnerability.

It was King Rigenos who saw it first. He screwed up his eyes and pointed through the smoke, his open mouth red in the blackness of his soot-covered face.

"There! See it, Erekosë? There!"

I saw a magnificent Eldren ship ahead of us, but I did not know why Rigenos singled it out.

"It is the Eldren flagship, Erekosë," Rigenos said. "It could be that their leader himself is aboard. If that cursed servant of Azmobaana does ride his own flagship and if we can destroy him, then our cause will be truly won. Pray that the Eldren prince rides her, Erekosë!"

Katorn snarled from behind us: "I would like to be the one to bring him down." He had a heavy crossbow in his mailed hands and he stroked its butt as another man might stroke a favourite kitten.

"Oh, let Prince Arjavh be there. Let him be there," hissed Rigenos thirstily.

I paid them little heed, but shouted the order for grappling irons to be readied.

Luck, it seemed, was still with us. Our huge vessel reared up on a surging wave at exactly the right moment and we rode it down upon the Eldren flagship, our timbers scraping its sides and turning it so that it lay in a perfect position for our grapples to seize it. The iron claws snaked out on thick ropes, clamped in the rigging, stabbed into the deck, snatched at the rails.

Now the Eldren craft was bound to us. We held it close, as a lover holds his mistress.

And that same smile of triumph began to cross my face. I had the sweet taste of victory on my lips. It was the sweetest taste of all. I, Erekosë, signed for a slave to run forward and wipe my face with a damp cloth. I drew myself up proudly on my deck. Just behind me was King Rigenos, on my right. On my left was Katorn. I felt a comradeship with them suddenly. I looked proudly down on the Eldren deck. The warriors looked exhausted. But they stood ready, with arrows strung on bows, with swords clenched in white fists and shields raised. They watched us silently; they did not attempt to cut the ropes, they waited for us to make the first move.

When two flagships locked in this way, there was always a pause before fighting broke out. This was to enable the enemy commanders to speak and, if both desired it, decide a truce and the terms of that truce.

Now King Rigenos bellowed across the rail of his high deck, calling out to the Eldren who looked up at him, their strange eyes smarting with the smoke as much as ours did.

"This is King Rigenos and his champion, the immortal Erekosë, your ancient enemy come again to defeat you. We, would speak with your commander for a moment, in the usual truce."

From beneath a canvas awning on his poop deck, a tall man now emerged. Through the shifting smoke I saw, dimly at first, a pointed, golden face with blue-flecked milky eyes staring sadly from the sockets of the slanting brow. An eldritch voice, like music, sang across the sea:

"I am Duke Baynahn, commander of the Eldren fleet. We will make no complicated peace terms with you, but if you let us sail away now, we will not continue to fight."

Rigenos smiled and Katorn snorted. "How gracious! He knows he is doomed."

Rigenos chuckled at this. Then he called back to Duke Baynahn.

"I find your proposal somewhat naive, Duke Baynahn."

Baynahn shrugged wearily. "Then let us finish this," he sighed. He raised his gloved hand to order his men to loose their arrows.

"Hold a moment!" Rigenos shouted. "There is another way, if you would spare your men.

Slowly Baynahn lowered his hand. "What is that?" His voice was wary.

"If your master, Arjavh of Mernadin, is aboard his own flagship — as he should be — let him come out and do battle with Lord Erekosë, Humanity's champion." King Rigenos spread out his palms. "If Arjavh should win, why, you will go in peace. If Erekosë should win, then you will become our prisoners."

Duke Baynahn folded his arms across his chest. "I have to tell you that our Prince Arjavh could not get to Paphanaal in time to sail with our fleet. He is in the West — in Loos Ptokai."

King Rigenos turned to Katorn.

"Kill that one, Katorn," he said quietly.

Duke Baynahn continued: "However, I am prepared to fight your champion if..."

"No!" I cried to Katorn. "Stop! King Rigenos, that is dishonourable — you speak during a truce."

"There is no question of honour, Erekosë, when exterminating vermin. That you will soon learn. Kill him, Katorn!"

Duke Baynahn was frowning, plainly puzzled at our muted argument, striving to catch the words.

"I will fight your Erekosë," he said. "Is it agreed?"

And Katorn brought up the crossbow and the bolt whirred and I heard a soft gasp as it penetrated the Eldren speaker's throat.

His hands went up toward the quivering bolt. His strange eyes filmed. He fell.

I was enraged at the treachery shown by one who so often spoke of treachery in his enemies. But now there was no time to remonstrate for already the Eldren arrows were whistling toward us and I had to ensure our defenses and prepare to lead the boarding party against the betrayed crew of the enemy ship.

I grasped a trailing rope, unsheathed my glowing sword and let the words come from my lips, though I was still full of anger against Katorn and the king.

"For Humanity!" I shouted. "Death to the Hounds of Evil!"

I swung down through the heated air that slashed against my face in that swift passage and I dropped, with howling human warriors behind me, among the Eldren ranks.

Then we were fighting.

My followers took care to stay away from me as the sword opened pale wounds in the Eldren foes, destroying all whom it even lightly cut. Many Eldren died beneath Kanajana, but there was no battle joy in me as I fought, for I was still furious with my own people's actions and there was no skill needed for such slaying — the Eldren were shocked at the death of their commander and they were plainly half dead with weariness, though they fought bravely.

Indeed, the slender ships seemed to hold more men than I had estimated. The long-skulled Eldren, well aware that my sword touch was lethal, flung themselves at me with desperate and ferocious courage.

Many of them wielded long-hafted axes, swinging at me out of reach of my sword. The sword was no sharper than any ordinary blade and, although I hacked at the shafts, I succeeded only in splintering them slightly. I had constantly to duck, stab beneath the whirling axe blades.

A young, golden-haired Eldren leaped at me, swung his axe and it smashed against my shoulder plate, knocking me off balance.

I rolled, trying desperately to regain my footing on the blood-smeared deck. The axe smashed down again, onto my breastplate, winding me. I struggled up into a crouching position, plunged forward beneath the axe and slashed at the Eldren's bared wrist.

A peculiar sobbing grunt escaped his lips. He groaned and died. The "poison" of the blade had done its work yet again. I still did not understand how the metal itself could be poisoned, but there was no doubting its effectiveness. I straightened up, my bruised body throbbing as I stared down at the brave young Eldren who now lay at my feet. Then I looked about me.

I saw that we had the advantage. The last pocket of fiercely fighting Eldren was on the main deck, back to back around their banner — a scarlet field bearing the silver basilisk of Mernadin.

I stumbled toward the fray. The Eldren were fighting to the last man. They knew they would receive no mercy from their human enemies.

I stopped. The warriors had no need of help from me. I sheathed my sword and watched as the Eldren were engulfed by our forces and, although all badly wounded, continued to fight until slain.

I looked about me. A peculiar silence seemed to surround the two locked ships, though in the distance the sound of cannon could still be heard.

Then Katorn, who had led the attack on the last Eldren defenders, snatched down their basilisk banner and flung it into the flowing Eldren blood. Insanely he began to trample the flag until it was completely soaked and unrecognizable.

"Thus will all the Eldren perish!" he screamed in his mad triumph. "All! All! All!"

He stumbled below to see what loot there was.

The silence returned. The drifting smoke began to dissipate and hang higher in the air above us, obscuring the sunlight.

Now that the flagship was ours, the day was won. Not a single prisoner would be taken. In the distance the victorious human warriors were busy firing the Eldren vessels. There seemed to be no Eldren ships left uncaptured, none fleeing over the horizon. Many of our own ships had been destroyed or were sinking in flames. Both sides' craft were stretched across a vast expanse of water and the ocean itself was covered by so great and thick a carpet of wreckage and corpses that it seemed as if the remaining ships were embedded in it.

I, for one, felt trapped by it. I wanted to leave this scene as soon as possible. The smell of the dead choked me. This was not the battle I had expected to fight. This was not the glory I had hoped to win.

Katorn re-emerged with a look of satisfaction on his dark face.

"You're empty-handed," I said. "Why so pleased?"

He wiped his lips. "Duke Baynahn had his daughter with him."

"Is she still alive?"

"Not now."

I shuddered.

Katorn stretched up his head and looked around him. "Good. We've finished them. I'll give orders to fire the remaining vessels."

"Surely," I said, "that is a waste. We could use their ships to replace those we have lost."

"Use these cursed craft? Never." He spoke with a twist of his mouth and strode to the rail of the Eldren flagship, shouting to his men to follow him back to their own vessel.

I came reluctantly, looking back to where the corpse of the betrayed Duke Baynahn still lay, the crossbow bolt projecting from his slender neck.

Then I clambered aboard our ship and I gave the orders to save what grapples we could and cut away the rest.

King Rigenos greeted me. He had taken no part in the actual fighting. "You did well, Erekosë. Why, you could have taken that ship single-handed."

"I could have," I said. "I could have taken the whole fleet single-handed."

He laughed. "You are very confident! The whole fleet!"

"Aye. There was one way."

He frowned. "What do you mean?"

"If you had let me fight Duke Baynahn — as he suggested — many lives and many ships would have been saved. Our lives. Our ships."

"You surely did not trust him? The Eldren will always try some trick like that. Doubtless, if you had agreed to his plan, you would have stepped aboard his ship and been cut down by a hundred arrows. Believe me, Erekosë, you must not be deceived by them. Our ancestors were so deceived — and look how we suffer now."

I shrugged. "Maybe you are right."

"Of course I am right." King Rigenos turned his head and called to our crew, "Fire the ship! Fire that cursed Eldren craft! Hurry, you laggards!"

He was in a good humour was King Rigenos. A great good humour.

I watched as blazing arrows were accurately shot into bales of combustible materials which had been placed in strategic parts of the Eldren ship.

The slender vessel soon caught. The bodies of the slain began to burn and oily smoke struck upward to the sky. The ship drifted away, its silver cannon like the snouts of slaughtered beasts, its glistening sails dropping in flaming ribbons to the already flaming deck. It gave a long shudder suddenly as if expiring the last of its life.

"Put a couple of shots below the waterline," Katorn shouted to his gunners. "Let's make sure the thing sinks once and for all."

Our brazen cannon snarled and the heavy shot smashed into the Eldren flagship, sending up gouts of water and crashing through the timbers.

The flagship yawed, but still seemed to be trying to stay upright. Her drifting went slower and slower as she settled lower in the water until she had stopped altogether. And then all at once she sank swiftly and was gone.

l thought of the Eldren duke. I thought of his daughter.

And something in me envied them. They would know eternal peace, just as it seemed I should know nothing but eternal strife.

Our fleet began to reassemble.

We had lost thirty-eight men-o'-war and a hundred and ten smaller craft of different types.

But nothing remained of the Eldren fleet.

Nothing but the burning hulks which we left, sinking, behind us as we sailed, in battle-thirsty glee, for Paphanaal.

T H I R T E E N
P A P H A N A A L

For the rest of our sailing toward Paphanaal, I avoided both Katorn and King Rigenos. Perhaps they were right and the Eldren could not be trusted. But should we not set some kind of example?

On the second night of the voyage after the big battle with the Eldren, Count Roldero visited me.

"You did well there," he said. "Your tactics were superb. And I hear you accounted well for youself in the hand-to-hand fighting." He looked about him in mock fear and whispered, jerking his thumb at a vague spot above him, "But I hear Rigenos decided that it was best he did not put the royal person in danger, lest we warriors lose heart."

"Oh," I said, "Rigenos has a fair point. He came with us, don't forget. He could have stayed behind. We all expected him to. Did you hear of the order he gave while the truce was on with the enemy commander?"

Roldero sniffed. "Had him shot by Katorn?"

"Yes."

"Well…" Roldero grinned at me. "You make allowances for Rigenos's cowardice and I'll make allowances for his treachery!" He burst into gusty laughter. "That's fair, eh ?"

l could not help smiling. But later, more seriously, I said: "Would you have done the same, Roldero?"

"Oh, I expect so. War, after all…"

"But Baynahn was prepared to fight me. He must have known his chances were slim. He must have known, too, that Rigenos could not be trusted to keep his word."

"If he did, then he would have acted as Rigenos acted. It was just that Rigenos was quicker. Merely tactics, you see — the trick is to gauge the exact moment to be treacherous."

"Baynahn did not look like one who would have acted treacherously."

"He was probably a very kind man and treated his family well. I told you, Erekosë, it is not Baynahn's character I dispute. I just say that, as a warrior, he would have tried what Rigenos succeeded in doing — eliminating the enemy's chief. It is one of the basic principles of warfare!"

"Do you say so, Roldero?"

"I do say so. Now drink up."

I did drink up. And I drank deep and I drank myself stupid. Now there were not merely the dream memories to contend with, but much more recent memories, too.

Another night came before we reached the harbour city of Paphanaal and we lay at anchor, a sea league or so offshore.

Then, in the shifting dawn of the morrow, we upped anchors and rowed in toward Paphanaal, for there was no wind to fill our sails.

Nearer we came to land.

I saw cliffs and black mountains rising.

Nearer.

I saw a flash of brighter colour to the east of us.

"*Paphanaal!*" shouted the lookout from his precarious perch in the top trees.

Nearer.

And there was Paphanaal.

She was undefended as far as we could make out. We had left her defenders on the bottom of the ocean, far behind.

There were no domes on this city, no minarets. There were steeples and buttresses and battlements, all close together. They made the city seem like one great palace. The materials of their construction were breathtaking. There was white marble veined with pink, blue, green and yellow. Orange marble, veined with black. Marble faced with gold, basalt and quartz and bluestone in abundance.

It was a shining city.

As we came closer, we saw no one on the quaysides, no one in the streets or on the battlements. I assumed that the city had been deserted.

I was wrong.

We put in to the great harbour and disembarked. I formed our armies into disciplined ranks and warned them of a possible trap, although I did not really believe there could be one.

The warriors had spent the rest of the voyage repairing their clothes and their armour, cleaning their weapons and making repairs to their ships.

All the ships crowded the harbour now, their flags waving in the light breeze that had come up almost as soon as we set foot on the cobblestones of the quay. Clouds came in with the breeze and made the day gray.

The warriors stood before King Rigenos, Katorn and myself. Rank upon rank they stood, their armour bright, their heavy banners moving sluggishly.

There were seven hundred divisions, each hundred divisions commanded by a marshal, who had as his commanders his captains, who controlled twenty-five divisions each, and his knights, who controlled one division.

The wine had helped fade the memory of the battle and I felt the return of my old pride as I stood looking at the paladins and armies of Humanity assembled before me. I addressed them.

"Marshals, Captains, Knights and Warriors of Humanity, you have seen me to be a victorious war leader."

"Aye!" they roared, jubilant.

"We shall be victorious here and elsewhere in the land of Mernadin. Go now, with caution, and search these buildings for Eldren. But be careful. This city could hide an army, remember!"

Count Roldero spoke up from the front rank.

"And booty, Lord Erekosë. What of that?"

King Rigenos waved his hand. "Take what booty you desire. But remember what Erekosë has said — be wary for such things as poisoned food. Even the wine cups could be smeared with poison. Anything in this damned city could be poisoned!"

The divisions began to march past us, each taking a different direction.

I watched them go and I thought that, while the city received them into its heart, it did not welcome them.

I wondered what we would find in Paphanaal. Traps? Hidden snipers? Everything poisoned, as Rigenos had said?

We found a city of women.

Not one Eldren man had remained.

Not one boy over twelve. Not one old man of any age.

We had slain them all at sea.

F O U R T E E N

E R M I Z H A D

I did not know how they slew the children. I begged King Rigenos not to give the order. I pleaded with Katorn to spare them — to drive them from the city if he must, but not to kill them.

But the children were slain. I do not know how many.

We had taken over the palace which had belonged to Duke Baynahn himself. He had, it transpired, been warden of Paphanaal.

I shut myself in my quarters while the slaughter went on outside. I reflected sardonically that for all their talk of the Eldren "filth", they did not seem to mind forcing their attentions on the Eldren women.

There was nothing I could do. I did not even know if there was anything I should do. I had been brought here by Rigenos to fight for Humanity, not to judge it. I had agreed to answer his summons, after all — doubtless with reason. But I had forgotten any reason.

I sat in a room that was exquisitely furnished with delicate furniture and fine, light tapestries on walls and floor. I looked at the Eldren craftsmanship and I sipped the aromatic Eldren wine and I tried not to listen to the cries of the Eldren children as they were butchered in their beds in the houses in the streets beyond the thin palace walls.

I looked at Kanajana, which I had propped in a corner, and I hated the poisoned thing. I had stripped myself of my armour and I sat alone.

And I drank more wine.

But the wine of the Eldren began to taste of blood and I tossed the cup away and found a skin that Count Roldero had given me and sucked it dry of the bitter wine it contained.

But I could not get drunk. I could not stop the screams from the streets. I could not fail to see the flickering shadows on the tapestries I had drawn over the windows. I could not get drunk and therefore I could not even begin to try to sleep, for I knew what my dreams would be and I feared those almost as much as I feared thinking of the implications of what we were doing to those who were left in Paphanaal.

Why was I here? Oh, why was I here?

There was a noise outside my door and then a knock.

"Enter," I said.

No one entered. My voice had been too low.

The knock sounded again.

I rose and walked unsteadily to the door and flung it open.

"Can you not leave me in peace?"

A frightened soldier of the Imperial Guard stood there. "Lord Erekosë, forgive me for disturbing you, but I bear a message from King Rigenos."

"What's the message?" I said without interest.

"He would like you to join him. He says that there are still plans to discuss."

I sighed. "Very well. I will come down shortly."

The soldier hurried off along the corridor.

At last, reluctantly, I rejoined the other conquerors. All the marshals were there, lounging on cushions and celebrating their victory. King Rigenos was there and he was so drunk that I envied him. And, to my relief, Katorn was not there.

Doubtless he was leading the looters.

As I came into the hall, a huge cheer went up from the marshals and they raised their wine-cups in a toast to me.

I ignored them and walked to where the king was seated alone, staring vacantly into space.

"You wish to discuss further campaigns, King Rigenos," I said. "Are you sure?"

"Ah, my friend Erekosë. The Immortal. The Champion. The saviour of Humanity. Greetings, Erekosë." He put a hand drunkenly on my arm. "You disapprove of my unkingly insobriety, I see."

"I disapprove of nothing," I said. "I have been drinking much myself."

"But you — an Immortal — can contain your" — he belched — "can contain your liquor."

I took pains to smile and said: "Perhaps you have stronger liquor. If so, let me try it."

"Slave!" screamed King Rigenos. "Slave! More of that wine for my friend Erekosë!"

A curtain parted and a trembling Eldren boy appeared. He was bearing a wineskin almost as large as himself.

"I see you have not slain all the children," I said.

King Rigenos giggled. "Not yet. Not while there are uses for them!"

I took the wineskin from the child and nodded to him. "You may go." I held the skin and put the opening to my lips and began to drink deeply. But still the wine refused to dull my brain. I hurled the skin away and it fell heavily and slopped wine over the tapestries and cushions covering the floor.

King Rigenos continued to giggle. "Good! Good!"

These people were barbarians. Suddenly I wished that I was John Daker again. Studious, unhappy John Daker, living his quiet, cut-off life in the pursuit of pointless learning.

I turned to leave.

"Stay, Erekosë. I'll sing a song. It's a filthy song about the filthy Eldren."

"Tomorrow."

"It's already tomorrow!"

"I must rest."

"I am your king, Erekosë. You owe your material form to me. Do not forget that!"

"I have not forgotten."

The doors of the hall burst open then and they dragged in the girl.

Katorn led them and he was grinning like a sated wolf.

She was a black-haired girl. Her alien features were composed against the fear she felt. She had a strange, shifting beauty which was always there but which seemed to change with every breath she took. They had torn her garments and bruised her arms and face.

"Erekosë!" Katorn followed his men in. He, too, was very drunk. "Erekosë — Rigenos, my lord king — *look!*"

The king blinked and looked at the girl with distaste. "Why should we take interest in an Eldren wanton? Get hence, Katorn. Use her as you will —

that is your private decision — but be sure she is not still alive when we leave Paphanaal."

"No!" laughed Katorn. "Look! Look at her!"

The king shrugged and inspected the wine swilling in his cup.

"Why have you brought her here, Katorn?" I asked quietly.

Katorn rocked with laughter. His thick lips opened wide and he roared in our faces. "You know not who she is, that's plain!"

"Take the Eldren wench away, Katorn!" The king's voice rose in drunken irritation.

"My lord king — this — this is *Ermizhad!*"

"What?" The king leaned forward and stared at the girl. "What? Ermizhad, that whore! Ermizhad of the Ghost Worlds!"

Katorn nodded. "The same."

The king grew more sober. "She's lured many a mortal to his death, so I've heard. She shall die by torture for her lustful crimes. The stake shall have her."

Katorn shook his head. "No, King Rigenos — at least, not yet. Forget you that she's Prince Arjavh's sister?"

The king nodded in a mockery of gravity. "Of course. Arjavh's sister."

"And the implications, my lord? We should keep her prisoner, should we not? She will make a good hostage, eh? A good bargaining counter, should we need one?"

"Ah, of course. Yes. You did right, Katorn. Keep her prisoner." The king grinned a silly grin. "No. It is not fair. You deserve to enjoy yourself further this night. Who does not wish to enjoy himself?" He looked at me. "Erekosë — Erekosë who cannot get drunk. She shall be put in your charge, Champion."

I nodded. "I accept the charge," I said. I pitied the girl, whatever terrible crimes she had committed.

Katorn looked at me suspiciously.

"Do not worry, Lord Katorn," I said. "Do as the king says — continue to enjoy yourself. Slay some more. Rape some more. There must be plenty left."

Katorn drew his brows together. Then his face cleared a little.

"A few maybe," he said. "But we've been thorough. Only she will live to see the sun rise, I think." He jabbed a thumb at his prisoner, then signed to his men. "Come! Let's finish our task."

He stalked out.

Count Roldero got up slowly and came toward me as I stood looking at the Eldren girl.

The king looked up. "Good. Keep her from harm, Erekosë," he said cynically. "Keep her from harm. She'll be a useful piece in our game with Arjavh."

"Take her to my apartments in the east wing," I told the guards, "and make sure she's unmolested and has no chance to escape."

They took her away and, almost as soon as she had left, King Rigenos made to stand up, swayed and fell with a crash to the floor.

Count Roldero gave a slight smile. "Our liege is not himself," he said. "But Katorn is right. The Eldren bitch will be useful to us."

"I understand her usefulness as a hostage," I said, "but I do not understand this reference to 'the Ghost Worlds.' I've heard them spoken of once before. What are they, Roldero?"

"The Ghost Worlds? Why, we all know of them. I should have thought that you would, too. But we do not often speak of them."

"Why so?"

"Humankind fear Arjavh's allies so much that they will rarely mention them, in terror of conjuring them up by their words, you understand."

"I do not understand."

Roldero rubbed his nose and coughed. "I am not superstitious, Erekosë," he said. "Like yourself."

"I know. But what are the Ghost Worlds?"

Roldero seemed nervous. "I'll tell you, but I'm uncomfortable about doing so in this cursed place. The Eldren know better than we what the Ghost Worlds are. We had thought, at first, that you yourself were a prisoner there. That was why I was surprised."

"Where are they?"

"The Ghost Worlds lie beyond Earth — beyond Time and beyond Space — linked to Earth only by the most tenuous of bonds."

Roldero's voice dropped, but he whispered on.

"There, on the torn Ghost Worlds, dwell the many-coiled serpents which are the terror and the scourge of the eight dimensions. Here, also, live ghosts and men — those who are manlike and those who are unlike men — those who know that their fate is to live without Time, and those who are unaware of their doom. And there, also, do kinfolk to the Eldren dwell — the halflings."

"But what *are* these worlds?" I asked impatiently.

Roldero licked his lips. "They are the worlds to which human sorcerers sometimes go in search of alien wisdom, and from which they draw helpers of horrible powers and disgusting deeds. It is said that within those worlds an

THE ETERNAL CHAMPION

initiate may meet his long-slain comrades, who may sometimes help him; his dead loves and his dead kin, and particularly his enemies — those whom he has caused to die. Malevolent enemies with great powers — or wretches who are half-souled and incomplete."

His whispered words convinced me, perhaps because I had drunk so much. Was it these Ghost Worlds that were the origin of my strange dreams? I wanted to know more.

"But what are they, Roldero? Where are they?"

Roldero shook his head. "I do not concern myself with such mysteries, Erekosë. I have never been much of a mystic. I believe — but I do not probe. I know of no answer to either of your questions. They are worlds full of shadow and gloomy shores upon which drab seas beat. The populace can sometimes be summoned by powerful sorcery to visit this Earth, to haunt, to help — or to terrorize. We think that the Eldren came, originally, from these half-worlds if they were not, as our legends say, spawned from the womb of a wicked queen who gave her virginity to Azmobaana in return for immortality — the immortality which her offspring inherited. But the Eldren are material enough, for all their lack of souls, whereas the Ghost Armies are rarely solid flesh."

"And Ermizhad?"

"The Wanton of the Ghost Worlds."

"Why is she called that?"

"It is said that she mates with ghouls," muttered Count Roldero. He shrugged and drank more wine. "And in return for giving her favours to them, she receives special powers over the halflings who are friends with the ghouls. The halflings love her, I'm told, as far as it's possible for such creatures to love."

I could not believe it. The girl seemed young. Innocent. I said as much.

Roldero gestured dismissively. "How do you tell the age of an Immortal? Look at yourself. How old are you, Erekosë? Thirty? You look no older."

"But I have not lived forever," I said. "At least, not in one body, I do not think."

"But how do you tell?"

I could not answer him, of course. "Well, I think there's a great deal of superstition mixed up in your tale, Roldero," I said. "I would not have expected it of you, old friend."

"Believe me or not," Roldero muttered. "But you would do better to believe me until I am proved a liar, eh?"

"Possibly you're right."

"I sometimes wonder at you, Erekosë," he said. "Here you are owing your own existence to an incantation, and you are the most sceptical man I know!"

I smiled at this. "Yes, Roldero. I should indeed believe more."

"Come," said Roldero, moving toward the prone king, who lay on his face in a pool of wine. "Let's get our lord to bed before he drowns."

Together we picked up the king and called for a soldier to help us as we hauled Rigenos up the stairs and dumped him on his bed.

Roldero put a huge hand on my shoulder. "And stop brooding, friend. It will do no good. Think you that I enjoy the slaughter of children? The rape of young girls?" He rubbed his mouth with the back of his hand as if to rid it of a foul taste. "But if it is not done now, Erekosë, it will be done at some time to our children and to our young girls. I know the Eldren are beautiful. But so are many snakes. So are some kinds of wolf that prey on sheep. It is braver to do what has to be done than it is to pretend to yourself that you are not doing it. You follow me?"

We stood in the king's bed chamber staring at each other.

"You are very kind, Roldero," I said.

"It's well-meant advice," he told me.

"I know it is."

"It was not your decision to slaughter the children," he said.

"But it was my decision to say nothing of it to King Rigenos," I replied.

At the mention of his name, the king stirred and began to mumble in his stupor.

"Come," grinned Roldero. "Let's get out of here before he remembers the words of that dirty song he promised to sing us."

We parted in the corridor outside the chamber. Count Roldero looked at me with some concern. "These actions must be made," he said. "It has befallen us to be the instruments of a decision made some centuries ago. Do not bother yourself with matters of conscience. The future may see us as bloody-handed butchers. But we know we are not. We are men. We are warriors. And we are at war with those who would destroy us."

I said nothing, but put my hand on his shoulder, then turned and walked back to my lonely apartments.

In my mental discomfort, I had all but forgotten the girl until I saw the guard at my door.

"Is the prisoner secure?" I asked him.

"There is no way out," the guard said. "No way, at least, Lord Erekosë, that a human could take. But if she were to summon her halfling allies…"

"We'll concern ourselves with those when they materialize," I told him. He unlocked the door for me and I entered.

There was only one lamp burning and I could barely see. I took a taper from a table and with it lit another lamp.

The Eldren girl lay on the bed. Her eyes were closed, but her cheeks were stained with tears.

So they cry like us, too, I thought.

I tried not to disturb her, but she opened her eyes and I thought I saw fear in them, though it was difficult to tell, for the eyes really were strange — without orbs and flecked with gold and blue. Seeing those eyes, I remembered what Roldero had told me and I began to believe him.

"How are you?" I asked inanely.

Her lips parted, but she did not speak.

"I do not intend to harm you," I said weakly. "I would have spared the children if I could. I would have spared the warriors in the battle. But I have only the power to lead men to kill each other. I have no power to save their lives."

She frowned.

"I am Erekosë," I said.

"Erekosë?" The name was music when she spoke it. She pronounced it more familiarly than I did myself.

"You know who I am?"

"I know who you were."

"I am reborn," I said. "Do not ask me how."

"You do not seem happy to be reborn, Erekosë."

I shrugged.

"Erekosë," she said again. And then she voiced a low, bitter laugh.

"Why do you laugh?"

But she would not speak again. I tried to converse with her further. She closed her eyes. I left the room and went to the bed next door.

The wine had worked at last — or something had — for I slept without dreaming.

FIFTEEN
THE RETURNING

Next morning I arose, washed myself, dressed and knocked on Ermizhad's door.

There was no reply.

Thinking that she had, perhaps, escaped and that Katorn would be instantly suspicious that I had helped her, I flung open the door and entered.

She had not escaped. She still lay on the bed, but now her eyes were open again as she stared at the ceiling. Those eyes were as mysterious to me as the star-flecked depths of the universe.

"Did you sleep well?" I asked.

She did not reply.

"Are you ill?" was my next, rather stupid question. But she had plainly decided to communicate with me no further. I made one last attempt and then left, going down to the great hall. Here Roldero was waiting for me and there were a few other marshals, looking the worse for wear, but King Rigenos and Katorn were not present.

Roldero's eyes twinkled. "There are no drums beating in your skull by the look of you."

He was right. I had not considered it, but I suffered no after effects from the huge quantities of wine drunk the night before.

"I feel very good," I said.

"Ah, now I believe you are an Immortal!" he laughed. "I have not escaped so lightly. Neither, it seems, have King Rigenos and Lord Katorn, or some of the others who were enjoying themselves so much last night." He drew closer and said quietly: "And I hope you are in better spirits today, my friend."

"I suppose that I am," I said. I felt drained of emotion, in fact.

"Good. And what of that Eldren creature? Still safe?"

"Still safe."

"She did not try to seduce you?"

"On the contrary, she will not speak to me at all!"

"Just as well." Roldero looked around impatiently. "I hope they get up soon. There's much to discuss. Do we carry on inland or what?"

"I thought we agreed that the best plan was to leave a good force here, strong enough to defend the city, and get back to the Two Continents to re-equip and to check any attempt to invade us while our fleet's at Paphanaal."

Roldero nodded. "It's the most sensible plan. But I do not like it very much. While it has logic, it does not suit my impatience to get at the enemy as soon as possible."

I agreed with him. "I would like to have done with this as soon as I am able," I told him.

But we had little clear idea where the rest of the Eldren forces were marshaled. There were four other major cities on the continent of Mernadin. The chief of these was Loos Ptokai, which lay near to the Plains of Melting Ice. This was Arjavh's headquarters and, from what the Eldren on the flagship had said, he was either there now or marching to recapture Paphanaal. It seemed to us that he would attempt this, because Paphanaal was the most important position on the coast. With it in our hands, we had a good harbour in which to bring our ships and land our men.

And if Arjavh did march against us, then all we had to do was save our energy and wait. We thought that we could leave our main force in Paphanaal, return to our own base at Noonos, bringing back the divisions of warriors who, because of insufficient ships, had been unable to come with us on the preliminary expedition.

But Roldero had something else on his mind. "We must not forget the sorcerous fortresses of the Outer Islands," he told me. "They lie at World's Edge. The Outer Islands should be taken as soon as possible."

"What exactly are the Outer Islands? Why are they so strategic?" I asked him. "And why haven't they been mentioned before in our plans?"

"Ah," said Count Roldero. "Ah, it is because of our reluctance, particularly when at home, to discuss the Ghost Worlds."

I made a sign of mock despair. "The Ghost Worlds again!"

"The Outer Islands lie in the gateway to the Ghost Worlds," Roldero said seriously. "From there the Eldren can summon their ghoulish allies. Perhaps, now Paphanaal is taken, we should concentrate on smashing their strength in the west — at World's Edge."

Had I been wrong to be so sceptical? Or was Roldero over-estimating the power of the Ghost World denizens? "Roldero, have you ever seen these halflings?" I asked him.

"Oh, yes, my friend," he replied. "You are wrong if you believe them legendary beings. They are, in one sense, real enough."

I became more convinced. I trusted Roldero's opinions more than most.

"Then perhaps we should alter our strategy slightly," I said. "We can leave the main army here to wait for Arjavh to march against the city and waste his strength trying to take it from the land side. We return to Noonos with the large portion of the fleet, add any new ships that are ready to our force, take fresh warriors aboard — and sail against the Outer Islands while, if we are right, Arjavh expends his own force trying to retake Paphanaal."

Roldero nodded. "It seems a wise plan to me, Erekosë. But what of the girl, our hostage? How shall we use her to our best advantage?"

I frowned. I did not like the idea of using her at all. I wondered where she would be safest.

"I suppose we should keep her as far away from here as possible," I said. "Necranal would be best. There is little chance of her people being able to rescue her and she would have a difficult time getting back if she managed to escape. What do you think?"

Roldero nodded. "I think you are right. That's sensible."

"We must discuss all this with the king, of course," I said gravely.

"Of course," said Roldero, and winked.

"And Katorn," I added.

"And Katorn," he agreed. "Especially Katorn."

It was well after noon before we had the chance to speak with Katorn or the king. Both were pale-faced and were quick to agree with our suggestions as if they would agree to anything as long as they were left alone.

"We'll establish our position here," I told the king, "and set sail back to Noonos within the week. We should waste no time. Now that we have gained Paphanaal, we can expect savage counterattacks from the Eldren."

"Aye," muttered Katorn. He was red-eyed. "And you are right to try to block off Arjavh's summoning of his frightful Ghost Armies."

"I am glad you approve of my plan, Lord Katorn," I said.

His smile was twisted. "You're proving yourself, my lord, after all. Still a little soft toward our enemies, but you're beginning to realize what they're like."

"I wonder," I said.

There were minor details of the plan to discuss and, while the victorious warriors continued to pleasure themselves on Eldren spoils, we talked of these matters until they were completely settled.

It was a good plan.

It would work if the Eldren reacted as we expected. And we were sure that they would.

We agreed that King Rigenos and I would return with the fleet, leaving Katorn to command the army at Paphanaal. Roldero also elected to return with us. The bulk of the warriors would remain behind. We had to hope that the Eldren did not have another fleet in the vicinity, for we would be sailing back with just the minimum crews and would be hard-pressed to defend ourselves if attacked at sea.

But there were risks to all the different possibilities and we had to decide which actions the Eldren were most likely to take and act accordingly.

The next few days were spent in preparation for the voyage back and soon we were ready to sail.

We sailed out of Paphanaal on a dawn tide, our ships moving sluggishly through the water, for they groaned with captured Eldren treasure.

Begrudgingly the king had agreed to give Ermizhad decent quarters next to mine. His attitude toward me seemed to have changed since the first drunken night in Paphanaal. He was reserved, almost embarrassed by my presence. Doubtless he remembered vaguely that he had made some sort of fool of himself. Perhaps he resented my refusal to celebrate our victory; perhaps the glory that I had won for him made him jealous, though the gods knew I wanted nothing of that tainted glory.

Or perhaps he sensed my own disgust with the war I had agreed to fight for him and was nervous that I might suddenly refuse to be the champion he felt he so desperately needed?

I had no opportunity to discuss this with him and Count Roldero could offer no explanation save to say, in the king's favour, that the slaughter might have wearied Rigenos just as it had wearied me.

I was not sure of this, for Rigenos seemed to hate the Eldren even more than before, as was made evident by his treatment of Ermizhad.

Ermizhad still refused to speak. She hardly ate and she rarely left her cabin. But one evening, as I strolled on deck, I saw her standing at the rail and staring down into the sea as if she contemplated hurling herself into its depths.

I increased my pace so that I should be near if she did attempt to throw herself overboard. She half-turned as I approached and then looked away again.

At this point the king emerged on the poop deck and called down to me.

"I see you've taken pains to make sure the wind's behind you when you get near to the Eldren bitch, Lord Erekosë."

I stopped and looked up. At first, I hardly understood the reference. I glanced at Ermizhad, who pretended not to have heard the king's insult. I, too, pretended I had not understood the significance of the remark and gave a slight, polite bow.

Then, deliberately, I walked past Ermizhad and paused near the rail, staring out to sea.

"Perhaps you have no sense of smell, Lord Erekosë," the king called. Again I ignored the remark.

"It seems a pity that we must tolerate vermin on our ship when we took such pains to scrub our decks free of their tainted blood," the king went on.

At last, furious, I turned around, but he had left the poop deck. I looked at Ermizhad. She continued to stare into the dark waters as they were pierced by our oars. She seemed almost mesmerized by the rhythm. I wondered if she really had not heard the insults.

There were several more occasions of that kind on board the flagship *Iolinda* as we sailed for Noonos. Whenever King Rigenos got the opportunity, he would speak of Ermizhad in her presence as if she were not there; speak disdainfully of her and his disgust for all her kind.

Increasingly, I found it harder to control my anger, but control it I did, and Ermizhad, for her part, showed no sign that she was offended by the king's crude references to her and her race.

I saw less of Ermizhad than I wished but, in spite of the king's warnings, came to like her. She was certainly the most beautiful woman I had ever seen. Her beauty was different from the cool beauty of Iolinda, my betrothed.

What is love? Even now, now that the whole pattern of my particular destiny seems to have been fulfilled, I do not know. Oh, yes, I still loved Iolinda, but I think that, while I did not know it, I was falling in love with Ermizhad, too.

I refused to believe the stories told about her and esteemed her, though, at that time, I had no thought of letting this affect my attitude toward her.

That attitude had to be of a jailer for his prisoner — an important prisoner, at that. A prisoner who could help decide the war against the Eldren in our favour.

I did pause, once or twice, to wonder about the logic of keeping her as a hostage. If, as King Rigenos insisted, the Eldren were coldhearted and unhuman, then why should Arjavh care that his sister would be murdered by us?

Ermizhad, if she were the creature King Rigenos believed her to be, showed no signs of her evil. Rather, she seemed to me to exhibit a singular nobility of soul that was in excellent contrast to the king's rude banter.

And then I wondered if the king realized the affection I felt for Ermizhad and was afraid that the union between his daughter and his immortal champion was threatened.

But I remained loyal to Iolinda. It did not occur to me to question that we should not be married on my return, as we had agreed.

There must be countless forms of love. Which is the form which conquers the rest? I cannot define it. I shall not try.

Ermizhad's beauty had the fascination of being an unhuman beauty, but close enough to my own race's ideal to attract me.

She had the long, pointed Eldren face that John Daker might have tried to describe as "elfin" and failed to do justice to its nobility. She had the slanting eyes that seemed blind in their strange milkiness, the slightly pointed ears, the high angular cheekbones and a slender body that was almost boyish. All the Eldren women were slender like this, small-breasted and narrow-waisted. Her red lips were fairly wide, curving naturally upwards so that she always seemed to be on the point of smiling when her face was in repose.

For the first two weeks of our voyage, she continued to refuse to speak, although I showed her elaborate courtesy. I saw that she had everything for her comfort and she thanked me through her guards, that was all. But one day I stood outside the set of cabins where she, the king and myself had our apartments, leaning over the rail and looking at a grey sea and an overcast sky, and I saw her approach me.

"Greetings, Sir Champion," she said half-mockingly as she came out of her cabin.

I was surprised.

"Greetings, Lady Ermizhad," said I. She was dressed in a cloak of midnight blue flung around a simple smock of pale blue wool.

"A day of omens, I think," she said, looking at the gloomy sky which boiled darkly now above us, full of heavy greys and dusty yellows.

"Why think you?" I enquired.

She laughed. It was lovely to hear — crystal and gold-strung harps. It was the music of heaven, not of hell. "Forgive me," she said. "I sought to disturb you — but I see you are not so prone to suggestion as others of your race."

I grinned. "You are very complimentary, my lady. I find their superstitions a trifle tedious, I must admit. As are their insults."

"One is not troubled by those," she said. "They are sad little insults, really."

"You are very charitable."

"We Eldren are a charitable race, I think."

"I have heard otherwise."

"I suppose you have."

"I have bruises that prove otherwise!" I smiled. "Your warriors did not seem particularly charitable in the sea fight beyond Paphanaal."

She bowed her head. "And yours were not charitable when they came to Paphanaal. Is it true? Am I the only survivor?"

I licked my lips. They were suddenly dry. "I believe so," I said quietly.

"Then I am lucky," she said, her voice rising a little.

There was, of course, no reply I could make.

We stood there in silence, looking at the sea.

Later she said quietly: "So you are Erekosë. You are not like the rest of your race. In fact, you do not seem wholly of that race."

"Aha," I replied. "Now I know you are my enemy."

"What do you mean?"

"My enemies — the Lord Katorn in particular — suspect my humanity."

"And are you human?"

"I am nothing else. I am sure of that. I have the uncertainties of any ordinary mortal. I am as confused as the rest, though my problems are, perhaps, different. How I came here, I do not know. They say I am a great hero reborn, come to aid them against your people. They brought me here by means of an incantation. But then it sometimes seems to me, in dreams, at night, that I have been many heroes."

"And all of them human?"

"I am not sure. I do not think my basic character has altered in any of those incarnations. I have no special wisdom, no special powers, so far as I know. Would you not think that an Immortal would have gathered a great store of wisdom?"

She nodded slightly. "I would think so, my lord."

　　　　THE ETERNAL CHAMPION

"I am not even sure where I am," I continued. "I do not know if I came here from the far future or from the far past."

"The terms mean little to the Eldren," she said. "But some of us believe that past and future are the same — that Time moves in a circle, so that the past is the future and the future is the past."

"An interesting theory," I said. "But a rather simple one, is it not?"

"I think I would agree with you," she murmured. "Time is a subtle thing. Even our wisest philosophers do not fully understand its nature. The Eldren do not think very much about Time — we do not have to, normally. Of course, we have our histories. But history is not Time. History is merely a record of certain events."

"I understand you," I said.

Now she came and stood by the ship's rail, one hand resting lightly upon it.

At that moment I felt the affection that I suppose a father might have for a daughter, a father who delights in his offspring's assured innocence. She could not have been, I felt, much more than nineteen. Yet her voice had a confidence that comes with knowledge of the world, her carriage was proud, also confident. I realized then that Count Roldero might well have spoken the truth. How, indeed, could you gauge the age of an Immortal?

"I thought at first," I said, "that I came from your future. But now I am not sure. Perhaps I come from your past — that this world is, in relation to what I call the 'twentieth century,' in the far future."

"This world is very ancient," she agreed.

"Is there a record of a time when only human beings occupied Earth?"

"We have no such records," she smiled. "There is an echo of a myth, the thread of a legend, which says that there was a time when only the Eldren occupied Earth. My brother has studied this. I believe he knows more."

I shivered. I did not know why, but my vitals seemed to chill within me. I could not, easily, continue the conversation, though I wanted to.

She appeared not to have noticed my discomfort.

At last I said: "A day of omens, madam. I hope to talk with you again soon." I bowed and returned to my cabin.

CONFRONTATION WITH THE KING

That night I slept without my usual precaution of a jug of wine to send me into deeper slumber. I did it deliberately, though with trepidation.

"EREKOSË..."

I heard the voice calling as it had called once before to John Daker. But this time it was not the voice of King Rigenos.

"Erekosë..."

This voice was more musical.

I saw green, swaying forests and great, green hills and glades and castles and delicate beasts whose names I did not know.

"Erekosë? My name is not Erekosë," I said. "It is Prince Corum. Prince Corum — Prince Corum Jhaelen Irsei in the Scarlet Robe — and I seek my people. O, where are my people? Why is there no cessation to this quest?"

I rode a horse. The horse was mantled in yellow velvet and hung about with panniers, two spears, a plain round shield, a bow and a quiver holding arrows. I wore a conical silver helm and a double weight of chain mail, the lower layer of brass and the upper of silver. And I bore a long, strong sword that was not the sword Kanajana.

"Erekosë."

"I am not Erekosë."

"Erekosë!"

"*I am John Daker!*"

"*Erekosë!*"

"*I am Jerry Cornelius.*"

"*Erekosë!*"

"*I am Konrad Arflane.*"

"*Erekosë!*"

"*What do you want?*" *I asked.*

"*We want your help!*"

"*You have my help!*"

"*Erekosë!*"

"*I am Karl Glogauer!*"

"*Erekosë!*"

"*I seek lost Tanelorn.*"

The names did not matter. I knew it now. Only the fact mattered. The fact that I was a creature incapable of dying. A creature eternal. Doomed to have many shapes, to be called many names, but to be forever battling.

And perhaps I had been wrong. Perhaps I was not truly human, but only assumed the characteristics of a human being if I were caught in a human body.

It seemed to me that I howled in misery then. What was I? What was I, if I were not a man?

The voice was still calling, but I refused to heed it. How I wished I had not heeded it before, as I lay in my comfortable bed, in the comfortable identity of John Daker.

I awoke and I was sweating. I had found out nothing more about myself and the mystery of my origin. It seemed I had only succeeded in confusing myself further.

It was still night, but I dared not fall asleep again.

I peered through the darkness. I looked at the curtains pulled across the windows, the white coverlet of the bed, my wife beside me.

I began to scream.

"EREKOSË — EREKOSË — EREKOSË."

"*I am John Daker!* " I screamed. "Look — I am John Daker!"

"EREKOSË."

"I know nothing of this name, Erekosë. My name is Elric, Prince of Melniboné. Elric Kinslayer. I am known by many names."

Many names — many names — many names...

How was it possible to possess dozens of identities all at the same time? To move from period to period at random? To move away from Earth itself, out to where the cold stars glared?

"I seek Tanelorn and peace. Oh, where lies Tanelorn?"

There was a rushing noise and then I plunged through dark, airless places, down, down, down. And there was nothing in the universe but drifting gas. No gravity, no colour, no air, no intelligence save my own — and perhaps, somewhere, one other.

Again I screamed.

And I refused to let myself know further.

Whatever the doom upon me I thought next morning, I would never understand it. And it was probably for the best.

I went on deck and there was Ermizhad, standing in the same place at the rail, as if she had not moved all night. The sky had cleared somewhat and sunlight pushed thick beams through the clouds, the rays slanting down on the choppy sea so that the world was half-dark, half-light.

A moody day.

We stood for a while in silence, leaning out over the rail, watching the surf slide by, watching the oars smash into the waters in monotonous rhythm.

Again, she was the first to speak.

"What do they plan to do with me?" she asked quietly.

"You will be a hostage against the eventuality of your brother, Prince Arjavh, ever attacking Necranal," I told her. It was only half the truth. There were other ways of using her against her brother, but there was no point in detailing them. "You will be safe — King Rigenos will not be able to bargain if you are harmed."

She sighed.

"Why did not you and the other Eldren women flee when our fleets put in to Paphanaal?" I asked. This had puzzled me for some time.

"The Eldren do not flee," she said. "They do not flee from cities that they build themselves."

"They fled to the Mountains of Sorrow some centuries ago," I pointed out.

"No." She shook her head. "They were driven there. That is the difference."

"That is a difference," I agreed.

"Who speaks of difference?" A new, harsher voice broke in. It was King Rigenos. He had come silently out of his cabin and stood behind us, feet apart on the swaying deck. He did not acknowledge Ermizhad but stared directly at me. He did not look well.

"Greetings, sire," I said. "We were discussing the meaning of words."

"You've become uncommon friendly with the Eldren bitch!" he sneered. What was it about this man who had shown himself kind and brave in many ways, that when the Eldren were concerned he became an uncouth barbarian?

"Sire," I said, for I could no longer be polite. "Sire, you speak of one, who, though our enemy, is of noble blood."

Again he sneered. "Noble blood! The vile stuff which flows in their polluted veins cannot be termed thus! Beware, Erekosë! I realize that you are not altogether versed in our ways or our knowledge, that your memory is hazy — but remember that the Eldren wanton has a tongue of liquid gold which can beguile you to your doom and ours. Pay no heed to her!"

It was the most direct and most portentous speech he had made thus far.

"Sire," I said.

"She'll weave such a spell that you'll be a fawning dog at her mercy and no good to any of us. I tell you, Erekosë, beware. Gods! I've half a mind to give her to the rowers and let them have their way with her before she's thrown over the side!"

"You placed her under my protection, my lord king," I said angrily. "And I am sworn to protect her against *all* dangers!"

"Fool! I have warned you. I do not want to lose your friendship, Erekosë — and more, I do not want to lose our war champion. If she shows further signs of enchanting you, I shall slay her. None shall stop me!"

"I am doing your work, my king," I said, "at your request. But remember you this — I am Erekosë. I have been many other champions. What I do is for the human race. I have taken no oath of loyalty to you or to any other king. I am Erekosë, the War Champion, Champion of Humanity — not Rigenos's Champion!"

His eyes narrowed. "Is this treachery, Erekosë?" It was almost as if he hoped it were.

"No, King Rigenos. Disagreement with a single representative of Humanity does not constitute treachery to mankind."

He said nothing, but just stood there, seeming to hate me as much as he hated the Eldren girl. His breathing was heavy and rasped in his throat.

"Give me no reason to regret my summoning of thee, dead Erekosë," he said at length and turned away, going back into his cabin.

"I think it would be for the best if we discontinued our conversation," said Ermizhad quietly.

"Dead Erekosë, eh?" I said, and then grinned. "If I'm dead, then I'm strangely prone to emotion for a corpse." I made light of our dispute, yet events had taken a turn which caused me to fear that he would not, among other things, allow me the hand of Iolinda — for he still did not know that we were betrothed.

She looked at me strangely and moved her hand as if to comfort me.

"Perhaps I am dead," I said. "Have you seen any creatures like me on the Ghost Worlds?"

She shook her head. "Not really."

"So the Ghost Worlds do exist?" I said. "I had been speaking rhetorically."

"Of course they exist!" She laughed. "You are the greatest sceptic I have ever met!"

"Tell me about them, Ermizhad."

"What is there to tell?" She shook her head. "And if you do not believe what you have heard already, then there's little point if I tell you more that you will not believe, is there?"

I shrugged. "I suppose not." I felt she was being unduly secretive, but I did not press the matter.

"Answer one thing," I said. "Would the mystery of my existence be found on the Ghost Worlds?"

She smiled sympathetically. "How could I answer that, Erekosë?"

"I don't know. I thought the Eldren knew more of — of sorcery…"

"Now you are showing yourself to be as superstitious as your fellows," she said. "You do not believe…"

"Madam," I said, "I do not know what I should believe. The logic of this world — both human and Eldren — is, I fear, a mystery to me."

SEVENTEEN
NECRANAL AGAIN

Although the king refrained from further outbursts against either myself or Ermizhad, it could not really be said that he warmed to me again, though he grew more relaxed as the shores of Necralala drew closer.

And eventually Noonos was sighted and we left the better part of the fleet there to refit and reprovision, and sailed back up the River Droonaa to come again to Necranal.

The news of our great sea victory was already in Necranal. Indeed, it had been amplified and it seemed that I had sunk some score of ships and destroyed their crews single-handedly!

I did nothing to deny the truth of this. I was worried King Rigenos would begin to work against me. The adulation of the people, however, meant that he could not be seen to deny me anything. My power had grown. I had achieved a victory, I had proved myself the champion the people wanted.

It now seemed that, if King Rigenos acted against me, he would arouse the wrath of the people against *him* — and that wrath would be so great it could lose him his crown — and his head.

This did not mean, of course, that he had to like me, but in fact, when we had once again reached the Palace of Ten Thousand Windows, he was almost in an affable mood.

Exhaustion makes us see threats from outside when really the threat is from within — the signals of failing physical powers: I think he had begun to see me as a threat to his throne, but the sight of his palace, his people and his daughter, the promise of rest and security, reassured him that he was still the king and would always be the king. I was not interested in his crown. I was interested only in his daughter.

Guards escorted Ermizhad away to her quarters when we arrived. She had departed before Iolinda came running down the stairs into the Great Hall, her face radiant, her carriage graceful, kissing first her father and then myself.

"Have you told Father of our secret?" she asked.

"I think he knew before we left." I laughed, turning to Rigenos, upon whose face there had come something of an abstracted look. "We would be betrothed, sire. Do you give us your consent?"

King Rigenos opened his mouth, wiped his forehead and swallowed before nodding. "Of course. My blessings to you. This will make our unity even stronger."

A slight frown came to Iolinda's brow. "Father — you are pleased, are you not?"

"Of c— yes, naturally I am pleased — naturally. But I am weary with travelling and with fighting, my dear. I need to rest. Forgive me."

"Oh, I am sorry, Father. Yes, you must rest. You do not look well. I will have the slaves prepare some food for you and you can dine in bed."

"Yes," he said, "yes."

When he had gone, Iolinda looked at me curiously. "You, too, seem to have suffered from the fighting, Erekosë. You are not hurt?"

"No. The battle was bloody. And I did not enjoy much of what we had to do."

"Warriors must kill. That is the way."

"But must they kill women, Iolinda? Must they kill children? Babies?"

She moistened her lips with her tongue. Then she said: "Come. Let's eat in my apartments. It is more restful there."

When we had eaten, I felt better, but was still not completely at ease.

"What happened?" she asked. "At Mernadin?"

"There was a great sea fight. We won it."

"That is good."

"Yes."

"You took Paphanaal. You stormed it and took it."

"Who told you we 'stormed' it?" I asked in astonishment.

"Why, you do — the returning warriors. We heard the news shortly before you came back."

"The city gave no resistance," I told her. "There were some women in Paphanaal and there were some children in Paphanaal and they were butchered by our troops."

"A few women and children always get harmed in the storming of a city," said Iolinda. "You must not blame yourself if…"

"We did not storm the city," I repeated. "It was undefended. There were no men there. Every one of the male inhabitants of Paphanaal had sailed with the fleet we destroyed."

She shrugged. Evidently she could not visualise the true picture. Perhaps it was just as well. But I could not resist one further comment:

"And, although we would have won anyway, part of our sea victory was due to our treachery," I said.

"You were betrayed, did you say?" She looked up eagerly. "Some treachery of the Eldren?"

"The Eldren fought honourably. We slaughtered their commander during a truce."

"I see," she said. Then she smiled. "Well, we must help you forget such terrible things, Erekosë."

"I hope you can," I said.

The king announced our betrothal the next day and the news was received with joy by the citizens of Necranal. We stood before them on the great balcony overlooking the city. We smiled and waved but, when we went inside again, the king left us with a curt word and hurried away.

"Father really does seem to disapprove of our match," Iolinda said in puzzlement, "in spite of his consent."

"A disagreement about tactics while at war," I said. "You know how important we soldiers think these things. He will soon forget."

But I was perturbed. Here was I a great hero, loved by the people, marrying the king's daughter as a hero should, and something was beginning to strike me as being not quite right. I had had the feeling for some time, but I could not trace the source. I did not know whether it was to do with my peculiar dreams, my worries concerning my origin or merely the crisis which seemed to be building between the king and myself. There again, I was still very weary and probably my anxiety was baseless.

Iolinda and I now went to the bridal bed together, as was the custom in the Human Kingdoms.

But, that first night, we did not make love.

Halfway through the night I felt my shoulder being touched and I straightened up almost instantly.

I smiled in relief.

"Oh, it is you, Iolinda."

"It is I, Erekosë. You moaned and groaned so in your sleep that I thought it better to wake you."

"Aye…" I rubbed my eyes. "I thank you." My memory was unclear, but it seemed to me that I had been experiencing the usual dreams.

"Tell me something of Ermizhad," Iolinda said suddenly.

"Ermizhad?" I yawned. "What of her?"

"You have seen much of her, I heard. You conversed with her. I have never conversed with an Eldren. Usually we do not take prisoners."

I smiled. "Well, I gather it's heresy to say so, but I found her quite — human."

"Oh, Erekosë. That's a joke in bad taste. They say she's beautiful. They say she has a thousand human lives to account for. She's evil, is she not? She has lured many men to their deaths."

"I did not ask her about that," I said. "Mainly we discussed broad matters of philosophy."

"She is very clever, then?"

"I do not know. She seemed almost innocent to me." Then I added hastily, diplomatically: "But perhaps that's her cleverness — to seem innocent."

Iolinda frowned. "Innocent! Ha!"

I was disturbed. "I only offer my impression, Iolinda. I have no opinions, really, concerning Ermizhad. Or for that matter the rest of the Eldren."

"Do you love me, Erekosë?"

"Of course."

"You would not betray me?"

I laughed and took her in my arms. "How could you fear such a thing?"

We fell again into sleep.

Next morning, King Rigenos, Count Roldero and myself got down to the serious business of planning our strategy. Concerning ourselves with maps and battle plans, the tensions between us began to relax. Rigenos was almost cheerful. We were in unison about what should be done. By now it was likely Prince Arjavh would be attempting to retake Paphanaal — and assuredly failing. Probably he would lay siege to it, but we could bring in supplies and weapons by ship, so he would waste his time. Meanwhile, our expedition to the Ghost Worlds would attack Eldren positions there and, Roldero and Rigenos assured me, make it impossible for them to call on their halfling allies.

The plan, of course, depended on Arjavh's attacking Paphanaal.

"But he would have been already on his way when we sailed in," Rigenos reasoned. "It would be pointless for him to turn back. What could he achieve by doing that?"

Roldero agreed. "I think it's pretty certain that he'll concentrate on Paphanaal," he said. "Another two or three days and our fleets will be ready to sail again. We'll soon have the Outer Islands subdued, then we move on to Loos Ptokai itself. With luck, Arjavh will still have his main force concentrated on Paphanaal. By the end of this year, every Eldren position will have fallen to us."

I was a trifle cynical about his overconfidence. Katorn at least would have been less sure. I half-wished, in fact, that Katorn was here. I respected his advice as a soldier and strategist.

Next day, while we still pored over maps, the news came.

It astonished us. It altered every plan we had made. It made nonsense of our strategy. It put us in a frightening position.

Arjavh, Prince of Mernadin, Ruler of the Eldren, had not attacked Paphanaal. A great proportion of our troops waited there to greet him, but he had not deigned to pay them a visit.

Perhaps he had never intended to march on Paphanaal.

Perhaps he had always planned to do what he had done now and it was we who were the dupes! We had been outmaneuvered!

"I said that the Eldren were clever," said King Rigenos when we received the news. "I told you, Erekosë."

"I believe you now," I said softly, trying to grasp the enormity of what had happened.

"Now how do you feel about them, my friend?" Roldero said. "Are you still divided?"

I shook my head. My loyalties lay with Humanity. There was no time for conscience, no point in trying to understand these unhuman people. I had underestimated them and now it seemed that Humanity itself might have to pay the price.

Eldren ships had beached on the coasts of Necralala, on the eastern seaboard and reasonably close to Necranal. An Eldren army was pushing toward

Necranal herself and, it was said, none could stand against It.

I cursed myself then. Rigenos, Katorn, Roldero, even Iolinda had all been right. I had been deceived by their golden tongues, their alien beauty.

And there was hardly a warrior in Necranal. Half our available force was in Paphanaal and it would take a month to bring them back. The fleet Eldren craft had probably crossed the ocean in half that time! We thought we had defeated their fleet at Paphanaal. We had only defeated a fraction of it!

There was fear on all our faces as we made hasty contingency plans.

"There's no point in recalling the troops in Paphanaal at this stage," I said. "By the time they got here, the battle would have been decided. Send a fast messenger there, Roldero. Tell them what has happened and let Katorn decide his own strategy. Tell him I trust him."

"Very well," Roldero nodded. "But our available warriors are scarce in number. We can get a few divisions from Zavara. There are troops at Stalaco, Calodemia and some at Dratarda. Perhaps they can reach us in a week. Then we have some men at Shilaal and Sinana, but I hesitate to recommend their withdrawal."

"I agree," I said. "The ports must be defended at all costs. Who knows how many other fleets the Eldren have?" I cursed. "If only we had some means of gathering intelligence. Some spies. . ."

"That's idle talk," Roldero said. "Who among our people could disguise himself as an Eldren? For that matter who would be able to stomach their company long enough?"

Rigenos said: "The only large force we have is at Noonos. We'll have to send for them and pray that Noonos is not attacked in their absence." He looked at me. "This is not your fault, Erekosë. We expected too much of you."

"Well," I promised him, "you can expect more of me now, King Rigenos. I'll drive the Eldren back."

Rigenos scowled thoughtfully. "There's one thing we have to bargain with," he said. "The Eldren bitch — Arjavh's sister."

And then an idea began to dawn on me. We had thought Prince Arjavh must certainly march on Paphanaal and he had not. We had never expected him to invade Necralala. But he had. Why?

"What of her?" I said.

"Could we not use her now? Tell Arjavh that, if he does not retreat, we will slay her?"

"Would he trust us?"

"That depends on how much he loves his sister, eh?" King Rigenos grinned, his spirits rising. "Yes. Try that, anyway, Erekosë. But do not go to him in weakness. Take all the divisions you can muster."

"Naturally," I said. "I have a feeling that Arjavh will not let sentiment stop him while there is a chance he can capture the capital."

King Rigenos ignored this. Even I wondered about the truth of it, particularly since I was beginning to think there might be something more to Arjavh's decision.

King Rigenos put his hand on my shoulder. "We have had our differences, Erekosë. But now we are united. Go. Do battle with the Hounds of Evil. Win the battle. Kill Arjavh. This is your opportunity to strike the head from the monster that is the Eldren. And if battle seems impossible — use his sister to buy time for us. Be brave, Erekosë, be cunning — be strong."

"I will try," I said. "I will leave at once to rally the warriors at Noonos. I'll take all available cavalry and leave a small force of infantry and artillery to defend the city."

"Do as you think fit, Erekosë."

I went back to our apartments and said farewell to Iolinda. She was full of sorrow.

I did not call on Ermizhad and tell her what we planned.

EIGHTEEN
PRINCE ARJAVH

I rode out in my proud armour at the head of my army. My lance flaunted my banner of a silver sword on a black field, my horse pranced, my stance was confident and I had five thousand knights at my back and no idea of the size of the Eldren army.

We rode from Noonos eastwards to where the Eldren were said to be marching. We planned to cut them off before they reached Necranal.

Well before we met Arjavh's forces, we heard stories of their progress from fleeing villagers and townspeople. Apparently the Eldren were marching doggedly for Necranal, avoiding any settlements they came to. There were no reports, so far, of Eldren atrocities. They seemed to be moving too fast to bother to waste time on civilians.

Arjavh appeared to have only one ambition — to reach Necranal in the shortest possible time. I knew little of the Eldren prince save that he was reputedly a monster incarnate, a slayer and torturer of women and children. I was impatient to meet him in battle.

And there was one other rumour concerning Prince Arjavh's army. They said it was partly comprised of halflings — creatures from the Ghost Worlds. This story had terrified my men, but I had tried to assure them that the rumours were false.

Roldero and Rigenos were not with me. Roldero had returned to supervise the defense of Necranal, should we be unsuccessful, and it was in Necranal that Rigenos also stayed.

For the first time now, I was on my own. I had no advisors. I felt I needed none.

The armies of the Eldren and the forces of Humanity saw each other at last when they reached a vast plateau known as the Plain of Olas, after an ancient city that had once stood there. The plateau was surrounded by the peaks of distant hills. It was green and the hills were purple and we saw the banners of the Eldren as the sun set and those banners shone as if they were flags of fire.

My marshals and captains were all for rushing upon the Eldren as soon as morning came. To our relief it seemed that their numbers were smaller than ours and it now looked likely we could defeat them.

I felt relieved. It meant that I did not need to use Ermizhad for bartering with Arjavh and I could afford to stand by the Code of War which the humans used among themselves but refused to extend to the Eldren.

My commanders were horrified when I told them, but I said: "Let us act well and with nobility. Let us set an example to them." Now there was no Katorn, no Rigenos — not even Roldero — to argue with me and tell me that we must be treacherous and quick where Eldren were concerned. I wanted to fight this battle in the terms that Erekosë understood, for I was following Erekosë's instincts now.

I watched our herald ride into the night under a flag of truce. I watched him ride away and then, on an impulse, spurred after him.

My marshals called after me: "Lord Erekosë — where do you go?"

"To the Eldren camp!" I called back, and laughed at their consternation.

The herald turned in his saddle, hearing the hoofbeats of my horse. "Lord Erekosë?" he said questioningly.

"Ride on, herald — and I'll ride with you."

And so, together, we came at last to the Eldren camp, and we stopped as the outer guards hailed us.

"What would you here, humans?" some low-ranking officer asked, peering with his blue-flecked eyes through the gloom.

The moon came out and shone silver. I took my banner from where it lay against my horse's side. I raised it and I shook it out. The moon picked up the motif.

"That is Erekosë's banner," said the officer.

"And I am Erekosë," I said.

A look of disgust crossed the Eldren's face. "We heard what you did at Paphanaal. If you were not here under the truce flag, I would..."

"I did nothing at Paphanaal I am ashamed of," I said.

"No. You would not be ashamed."

"My sword was sheathed during the whole stay at Paphanaal, Eldren."

"Aye — sheathed in the bodies of babes."

"Think what you will," I said. "Lead me to your master. I'll not waste time with you."

We rode through the silent camp until we came to the simple pavilion of Prince Arjavh. The officer went inside.

Then I heard a movement in the tent and from it stepped a lithe figure, dressed in half-armour, a steel breastplate strapped over a loose shirt of green, leather hose beneath leg greaves, also of steel, and sandals on his feet. His long black hair was kept away from his eyes by a band of gold bearing a single great ruby.

And his face — his face was beautiful. I hesitate to use the word to describe a man, but it is the only one that will do justice to those fine features. Like Ermizhad, he had the tapering skull, the slanting, orbless eyes. But his lips did not curve upwards as did hers. His mouth was grim and there were lines of weariness about it. He passed his hand across his face and looked up at us.

"I am Prince Arjavh of Mernadin," he said in his liquid voice. "What would you say to me, Erekosë, you who abducted my sister?"

"I came personally to bring the traditional challenge from the hosts of Humanity," I said.

He raised his head to look about him. "Some plot, I gather. Some fresh treachery?"

"I speak only the truth," I told him.

There was melancholy irony in his smile when he replied. "Very well, Lord Erekosë. On behalf of the Eldren, I accept your gracious challenge. We will battle, then, shall we? We will kill each other tomorrow, shall we?"

"You may decide when to begin," I said. "For it is we who made the challenge."

He frowned. "It has been perhaps a million years since the Eldren and Humanity fought according to the Code of War. How can I trust you, Erekosë? We have heard how you butchered the children."

"I butchered no children," I said quietly. "I begged that they be spared. But at Paphanaal I was advised by King Rigenos and his marshals. Now I control the battle forces and I choose to fight according to the Code of War. The Code of War, I believe, that I originally drew up."

"Aye," Arjavh said thoughtfully. "It's sometimes called Erekosë's Code. But you are not the true Erekosë. He was a mortal like all men. Only the Eldren are immortal."

"I am mortal in many respects," I said shortly, "and immortal in others. Now, shall we decide the terms of battle?"

Arjavh spread his arms. "Oh, how can I trust all this talk? How many times have we agreed to believe you humans and have been betrayed time after time? How can I accept that you are Erekosë, the Champion of Humanity, our ancient enemy whom, even in our legends, we respect as a noble foe? I wish to believe you, you who calls himself Erekosë, but I cannot afford to."

"May I dismount?" I asked. The herald glanced at me in astonishment.

"If you will."

I clambered from the back of my armoured horse and unbuckled my sword and hung it over the pommel of the saddle and I pushed the horse to one side and walked forward and stood there confronting Prince Arjavh face to face.

"We are a stronger force than you," I said. "We stand a good chance of winning the battle tomorrow. It is possible that within a week even the few who escape the battle will be dead at the hands of our soldiers or our peasants. I offer you the chance to fight a noble battle, Prince Arjavh. A fair battle. I suggest that the terms can include the sparing of prisoners, medical treatment for all captured wounded, a counting of the dead and of the living." I was remembering it all as I spoke.

"You know Erekosë's Code well," he said.

"I should."

He looked away and up at the moon. "Is my sister still alive?"

"She is."

"Why did you come thus with your herald to our camp?"

"Curiosity, I suppose," I told him. "I have spoken much with Ermizhad. I wanted to see if you were the devil I heard you were — or the person Ermizhad described."

"And what do you see?"

"If you are a devil, you are a weary one."

"Not too weary to fight," he said. "Not too weary to take Necranal if I can."

"We expected you to march on Paphanaal," I told him. "We thought it logical that you would try to recapture your main port."

"Aye — that's what I planned. Then I learned that you had abducted my sister." He paused. "How is she?"

"Well," I said. "She was placed under my protection and I have seen to it that she has been treated with courtesy wherever possible."

He nodded.

"We come, of course, to rescue her," he said.

"I wondered if that was your reason." I smiled a little. "We should have expected it, but we did not. You realise that they will, should you win tomorrow's battle, threaten to kill her if you do not retreat."

Arjavh pursed his lips. "They will kill her, anyway, will they not? They will torture her. I know how they treat Eldren prisoners."

I could say nothing to the contrary.

"If they kill my sister," Prince Arjavh said, "I will burn down Necranal though I am the only one left to do it. I will kill Rigenos, his daughter, everyone."

"And so it goes on," I said softly.

Arjavh looked back at me. "I am sorry. You wished to discuss the terms of battle. Very well, Erekosë, I will trust you. I agree to all your proposals — and offer a term of my own."

"That is?"

"Deliverance of Ermizhad from captivity if we should win. It will save you and us many lives."

"It would," I agreed, "but it is not for me to make that bargain. I regret it, Prince Arjavh, but it is the king who holds her. If she were my prisoner and not just under my protection, I would do as you suggest. If you win, you must go on to Necranal and lay siege to the city."

He sighed. "Very well, Sir Champion. We shall be ready at dawn tomorrow."

I said hurriedly: "We outnumber you, Prince Arjavh. You could go back now — in peace."

He shook his head. "Let the battle be fought."

"Until dawn, then, Prince of the Eldren."

He moved his hand tiredly in assent. "Farewell, Lord Erekosë."

"Farewell." I mounted my horse and rode back to our camp in a sorrowful mood, the puzzled herald at my side.

Once again I was divided. Were the Eldren so clever they could deceive me so easily?

Tomorrow would tell.

That night in my own pavilion I slept as badly as ever, but I accepted the dreams, the vague memories, and I did not attempt to fight them, to interpret them. It had become clear to me that there was no point to it. I was what I was — I was the Eternal Champion, the Everlasting Wager of War. I would never know why.

Before dawn our trumpets warned us to awake and make ourselves ready. I buckled on my armour, my sword and my lance's cover was ripped off to reveal the long, metal-shod spear.

I went out into the chill of the dying night. The day was not yet with us. Silhouetted against what little light we had, my cavalry was already mounting. There was a cold, clammy sweat on my forehead. I wiped It with a rag time after time, but it remained there. I raised my helm and brought it down over my head, strapping it to my shoulder plates. My squires handed me my gauntlets and I pulled them on. Then, stiff-legged in my armour, I stalked toward my steed, was helped into the saddle, was handed my shield and my lance, and cantered up the line to the head of my troops.

It was very quiet when we began to move — a steel sea lapping at the coast that was the Eldren camp.

As the watery dawn broke, our forces sighted each other. The Eldren were still by their camp but, when they saw us, they too began to move. Very slowly, it seemed, but implacably.

I lifted my visor to get a wider view of the surroundings. The ground seemed good and dry. There appeared to be no places with superior advantages.

The horses' hooves thumped the turf. The arms of the riders clattered at their sides. Their armour clashed and their harness creaked. But in spite of this a silence seemed to fill the air.

Nearer we came and nearer.

A flight of swallows flew high above us and then glided away toward the far-off hills.

I closed my visor. The back of the horse jogged beneath me. The cold sweat seemed to cover my body and clog my armour. The lance and the shield were suddenly very heavy.

I smelled the stink of other sweating men and horses. Before long, I would smell their blood, too.

Because of our need for speed, we had brought no cannon. The Eldren, also wishing to travel rapidly, had no artillery either. Perhaps, I thought, their siege machines were following behind at a slower pace.

Nearer now. I could make out Arjavh's banner and a little cluster of flags that were those of his commanders.

I planned to depend upon my cavalry. They would spread out on two sides to surround the Eldren while another arrowhead of horsemen pierced the centre of their ranks and pushed through to the rear so that we would surround them on all sides.

Nearer still. My stomach grumbled and I tasted bile in my mouth.

Close. I reined in my horse and raised my lance and gave the order for the archers to shoot.

We had no crossbows, only longbows, which had greater range and penetrating power and could shoot many more arrows at a time. The first flight of arrows screamed overhead and thudded down into the Eldren ranks and then were almost instantly followed by another flight and then another.

Our shafts were answered by the slim arrows of the Eldren. Horses and men shrieked as the arrows found their marks and for a moment there was consternation among our men as their ranks became ragged. But then, with great discipline, they re-formed.

Again I raised my lance on which fluttered my black and silver pennant.

"Cavalry! Advance at full gallop!"

The trumpets shouted the order. The air was savaged by the sound. The knights spurred their war steeds forward and began, line upon line of them, to fan out on two sides while another division rode straight toward the centre of the Eldren host. These knights were bent over the necks of their fast-moving horses, lances leaning at an angle across their saddles, some held under the right arm and aimed to the left and others secure under left arms, aimed at the right. Their helmet plumes fluttered behind them as they bore down on the Eldren. Their cloaks streamed out, and their pennants waved and the dim sunlight gleamed on their armour.

I was almost deafened by the thunder of hooves as I kicked my charger into a gallop and, with a band of fifty picked knights behind me, they themselves surrounding the twin standards of Humanity, rode forward, straining my eyes for Arjavh, whom, at that moment, I hated with a terrible hatred.

I hated him because I must fight this battle and possibly kill him.

With a fearful din made up of shouts and clashing metal, we smashed into the Eldren army and soon I was oblivious to all but the need to kill and defend my life against those who would kill me. I broke my lance early on. It smashed right through the armoured body of an Eldren noble and split with the impetus. I left it in him and drew my sword.

Now I hewed about me with savage intensity, seeking sight of Arjavh. At last I saw him, a huge mace swinging from his gauntleted hand, battering at the infantrymen who sought to pull him from his saddle.

"*Arjavh!*"

He glimpsed me from the corner of his eye as I waited for him. "A moment, Erekosë, I have work here."

"*Arjavh!*" The name I screamed was a challenge, nothing else.

Arjavh finished the last of the foot soldiers and he kicked his horse toward me, still flailing around him with his giant mace as two mounted knights came at him. Then the men drew back as they saw we were about to engage.

We came close enough to fight now. I aimed a mighty blow at him with my poisoned sword, but he pulled aside in time and I felt his mace glance off my back as I leaned so far forward in my saddle after the wasted blow that my sword almost touched the churned ground.

I brought the sword up in an underarm swing and the mace was there to deflect it. For several minutes we fought until, in my astonishment, I heard a voice some distance away.

"RALLY THE STANDARD! RALLY, KNIGHTS OF HUMANITY!"

We had not succeeded in our tactics! That was obvious from the cry. Our forces were attempting to consolidate and attack afresh. Arjavh smiled and lowered his mace.

"They sought to surround the halflings," he said and laughed aloud.

"We'll meet again soon, Arjavh," I shouted as I turned my horse back and spurred it through the press, forcing my way through the milling, embattled men toward the standard which swayed to my right.

There was no cowardice in my leaving and Arjavh knew it. I had to be with my men when they rallied. That was why Arjavh had lowered his weapon. He had not sought to stop me.

N I N E T E E N

THE BATTLE DECIDED

Arjavh had mentioned the halflings. I had noticed no ghouls amongst his men. What were they, then? What kind of creatures could not be surrounded?

The halflings were only part of my problem. Fresh tactics had to be decided upon hurriedly or the day would be soon lost. Four of my marshals were desperately trying to get our ranks reformed as I came up to them. The Eldren enclosed us where we had planned to enclose them and many groups of our warriors were cut off from the main force.

Above the noise of the battle I shouted to one of my marshals: "What's the position? Why did we fail so quickly? We outnumber them."

"It's hard to tell what the position is, Lord Erekosë," the marshal answered, "or how we failed. One moment we had surrounded the Eldren and the next moment half their forces were surrounding us — they vanished and reappeared behind us! Even now we cannot tell which is material Eldren and which is halfling." The man who answered me was Count Maybeda, an experienced old warrior. His voice was ragged and he was very much shaken.

"What other qualities do these halflings possess?" I asked.

"They are solid enough when fighting, Lord Erekosë, and they can be slain by ordinary weapons — but they can disappear at will and be wherever they wish on the field. It is impossible to plan tactics against such a foe."

"In that case," I decided, "we had best keep our men together and fight a defensive action. I think we still outnumber the Eldren and their ghostly allies. Let them come to us!"

The morale of my warriors was low. They were disconcerted and were finding it difficult to face the possibility of defeat when victory had seemed so certain.

Through the milling men I saw the basilisk banner of the Eldren approaching us. Their cavalry poured in swiftly with Prince Arjavh at their head.

Our forces came together again and once more I was doing battle with the Eldren leader.

He knew the power of my sword — knew that the touch of it could slay him if it fell on a break in his armour — but that deadly mace, wielded with the dexterity with which another would wield a sword, warded off every blow I aimed.

I fought him for half an hour until he showed signs of dazed weariness and my own muscles ached horribly.

And again our forces had been split! Again it was impossible to see how the battle went. For most of the time I was uncaring, oblivious to the events around me as I concentrated on breaking through Arjavh's splendid guard.

Then I saw Count Maybeda ride swiftly past me, his golden armour split, his face and arms bloody. In one red hand he carried the torn banner of Humanity and his eyes stared in fear from his wounded head.

"Flee, Lord Erekosë!" he screamed as he galloped past. "Flee! The day is lost!"

I could not believe it, until the ragged remnants of my warriors began to stream past me in ignominious flight.

"Rally, Humanity!" I called. "Rally!" But they paid me no heed. Again Arjavh dropped his mace to his side.

"You are defeated," he said.

Reluctantly I lowered my sword.

"You are a worthy foe, Prince Arjavh."

"You are a worthy foe, Erekosë. I remember our battle terms. Go in peace. Necranal will need you."

I shook my head slowly and drew a heavy breath. "Prepare to defend yourself, Prince Arjavh," I said.

He shrugged, swiftly brought up the mace against the blow I aimed at him and then brought it down suddenly upon my metal-gauntleted wrist. My whole arm went numb. I tried to cling to the sword, but my fingers would not respond. It dropped from my hand and hung by a thong from my wrist.

With a curse, I flung myself from my saddle straight at him, my good hand grasping at him, but he turned his horse aside and I fell, face forward, in the bloody mud of the field.

I attempted once to rise, failed, and lost consciousness.

WHO AM I?
You are Erekosë, the Eternal Champion.
WHAT IS MY REAL NAME?
Whatever it happens to be.
WHY AM I AS I AM?
Because that is what you have always been.
WHAT IS "ALWAYS"?
Always.
WILL I EVER KNOW PEACE?
You will sometimes know peace.
FOR HOW LONG ?
For a while.
WHERE DID I COME FROM?
You have always been.
WHERE WILL I GO?
Where you must.
FOR WHAT PURPOSE?
To fight.
TO FIGHT FOR WHAT?
To fight.
FOR WHAT?
Fight.
FOR WHAT?

I shivered, aware that I was no longer clad in my armour. I looked up. Arjavh stood over me.

"I wonder why he hated me then," he was murmuring to himself. Then he realised I was awake and his expression altered. He gave a light smile. "You're a ferocious one, Sir Champion."

I looked into his moody, milky eyes.

"My warriors," I said, "what…?"

"Those that were left have fled. We released the few prisoners we had and sent them after their comrades. Those were the terms, I believe?"

I struggled up. "Then you are going to release me?"

"I suppose so. Although…"

"Although?"

"You would be a useful bargaining prisoner."

I took his meaning and relaxed, sinking back onto the hard bed. I thought deeply and fought the idea which came to me. But it grew too large in me. At length I said, almost against my will: "Trade me for Ermizhad."

His cool eyes showed surprise for an instant. "You would suggest that? But Ermizhad is such a strong hostage for Humanity."

"Damn you, Eldren. I told you to trade me for her."

"You're a strange human, my friend. But with your permission granted, that is what I shall do. I thank you. You really do remember the old Code of War, don't you? I think you are who you say you are."

I closed my eyes. My head ached.

He left the tent and I heard him instructing a messenger.

"Make sure the people know!" I shouted from the bed. "The king may not agree, but the people will force his hand. I'm their hero! They'll willingly trade me for an Eldren — no matter who that Eldren is."

Arjavh instructed the messenger accordingly. He came back into the tent.

"It puzzles me," I said at length. He was sitting on a bench on the other side of the tent. "It puzzles me that the Eldren have not conquered Humanity before now. With those halfling warriors, I should think you'd be invincible."

He shook his head. "We rarely make use of our allies," he said. "But I was desperate. You can understand that I was prepared to go to almost any measures to rescue my sister."

"I can," I told him.

"We would never have invaded," he continued, "had it not been for her." It was said so simply that I believed him. I had already been fairly certain of that.

THE ETERNAL CHAMPION 117

I took a deep breath. "It is hard for me," I said. "I am forced to fight like this, with no clear idea about the rights or the wrongs of that fighting, with no true knowledge of this world, with no opinions of those who inhabit it. Simple facts turn out to be lies — and unbelievable things turn out to be true. What are the halflings, for instance?"

Again he smiled. "Sorcerous ghouls," he said.

"That is what Count Roldeco told me. It is no explanation."

"What if I told you they were capable of breaking up their atomic structure at will and assembling again in another place? You would not understand me. Sorcery, you would say."

I was surprised at the scientific nature of his explanation. "I would understand you better," I said slowly.

He raised his slanting eyebrows.

"You *are* different," he said. "Well, the halflings, as you have seen, are related to the Eldren. Not all the dwellers on the Ghost Worlds are our kin — some are more closely related to men, and there are other, baser forms of life.

"The Ghost Worlds are solid enough, but exist in an alternate series of dimensions to our own. There are many such series, our philosophers believe — possibly an infinite series. On the worlds we know, the halflings have no special powers — no more than we have — but here they have. We do not know why. They do not know why. On Earth different laws seem to apply for them. More than a million years ago we discovered a means of bridging the dimensions between Earth and these other worlds. We found a race akin to our own who will, at times, come to our aid if our need is especially great. This was one of those times. Sometimes, however, the bridge ceases to exist when the Ghost Worlds move into another phase of their weird orbit, so that any halflings on Earth cannot return and any of our people are in the same position if they are on the Ghost Worlds. Therefore, you will understand, it is dangerous to stay on either side overlong."

"Is it possible," I asked, "that the Eldren came originally from these Ghost Worlds?"

"I suppose it is possible," he agreed. "There are no records, though."

"Perhaps that is why the humans hate you as aliens," I suggested.

"That is not the reason," he told me, "for the Eldren occupied Earth for ages before humankind ever came here."

"What!"

"It is true," he said. "I am an immortal and my grandfather was an immortal. He was slain during the first wars between the Eldren and Humanity. When the humans came to Earth, they had incredible weapons of terrible destructive potential. In those days we also possessed similar weapons. The wars created such destruction the Earth seemed like a blackened ball of mud when the wars were ended and the Eldren defeated. So terrifying was the destruction that we swore never again to use our weapons, whether we were threatened with extermination or not. We could not assume the responsibility for destroying an entire planet."

"You mean you still have these weapons?"

"They are locked away, yes."

"And you have the knowledge to use them?"

"Of course. We are immortal. We have many people who fought in those ancient wars, some even built new weapons before our decision was made."

"Then why...?"

"I have told you. We swore not to."

"What happened to the humans' weapons — and their knowledge of them? Did they make the same decision?"

"No. The human race degenerated. Wars occurred among themselves. At one time they almost wiped themselves out completely, at another they were barbarians, and at another they seemed to have matured, to have conquered their monstrous egos and found self-respect at last, to be at peace with their own souls and with one another. During one of those stages they lost the knowledge and the remaining weapons. In the last million years they have climbed back from absolute savagery — the peaceful years were short, a false lull — and I'd predict they'll sink back again soon enough. They seem bent on their own destruction as well as ours. We have wondered if the humans, who must surely exist in other planes, are the same. Perhaps not."

"I hope not," I said. "How do you think the Eldren will fare against the humans?"

"Badly," he said. "Particularly since the humans are inspired by your leadership and the gateway to the Ghost Worlds is due soon to close again. Previously Humanity was split by quarrels, you see. King Rigenos could never get his marshals to agree and he was too uncertain of himself to make the large decisions. But you have made decisions for him and you have united the marshals. You will win, I think."

"You are a fatalist," I said.

"I am a realist," he said.

"Could not peace terms be arranged?"

He shook his head. "What use is it to talk?" he asked me bitterly. "You humans, I pity you. Why will you always identify our motives with your own?

We do not seek power — only peace. But that, I suppose, this planet shall never have until Humanity dies of old age."

I stayed with Arjavh for a few more days before he released me, on trust, and I rode back toward Necranal. It was a long, lonely ride and I had a great deal of time to think.

I was hardly recognized this time, for I was dusty and my armour was battered and the people of Necranal had become used to seeing beaten warriors returning to the city.

I reached the Palace of Ten Thousand Windows. A gloomy quiet had settled on it. The king was not in the Great Hall and Iolinda was not in her quarters.

In my old apartments, I stripped off my armour. "When did the Lady Ermizhad leave?" I asked a slave.

"Leave, master? Is she not still here?"

"What? Where?"

"In the same quarters, surely."

I still had my breastplate on and I donned my sword as I strode through the corridors until I got to Ermizhad's apartments and brushed past the guard on the door.

"Ermizhad — you were to be traded for me. Those were the terms. Where is the king? Why has he not kept his word?"

"I knew nothing of this," she said. "I did not know Arjavh was so close, otherwise…"

I interrupted her. "Come with me. We'll find the king and get you on your journey back."

I half dragged her from room to room of the palace until at last I found the king in his private apartments. He was in conference with Roldero as I burst in upon them.

"King Rigenos, what is the meaning of this? My word was given to Prince Arjavh that Ermizhad was to leave here freely upon my release. He allowed me to leave his camp on trust and now I return to find the Lady Ermizhad still in captivity. I demand that she be released immediately."

The king and Roldero laughed at me.

"Come now, Erekosë," said Roldero. "Who needs to keep his word to an Eldren jackal? Now we have our war champion back and still retain our chief hostage. Forget it, Erekosë. There is no need to regard the Eldren as human!"

Ermizhad smiled. "Do not worry, Erekosë. I have other friends." She closed her eyes and began to croon. At first the words came softly, but the volume rose until she was giving voice to a weird series of harmonies.

Roldero jumped forward, dragging out his sword.

"Sorcery!"

I stepped between them.

Roldero said urgently: "Erekosë! The bitch invokes her demon kind!"

I drew my own sword and held it warningly in front of me, protecting Ermizhad. I had no idea what she was doing, but I was going to give her the chance, now, to do whatever she wanted.

Her voice changed abruptly and then stopped. Then she cried: "Brethren! Brethren of the Ghost Worlds — aid me!"

TWENTY-ONE
AN OATH

Quite suddenly there materialized in the chamber some dozen or so Eldren, their faces but slightly different from others I had seen. I recognized them now as halflings.

"There!" shouted Rigenos. "Evil sorcery. She is a witch. I told you! A witch!"

The halflings were silent. They surrounded Ermizhad until all their bodies touched hers and one another's. Then Ermizhad shouted: "Away, brethren — back to the camp of the Eldren!"

Their forms began to flicker so that they seemed half in our dimension, half in some other. "Goodbye, Erekosë," she cried. "I hope we shall meet in happier circumstances."

"I hope so!" I shouted back. And then she vanished.

"Traitor!" cursed King Rigenos. "You aided her escape!"

"You should die by torture!" added Roldero, disgusted.

"I'm no traitor, as well you know," I said evenly. "You are traitors — traitors to your words, to the great tradition of your ancestors. You have no case against me, you stupid — stupid brutes."

I stopped, turned on my heel and left the chamber.

"You lost the battle — War Champion!" screamed King Rigenos after me as I stalked out. "The people do not respect defeat!"

I went to find Iolinda.

She had been walking in the balconies and had now returned to her apartments. I kissed her, needing at that moment a woman's friendly sympathy, but I seemed to meet a block. She was not, it seemed, prepared to give me help, although she kissed me dutifully. At length I ceased to embrace her and stood back a little, looking into her eyes.

"What's wrong?"

"Nothing," she said. "Should there be? You are safe. I had feared you dead."

Was it me, then? Was it? I pushed the thought from me. But can a man force himself to love a woman? Can he love two women at the same time? I was desperately clinging to the strands of the love I had felt for her when first we met.

"Ermizhad is safe," I blurted. "She called her halfling brothers to her aid and, when she returns to the Eldren camp, Arjavh will take his forces back to Mernadin. You should be pleased."

"I am," she said, and then: "And you are pleased, no doubt, that our hostage escaped!"

"What do you mean?"

"My father told me how you'd been enchanted by her wanton sorcery. You seemed to be more anxious for her safety than ours."

"That is foolish talk."

"You seem to like the company of the Eldren, too. Holidaying with our greatest enemy..."

"Stop!"

"I think my father spoke true, Erekosë." Her voice was subdued now. She turned from me.

"But, Iolinda, I love you. You alone."

"I do not believe you, Erekosë."

What is it in me that I should become what I became then? At that moment I gave an oath which was to affect all our destinies. Why, as my love for her began to fade and I saw her as a selfish, grasping fool, did I yet protest a greater love for her?

I do not know. I only know that I did it.

"I love you more than life, Iolinda!" I said. "I would do anything for you!"

"I do not believe you!"

"I do. I will prove it!" I cried in agony.

She turned. There was pain and reproach in her eyes. There was a bitterness that went so deep it had no bottom. There was anger and there was revenge.

"How will you prove it, Erekosë?" she said softly.

"I swear I shall kill all the Eldren."

"All?"

"Every single Eldren."

"You will spare none?"

"None! None! I want it to be over. And the only way I can finish it is to kill them all. Then it will be over — only then!"

"Including Prince Arjavh and his sister?"

"Including them!"

"You swear this? You swear it?"

"I swear it. And when the last Eldren dies, when the whole world is ours, then I will bring it to you and we shall be married."

She nodded. "Very well, Erekosë." She went swiftly from the room.

I unstrapped my sword and flung it savagely to the floor. I spent the next few hours fighting my own agony of spirit.

But I had made the oath now.

Soon I became cold. I meant what I had said. I would destroy all the Eldren. Rid the world of them. Rid myself of this continual turmoil in my mind.

TWENTY-TWO

THE REAVING

The less of a man I became, and the more of an automaton, so the dreams and half-memories ceased to plague me. It was as if they had deliberately driven me into this mindless role; so long as I continued to be a creature without remorse or conscience they would reward me with their absence. If I again showed signs of ordinary humanity, then they would punish me with their presence.

But that is a notion. It is no nearer the truth, I suppose, than any other. One might also argue that I was about to achieve the catharsis that would rid me of any ambivalence; banish my nightmares; cleanse my psyche.

In the month I spent preparing for the great war against the Eldren, I saw but little of my betrothed and, finally, ceased to seek her out, concentrating instead on the plans for the campaigns we intended to fight.

I developed the strictly controlled mind of the soldier. I allowed no emotion, whether it was love or hate, to influence me.

I became strong. And in my strength I became virtually inhuman. I knew people remarked upon it — but they also saw in me the qualities of a great battle leader and, while all avoided my company socially, they were very glad that Erekosë led them.

Arjavh and his sister returned to their ships and in their ships went back to their own land. Now, doubtless, they awaited us, readying themselves for the next battle.

We continued with our original plans and at length were ready to sail for the Outer Islands at World's Edge. The gateway to the Ghost Worlds which we intended to close.

Then we sailed.

It was a long and arduous sailing, that one, before we sighted the bleak cliffs of the Outer Islands and prepared ourselves for the invasion.

Roldero was with me. But it was a grim Roldero, a silent Roldero who had made himself, as I had, into nothing but an instrument of war.

Warily we sailed in. The Eldren, however, had known of our coming and had all but deserted their towns. This time there were no women and no children, naught but a few handfuls of Eldren warriors whom we slew. And of halflings there were none. Arjavh had spoken the truth when he said the gates were closing to the Ghost Worlds.

We ripped the towns to rubble, burning and pillaging as a matter of course, but without lust. We tortured captured Eldren to discover the meaning for this desertion and they told us nothing intelligible; but secretly I knew the meaning. Our troops became morose, possessed of a sense of anticlimax and, though we left no building standing, no Eldren alive, the men could not rid themselves of the notion that they had been thwarted in some inexplicable way — as an ardent lover is innocently thwarted by a coy maiden.

And, because of the Eldren's refusal to give them a mighty battle, our soldiers grew to hate the Eldren that much more.

When our work was done in the Outer Islands, and every building was dust, every Eldren a corpse, we sailed almost immediately for the continent of Mernadin and put into Paphanaal, which was still held by our forces under the Lord Katorn. But, in the meantime, King Rigenos had joined them and was waiting for us to arrive. We landed our troops and pushed outwards across the continent, bent on conquest.

I remember few incidents in detail. Days merged one into the other and wherever we went we slew Eldren. There was no Eldren fortress which could withstand our grim thrusting.

I was tireless in my murdering; insatiable in my bloodlust. Humanity had wanted such a wolf as I, and now they had him and they followed him, and they feared him.

It was a year of fire and steel and ruined flesh; Mernadin seemed at times to be nothing but a sea of smoke and blood. The troops were all physically weary, but the spirit of slaughter was in them and it gave them a horrible vitality.

A year of pain and death. Everywhere that the banners of Humanity met the standards of the Eldren, the basilisk standards would be torn down and trampled.

We put all we found to the sword. We mercilessly punished deserters in our own ranks, we flogged our troops to greater endurance.

We were the horsemen of death: King Rigenos, Lord Katorn, Count Roldero and myself. We grew as gaunt as hungry dogs and it seemed we fed on Eldren flesh, drank only Eldren blood. Fierce dogs we were. Wild-eyed and panting dogs, sharp-fanged dogs forever restless for the scent of fear and death.

Towns burned behind us, cities fell and were crushed, stone by stone, to the ground. Eldren corpses littered the countryside and the fairest of our camp followers were fat carrion birds and sleek-coated jackals. A year of bloodshed. A year of destruction. But was it Mernadin I wished to destroy, or was it myself? If I could not force myself to love, then I could force myself to hate; and this I did. All feared me, humans and Eldren alike, as I turned beautiful Mernadin into a funeral pyre on which I sought, in terrible bewilderment and grief, to burn the decaying vestiges of my own humanity.

I cannot justify my actions. Roldero had said that men must be judged by their deeds, not their motives. I offer such speculation only in the hope that by understanding our motives we may thus control our deeds.

It was in the Valley of Kalaquita, where stood the garden city of Lakh, that King Rigenos was killed.

The city looked peaceful and deserted, and we rode down upon it with little caution. We howled one great, concerted war-cry and, in place of the disciplined army which had landed at Paphanaal, we were one mass of blood-encrusted armour and dust-ingrained flesh, waving our weapons and galloping wildly upon that garden city of Lakh.

It was a trap.

The Eldren were in the hills and had used their beautiful city as bait. Silver-snouted cannon suddenly shouted from surrounding copses and sent a searing shower of shot into our astonished soldiers' midst! Slender arrows whistled in a wave of sharp-tipped terror as the hidden Eldren archers took their vengeance with their bows.

Horses fell. Men screamed. We turned in confusion. But then our own bowmen began to retaliate, concentrating not on the enemy archers, but on their cannoneers. Gradually the silver guns went silent and the archers melted back into the hills, retreating again to one of their few remaining fortresses.

I turned to King Rigenos, who sat beside me on his big war steed. He was rigid, staring up at the sky. And then I saw that an arrow had pierced his thigh and imbedded itself in his saddle, pinning him to his horse.

"Roldero!" I shouted. "Get a doctor for the king if we have one."

Roldero rode up from where he had been taking account of our dead. He pushed back the king's visor and shrugged. Then he stared significantly at me. "He has not breathed for several minutes by the look of him."

"Nonsense. An arrow in the thigh doesn't kill. Not normally, at any rate — and not so quickly. Get the doctor.

A peculiar smile crossed Roldero's bleak features. "It was the shock, I think, that killed him." Then he laughed brutally and pushed at the armoured corpse with his hand so that it tilted over, wrenching the arrow free, and crashing into the mud. "Your betrothed is queen now, Erekosë," said Roldero, still laughing. "I congratulate you."

My horse stirred as I stared down at Rigenos's corpse. Then I shrugged and turned my steed away.

It was our habit with the dead to leave them, no matter who they had been, where they lay.

We took Rigenos's horse with us. It was a good horse.

The loss of the king did not worry our warriors much, though Katorn himself seemed a little perturbed, perhaps because he had had such great influence over the monarch. But the king had possessed no real authority in this last year, for Humanity followed a grimmer chief, who some thought might be Death Himself.

Dead Erekosë is what they called me. The vengeful, mindless Sword of Humanity.

I did not care what they called me — Reaver, Bloodletter, Berserker — for my dreams no longer plagued me, my own hypocrisy did not disturb me, and my ultimate goal came closer and closer.

It was the last fortress of the Eldren left undefeated. I dragged my armies behind me as if by a rope. I dragged them toward the principal city of Mernadin, by the Plains of Melting Ice, Arjavh's capital — Loos Ptokai.

And at last we saw its looming towers silhouetted against a red evening sky. Of marble and black granite, it rose mighty and seemingly invulnerable above us.

But I knew we should take it.

I had Arjavh's word for it, after all. He had told me we should win.

The night after we had camped beneath the walls of Loos Ptokai, I sprawled in my chair and could not sleep. Instead I stared into the darkness. This was not my habit. Normally I would now slump into my bed and snore till dawn, wearied by the day's killing.

But tonight I brooded.

And then, at dawn the next day, my features cold as stone, I rode beneath my banner as I had ridden a year before into the camp of the Eldren, with my herald at my side.

We came close to the main gate of Loos Ptokai and then we stopped. A few Eldren looked down from distant battlements but I could not read their expressions.

My herald raised his golden trumpet to his lips and blew an eerie blast upon it which echoed among the black and white towers of Loos Ptokai.

"Eldren prince!" I called in my dead voice. "Arjavh of Mernadin, I have come to slay you."

Then on the battlements directly over the great main gate I saw Arjavh appear. He peered down at me and there was a sadness in his strange eyes.

"Greetings, old enemy," he called. "You will have a long siege before you break this, the last of our strength."

"So be it," I said, "but break it we shall."

Arjavh paused. Then he said: "We once agreed to fight a battle according to the Erekosian Code of War. Do you wish to discuss terms again?"

I shook my head. "We shall not stop until every Eldren is slain. I have sworn an oath, you see, to rid Earth of all your kind."

"Then," said Arjavh, "before the battle commences, I invite you to enter Loos Ptokai as my guest and refresh yourself. You would seem in need of refreshment."

At this I bridled, but then my herald sneered. "They become ingenuous in their defeat, master, if they think they can deceive you by such a simple trick."

My mind had once again suddenly become a battleground of conflicting emotions. "Be silent!" I ordered the herald. I took a deep breath.

"Well?" called Arjavh.

"I accept," I said hollowly. And then I added: "Is the Lady Ermizhad therein?"

"She is — and is eager to see you again." There was an edge to Arjavh's voice as he answered this last question. For a moment I was again suspicious; did I detect the threat of treachery?

Arjavh must have been aware of my own affection for his sister: the affection I did not admit; but which secretly contributed to my decision to enter Loos Ptokai.

The herald said in astonishment: "My lord, surely you cannot be serious? As soon as you are inside the gates, you will be slain. There were stories once that you and Prince Arjavh were on not unfriendly terms, for enemies, but after the havoc you have caused in Mernadin, he will kill you immediately. Who would not?"

I shook my head. I was in a new and quieter mood. "He will not," I said. "And this way I can find an opportunity to judge the Eldren strength. It will be useful to us."

"But disastrous for us, if you should die."

"I will not die," I said, and then, incredibly, all the ferocity, the hate, the mad battle-anger, rushed out of me, leaving me, as I turned away from the herald so he should not see, with tears in my eyes.

"Open your gates, Prince Arjavh," I called in shaking tones. "I come to Loos Ptokai as your guest."

TWENTY-THREE
IN LOOS PTOKAI

I rode my horse slowly into the city, having left my sword and lance with the herald, who was now, in astonishment, galloping back to our own camp to give the news to the marshals.

The streets of Loos Ptokai were silent, as if in mourning. And when Arjavh came down the steps from the battlements to greet me, I saw, that he, too, wore the expression which showed upon my own harsh features. His step was not so lithe and his voice not quite so lilting as when we had first met a year before.

I dismounted. He gripped my arm.

"So," he said in attempted gaiety, "the barbarian battlemonger is still material. My people had begun to doubt it."

"I suppose they hate me," I said.

He seemed a little surprised. "The Eldren cannot hate," he said as he led me toward his palace.

I was shown by Arjavh to a small room containing a bed, a table and a chair of wonderful workmanship, all slender and seemingly of precious metal but in fact of cunningly wrought wood. In one corner was a sunken bath with water steaming in it.

When Arjavh had gone, I stripped off my blood- and dust-encrusted armour and climbed out of the underclothes I had worn for much of the past year. Then I sank gratefully into the water.

Since the initial emotional shock I had received when Arjavh had issued his invitation, my mind had become numbed. But now, for the first time in a year, I relaxed, mentally and physically, washing all the grief and hatred from me as I washed my body. So suddenly did the tension leave me that it might have been the result of Eldren sorcery; but I think now that I relaxed because I did not have to deceive myself in Loos Ptokai.

I was almost cheerful as I donned the fresh clothes which had been laid out for me and when someone knocked at my door, called lightly for them to enter.

"Greetings, Erekosë." It was Ermizhad.

"My lady." I bowed.

"How are you faring, Erekosë?"

"In war, as you know, I am faring well. And personally I feel better for your hospitality."

"Arjavh sent me to bring you to the meal."

"I am ready. But first tell me how you have fared, Ermizhad."

"Well enough — in health," said she. Then she came closer to me. Involuntarily I leaned back slightly. She looked at the ground and raised her hands to touch her throat. "And tell me — are you now wed to Queen Iolinda?"

"We are still betrothed," I told her.

Deliberately, then, I looked into Ermizhad's eyes and added as levelly as I could: "We are to be married when…"

"When?"

"When Loos Ptokai is taken."

She said nothing.

I stepped forward so that we were separated by little more than an inch. "Those are the only terms on which she will accept me," I said. "I must destroy all the Eldren. Your trampled banners will be my wedding gift to her."

Ermizhad nodded and gave me a queer, sad and sardonic look. "That is the oath you swore. You must abide by it. You must slay every Eldren. Every one."

I cleared my throat. "That is the oath."

"Come," she said. "The meal grows cold."

At dinner, Ermizhad and I sat close together and Arjavh spoke wittily of some of the stranger experiments of his scientist ancestors and for a little while we managed to drive away the knowledge of the forthcoming battle. But later, as

Ermizhad and I talked softly to one another, I caught a look of pain in Arjavh's eyes and for a moment he was quiet. He broke into our conversation suddenly:

"We are beaten, as you know, Erekosë."

I did not want to speak of these things any more. I shrugged and tried to continue the lighter talk with Ermizhad. But Arjavh was insistent.

"We are doomed, Erekosë, to fall beneath the swords of your great army."

I drew a deep breath and looked him full in the face. "Yes. You are doomed, Prince Arjavh."

"It is a matter of time before you raze our Loos Ptokai."

This time I avoided his urgent gaze and merely nodded.

"So — you..." He broke off.

I became impatient. Many emotions mingled in me. "My oath," I reminded him. "I must do what I swore I would do, Arjavh."

"I do not fear to lose my own life..." he began.

"I know what you fear," I told him.

"Could not the Eldren admit defeat, Erekosë? Could they not acknowledge mankind's victory? Surely, one city... ?"

"I swore an oath." Now sadness filled me.

"But you cannot..." Ermizhad gestured with her slim hand. "We are your friends, Erekosë. We enjoy each other's company. We — we *are* friends."

"We are of different races," I said. "We are at war."

"I am not asking for mercy," Arjavh said.

"I know that," I replied. "I do not doubt Eldren courage. I have seen too many examples of it."

"You abide by an oath given in anger, offered to an abstraction, that leads you to slay those you love and respect. An oath made to strengthen an already faltering resolve. You hated killing. I know you did!" Ermizhad's voice was puzzled. "Are you tired of killing, Erekosë?"

"I am very tired of killing," I told her.

"Then...?"

"But I began this thing," I continued. "Sometimes I wonder if I really do lead my men — or if they push me ahead of them. Perhaps I am wholly their creation. The creation of the will of Humanity. Perhaps I am a kind of patchwork hero that they have manufactured. Perhaps I have no other existence and when my work is done, I will fade as their sense of danger fades."

"I think not," said Arjavh soberly.

I shrugged. "You are not me. You have not had my strange dreams."

"You still have those dreams?" Ermizhad asked.

"Not recently. Since I began this campaign, they have gone away. They only plague me when I attempt to assert my own individuality. When I do what is required of me, they leave me in peace. I am a ghost, you see. Nothing more."

Arjavh sighed. "I do not understand this. I think you are suffering from a terrible self-deception, Erekosë. You could assert your own will — but you are afraid to! Instead, you abandon yourself to hate and bloodshed, to this peculiar melancholia of yours. You are depressed because you are *not* doing what you really desire to do. The dreams will come again, Erekosë. Mark my words — the dreams will come again and they will be more terrible than any you have experienced before."

"Stop!" I shouted. "Do not spoil this last meeting of ours. I came here because…

"Because?" Arjavh raised a slim eyebrow.

"Because I needed some civilized company."

"To see your own kind," Ermizhad said softly.

I turned on her, rising from the table. "You are not my own kind! My race is out there, beyond those walls, waiting to vanquish you!"

"We are kin in spirit," Arjavh said. "Our bonds are finer and stronger than bonds of blood."

My face twisted and I buried it in my hands. "NO!"

Arjavh put a hand on my shoulder. "You are more substantial than you will allow yourself to be, Erekosë. It would take a great deal of a particular kind of courage if you would pursue the implications of another course of action."

I let my hands fall to myself. "You are right," I told him. "And I do not have that courage. I am just a sword. A force, like a whirlwind. There is nothing else to me — nothing I would allow. Nothing I am allowed…"

Ermizhad interrupted fiercely. "For your own sake, you must allow that other self to rule. Forget your oath to Iolinda. You do not love her. You have nothing in common with the bloodthirsty rabble that follows you. You are a greater man than any you lead — greater than any you fight."

"Stop it! This is Eldren sophistry. You would save your skins with words, having failed with swords!"

"She is right, Erekosë," Arjavh said. "It is not for *our* lives that we argue. It is for *your* spirit."

I slumped down into my seat. "I sought to avoid confusion," I said, "by taking a simple course of action. It is true that I feel no kinship with those I lead — or those who thrust me before them — but undeniably they *are* my kin. My duty…"

"Let them fare how they will," Ermizhad said. "Your duty is not to them. It is to yourself."

I sipped some wine. Then I said quietly: "I am afraid."

Ajavh shook his head. "You are brave. It is not your fault."

"Who knows?" I said. "Perhaps at some stage in one of my incarnations I committed an enormous crime. And now I am paying the price."

"That is self-pitying speculation," Arjavh reminded me. "It is not — it is not — manly, Erekosë."

I inhaled deeply. "I suppose not." Then I looked at him. "But if Time is cyclic — in some form, at least — it could be that I have not yet committed that crime."

"It is idle to speak of 'crime' in this way," Ermizhad said impatiently. "What does your heart tell you to do?"

"My heart? I have not listened to it for many months."

"Listen to it now!" she said.

I shook my head. "I have forgotten how to listen to it, Ermizhad. I must finish what I set out to do. What I was called here to do."

"Are you sure it was King Rigenos who called you?"

"Who else?"

Arjavh smiled. "This, too, is idle speculation. You must do what you must do, Erekosë. I will plead for my people no longer."

"Thank you for that," I said. I rose, staggered slightly and screwed up my eyes. "Gods! I am so *weary!*"

"Rest here tonight," Ermizhad said quietly. "Rest with me."

I looked at her.

"With me," she said.

Arjavh began to speak, changed his mind and left the room.

I realized then that I wanted nothing else but to do as Ermizhad suggested. Yet I shook my head. "It would be weakness."

"No," she said. "It would give you strength. It would enable you to make a clearer decision."

"I have made my decision. Besides, my oath to Iolinda…"

"You swore no oath of faithfulness."

I spread my hands. "I cannot remember."

She moved toward me and stroked my face. "Perhaps it would end something," she suggested. "Perhaps it would restore your love for Iolinda."

Now physical pain seemed to seize me. I even wondered for a moment if they had poisoned me. "No."

"It would help," she said. "I know it would help. How, I am not sure. I do not even know if it suits my own desires, but…"

"I *cannot* weaken now, Ermizhad."

"Erekosë, it would not be weakness!"

"Still…"

She turned away from me and said in a soft, strange tone, "Then rest here anyway. Sleep in a good bed so that you will be fit for tomorrow's fighting. I love you, Erekosë. I love you more than I love anything. I will aid you in whatever course of action you decide upon."

"I have already decided," I reminded her. "And you cannot aid me there." I felt dizzy. I did not want to return to my own camp in that condition, for they would be sure I had been drugged and would lose all confidence in me. Better to stay the night and greet my troops refreshed. "Very well, I will stay here tonight," I said. "Alone."

"As you wish, Erekosë." She moved toward the door. "A servant will come to show you where to sleep."

"I'll sleep in this room," I told her. "Have someone bring in a bed."

"As you wish."

"It will be good to sleep in a real bed," I said. "My thoughts will be sharper in the morning."

"I hope so. Good night, Erekosë."

Had they known that the dreams would return that night? Was I the victim of immense and subtle cunning such as only the unhuman Eldren possessed?

I lay on my bed in the Eldren fortress city and I dreamed.

But this was not a dream in which I sought to discover my true name. I had no name in this dream. I did not want a name.

I watched the world turning and I saw its inhabitants running about its surface like ants in a hill, like beetles in a dung heap. I saw them fighting and destroying, making peace and building — only to drag those buildings down again in another inevitable war. And it seemed to me that these creatures had evolved only so far from the beast state and that some quirk of destiny had doomed them to repeat, over and over again, the same mistakes. And I realised that there was no hope for them — these imperfect creatures that were halfway from the animals, halfway from the gods — that it was their fate, like mine, to struggle forever and forever fail to be fulfilled. The paradoxes that existed in me existed in the whole race. The problems for which I could find no solution in fact had no solution. There was no point in seeking an answer; one could only accept what existed or else reject it, as one pleased. It would always be the same. Oh, there was much to love them for and nothing at all to hate them for. How could they be hated, when their errors resulted from the quirk of fate that had made them the half-creatures that they were — half-blind, half-deaf, half-dumb?

I woke up and felt very calm. And then, gradually, a sense of terror possessed me as the implications of my thoughts began to dawn on me.

Had the Eldren sent this dream — with their sorcery?

I did not think so. This dream was the dream that the other dreams had sought to hide from me. I was sure of it. This was the stark truth.

And the stark truth horrified me.

It was not my fate to wage eternal war — it was the fate of my entire race. As part of that race — as its representative, in fact — I, too, must wage eternal war.

And that is what I wished to avoid. I could not bear the thought of fighting forever, wherever I was required. And yet whatever I did to try to end the cycle would be hopeless. There was only one thing I could do.

I buried the thought.

But what else?

Try for peace? See if it would work? Let the Eldren live?

Arjavh had expressed impatience with idle speculation. But this, too, was idle speculation. The human race was sworn to destroy the Eldren. This done, of course, it would then turn upon itself again and begin the perpetual squabbling, the constant warring that its peculiar destiny decreed for it.

And yet — should I not, at least, attempt to make the compromise?

Or should I continue with my original ambition, destroy the Eldren, let the race resume its fratricidal sport? In a way it seemed to me that, while some Eldren lived, the race might hold together. If the common enemy remained, at least some sort of unity would exist in the human kingdoms. It seemed critical to me then that some Eldren be spared — for the sake of Humanity.

I suddenly realised that there was no contradiction in my loyalties at all. What I had thought was contradictory was, in fact, two halves of a whole. The dream had merely helped me unite them and see everything clearly.

Perhaps this was a complex piece of rationalisation? I shall never know. I feel that I was right, though it is possible that subsequent events proved me wrong. At least I tried.

I sat up in my bed as a servant came in with water for me to wash and my own clothes freshly laundered. I washed, dressed myself and, when a knock came at the door, I called out for the person to enter.

It was Ermizhad. She brought me my breakfast and set it on the table. I thanked her and she looked at me oddly.

"You seem to have changed since last night," she said. "You seem more at one with yourself."

"I think I am," I told her as I ate. "I had another dream last night."

"Was it as terrifying as the others?"

"More terrifying in certain aspects," I said. "But it did not raise problems, this time. It offered me a solution."

"You feel you can fight better."

"If you like. I think it would be in the interest of my race if we made peace with the Eldren. Or, at least, declared a permanent truce."

"You have realised at last that we offer you no danger."

"On the contrary, it is the very danger you offer that makes *your* survival necessary to my race." I smiled, remembering an old aphorism from somewhere. "If you did not exist, it would be necessary to invent you."

A look of intelligence brightened her face. She smiled, too. "I think I understand you."

"Therefore, I intend to present this conclusion to Queen Iolinda," I said. "I hope to persuade her that it is in our interest to end this war against the Eldren."

"And your terms?"

"I see no need to make terms with you," I said. "We will merely stop fighting and go away."

She laughed. "Will it be so easy?"

I looked squarely at her, deliberated for a moment, and then I shook my head. "Perhaps not. But I must try."

"You have become very rational suddenly, Erekosë. I am glad. Your sleep here did do you some good, then."

"And the Eldren, too, perhaps."

She smiled again. "Perhaps."

"I will return to Necranal as soon as possible and speak with Iolinda."

"And if she agrees, you will marry her?"

I felt weak, then. At last I said: "I must do that. Everything would be negated if I did not. You understand?"

"Entirely," she said and there were tears in her eyes as she smiled.

Arjavh came in a few minutes later and I told him what I intended to do. He received the news rather more sceptically than Ermizhad.

"You do not think I mean what I say?" I asked him.

He shrugged. "I believe you completely, Erekosë. But I do not think the Eldren will survive."

"What is it? Some disease? Something in you that…?"

He laughed shortly. "No, no. I think you will propose a truce and that the people will not let you make it. Your race will only be satisfied when every Eldren has perished. You said that it is their destiny always to fight. Could it not be that secretly they resent the Eldren because the presence of the Eldren means that they cannot go about their normal activities — I mean by that their fighting amongst themselves? Could this be nothing more than a pause before they wipe us out? And if they do not wipe us out now, they will do it very soon, whether you lead them or no."

"Still, I must try," I said.

"Try by all means. But they'll hold you to your vow, I'm sure."

"Iolinda is intelligent. If she listens to my arguments . . ."

"She is one of them. I doubt if she will listen. Intelligence has little to do with it. Last night when I pleaded with you, I was not myself — I panicked. I know, really, that there can be no peace."

"I must try."

"I hope you succeed."

Perhaps I had been beguiled by the charms of the Eldren, but I did not think so. I would do my best to bring peace to the wasted land of Mernadin, though it meant I could never see my Eldren friends again — never see Ermizhad.

I put the thought from my head and resolved to dwell upon it no longer.

Then a servant entered the room. My herald, accompanied by several marshals, including Count Roldero, had presented himself outside the gates of Loos Ptokai, half-certain that I had been murdered by the Eldren.

"Only sight of you will reassure them," Arjavh murmured. I agreed and left the room.

I heard the herald calling as I approached the city wall. "We fear that you have been guilty of great treachery. Let us see our master — or his corpse." He paused. "Then we shall know what to do."

Arjavh and I mounted the steps to the battlements and I saw relief in the herald's eyes as he noted I was unharmed.

"I have been talking with Prince Arjavh," I said. "And I have been thinking deeply. Our men are weary beyond endurance and the Eldren are now only a few, with just this city in their possession. We could take Loos Ptokai, but I see no point to it. Let us be generous victors, my marshals. Let us declare a truce."

"A truce, Lord Erekosë!" Count Roldero's eyes widened. "Would you rob us of our ultimate prize? Our final, fierce fulfillment? Our greatest triumph? *Peace!*"

"Yes," I said, "peace. Now go back. Tell our warriors I am safe."

"We can take this city easily, Erekosë," Roldero shouted. "There's no need to talk of peace. We can destroy the Eldren once and for all. Have you succumbed to their cursed enchantments again? Have they beguiled you with their smooth words?"

"No," I said, "it was I who suggested it."

Roldero swung his horse around in disgust.

"Peace!" he spat as he and his comrades headed back to the camp. "Our Champion's gone mad!"

Arjavh rubbed his lips with his finger. "Already, I see, there is trouble."

"They fear me," I told him, "and they'll obey me. They'll obey me — for a while, at least."

"Let us hope so," he said.

TWENTY-FOUR

THE PARTING

This time there were no cheering crowds in Necranal to welcome me, for news of my mission had gone ahead of me. The people could hardly believe it, but where they did believe it, they disapproved. I had shown weakness, in their eyes.

I had not seen Iolinda, of course, since she had become queen. She had a haughty look now as she strode about her throne room, awaiting me.

Privately I was a little amused. I felt like the man who, as an old rejected suitor, returns to see the object of his passion married and become a shrew. I was, therefore, somewhat relieved.

It was a small relief.

"Well, Erekosë," she said. "I know why you are here — why you have forsaken your troops, gone against your word to me that you would destroy every Eldren. Katorn has told me."

"Katorn is here?"

"He came here as soon as he heard your pronouncement from the battlements of Loos Ptokai, where you stood with your Eldren friends."

"Iolinda," I said urgently. "I am convinced that the Eldren are weary of war, that they never intended to threaten the Two Continents at all. They want only peace."

"Peace we shall have. When the Eldren race has perished."

"Iolinda, if you love me, you will listen to me, at least."

"If I love *you*? And what of the Lord Erekosë? Does he still love his queen?"

I opened my mouth, but I could not speak.

And suddenly there were tears in her eyes. "Oh, Erekosë." Her tone softened. "Can it be true?"

"No," I said thickly. "I still love you, Iolinda. We are to be married."

But she knew. She had suspected; but now she knew. However, if peace could result from my action, I was still prepared to pretend, to lie, to declare my passion for her, to marry her.

"I still want to marry you, Iolinda," I said.

"No," she said. "No. You do not."

"I will," I said desperately. "If peace with the Eldren comes about. . ."

Again her wide eyes blazed. "You insult me, my lord. Not on those terms, Erekosë. Never. You are guilty of high treason against us. The people already speak of you as a traitor."

"But I conquered a continent for them. I took Mernadin."

"All but Loos Ptokai — where your wanton Eldren bitch waits for you."

"Iolinda! That is not true!"

But it was almost true.

"You are unfair..." I began.

"And you are a traitor! Guards!"

As if they had been prepared for this, a dozen of the Imperial Guards rushed in, led by their captain, Lord Katorn. There was a hint of triumph in his eyes and then I knew for certain that he had always hated me because he desired Iolinda.

And I knew, whether I drew my sword or not, he would slay me where I stood.

So I drew my sword. The sword Kanajana. It glowed and the glow was reflected in Katorn's black eyes.

"Take him, Katorn!" cried Iolinda. And her voice was a scream of agony. I had betrayed her. I had failed to be the strength she needed so desperately. "Take him. Alive or dead. He is a traitor to his kind!"

I was a traitor to her. That was what she really meant. That was why I must die.

But I still hoped to save something. "It is untrue..." I began. But Katorn was already cautiously advancing, his men spreading out behind him. I backed to a wall, near a window. The throne room was on the first story of the palace. Outside were the private gardens of the queen. "Think, Iolinda," I said. "Retract your command. You are driven by jealousy. I'm no traitor."

"Slay him, Katorn!"

But I slew Katorn. As he came rushing at me, my sword flicked across his writhing, hate-filled face. He screamed, staggered, his hands rushed up to his head and then he toppled in his golden armour, toppled and fell with a crash to the flagstones.

He was the first human I was to slay.

The other guards came on, but more warily. I fought off their blades, slew a couple more, drove the others back, glimpsed Queen Iolinda watching me, her eyes full of tears, and leaped to the sill of the window.

"Goodbye, Queen. You have lost your champion now."

I jumped.

I landed in a rosebush that ripped at my skin, broke free and ran toward the gate of the garden, the guards behind me.

I tore the gate open and rushed down the hill and into the twisting streets of Necranal, with the guards in pursuit, their ranks joined by a howling pack of citizens who had no idea why I was wanted or even who I was. They chased me for the sheer pleasure of the hunt. My situation reflected more than ever the perpetual paradox of my life since I had obeyed Humanity's summons. Not long since I had led them. I had been the most powerful man in the world. And now, suddenly, I was a fugitive, running through the streets like a common pickpocket.

So it was thus that things turned. Iolinda's pain and jealousy had clouded her mind. And soon her decision would be the cause of more bloodshed than even she had demanded.

I ran, blindly at first, and then toward the river. My crew, I hoped, would still be loyal to me. If they were, then there was a faint chance of escape. I gained the ship just before my pursuers. I leaped aboard screaming:

"Prepare to sail!"

Only half the crew was aboard. The rest was on shore, in the taverns, but those remaining hurriedly shipped out the oars while we held the guards and the citizens at bay.

Then we shoved off and began our hasty flight down the Droonaa River.

It was some time before they managed to commandeer a ship for pursuit and by that time we were safely outdistancing them. My crew asked no questions. They were used to my silences, my actions which sometimes seemed peculiar. But, a week after we were on course over the sea, bound for Mernadin, I told them briefly that I was now an outlaw.

"Why, Lord Erekosë?" asked my captain. "It seems unjust."

"It is unjust, I think. Call it the queen's malice. I suspect Katorn spoke against me, making her hate me."

They were satisfied with the explanation and, when we put in at a small cove near the Plains of Melting Ice, I bade them farewell, mounted my horse and rode swiftly for Loos Ptokai, knowing not what I should do when I got there. Knowing only that I must let Arjavh know the turn events had taken.

He had been right. Humanity would not let me show mercy.

My crew bid me farewell with a certain amount of affection. They did not know — and neither did I — that they were soon to be killed because of me.

Now I crept into Loos Ptokai. I sneaked through the great siege camp that we had constructed there and, at night, entered the city of the Eldren.

Arjavh rose from his bed when he heard I had returned.

"Well, Erekosë?" He looked searchingly at me. Then he said: "You were not successful, were you? You have been riding hard and you have been fighting. What happened?"

I told him.

He sighed. "Well, our advice was foolish. Now you will die when we die."

"I would rather that, I think," I said.

Two months passed. Two ominous months in Loos Ptokai. Humanity did not attack the city immediately and it soon emerged that they were awaiting orders from Queen Iolinda. She, it appeared, had refused to make a decision.

The inaction was oppressive in itself.

I fretted often at the battlements, looking out over the great camp and wishing that the thing would start and be finished. Only Ermizhad eased my unhappiness. We openly acknowledged our love now.

And because I loved her, I began to want to save her.

I wanted to save her and I wanted to save myself and I wanted to save all the Eldren in Loos Ptokai, for I wanted to stay with Ermizhad forever. I did not want to be destroyed.

Desperately I tried to think of ways in which we could defeat that great force, but every plan I made was a wild one and could not work.

And then, one day, I remembered a conversation I had had with Arjavh on the plateau after he had defeated me in battle.

I went looking for him and found him in his study. He was reading from one of the beautifully decorated Eldren scrolls.

"Erekosë? Are they beginning their attack?"

THE ETERNAL CHAMPION

"No, Arjavh. But I recall that you told me once about some ancient weapons your race had — that you still have."

"What?"

"The old terrible weapons," I said. "The ones you swore never to use again because they could destroy so much!"

He shook his head. "Not those."

"Use them this once, Arjavh," I begged him. "Make a show of strength, that is all. They will be ready to discuss peace then."

He rolled up his scroll. "No. They will never discuss peace with us. They would rather die. I do not think that even this situation merits the breaking of that ancient vow."

"Arjavh," I said. "I respect the reasons for refusing to use the weapons. But I have grown to love the Eldren. I have already broken one vow. Let me break another — for you."

He still shook his head.

"Just agree to this, then," I said. "If the time comes when I feel we could use them, will you let me decide — take the decision out of your hands, make it my responsibility?"

He looked searchingly at me. The orbless eyes seemed to pierce me.

"Perhaps," he said.

"Arjavh — will you?"

"We Eldren have never been motivated as much by self-interest as you humans — and never to the extent of destroying another race, Erekosë. Do not confuse our values with those of mankind."

"I am not," I replied. "That is my reason for asking you this. I could not bear to see your noble race perish at the hands of those beasts beyond our walls!"

Arjavh stood up and replaced the scroll in the shelves. "Iolinda spoke the truth," he said quietly. "You are a traitor to your own race."

"'Race' is a meaningless term. It was you and Ermizhad who told me to be an individual. I have chosen my loyalties."

He pursed his lips. "Well…"

"I seek only to stop them continuing in their folly," I said.

He clenched his thin, pale hands together.

"Arjavh. I asked you because of the love I have for Ermizhad and the love she has for me. Because of the great friendship you have given me. For all Eldren left alive, I beg you to let me take the decision if it becomes necessary."

"For Ermizhad?" he raised his slanting eyebrows. "For you? For me? For my people? Not for revenge?"

"No," I said quietly. "I do not think so."

"Very well. I leave the decision to you. I suppose that is fair. I do not want to die. But remember — do not act as unwisely as others of your kind."

"I will not," I promised.

I think I kept that particular promise.

TWENTY-FIVE
THE ATTACK

And the days continued to pass. Gradually the air began to chill; night came sooner. Winter threatened. If winter arrived before Count Roldero, we would be safe until spring, for the invaders would be fools to attempt a heavy siege.

They realized this, too, and it seemed Iolinda must have come to a decision. She gave them permission to attack Loos Ptokai.

After much bickering among themselves, I learned, the marshals elected one of themselves, the most experienced, to act as their war champion.

They elected Count Roldero.

The siege commenced in earnest.

Their massive siege engines were brought forward, including the giant cannon known as the Firedrakes — great black things of iron, decorated with fierce reliefs.

Roldero rode up and his herald announced his presence. I went to speak with him from the battlements.

"Greetings, Erekosë the Traitor!" he called. "We have decided to punish you — and all the Eldren within these walls. We would have slaughtered the Eldren cleanly, but now we intend to put to slow death all those we capture."

I was saddened.

"Roldero, Roldero," I begged. "We were friends once. You were perhaps the only true friend I had. We drank together and fought together, made jokes together. We were comrades, Roldero. Good comrades."

His horse fidgeted beneath him, pawing at the earth.

"That was an age ago," he said without looking up at me.

"Little more than a year, Roldero."

"But we are not those two friends any longer, Erekosë." He looked up, shielding his eyes with a gauntleted hand. I saw that his face had grown old and it bore many new scars. Doubtless I looked as changed as he. "We are different men," Roldero said, and wrenching at his reins drove his horse away, digging his long spurs savagely into its flanks. Now there was nothing we could do but fight.

The Firedrakes boomed and their solid shot slammed against the walls. Blazing fireballs from captured Eldren artillery (we had become less fastidious as the war went on) screamed over the walls and into the streets. These were followed by thousands of arrows that came in a black shower, blotting out the light.

And then a million men rushed against our handful of defenders.

We replied with what cannon we had, but we relied mainly on archers to meet that first wave, for we were short of shot.

And we repelled them. After ten hours of fighting they fell back.

Then, next day and the day after, they continued to attack. But Loos Ptokai, the ancient capital of Mernadin, held firm.

Battalion upon battalion of yelling warriors mounted the siege towers and we again replied with arrows, with molten metal and, economically, with the fire-spewing cannon of the Eldren. We fought bravely, Arjavh and I leading the defenders and, whenever they sighted me, the warriors of Humanity screamed for vengeance and died striving for the privilege of slaying me.

We fought side by side, like brothers, Arjavh and I, but our Eldren warriors were tiring and, after a week of constant barrage, we began to realise that we could not much longer hold back that tide of steel.

That night we sat together after Ermizhad had gone to bed. We massaged our aching muscles and we spoke little.

Then I said: "We shall all be dead soon, Arjavh. You and I. Ermizhad. The rest of your folk."

He continued to dig his fingers into his shoulder, kneading it to loosen it. "Yes," he said. "Soon."

I wanted him to raise the subject that was on the tip of my tongue, but he would not.

The next day, scenting our defeat, the warriors of Humanity came at us with greater vigour than ever. The Firedrakes were brought in closer and began

148   THE ETERNAL CHAMPION

steadily to bombard the main gates.

I saw Roldero, mounted on his great black horse, directing the operation and there was something about his stance that made me realise that he was sure he would break our defenses that day.

I turned to Arjavh, who stood beside me on the wall, and I was about to speak when several of the Firedrakes boomed in unison. The black metal shook, the shot screamed from their snouts, hit the main gates, which were of metal, and split the left one down the middle. It did not fall, but it was so badly weakened that one more cannonade would bring it completely down.

"Arjavh!" I yelled. "We must break out the old weapons. We must arm the Eldren!"

His face was pale, but he shook his head.

"Arjavh! We must! Another hour and we'll be driven off these battlements! Another three and we'll be overwhelmed entirely!" He looked to where Roldero was directing the cannoneers and this time he did not remonstrate. He nodded. "Very well. I agreed that you would decide. Come."

He led me down the steps.

I only hoped he had not overestimated their power.

Arjavh led me to the vaults that lay at the core of the city. We moved along bare corridors of polished black marble, lighted by small bulbs which burned with a greenish glow. We came to a door of dark metal and he pressed a stud beside it. The door moved open and we entered an elevator, which bore us yet farther downward.

I was again astonished at the Eldren. They had deliberately given up all these marvels to satisfy their ideals of justice and honour.

Then we stepped into a great hall full of weirdly wrought machines that looked as if they had just been manufactured. They stretched for nearly half a mile ahead of us.

"These are the weapons," said Arjavh bleakly.

Around the high walls were arranged handguns of various kinds; there were rifles and objects that looked to John Daker's eye like antitank weapons. There were squat war machines on caterpillar treads, with glass cabins and couches for a single man to lie flat upon and operate the controls. I was surprised that there were no flying machines of any kind — or none that I recognized as such. I mentioned this to Arjavh.

"Flying machines! It would be interesting if such things could be invented. But I do not think it is possible. We have never, in all our history, been able to develop a machine that will safely stay in the air for any length of time."

I was amazed at this odd gap in their technology, but I commented on it no further.

"Now you have seen these fierce things," he said, "do you still feel you should use them?"

He doubtless thought such weapons were not familiar to me. They were not so very different to the war machines John Daker had known. And, in my dreams, I had seen much stranger weapons.

"Let us ready them," I said to him.

We returned to the surface and there instructed our warriors to transport the weapons to the surface.

Roldero had smashed in one of our gates now and we had had to bring up cannon to defend it, but the warriors of Humanity were beginning to press in and some hand-to-hand fighting was going on at the approach to the gates.

Night was falling. I hoped that, in spite of their gain, the human army would retreat at dark and give us the time we needed. Through the gap in the gate I saw Roldero urging his men in. Doubtless he hoped to consolidate his advantage before the twilight ended.

I ordered more men to the breach.

Already I was beginning to doubt my own decision.

Perhaps Arjavh was right and it was criminal to let the power of the ancient weapons loose. But then, I thought, what does it matter? Better destroy them and half the planet than let them destroy the beauty that was the Eldren.

I was forced to smile at this reaction in myself. Arjavh would not have approved of it. Such a thought was alien to him.

I saw Roldero bring in more men to counter our forces and I swung into the saddle of a nearby horse, spurring it toward the crucial breach.

I drew my poison sword, Kanajana, and I voiced my battle cry — the battle cry that only a short while ago had urged these warriors I attacked into battle against those I now led. They heard it and, as I suspected, were disconcerted.

I leaped my horse over the heads of my own men and confronted Roldero. He looked at me in astonishment and pulled his horse up short.

"Would you fight me, Roldero?" I said.

He shrugged. "Aye. I'll fight you, traitor."

And he rushed at me with his reins looped over his arm and both hands around the hilt of his great sword. It whistled over my head as I ducked.

Everywhere about us, beneath the broken walls of Loos Ptokai, human and Eldren fought desperately in the fading light.

Roldero was tired, more tired than I was, but he battled valiantly on and I could not get through his guard. His sword caught me a blow on my helmet and I reeled and struck back and caught *him* on the helmet. My helmet stayed on, but his was half-pulled off. He wrenched it off all the way and flung it aside. His hair had turned completely white since I had last seen him bareheaded.

His face was flushed and his eyes bright, his lips drawn back over his teeth. He tried to stab his sword through my visor, but I ducked under the blow and he fell forward in his saddle and I brought up my sword and drove it down into his breastbone.

He groaned and then his face lost all its anger and he gasped: "Now we can be friends again, Erekosë…" and he died.

I looked down at him as he collapsed over the neck of his horse. I remembered his kindness, the wine he had brought me to help me sleep, the advice he had tried to give me. And I remembered him pushing the dead king from his saddle. Yet, Count Roldero was a good man, a good man forced by history to do evil. By his own rule he had been condemned.

His black horse turned and began to canter back toward the count's distant pavilion.

I raised my sword in salute and then shouted to the humans who fought on. "Look, warriors of Humanity! Look! Your war champion is defeated!"

The sun was setting.

The warriors began to withdraw, looking at me in hatred as I laughed at them, but not daring to attack me while the bloody sword Kanajana was in my hand.

One of them did call back, however.

"We are not leaderless, Erekosë, if that is what you think. We have the queen to send us into battle. She has come to be witness to your destruction tomorrow!"

Iolinda was with the besiegers!

I thought swiftly and then yelled: "Tell your mistress to come tomorrow to our walls. Come at dawn to parley!"

Through the night we worked to reinforce the gate and to position the newfound weapons. They were raised wherever they would fit and the Eldren soldiers were armed with the hand weapons.

I wondered if Iolinda would get the message and, if she did get it, whether she would deign to come.

She came. She came with her remaining marshals in all their proud panoply of war. That panoply seemed so insignificant now, against the power of the ancient Eldren weapons.

We had set one of the new cannon pointing up at the sky so that we could demonstrate its fearful potential.

Iolinda's voice drifted up to us.

"Greetings, Eldren — and greetings to your human lap-dog. Is he a well-trained pet now?"

"Greetings, Iolinda," I said, showing my face. "You begin to show your father's penchant for poor insults and obvious irony. Let's waste no further time."

"I am already wasting time," she said. "We are going to destroy you all today."

"Perhaps not," I said. "For we offer you a truce — and peace."

Iolinda laughed aloud. "*You* offer us peace, traitor! You should be begging for peace — though you'll get none!"

"I warn you, Iolinda," I shouted desperately. "I warn you all. We have fresh weapons — weapons which once came near to destroying this whole Earth! Watch!"

I gave the order to fire the giant cannon.

An Eldren warrior depressed a stud on the controls.

There came a humming from the cannon and all at once a tremendous blinding bolt of golden energy gouted from its snout. The heat alone blistered our skins and we fell back, shielding our eyes.

Horses shrieked and reared. The marshals' faces were grey and their mouths gaped. They fought to control their mounts. Only Iolinda sat firmly in her saddle, apparently calm.

"That is what we offer you if you will not have peace," I shouted. "We have a dozen like it and there are others that are different, but as powerful, and we have hand cannon which can kill a hundred men at a sweep. What say you now?"

Iolinda raised her face and stared directly up at me.

"We fight," she said.

"Iolinda," I pleaded. "For our old love, for your own sake — do not fight. We will not harm you. You can go home, all of you, and live in security for the rest of your lives. I mean it."

"Security!" She laughed bitterly. "Security, while such weapons as these exist!"

"You must believe me, Iolinda!"

"No," she said. "Humanity will fight to the end and, because the Good One favours us, doubtless we will win. We are pledged to wage war on sorcery and there was never greater sorcery than what we have seen today."

"It is not sorcery. It is science. It is only like your cannon, but more powerful."

"Sorcery!" Everyone was murmuring it now. They were like savages, these fools.

"If we continue to fight," I said, "it will be a fight to the finish. The Eldren would prefer to let you go, once this battle is won. But if we win, I intend to clean the planet of your kind, just as you swore you would do to the Eldren. Take the chance. A peace! Be sane."

"We will die by sorcery," she said, "if we have to. But we will die fighting it."

I was too weary to continue. "Then let us finish this business," I told her.

Iolinda wheeled her horse away and, with her marshals in her wake, galloped back to order the attack.

I did not see Iolinda perish. There were so many that perished that day.

They came and we met them. They were helpless against our weapons. Energy spouted from the guns and seared into their ranks. How quickly they fell and how tragically they died. We all felt sorrow as we let loose the howling waves of force which swept across them and destroyed them, turning proud men and beasts to blackened rubble.

We did as they had predicted we would do. We destroyed them all.

I pitied them as they came on, the cream of Humanity's menfolk. Each wave was burned down as soon as it came within two hundred yards of our walls. We begged them to retreat. They came again. I began to guess that they wished to die. They sought rest in death.

It took two hours to destroy a million warriors.

When the extermination was over, I was filled with a strange emotion which I could not then and cannot now define. It was a mixture of grief, relief and triumph. I mourned for Iolinda. She was somewhere there in the heap of blackened bone and smouldering flesh — one piece of ruined meat amongst many, her beauty gone in the same instant as her life.

And it was then that I made my final decision. Or did I, indeed, make it at all? Was it not what I had been brought here to do?

Or was it the crime I had mentioned earlier? Was this the crime I committed that doomed me to be what I was?

Was I right?

In spite of Arjavh's constant antagonism to my plan, I ordered the machines out of Loos Ptokai and, mounted in one of them, led them overland.

This is what I did.

Two months before, I had been responsible for winning the cities of Mernadin for Humanity. Now I reclaimed them in the name of the Eldren.

I reclaimed them in a terrible way. I destroyed every human being occupying them.

A week and we were at Paphanaal, where the fleets of mankind lay at anchor in the great harbour.

I destroyed those fleets as I destroyed the garrison — men, women and children perished. None were spared.

And then, for many of the machines were amphibious, I led the Eldren across the sea to the Two Continents, though Arjavh and Ermizhad were not with me.

These cities fell: Noonos of the jewel-studded towers fell. Tarkar fell. The wondrous cities of the wheatlands, Stalaco, Calodemia, Mooros and Ninadoon, all fell. Wedmah, Shilaal, Sinana and others fell, crumbling in an inferno of gouting energy. They fell in a few moments.

In Necranal, the pastel-colored city of the mountain, five million citizens died and all that was left of Necranal was the scorched, smoking mountain itself.

But I was thorough. Not merely the great cities were destroyed. Villages were destroyed. Hamlets were destroyed. Towns and farms were destroyed.

I found some people hiding in caves. The caves were destroyed.

I destroyed forests where they might flee. I destroyed the very stones they might creep under.

I would doubtless have destroyed every blade of grass if Arjavh had not come hurrying over the ocean to stop me.

He was horrified at what I had done. He begged me to stop.

I stopped.

There was no more killing to do.

We made our way back to the coast and we paused to look at the smouldering mountainside that had been Necranal.

"For one woman's wrath," said Prince Arjavh, "and another's love you did this?"

I shrugged. "I do not know. I think I did it for the only kind of peace that will last. I know my race too well. This Earth would have been forever rent by strife of some kind. I had to decide who best deserved to live. If they had destroyed the Eldren, they would have soon turned on each other, as you know. And they fight for such empty things, too. For power over their fellows, for a bauble, for an extra acre of land that they will not till, for possession of a woman who doesn't want them."

"You decided that! You took this vast responsibility onto your own shoulders? You judged them and executed them according to your own interpretation of justice?" Arjavh said quietly. "Really, Erekosë, I do not think you know yet what you have done."

I sighed. "But it is done," I said.

"Yes." His eyes were full of a profound pity for me. He gripped my arm. "Come, friend. Back to Mernadin. Leave this stink behind. Ermizhad awaits you."

I was an empty man, then, bereft of emotion. I followed him toward the river. It moved sluggishly now. It was choked with black dust, with burned flesh.

"I think I did right," I said. "It was not my will, you know, but something else. I think it might have been my fate from the beginning. I think it was another will than mine which dragged me here — not Rigenos. Rigenos, like me, was a puppet — a tool used, as I was used. It was pre-ordained that Humanity should die on this planet."

"It is better that you think that," he said. "Come now. Let us go home."

E P I L O G U E

The scars of that destruction have healed now, as I end my chronicle.

I returned to Loos Ptokai to wed Ermizhad, to have the Eldren secret of immortality conferred upon me, to brood for a year or two until my brain cleared.

It is clear now. I feel no guilt for what I did. I feel more certain than ever that it was not my decision.

Perhaps that is madness? Perhaps I have rationalised my guilt? If so, I am at one with my madness, it does not tear me in two as my dreams used to. I have those dreams rarely these days.

So we are here, the three of us — Ermizhad, Arjavh and I. Arjavh is undisputed ruler of the Earth, an Eldren Earth, and we rule with him.

We cleansed this Earth of humankind. I am its last representative. And in so doing I feel that we knitted this planet back into the pattern, allowed it to drift, at last, harmoniously with a harmonious universe. For the universe is old, perhaps even older than I, and it could not tolerate the humans who broke its peace.

Did I do right?

You must judge for yourself, wherever you are.

For me, it is too late to ask that question. I have sufficient control nowadays never to ask it. The only way in which I could answer it would involve destroying my own sanity.

One thing puzzles me. If, indeed, Time is cyclic, in some manner, and the universe we know will be born again to turn another long cycle, then Humanity will one day arise again, somehow, on this Earth and my adopted people will disappear from the Earth, or seem to.

THE ETERNAL CHAMPION

And if you are human who reads this perhaps you know. Perhaps my question seems naive and you are at this moment laughing at me. But I have no answer. I can imagine none.

I am not to be the father of your race, human, for Ermizhad and I cannot produce children.

Then how shall you come again to disrupt the harmony of the universe?

And will I be here to receive you? Will I become your hero again or will I die with the Eldren fighting you?

Or will I die before then and be the leader who brings disrupting Humanity to Earth? I cannot say.

Which of the names will I have next time you call?

Now Earth is peaceful. The silent air carries only the sounds of quiet laughter, the murmur of conversation, the small noises of small animals. We and Earth are at peace.

But how long can it last?

Oh, how long can it last?

THE UNNEXED WORLDS

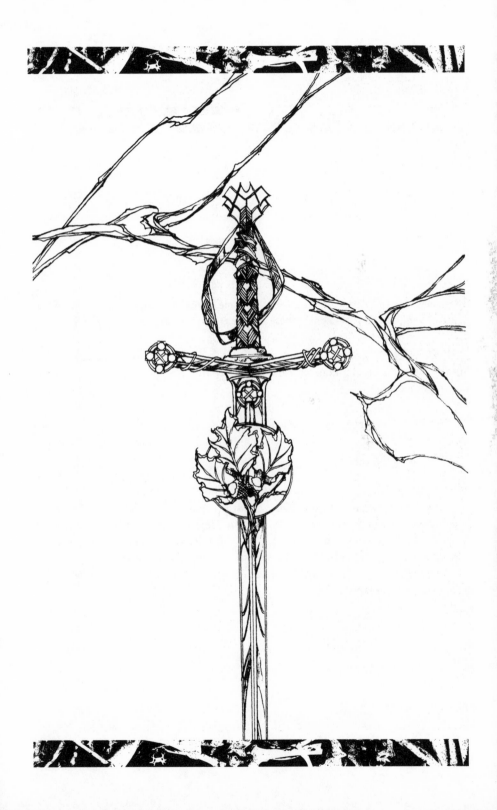

L I M B O

I dreamed I lay in a dark valley and all around me were the titanic forms of archangels. I heard distant voices and I knew these supernatural warriors were chanting a litany...

"We are the Warriors at the End of Time. We are the lost, the last, the unkind. We are the Warriors on the Edge of Time and we're tired, we're tired... We're tired of making love..."

And in my dream I walked away from those vast beings and came at length to a new place where the unshaded force of a star beat against my eyes and I saw one who was myself and not myself.

I dreamed this dream many times in those years when I clung to my good fortune and my love with a joy mixed with trepidation. I knew that it must all inevitably end.

The man of whom I dreamed was almost my double, but I lacked his skills, his experience or his faith. He was a *mukhamir*, an adept—an expert player in the great Game of Time. He ranged the mighty highways of interstellar space and had a bizarre, momentous destiny. His full name was Renark von Bek, Count of the Rim...

I was in a place of roads—silver spiderwebs of roads which wound between all the Realms of the multiverse...

THE ETERNAL CHAMPION

PROLOGUE

Count Renark was a wanderer in the galaxy for two years — but he was not lonely. Renark could never be lonely, for the galaxy was his omnipresent friend and he was aware of its movements. Even the peculiar control exercised on it by forces which he could not sense was as comforting as its presence. He moved about in it and contained awareness of every atom of it in his long, thin-boned skull. He wandered purposely through the teeming galaxy for two swift years and then, when ready, journeyed again towards the Rim...

BOOK ONE:

THE FRACTURED UNIVERSE

O   N   E

HIS NAME WAS Renark von Bek, Count of the Rim, scion of an ancient family and keeper of more than one dangerous secret.

The three of them met, at last, in a terrible town called Migaa on the harsh, bright edge of a wilderness. Both town and planet were called Migaa and it was the last chance planet for the galaxy's fugitives.

Count Renark disembarked from his cruiser, uncomfortable under the glare of the diamond-bright sun. He threaded his way through the great looming shapes of a hundred other ships, his mind searching the town ahead for his two friends. His skilled brain probed the shapes of streets and buildings, people and objects until at last he had located them, half a mile away on the other side of the town.

He strode briskly from the spaceport and there were no Customs officers to stop him here. He kept his friends' forms firmly fixed in his mind as he hurried in their direction. They were agitated and he guessed they might be in trouble.

People stared at him as he passed, a very tall, very gaunt man with deep-set black eyes in a long skull, a brooding face in repose. But they didn't stare at his face — they thought him remarkable mainly because he wore no apparent weapon. Almost all the men and women who came to Migaa came hurriedly — but they also came armed.

Only Count Renark walked purposefully along the metal-paved streets, through the glinting steel buildings. The others moved aimlessly, wearing dark lenses to ward off the glare of the desert reflected in the steel and chrome of the buildings. He noted little transport on the streets, and what there was moved lazily. He thought the town had an exhausted air — yet at the same time it possessed an atmosphere of expectancy. It was a peculiar mood — and it smothered Migaa.

He noted also a shared quality in the faces of the men and women, a set expression which tried vainly to disguise the hope lurking in their eyes. They seemed afraid of hoping, yet evidently could do nothing else. Migaa — or what Migaa offered — was their last chance. It was Renark's too, but for other, less selfish, reasons.

When he reached the building where he sensed his two friends were, it wasn't the tavern he'd expected. This was called *The Last Break Inn*, like hundreds of other taverns throughout the galaxy, but this one's name had a special significance.

He walked in to find tumult.

A fight was going on. He recognized several who could be either thieves or spacehands, judging by the white, metal-studded plastileather overalls they wore. They were thick, brutal, shouting men and they were attacking two others, not of their kind.

Renark recognized the pair — Paul Talfryn and young Asquiol of Pompeii, their backs against the far wall of the noisy, overcrowded public room. For a moment he felt the urge to leave them to it, confident that they would survive, but then he decided to help them. He wanted them to be as fit as possible for the forthcoming journey.

As he moved forward, a spacehand, using the whole of his metal-studded body as a weapon, launched himself at Renark. The spacehand had obviously learned his fighting techniques aboard ship or on a low-gravity planet. Migaa wasn't a low-grav world and the man's method of charging in an attempt to buffet Renark against the far wall didn't work. Renark skipped aside and the hand blundered past. Renark kicked against the base of the man's spine with a pointed boot. The spacehand collapsed backwards and Renark kicked him sharply in the head, knocking him out.

Swiftly Renark pushed towards his friends.

Talfryn looked almost panic-stricken as he warded off the blows of his attackers, but Asquiol — flamboyant, grinning and vicious — was enjoying himself. A set of knuckle-spikes gleamed on his right fist, and there was blood on them. One of Asquiol's opponents blundered back into Renark, clutching at a bleeding eye-socket.

"We're wasting time!" Renark shouted as the others saw him.

He moved into the crowd, pulling the tumbling space-men aside with his large, ugly hands. Together, Talfryn and Asquiol punched their way towards him.

A growling giant swung a pocket-mace at Asquiol, who ducked, crouched, then shot out his spike-covered fist deep into the spacehand's belly. The giant shrieked and the mace dropped from his hand as he fell to his knees.

The trio burst from the tavern and ran up a narrow side street until they saw the spacehands abandon the chase, shouting cat-calls from behind them. They turned into an alley, running between the backs of the buildings, their boots ringing on the metal.

"Which way to *The Salvation Inn?*" Renark said.

"Thanks for breaking that up," Asquiol grinned. "I thought you Guide Sensers could tell where anything was. It's this way. Not far."

Renark didn't bother to use his space-sensing ability. The image of what he had done to the spacehand was still sharp in his mind. He didn't like violence.

Asquiol led them back onto a main way. As they walked, Talfryn turned to Renark, his expression embarrassed.

"Sorry about that," he said. "Those hands were looking for trouble. They picked on Asquiol because of his clothes. We had to fight. We managed to avoid a dozen others, but couldn't get out of this one. The whole damned town's the same — tense, nervous, impatient."

"I'm afraid I encouraged them," Asquiol said. "Really, one can't have one's dress insulted by such a vulgar breed!" He collapsed his knuckle-spikes and put them away.

Lonely and time-begrimed despite his youth, Asquiol dressed with careful flamboyance. He wore a high-collared, quilted jacket of orange nyb-fur and tight slacks of purple stuff which fitted over his pointed, carbon-glass boots. His face was pale and tapering, his black hair cut short in a fringe over his forehead. He carried a slender, anti-neutron beamer — an outlawed weapon.

Asquiol had once been a prince — independent Overlord of Pompeii, before the Galactic Council enforced its extraordinary powers and brought the planet into the Union.

Renark remembered that Asquiol had lost his title and estates for protecting him, and he was grateful.

He noticed that the younger man had lapsed into a brooding mood. It was his usual reaction and because of it many people thought him unbalanced, though Renark knew that Asquiol was the very opposite. His was a fine, delicate balance which only his will maintained.

Talfryn, lean-faced like his two friends, sensitive and bearded, was an unlicensed explorer and therefore a criminal. He was dressed conservatively — sleeveless jerkin of unstained hide, blue shirt and black trousers — and carried a heavy power-gun. He looked curiously at Renark, but since he said nothing Renark remained silent.

Then he smiled. His thin, grim lips quirked upwards and he straightened his back, turning his long head and looking hard at Talfryn.

Talfryn seemed disturbed by the look, and felt obliged to speak so he said: "When do we leave? I'm impatient to get started."

Renark did not respond for a moment, and just kept looking.

Talfryn said: "I can't wait."

"I'm not sure yet," Renark said.

As they reached the tall, many-windowed structure of *The Salvation Inn*, on the edge of town, Talfryn said to Renark: "You told us we were wasting time back there. How much time have we, roughly?"

"Maximum, thirty-six hours," the Guide Senser replied.

Asquiol looked up, startled out of his mood. He seemed troubled. "Is that all?"

"That's all — probably less. I can feel it coming closer to this continuum all the time, but it's difficult to keep a fix on it always. It takes most of my energy."

They entered the wide, high-roofed public hall of *The Salvation Inn*. Asquiol looked around him, seeking someone in the crowd, but was disappointed. The huge windows which stretched up one high wall lighted several tiered galleries and looked out onto the bright black and white carbon desert of the planet.

They pushed through the crowd of men and women of many types. There were richly clad men; ragged men; women who drank heavily and women who sipped at a single drink; vociferous men and quiet women. Here, as in the rest of the town, there was an air of tired, tense expectancy — an atmosphere which had lasted, this era, for thirty-seven years. All the residents glanced often at the big scanner screens suspended in the middle of the hall.

The screens would come to life only on particular occasions — when what they awaited entered the area of space on which they were always focused. When that happened — if it happened — there would be a rush for the spaceport and Migaa would be deserted again. Some people had been waiting in Migaa for over thirty years; others had died before their chance came.

The three climbed a narrow, winding stair until they reached a gallery occupied by a table and three chairs. They sat down.

"I had this reserved," Asquiol said as he craned his neck to peer into the public hall.

Renark looked at him quizzically. "I'm having the ship checked and re-checked," he said. "It's got to be ready very soon. The Shifter could materialize well before the maximum thirty-six hours I mentioned. Though it shouldn't be here for another twelve hours — judging by the rate it's been moving towards us since I contacted it twenty days ago."

Renark paused, staring out across the terrible desert, screwing his eyes against the glare which penetrated even the poparoid windows.

"We've got to be ready," he said. "I can't tell how long it will remain in this continuum. There's also the possibility that it will rip through the continuum at speed and we won't have a chance to get there before it travels on."

"So we could have come to Migaa for nothing," Talfryn shrugged. "Well, my time's my own."

"Mine isn't." Renark did not expand on that remark.

He was the only man in the entire galaxy capable of knowing when the Shifter System would materialize. Others who came to Migaa took the chance that the bizarre, continuum-travelling system would appear in the space-time during their own life, but it was a gamble. This was the only reason Migaa existed, built on the nearest halfway habitable planet to where the Shifter would materialize. So the outlawed and the damned, the searching and the hunted came to Migaa when there was nowhere else to go. And they waited.

Renark knew he did not need to wait, for he was a Guide Senser with a peculiar instinct, developed to the level of a science. He could locate, given only the vaguest direction and description, anything in the galaxy, whether it was a planet or a lost penny.

Needing no maps or coordinates, he could lead a person anywhere he or she wanted to go. He was a human direction-finder, and because of this he knew the Shifter was coming closer, for he had trained himself to see past his own space and out into other dimensions lying beyond, where there seemed to be hazy ghosts of planets and suns almost, but not quite, like his own, each one replicating itself, level upon level, and each replica slightly different to the last, into infinity.

He had trained himself to see them, to prove a theory concerning the nature of the weird Shifter System which had been known to materialize — just suddenly appear in space and then vanish again without trace — only five times since mankind had reached the Rim.

Little else was generally known about it.

The few explorers and scientists who had managed to reach the Shifter before it vanished again had not returned. It was impossible to say how long it would stay at any one time. The mystery system seemed to have a wildly erratic orbit, and Renark's theory that it moved on a course different from the rest of the universe — a kind of *sideways* movement — had been postulated years before when, as Warden of the Rim Worlds, he had been given the responsibility of sensing it — as he sensed the world and suns within his own continuum.

The time of the Shifter's stay varied between a few hours and a few days. It was never certain when it would appear or disappear. The desperate men who came to Migaa were optimists, hoping against hope that they would have the luck to be there when the Shifter arrived.

Though the Shifter received its title from Count Renark's own theory, it had several other names — Ghost Worlds was a popular one — and certain religious-minded people ascribed some more dramatic significance to the system, declaiming that it had been cast from the universe for some sin its inhabitants had committed. These fanatics also had a name for the system — the Sundered Worlds.

And so a whole framework of myth had developed around the system, but very few dared investigate it for fear of being stranded. For the most part only criminals were willing to take the risk.

Count Renark stared down at the seething public hall. The Galactic Union's government machinery was near-perfect, its institutions difficult to abuse. This meant they could guarantee a greater degree of personal freedom for their citizens. But, because the government worked so well, criminals were hard put to escape the Union's laws. Migaa was their only hope. From Migaa they had the chance of escaping right out of the universe — unless the Galactic Police — the Geepees — made one of their sudden swoops on the town. For the most part the Geepees were content to leave well alone, but sometimes they hunted a criminal when he possessed some particular item or piece of information which they wanted. Then, if he eluded them long enough, they would come to Migaa looking for him.

Count Renark knew the Council sought him, that Musef Mordan, Captain in Chief of the Galactic Police, had his men scouring the galaxy for him. He wondered how long it would be before Mordan thought of Migaa.

Asquiol put his head in his hands and stared at Renark. "Isn't it time we had your reasons for this trip, Renark?" He turned his head and searched among the crowd below. "What made you quit your position as Rim Warden? Why wouldn't you tell the Council what you learned from that mysterious spaceship which landed on Golund three years ago? And why the passion to visit the Shifter?"

"I don't want to answer yet," Renark told him. "In fairness I should, but if I did it would give rise to further questions I can't possibly answer yet. All I can tell you right now is what you've guessed — I've been waiting three years to get to the Shifter, ever since I learned something of great importance from the crew of that spaceship on Golund. Indirectly what they told me caused me to resign as Warden. As for the answers I don't have — I hope the Shifter will give me them."

"We're your friends, Renark," Talfryn said, "and we're willing to go with you for that reason alone. But if you don't find the answers you want out there, will you answer the original questions?"

"There'll be nothing to lose if I do," Renark agreed. "But if you decide you don't want to come, then say so now. It's dangerous, we know that much. We might perish before we even reach the Shifter, and once there we may never be able to return."

Both men moved uncomfortably but said nothing.

Renark continued: "I owe you both debts of friendship. You, Paul, helped me in my research on variable time flows and were responsible finally for crystallizing my theory. Asquiol saved me from the attentions of that police patrol on Pompeii, sheltered me for six months and, when the Council found out, was forced, under the terms of his agreement, to give up his birthright. You have both made big sacrifices on my behalf."

"I'm curious enough, anyway, to explore the Ghost Worlds," smiled Talfryn, "and Asquiol has nothing to keep him here unless it's his new-found attraction for Willow Kovacs."

Willow owned *The Salvation Inn*. She was reputed to be beautiful.

Asquiol appeared displeased, but he only shrugged and smiled faintly. "You're right, Talfryn — if tactless. But don't worry, I'll still go when the time comes."

"Good," said Renark.

A woman came up the narrow stair leading to the gallery.

She moved in full knowledge of her slim beauty and her lips were curved in a soft smile. She was wearing the spoils of her conquests — her emerald-coloured dress was covered with jewels mined on a thousand planets. They flashed brightly, challenging the very brilliance of the desert. Her hands, heavy with rings, held a tray of hot food.

As she reached the table, Asquiol looked up at her and took the tray, making sure he touched her hands as he did so.

"Thanks," she said. "And hello — you must be the famous Warden Renark von Bek."

"Ex-Warden," he said. "And you're the young woman who has so disturbed our proud friend here."

She didn't reply to that.

"Eat well, gentlemen," she said, then returned down the staircase. "We'll meet later, Asquiol," she called over her shoulder as she made her way across the crowded floor of the great tavern.

Count Renark felt slightly troubled by this new intrusion. He hadn't been prepared for it. Although his loyalty to both his friends was great, he wanted Asquiol on the trip much more than he wanted Talfryn.

Asquiol was young, reckless, inclined to vindictive acts of cruelty at times; he was arrogant and selfish and yet he had a core of integrated strength which was hard to equate with his outward appearance.

But a woman. A woman could either complement that strength or destroy it. And Renark wasn't sure about Willow Kovacs.

Philosophically, and for the moment, Renark accepted the situation and turned his mind to the problem in hand.

"I think we should give the ship another check," he suggested when they had eaten. "Shall we go out to the pads now?"

Talfryn agreed, but Asquiol said: "I'll stay here. I'll either join you out there or see you when you return. How long will you be?"

"I've no idea," Renark said, rising. "But stay here so that we can contact you if necessary."

Asquiol nodded. "Don't worry — I wasn't thinking of leaving the inn."

Renark restrained an urge to tell Asquiol to be wary, but the Guide Senser respected his friend. It was up to the Prince of Pompeii to conduct his own affairs without advice.

Renark and Talfryn walked down the stairs, pushed their way through the throng and made for the door.

Outside there was a buzz of excited conversation. The two men caught some of it as they walked along the metal-paved streets.

"It seems there's a rumour that the Geepees are on their way in," Talfryn said worriedly.

Renark's face was grim. "Let's hope they don't get here before the Shifter." Talfryn glanced at him. "Are they after you?"

"They've been after me for two years. Oh, it's not for any crime. But the Council came to the conclusion that I might know something of use to them and have been trying to get hold of me."

"And do you know something of use to them?"

"I know something," Renark nodded, "but it's in their interest and mine that they don't find out about it."

"That's part of your secret?"

"Part of the secret," Renark agreed. "Don't worry — if we reach the Shifter, I'll let you know it, for better or worse."

He let his mind reach out into the void beyond the Rim. It was out there, coming closer. He could sense it. His mind trembled. He felt physically sick.

It was so wrong — *wrong!*

Implacably, the impossible system was shifting in. Would it stay long enough for them to get to it? And could they reach it? If only he knew a little more about it. It was a big gamble he was taking and there was just a slim chance of it paying off.

Only he knew what was at stake. That knowledge was a burden he had had to strengthen himself to bear. Most men could not have begun to bear such a burden.

As he walked along, glancing at the wretches who had so hopefully come to Migaa, he wondered if it was worth the attempt after all. But he shrugged to himself. You had to accept that it was worth it, he told himself, and act on the understanding.

There were none there who might have been properly described as extra-terrestrials. One of the discoveries humans had made when settling the galaxy was that they represented the only highly developed, intelligent life-form. There were other types of animal life, but Earth, throughout the galaxy, had been the only planet to bear a beast that could reason and invent. This was an accepted thing among most people, but philosophers still wondered and marvelled and there were many theories to explain the fact.

Two years previously Renark had suddenly resigned from his position as Warden of the Rim Worlds. It had been an important position and his resignation had given rise to speculation and gossip. The visit of an alien spaceship, supposedly an intergalactic craft, had not been admitted by the Galactic Council. When pressed for information they had replied ambiguously. Only Renark had seen the aliens, spent much time with them.

He had given no explanation to the Council and even now they still sought him out, trying to persuade him to take over a job which he had done responsibly and imaginatively. Space Sensers were rare, rarer even than other psi-talents — and a Guide Senser of Renark's stature was that much rarer. There were only a few G.S.s in the entire galaxy and their talents were in demand. For the most part they acted as pilots and guides on difficult runs through hyperspace, keeping, as it were, an anchor to the mainland and giving ships exact directions how, where and when to enter normal space. They were also employed on mapping the galaxy and any changes which occurred in it. They were invaluable to a complicated, galaxy-travelling civilization.

So the Council had begged Renark to remain Warden of the Rim even if he would not tell them who the visitors to Golund had been. But he had refused, and two years had been spent in collecting a special knowledge of what little information was known about the Shifter. In the end they had resorted to sending the Geepees after him, but with the help of Talfryn and Asquiol he had so far evaded them. He prayed they wouldn't come to Migaa before the Shifter materialized.

Renark had fitted his ship with the best equipment and instruments available. This equipment, in his eyes, included the dynamic, if erratic, Asquiol and the easygoing Paul Talfryn.

Several hundred ships were clustered in the spaceport. Many had been there for years, some for a century or more, their original owners having died, disappointed and frustrated, never having achieved their goal.

Renark's great spacer was a converted Police Cruiser which he had bought cheaply and illegally, rebuilt and re-equipped. It could be ready for take-off in half a minute. It was also heavily armed. It was against the law to own a police ship or to own an armed private vessel. The Union owned and leased all commercial craft.

The spacer required no crew. It was fully autosentient and had room for thirty passengers. Already, since landing, Renark had been pestered by people offering huge sums to guarantee them passage to the Shifter, but he had refused. Renark had little sympathy for most of those who gathered in Migaa. They would have received more mercy from the enlightened Legal Code, of which the Union was justly proud, than from Renark of the Rim.

Although Migaa itself was thick with criminals of all kinds, there were few in relation to the huge human population of the galaxy. For nearly two centuries the galaxy had been completely at peace, although the price of peace had, in the past, been a rigid and authoritarian rule which, in the last century, had thawed into the quasi-anarcho-socialist system which now served the galaxy.

Renark had no hatred for the Union which pestered him. He had served it loyally until he had acquired that certain knowledge which he had withheld from the Galactic Council. They had asked many times for the information he possessed, but he had refused; and he was cautious, also, never to let his whereabouts be known.

He glanced up into the blazing white sky as if expecting to see a Geepee patrol falling down upon them.

Slowly, the two men walked across the pad towards the cruiser.

Mechanics were at work on Renark's ship. They had long since completed their initial check and found the ship completely spaceworthy. But Renark had not been satisfied. Now they checked again. Renark and Talfryn entered the elevator and it took them into the center of the ship, to the control cabin.

Talfryn looked admiringly around the well-equipped cabin. He had the scientist's eye that could appreciate the ingenuity, the skill, the energy, the pure passion which had gone into its construction.

Once, a year ago, Renark had said in a talkative moment: "Take note of these instruments, Talfryn — they represent our salvation. They represent the power of the mind to supersede the limitations of its environment, the power of every individual to control, for the first time, their own destiny."

Renark hadn't been referring to his own particular instruments and Talfryn knew that.

Now, Talfryn thought, the mystique attached to science had made it at once a monster and a salvation. People believed it capable of anything, because they had no idea any more what it was. And they tended to think the worst of it. More men like Renark were needed — men who could not take the simple workings of a turbine for granted, yet, at the same time, could accept the whole realm of science.

Just then another thought occurred to Talfryn — a thought more immediately applicable to their present situation. He said: "How do we know that our drive — or any of our other instruments — will work in the Shifter, Renark?" He paused, looking around him at the tall, heaped banks of instruments. "If, as you think might be possible, different laws of space and time apply, then we may find ourselves completely stranded in the Shifter's area of space — cut adrift without control over the ship."

"I admit we don't know whether our instruments will work out there," Renark agreed, "but I'm prepared to risk the chance that we share certain laws with the Shifter. Maybe I'll be able to tell when it's closer, but my judgment won't be infallible."

As a Space Senser, Renark needed no equipment to heighten his powers, but he did need to concentrate, and he therefore used an energy-charger, a machine which replaced natural, nervous and mental energy as it was expended. It was equipment normally only issued to hospitals.

Now, as Talfryn studied the recordings which had been made of the Shifter and became increasingly puzzled, Renark got into a comfortably padded chair and attached electrodes to his forehead, his chest and other parts of his body. He held a stylus and a writing screen on the small ledge in front of him.

Calmly, he switched on the machine.

T W O

Renark concentrated all his powers.

He could feel the presence of the galaxy, spreading inwards from his own point in space; layer upon layer of it, time upon time, scale upon scale.

He was aware of the galaxy as a whole and at the same time felt the presence of each individual atom in its structure — each atom, each planet, each star, each nova, each nebula, each spiral. Through space, where matter was of minimum density, little cores of denser matter moved. Spaceships.

Faintly, beyond the limits of his own galaxy, he sensed the lesser density of intergalactic space, and beyond that he picked up faraway impressions of other galaxies.

There was something unpleasant happening out there — something he already knew about. Something he was pledged to challenge.

Then he adjusted his mind so that, instead of sensing the components of the galaxy, he sensed it as a whole. He widened his reception to take in a small area beyond the galaxy and immediately the entire structure of time and space, as he knew it, was flawed.

There was something there that was alien — something that did not fit. It was as if a body had moved through that small area and had torn a hole in the very fabric of the universe. His mind and body trembled as he sought to adjust to this new, unnatural factor. It was a binary star with eleven planets equidistantly encircling it.

It did not exist. Not in relation to the universe Renark knew. As yet, he could make no close assessment of its components. It was wrong! Renark controlled his mind against the thought and concentrated on judging the system's progress. It was, in relation to itself, travelling through space in the same manner as ordinary stars and planets travelled. But it also travelled through a series of dimensions of which Renark had no experience whatsoever. And its course, its orbit through the dimensions, was bringing it closer to Renark's own continuum.

He opened his eyes, gasping.

Quickly, he jotted down an equation; closed his eyes and re-adjusted his mind.

It continued towards them. It shifted through myriad alien dimensions, moving through a whole series of continua, progressing imperturbably onwards in an orbit as constant as the orbits of its planets about its stars. Soon now it would be passing through Renark's own space-time.

But how long would it stay there? Renark could not tell without knowing a little of the universes which lay beyond his own — and of these he had much to find out. His future plans depended on it.

In less than twenty minutes, Renark was finished. He looked over Talfryn's shoulder at the records. "She's coming closer," he said. "Between twelve to fifteen hours and she'll be here. That's if my calculations are right. I think they are. As far as I can tell, she's travelling at a regular rate. I can't explain why the periods spent in this continuum have varied so much, though, if her speed is as constant as it seems to be."

"Well, you've narrowed it, anyway." Talfryn's body seemed to tense.

"Yes." Renark moved about the control room reading displays.

"And you're certain it won't miss this space-time altogether?"

"That's possible — but unlikely."

Count Renark stared at a bank of gauges for a moment and then he moved towards a chrome and velvet chair which had a whole bank of manual levers and switches in front of it, a V-screen above it. This was the gunnery control panel.

Again he began to move uneasily about the great cabin. Again he volunteered a suggestion.

"We don't know all the directions in which our own universe moves," he said. "It may also, for all we know, have a "sideways" movement through the dimensions at an angle different from the Shifter. This would explain to some extent any inconsistency in the length of time the system stays in our space-time continuum."

Talfryn shook his head. "I've never been able to grasp any of those theories about the system. I don't even understand your ability to sense its approach. I know that, with training, Space Sensers can locate planets and even smaller

THE ETERNAL CHAMPION

bodies in normal space-time, but I wasn't aware that they could sense things outside, beyond, in different dimensions — wherever it is."

"Normally they can't," Renark said, "but many who have probed the perimeter of space outside the galaxy have mentioned that they have sensed something else, something not in keeping with any recognized natural laws. Others have had the illusion of sensing suns and worlds within the galaxy — where suns and worlds just can't be! This has given rise to the theory of the "multiverse", the multi-dimensional universe containing dozens of different universes, separated from each other by unknown dimensions…"

He paused. How could he explain in calm, logical words the sense of apartness, of alienness, he had received? How could he describe that shock, that experience which contradicted all he accepted with every sense he possessed, something that struck at the id, the ego, the emotions — everything?

He opened his mouth, trying to find words. But the words did not exist. The nearest way of expressing what he felt was to give vent to a shout of horror, agony — triumph. He didn't feel inclined to try.

So he shut his mouth and continued to pace the cabin, running his ugly hand over the firing arm of the big anti-neutron gun which had never been used. It was a savage weapon and he hoped it would never be needed.

Nuclear weapons of any sort made him uncomfortable. His strange sixth sense was as aware of the disruption of atoms as it was of their presence in natural state. It was an experience close to agony to sense the disruptive blast of atomic weapons. The anti-neutron cannon, beaming particles of anti-matter, was an even more terrible experience for him.

Once, as a child, he had been close to the area of a multi-megaton bomb explosion and his whole mind had blanked out under the strain of the experience. It had taken doctors a year to pull him back to sanity. Now he was stronger, better coordinated — but it was still not pleasant to be in a space fight.

Also, he loathed violence. It was the easy way out and, like many easy ways out, not a way out at all but only a continuation of a vicious circle. So whenever possible he avoided it.

However, he was prepared, in this case, to use it — if it meant using it against anything in the Shifter which attempted to stop him in his avowed objective.

Renark had geared himself to drive towards one aim, and one only. Already he was driving towards it and nothing — nobody — would stop him. He was dedicated, he was fanatical — but he was going to get results if that was possible. If it wasn't possible, then he'd die trying to make it possible.

Soon, now — very soon — the Shifter would enter their area of space. He was going there. The Shifter offered the only chance in the universe of supplying him with the information he needed.

He glanced back at Talfryn, who was still studying the records. "Any clearer?" he asked.

Talfryn shook his head and grinned. "I can just understand how the Shifter orbits through dimensions hitherto unknown to us, in the same way as we orbit through time and space, but the implications are too big for me. I'm bewildered. I'm no physicist."

"Neither am I," Renark pointed out. "If I were I might not be so affected by the Shifter. For instance, there's something peculiar about any system comprising a G-type binary star and eleven planets all equidistant from it — something almost artificial. If it is artificial — how did it happen?"

"Maybe it's the other way about," Talfryn suggested vaguely. "Maybe the planets all being the same distance away from the parent suns has something to do with the peculiar nature of the system. If they are a natural freak, could this have caused the Shifter's orbit?"

Renark nodded. He thought for a moment before he said: "If you take for granted that Time is cyclic in accordance with the other known laws of the universe — although, as you well know, my own experiments seem to prove that there is more than one particular time flow operating in our own universe — if you take that for granted, however, we can describe the rest by means of circles."

He walked to the chair where he had left his stylus and pad, picked them up and moved over the chart table.

"The Shifter orbits this way" — he drew a circle — "whereas we progress this way." He drew a half-circle cutting horizontally through the first circle.

"Imagine that we have a finite number of space-time continua, each with some mutually shared laws." He drew a number of other half-circles below and above the first. "They're all, like us, travelling this way. There is no contact between us but we exist side by side without being aware of each other's presence, all revolving in different sets of dimensions."

Talfryn nodded.

"Imagine that the normal continua, as we understand the word normal, are orbiting horizontally, as it were. Then imagine that the Shifter is orbiting *vertically*. Therefore, instead of going its way without ever touching other alternate universes, its course takes it through them."

"But wouldn't it take millions of years to complete a cycle like that?"

"Not necessarily. We know it doesn't, because we can't use temporal and spatial values and apply them to something as different as the Shifter. It has rules of its own which seem chaotic to us but are probably as ordered in relation to itself as ours are to us."

"You've got to take quite a bit for granted," Talfryn sighed.

"Our scientists have been doing extensive research into the "multiverse" theory. They're pretty convinced."

"Life and the universe," said Talfryn, seating himself in a chair, "are getting too complicated."

Renark laughed shortly. "One thing's clear, Talfryn — there are going to be a lot of mysteries solved and a lot of new ones started when we reach the Shifter. No one has ever returned from it."

He glanced up suddenly. A light was blinking on the control panel.

"That's the intercom," he said. "Might be Asquiol or one of the engineers. Could you deal with it, Paul?"

Talfryn walked over and picked up the instrument. He murmured a command but no picture appeared on the screen. He listened briefly and then turned back to regard Renark. "Asquiol's here — and he's brought that girl with him."

"What?" Renark for a moment lost his equilibrium. "Why?"

"That's the other thing — that's why they came here so fast. The Geepees have arrived — they're looking for you!"

Renark pursed his lips. He should have been ready for a police raid but he had been too busy explaining the Shifter to Talfryn.

Asquiol and Willow Kovacs stepped out of the elevator.

Asquiol said nervously: "Sorry about this, Renark — but these are my terms."

Renark shrugged. "Terms?" He leant over the control panel adjusting dials. "What's happening out there?"

"The Geepees are scouring Migaa asking if you're there. I got out as fast as I could. They'd be likely to recognize me and connect me with you."

"Good."

"You're willing to have Willow along on the trip?"

"You've told her the risks?"

"Yes."

Renark sighed. "I thought this might happen — knowing you. But I want you with us."

Renark forced away his irritation. There was no room for petty emotions in his plans. Only he knew what hung on his reaching the Shifter and discovering its nature and its cause. Matters of personalities could not be considered. Action, not argument, was required of him now.

He had to pray that the Geepees wouldn't discover him before the Shifter materialized. They'd have to sit tight and wait it out. With any luck the Geepees wouldn't make a search of the ships on the pads until after they had scoured the town.

Renark beamed a message to the engineers, telling them to clear away their equipment and leave the ship in readiness for take-off.

Then he sat in his chair and waited.

An hour passed.

Willow seemed uncomfortable, sitting there in her immaculate sheath dress, listening to the men talking and going over the equations Count Renark had made, the records of the Shifter, theories which had been put forward.

Count Renark said: "Rumour has it that *this* planet has a large human colony. I think we should head for that — number eight by my reckoning. You can see I've marked it."

He glanced at Willow, who appeared pensive and moved nervously on her seat. Normally nothing could break her self-contained attitude — an attitude that had been necessary in a town like Migaa. But here, for the first time, she was in the company of those even more self-contained than she was. And it disquieted her.

At last Asquiol saw her discomfort and said half-apologetically: "Anything troubling you?"

She smiled without amusement, then, shrugging, she left the control room.

Willow had always been curious about the Ghost Worlds, living as she had in their shadow all her life. But she had never seen them. For some reason the Ghost Worlds had allowed her to dominate all the many men in her life, for they had seemed to have a hunger which she could not satisfy — though they had sought in her that satisfaction and had, therefore, put themselves in her power, thinking she had a secret she did not, in fact, possess.

Now she was going to the Shifter ... on Asquiol's instigation. She was glad. These men, all three, offered her something she was unused to. A strength of character, perhaps, that she had never found in all the others who had come to Migaa, a peculiar mixture of detachment and passion. She had acted impulsively, however, and was now not sure she wished to go with them. She wondered if what she felt was called "fear."

Looking up from the charts, Talfryn glanced at the scanner screen. He swore and moved towards the controls.

"Something's gone wrong with the V-screen. I'll try and..."

"Don't touch those controls!"

Renark's brain seemed to swell within his skull, excitement pulsing through him, his body pounding. He paused for a second, frowned, controlled himself and then said calmly: "It's coming, Talfryn."

He sent his mind out, probing. He felt the sudden presence of the alien system grow as it merged into his own space-time — a whole system plunging towards them out of the hazy twilight of the universe, rupturing time and space on its rogue orbit. Elation flooded through him as he ran towards the V.

The other two stood close behind him.

He watched as visible lines of energy swept across the area of space where his calculations indicated the Shifter would appear.

Space seemed to peel back on itself. Great, blossoming splashes of colour poured through as if from the broken sides of a vat, merging with the darkness of space and making it iridescent so that sections shone like brass and others like silver, gold or rubies, the whole thing changing, changing constantly, erupting, flickering, vanishing, reappearing, patterns forming and reforming.

Then, faintly at first, as if through rolling, multi-coloured clouds, the Shifter itself began to materialize, coming into sharper focus.

And then it was hanging there, as solid as anything else in the universe, the clouds which had heralded its approach fading away. A new system had joined the galaxy.

But for how long, Renark wondered, would the eleven planets hang, equidistant, around the blazing blue binary star?

He rushed back to the control panel, pressed a single stud activating the ship's automatic circuits.

The ship lifted. It shrieked away from the spaceport, away from the Geepee vessels, and within minutes was in deep space straining towards the Shifter.

Moving to a single-minded, prearranged pattern, Renark acted like a zombie, his eyes fixed on the weird system ahead, his body one with the streaking ship which leapt the space between the edge of the galaxy and the mystery worlds.

Willow came out, startled, saw the screen and began to tremble.

Asquiol looked at her, but she glanced away and hurried back to the passenger accommodation.

Renark seated himself in the pilot's chair, his arms stretched over the complicated control board, checking every slight tendency for the ship to veer away from the Shifter.

At this distance the planets seemed, apart from their ordered positions around the suns, to be no different from any other system in the galaxy.

Yet they glowed like carefully set diamonds around the sapphire suns. The ship sped closer and Renark could observe the rotation of the planets around the twin star. They appeared to be moving very slowly. Yet the closer they came the faster the planets seemed to move.

The other two had taken their places. The ship's drive, buried in the core of the ship, could be heard now, humming with the strain.

Renark shouted: "Talfryn, keep all communication equipment on *Receive*. Asquiol, don't use those guns at random — wait until I order you to, if it's necessary."

He turned in his seat for a moment, stared at Asquiol. "And don't, on any account, use the anti-neutron cannon."

Asquiol grimaced.

Talfryn flipped switches.

Willow reappeared, bewildered by the suddenness of events. She was frustrated, wanting something to do. The men worked, with concentration and efficiency, to their prearranged plan. Asquiol was oblivious of her presence.

The planets came closer. There was something peculiar about several of them, particularly one at nadir-south-east of the binary.

As the Shifter got larger on the screen, the communications panel began to squeal and moan.

"We're picking up its static, anyway," Talfryn commented.

"They must be panicking on Migaa," Asquiol grinned. "The quicker we move the less chance we've got of getting caught up with the mob when they come out."

"They'll be fighting the Geepees right now," Renark said. "They won't even let a fleet of battlewagons stop them reaching the Shifter after waiting so long."

"That'll delay both sides for a while," Asquiol said.

"Let's hope the delay will be a long one." Renark stared at his screen. "What's ahead of us to starboard, Talfryn? Looks like a small fleet of some sort."

Talfryn moved dials. "You're right. Spaceships. A kind I don't recognize. We'd better head for the nearest planet and try to escape them. They don't look friendly."

The twin star was very close and bright now, blacking out the planets on Renark's screen.

Asquiol broke the energy seals on the guns with the key Renark handed him.

About ten of the weird ships came jolting closer, the metal of their hulls giving off a peculiar, yellowish glint. They pulsed through space and there was something menacing in their approach. Then they veered away, describing a long curve, and began to circle the area through which Renark's cruiser would have to pass.

Then, with a jerk which ripped at their nerves and muscles and threatened to turn their bodies inside out, they entered alien space. They were in the Shifter's territory now. That was why the other ships had come no further, but awaited them. Their minds blanked momentarily. They felt dizzy, sick. Renark, his senses going, sent out a desperate tendril of mental energy, anchoring himself to the Shifter ahead. He felt the presence of the darting alien ships. The metal of their construction was unfamiliar to him.

Then, suddenly, his whole mind seemed to explode as the fabric of space was ripped apart.

He gasped with the agony, forced his eyes open. He looked at the screen, and the planets, no longer whirling so rapidly around the binary, were moving at a more leisurely pace.

An inhuman growl rumbled through the control room. Talfryn worked the receiver, trying to pick up a picture, but couldn't. The growl came again but the language was unrecognizable. The leading vessel of the yellow fleet moved.

It seemed to turn over on itself, described a couple of somersaults, and then sent a coiling blast of energy before the humans' ship.

Renark blocked his mind and tensed his body. "Screens!" he yelled.

But Asquiol had already raised them.

The ship shuddered and the screens proved effective against the alien weapons — but only just. Asquiol aimed the energy-laden guns on the leading ship.

"The anti-neutron cannon would dispose of them quickly enough," he said wistfully.

"And probably the system as well," Talfryn added as Asquiol's rapid shots bit into the alien ship, and it exploded to form, almost immediately, nothing more than a ball of ragged metal.

Now the other ships came on in formation. But Asquiol bent over his guns and grimly pressed his fingers down on all studs. The ship took the enemy retaliation, but shuddered horribly. His own fire damaged two, which spiralled away from their comrades.

Then the whole fleet sailed up in the strange, somersaulting motion and fired together.

"We can't take this attack!" Talfryn screamed.

Asquiol's eyes were intent on the enemy craft. He sent another great blast of energy slamming through space as the force of the joint attack hit the cruiser.

The ship shook, shuddered, groaned and came to a dead stop. Lazily it began to spiral through space while more of the alien ships came flooding up from the nearest planet. Asquiol did what he could to halt them, but with the ship out of control it was difficult to aim.

Renark was fighting the controls.

"We took it," he shouted, "but it's thrown our circuits crazy. Talfryn, get down there and see what you can do with the Master Coordinator!"

Talfryn scuttled from his seat and entered the elevator, dragging a space suit with him.

Asquiol, eyes narrowed, aimed his guns carefully, cursing.

He cut down several more. But these ships didn't seem to care whether they were destroyed or not. Momentarily Asquiol wondered if they had living crews aboard.

Something was wrong with the quality of the void. It did not have its normal sharpness. Rivers of colour, very faint, seemed to run through, and shapes seemed to move just beyond the limit of his vision. It was tantalizing, it was maddening…

Willow, pale and tense, clung to a bulkhead, her eyes fixed on the big screen. Space was alive with boiling energy. It swirled and coiled and lashed through the disturbed vacuum. To her, it was as if the binary had suddenly gone nova, for she could not see through the multi-coloured patterns of force which obscured everything but the yellow, darting shapes of the enemy ships.

Slowly the patterns faded, but the alien vessels came on.

Renark realized that the hideous nature of the void was not created by the force released in the battle. It was something else. Something much more ominous.

Asquiol kept up a rapid continuous fire. The screens took the brunt of the energy, but suddenly the ship was agonizingly hot.

Renark spoke into his PV. "Talfryn, are you down there now?"

Talfryn's worried voice groaned back to him. "I'm doing what I can. With any luck I should have fixed up most of the masters in five minutes."

"Do it sooner," Renark ordered, "or you'll be dead."

What were these aliens? Why were they so savagely attacking a ship when they hadn't even bothered to discover whether it was friend or enemy?

They came on with implacable ferocity.

Asquiol's lean face ran with sweat. Willow was on the floor now, her eyes wide, still fixed on the screens.

"Get into a suit, Willow," he shouted. "Get into a suit!"

She staggered up and walked unsteadily towards the locker from which she had seen Talfryn take a suit. Slowly she opened it, hissing with pain as the metal burned her hand, struggled to release a suit and clamber into it, its fabric automatically adjusting to the shape of her body.

Renark pulled on heavy gauntlets. The controls were now too hot for him to manipulate with bare hands.

Again and again the alien craft somersaulted and sent charges of energy towards the ship.

Asquiol felt his skin blister as he returned the fire and had the satisfaction of seeing another three alien ships collapse into scrap.

Then Renark felt the ship responding again to the controls. Talfryn had fixed the Master Coordinator. He sent the ship veering away from the alien vessels. "Vardy Dan!" he commanded in ship's pidjin.

Talfryn came rushing from the elevator, tearing off his helmet. He flung himself into his seat.

"Christ!" he shouted. "More of them!"

Another fleet, larger than the one that had already attacked them, was coursing in to join the fight. As it got nearer, Talfryn noticed that the ships were not of the same design as the first fleet. In fact, not one of these ships was of identical design. The weirdly assorted fleet fanned out — to engage not their ship but the enemy!

Pale rays stranded out and twined around the enemy craft, which vanished.

"By God, they're on our side!" Asquiol cried joyously as Renark eased his ship away from the area of the fight.

Suddenly a clear voice came over the speakers. It began giving directions. Talfryn moved the keys. "I can't find the source," he said. The voice, speaking their own language, although a slightly archaic version, began to repeat the directions in exactly the same tone as before — velocity, trajectory and so forth.

The ship was beginning to cool. The people inside relaxed somewhat.

"Don't bother finding the source," Renark said. "It sounds like a recording, anyway — an automatic instruction to visitors. We'll do as it says."

Following the directions they found themselves shooting towards a rust planet — small, ominous. The ships which had aided them now surrounded them, a motley assortment, but fast enough to stay with Renark's speedy cruiser.

When they were on course, a new voice broke into the taped instruction recital.

"Welcome to Entropium. We saw that you were in trouble and sent help. Forgive us for not doing so earlier, but you were then beyond our boundaries. You put up a pretty good fight."

"Thanks," Asquiol said softly, "but we could have done with that help sooner." Except in rare instances, Asquiol was not a grateful young man.

"That was out of the question," the voice said lightly. "But you're all right now, barring accidents…"

They sped down into the glowing red shroud of the planet.

"… *barring accidents*…"

Again and again they went through the same action, unable to do anything, trapped into it, as if they were on a piece of film being run many times through a projector.

Every time they appeared to reach the planet's surface they found themselves heading through the red mist again.

Then they were in the mist and motionless, the voice speaking amusedly: "Don't worry, this will probably last a short while."

Exhausted as he was, Renark had to use his special space sense to get some kind of grip on the situation. But it was virtually impossible. One moment he felt the presence of the rust planet, the next it was gone and there was nothing in its place.

Several times they repeated their action of dropping down towards the surface until, quite suddenly, they were flashing through the fog and emerged into daylight — pinkish daylight — observing the jagged face of a sombre-coloured planet which, in its wild texture, was like a surrealist landscape painted by an insane degenerate.

Willow lay on the floor in her space suit, her eyes closed, and even the men fought to control their minds and emotions as they jarred and shuddered at the sight of the alien planet. It was unlike any other they had ever seen, unlike any planet in the galaxy they knew.

Why?

It wasn't simply the quality of the light, the texture of the surface. It was something that made them uncomfortable in their bones and their brain.

It seemed unsafe, insecure, as if about to collapse beneath them, to break up like a rotten melon.

"Follow the scarlet vessel," said the voice on the intercom.

Then Asquiol, Willow and Talfryn had vanished and only Renark was in the ship moving down once again into the red fog of the planet.

Where were they?

Desperately he quested around him with his mind, but the madness of disordered space and time was all about him — a whirlpool of *wrongness*.

Talfryn reappeared.

Renark said: "Where were you — what happened?" Then Willow reappeared, and Asquiol reappeared.

And suddenly they were back over the surface of the planet again.

"Follow that scarlet vessel," the voice instructed.

This time they noted a sardonic quality. Asquiol smiled, sensing that out there was a fellow spirit, as malicious as himself.

Willow had been seriously affected by the phenomenon, particularly when she had found herself momentarily alone in the ship. How many ships had there been in those few moments?

The scarlet vessel was at the point of the phalanx of slim, round, squat or square spaceships surrounding them. It broke away from the main fleet and headed across the planet in a south-westerly direction. Renark turned his own ship after it. The scarlet vessel slowed and Renark adjusted his speed. There was a break and for a few seconds the ship travelled backwards, then lurched and was moving forwards again after the scarlet ship. Ahead of them now they could make out the towers of a city.

The whole situation was taking on the aspect of a confused nightmare. Whether it was illusion or some physical distortion of reality, Renark simply couldn't tell.

Even the outline of the city ahead did not remain constant but wavered and changed.

Perhaps, Renark guessed, these hallucinations or whatever they were were the effect of adjusting to the different laws which applied to the Shifter System. Their senses had been thrown out of gear by the change and were having to adapt.

He hoped, for the sake of his mission, that he could adapt.

"Entropium," said the voice on the laser.

The scarlet craft arched upwards until it was vertical over the planet, and began to shudder downwards on an invisible repulsion field. Renark followed its example.

Cautiously, he nursed the ship towards the ground, still not sure that the planet would not suddenly disappear from around them and they would be once again in the thick of battle with the alien ships. The experiences of the past half-hour had shattered his nerves, almost sapped his confidence.

They landed on a mile-square field which was bare but for a collection of small buildings at its far end.

"What now?" Willow said.

"We disembark — we got here comparatively safely and we were aided. They'd be unlikely to go to all the trouble they did if they wished us harm. Also I'm curious to find out about the people of 'Entropium'." Renark pushed his big frame into a space suit and the others followed his example.

"What happened back there?" Talfryn said a trifle shakily.

"I should imagine we experienced some sort of space-time slip. We know nothing of this system to speak of. We must be prepared for anything and everything — we can't even be certain that actions we make here will have the results and implications they would have in normal space-time. We could, for instance, walk forward and discover that we were one step backwards, could jump and find ourselves buried in rock. Be careful, though — I doubt if anything as drastic as that will happen here, particularly since human beings seem to inhabit the world and have built a city here. But we must go warily."

T H R E E

The scarlet spacecraft was the only other ship on what was obviously a landing field. They wondered where the rest of the fleet had gone. As they cautiously disembarked, they saw that the crew of the scarlet ship were doing the same. Some of the figures were human.

And, for the first time, they were seeing alien and obviously intelligent life-forms.

Renark checked his wrist gauge. "Looks as if we don't need suits," he said, "but it's just as well to be careful."

He was tense as he walked across the charred ground towards the other group. He studied the aliens mingled with the human beings.

There were two sextupeds with four arms each and completely square heads containing a row of tiny eyes and beneath them a small mouth; several hopping creatures similar to kangaroos but obviously reptilian; a long-legged creature who towered over the others with a body proportionately smaller, a round body supporting long, swinging arm tentacles and a round head.

The leader of the six human beings was young, smiling, fair and dressed in a style which had been out of fashion in the galaxy for two hundred years — a loose blue shirt, baggy trousers tucked into green gaiters, and mauve pumps on his feet. Over the shirt was a pleated coat fanning out from his waist and dropping to his calves. His weapons included an unfamiliar pistol and a rifle slung over his shoulder. He swaggered.

"Move high, you load," he said in a peculiar accent. "How strong goes galaxy — same?"

"It's changed," replied Renark, recognizing in the youth's archaic slang a patois once used by the old CMG — the Criminal Musicians' Guild — which, two hundred years before, had been composed of men outlawed because they refused to play the specific kinds of music deemed "healthy" by the music censors.

But, two hundred years ago, the Shifter had been unheard of and Migaa not settled. Renark was curious. He could understand that two centuries hadn't passed as far as the young man was concerned, the flow of time being different here. Yet there was something wrong.

"You're after me, aren't you?" the young man said. "I blew the long note around two-twenty W.W. Three. You?"

"This is now four hundred and fifty-nine years after World War Three on Earth," Renark said. "We use a new reckoning, though. How did you get here? Mankind had only just reached the Rim when you were around."

"Accident, com. We were on the run — chased by Geepee ships — ran straight here. Found strange mixture, man — I inform you — and everyone from future. You're the farthest into the future I've met. Kol Manage is my name. Let's go."

"Go where?"

"Entropium." He pointed at the city. "Come on, it's a long blow."

The city could be seen about two miles away, scarring the skyline with a peculiar assortment of massive structures, some horribly ugly. But at least its outline now seemed firm and definite.

"Haven't you got ground transport?" Talfryn asked.

"Sometimes, com — not today. We scrap it all. Too square…"

"Why was that?"

"It palled, you know — we build something different sometime."

Renark fumed inwardly. This casual attitude was aggravating when he needed clear, definite answers to the questions concerning him.

There was little time to lose. Now that they were here he wanted to get started on his investigations. Yet the careless attitude of the Entropites threatened to slow him down, even though they didn't deliberately try to curtail him.

"Who runs the planet?" he asked Kol Manage as the group began to straggle towards the city.

"We all do. I guess you'd call Ragner Olesson boss. That's where we're going now — he wants to see you. He likes to see all newcomers."

"Can't we get there faster? I'm in a hurry."

"Well, stop hurrying, man — you've come to the end of the track. Ease up — there's nowhere to hurry to."

"What do you mean?" Renark's tense mouth was grim.

"What do you think? You didn't like it there — you'll have to like it here. Simple." And Kol Manage refused to answer any further questions.

They reached the suburbs of the city and were watched incuriously by some of the inhabitants, human and unhuman.

The population and the buildings comprised a disordered rabble which Renark found distasteful.

They walked through dirty streets which didn't seem to lead anywhere and it was nearly dark before they got to a square skyscraper, alive with light in its many windows.

The peculiar apathetic atmosphere of the city was as strong here as anywhere, but Renark hoped that at least some answers to his questions would be forthcoming. The atmosphere, he noted, was similar to Migaa's — only ten times worse.

The youth's companions dispersed but Manage led Renark and the others into the skyscraper and up a couple of flights of grubby stairs. They came to a door and Manage pushed it open.

The four people stayed uncertainly in the entrance to the big chamber, which was an untidy combination of control room and living quarters. Manage walked across it.

Two men looked up coolly at his approach. Both were middle aged. One was rugged and handsome.

Renark glanced in distaste at the place. Computers and other equipment lined one wall of the room. The floor was littered with carpets of clashing designs, papers, clothing and various objects — a couple of rifles, a flower vase, cups, files and books. Tables, chairs and couches were placed here and there in apparent disorder. The two men sat on a long couch near the largest computer. A door behind them opened on to another room.

"Enter," said the handsome man casually to the four. "We watched you come in — you made the quickest start I've ever seen. The rest shouldn't be here for a little while yet."

"They're probably having trouble with a police patrol," Count Renark said, entering with a degree of caution.

"I'm Ragner Olesson," said the big man. He looked hard at Renark, obviously seeing something unfamiliar in the Guide Senser's stern expression — perhaps, erroneously, sensing a rival to his leadership.

"Count Renark von Bek," said the ex-Warden, "these are my friends." He didn't introduce them.

"Well, Count Renark, all you need to know is this. Don't try to change things here. We like it as it is. You can do what you want in Entropium, anything you want at all — but don't interfere with us."

Renark frowned, feeling himself growing increasingly angry. This wasn't the reception he'd expected, and casualness and disorder of the kind he saw was annoying in his present frame of mind. His whole being was geared to one thing, one object.

He said: "Are you the boss of Entropium?"

"If you like. But I don't push anyone around as long as they keep to themselves any ideas they've got of taking over or changing things radically. Get it?"

"Now, listen," said Renark. "I'm looking for information, that's all. Maybe you can help me."

The man laughed, then sneered. He got up and swaggered closer to Renark, seeming a trifle agitated, however, as if Renark's statement was unprecedented.

"What kind of information, mister? We've got plenty of space to move around here, so go and look for it somewhere else. I don't like being disturbed. If you try to make troubles you can get off the planet" — he smiled sardonically — "or get killed. Your choice."

Controlling himself, Renark said calmly: "So what's expected of us now?"

"Look, you do what you like — so long as you don't bother anyone. Right now you're bothering me."

"Aren't you interested in why we're here? You helped us fight off the fleet that attacked us. Why did you do that?"

"You're here like everyone else who comes, because you don't like it where you came from. Right? We sent our fleet to help you because the more of us there are and the more ships we've got, the less chance the Thron — it was their ships that attacked you — have of invading us. Simple."

"I'm here," said Renark impatiently, "to discover the nature of this system — what makes it work. I'm not a criminal on the run and I'm not just a casual explorer. The very future of humanity may well hang on what I discover or fail to discover here. Is that clear?"

Olesson's companion got up. He was an intelligent-looking man with a tired face. His whole attitude was one of weariness and boredom.

"I'm Klein — I used to be a scientist of sorts. You won't find out anything about the Shifter, my friend. There's no line of inquiry you can follow that leads anywhere. Every fact you uncover is a contradiction of anything you've learned previously."

Renark's voice was savage. "I'm going to force the truth out of this system, Mr Klein."

His companions moved uncomfortably and Asquiol's slender right hand rested on the butt of his anti-neutron beamer. They were well aware that they were outnumbered here. They didn't feel Renark's anxiety and were therefore less ready to alienate their hosts.

But Klein smiled slightly, showing no annoyance. "There have been many who've tried — and all failed. The concept is too alien for us to grasp, don't you understand? It isn't a question of your capacity for reasoning or anything else. Why not just accept the fact that you're safe from the cares of the universe — the multiverse. Find yourself a niche and settle down. You can be quite comfortable here — nobody expects anything of you."

"There must be *some* questions you can answer to give me a clue, a starting point?"

"Harry," Olesson said impatiently, "forget these bums, will you? Let them do what they like so long as they stop worrying us. Let them make their "investigations." They won't get anywhere."

"I'm easy," Klein said to Renark, ignoring his companion. "But there's not much I can tell you. What do you want to know?"

"For a start, tell me something about the Shifter as you know it from living on it."

Klein shrugged and sighed. "We pick up all kinds of intelligent life-forms as we travel. Usually fugitives, sometimes explorers. They've settled on planets — if you can call it settled — that suit them best. Once on a planet, only a fool leaves it."

"Why?"

"Because if the planets are wild, then space outside is wilder. A trip outside the atmosphere sends anyone quite mad. Why do you think nobody leaves the planets? Only the Thron are insane enough already to do it. You've seen it at its best — when it's been calmer. That's why we had to wait so long before sending out help — not many people dare to risk travelling in space most of the time. It's usually worse near the perimeter, too. You were lucky to get help at all."

"What's wrong with it?"

"Nobody knows — but, most of the time, space out there is filled with chaos. Things appear and disappear, time becomes meaningless, the mind breaks..."

"But it wasn't too bad while we were coming here."

"Sure. The Thron had something to do with that, I guess. They seem to know a bit more about controlling whatever it is."

"Then, if that's so, there must be some means of discovering the real nature of the Shifter."

"No. I reckon the Thron have just been lucky." Klein stared with curiosity at Renark. "What exactly do you want to know — and why?"

"That's my business."

"You've got a bigger reason than mere curiosity. You said so. You tell me and maybe I'll decide to go on. If not, I don't want to bother. I want to see what you're leading up to."

"You can tell us now, Renark, surely," urged Talfryn. The ex-Warden sighed.

"All right. About three years ago I made contact with the crew of an intergalactic spaceship. Though it had come from another galaxy, it wasn't so very different from ours — and the crew was human. This in itself was astonishing. They had no knowledge of our history, just as we had none of theirs. They landed on Golund, a backwater planet under my jurisdiction. I went out to meet them. We learned one another's language and we talked. One of the things they told me was that, in their galaxy, human beings were the only intelligent life-form."

"Just like ours," Klein nodded.

"And, I suspect, just like any other galaxy in our particular universe. Tell me, Klein, where do the aliens we've seen come from?"

"Different space-time continua. Every STC seems to have only one dominant, intelligent life-form. I can't explain it."

"It must mean something. That's what I suspected, anyway. A phenomenon natural to every STC universe. But what isn't happening, I hope, in every STC, is what is happening in our particular universe."

"Happening?" Talfryn spoke.

"The visitors from the other galaxy came to warn us. Their news was so terrible that I had to keep it to myself. To have released it would have been to start galaxy-wide panic."

"What the hell is happening?" Even Olesson became interested.

"The end of the universe," Renark said.

"*What!*" Talfryn gasped.

"The end of the universe — so far as humanity's concerned, at any rate."

"And the Gee-Council don't know?" Asquiol said. "You didn't tell them — why?"

"Because I was counting on the Shifter to offer a clue that might save us."

"Not just the end of a galaxy," Klein said softly, "but an entire universe. Our universe. How do you know, Renark?"

"The visitors gave me proof — my own space-sensing ability did the rest. I'm convinced. The universe has ceased to expand."

"That's a problem?" Olesson said.

"Oh, yes — because, not only has it ceased expanding, it is now contracting. All matter is falling back to its source. All the galaxies are rapidly drawing together — and at a far greater speed than they expanded. And the speed increases as all matter is drawn back to the hub of our universe! Soon all the galaxies will exist as a single mote of matter in the vastness of space. Then even that mote may vanish, leaving — vacuum. So far this inward movement is restricted to the galaxies, but, soon, when they all come together, it will involve the stars, the planets — everything."

"This is theory," Klein spoke softly.

"Fact," said Renark. "My visitors' experiments are conclusive. They have tested the theory in their laboratories and found that when the matter has contracted as much as it can and it forms a pellet of astounding density it just disappears. They believe that when it reaches the final stage it enters other dimensions as a photon, possibly in some greater universe — the one encompassing the multiverse, itself, perhaps."

"So it disappears — like the Shifter?"

"That's right."

"I still don't know why you came here," Klein said. "Because it's safe? We are safe, aren't we?"

"I came here," said Renark, more calmly now, "in the hope of discovering a means of travelling into another universe."

"You think because the Shifter travels through the multiverse that you can find out how it works and build some kind of machine that will do the same — is that it?" Klein seemed interested, even enthusiastic.

"That's it. If I can discover the Shifter's secret, I may be able to return to our universe. As a Guide Senser I could probably find it — and warn them of what's happening and offer them a means of escaping into a universe which isn't undergoing this change."

Olesson put in: "Whatever happens, we're all right, eh?"

Renark nodded. "Yes. But that doesn't appeal much to me."

The others didn't reply. Although horrified, they also seemed relieved.

Renark sensed this. "You're still with me?" he said to his friends.

"We've nothing to lose," Talfryn said uncomfortably.

"Nothing," agreed Asquiol.

The equipment beside them squealed. Olesson moved ponderously towards it, tuned in the receiver, got sound and a picture. "Yes."

The face on the screen said: "More visitors, Ragnar — a big load from Migaa are coming in now."

"The usual routine," said Olesson, shutting off the receiver.

F O U R

Renark and his companions watched the screens as the shoals of craft from Migaa entered the Shifter's area of space.

Then the Thron ships came slashing upwards from their planet — like sharks. There was an insane, inexplicable anger in their ferocity.

From other directions a large, motley force of Entropium warships helped the Migaan craft dispose of the outnumbered Thron vessels. The fight was much shorter than Renark's.

"They're just in time," commented Olesson, watching the screen. "The system's due to begin transition again pretty soon. Better wave your universe goodbye, Renark. You won't be seeing it again for some time if at all." He grinned callously.

Ignoring the big man, Renark turned to his friends.

"We'll have to split up. There must be people here who aren't just criminals — people who've made some attempt to explore or analyse the system. They can help us. Move about the city — ask questions."

There was a peculiar note in Klein's voice. "Go to see Mary the Maze, Renark. I can't guarantee she'll help. but she'll serve as a warning to you. She was an anthropologist, I hear. She explored as much of the Shifter as she was able. But go and see where her curiosity got her, Renark."

"Where is she?"

"I'm not sure — but everyone knows her on Northside. You'll find her soon enough if you ask."

"Okay, I will." He said to the others: "You take other parts of the city. Don't ignore any piece of information, speculation or rumour — it could all be useful. We've got to work fast!"

"But fast," sneered Olesson as they left.

Walking out of the untidy building, they saw the bright arrows of fire searing down on the landing field two miles away. They split up.

Renark had chosen the worst possible time to look for anyone.

As he went from hotel to hotel, from bar to bar on the north side of Entropium, the men and women from Migaa began to pour exuberantly in.

They got drunk quickly and the whole city came alive and excited. Not only human beings celebrated the new "shipment's" arrival. Aliens of many kinds joined in with their own forms of merry-making.

Once, a creature like a giant cross between a slug and a caterpillar addressed him in high-pitched Terran, but he ignored it and moved on, searching, asking questions, getting incoherent or facetious replies.

And then the nightmare really began.

Quite suddenly Renark felt nausea flood through him, felt his vision blur and sent out a mind-probe which took in the whole of the system and part of the galaxy beyond it. His mind just refused to accept some of the information it received — he couldn't take it in.

The galaxy seemed distant, and yet retained the same point in space in relation to the Shifter.

Then the whole planet seemed suddenly engulfed by a weird, greyish mist. The darkness gave way to it.

For an instant, Renark thought he saw the buildings of the city begin to fade again. He felt weightless and had to cling to the side of a house. The house seemed solid enough, but its components moved beneath his hands and his own body seemed diffused, lacking its normal density. As his mind swirled, he returned it to the comforting reality of the galaxy, as he habitually did in times of stress. But the galaxy was no longer real.

It seemed ghostly; he was losing touch with it. He very nearly panicked, but controlled himself desperately.

Then he understood what was happening.

They were leaving the galaxy — leaving the universe Renark loved, that he was prepared to die for. He had an unreasoning sense of betrayal — as if the galaxy were leaving him rather than the reverse. He breathed heavily. He felt like a drowning man and sought for something to grab — physically and mentally. But there was nothing. Nothing constant. Nothing that did not change as he sensed or saw it.

The grey city seemed to tilt at an angle and he even felt himself sliding. He staggered on down the crazily angled street, his hands before him as if to ward off the maddening horror of all nature gone wrong.

The only thing he could cling to was abstract — something that could become disastrous reality — his reason for coming here. So he fought to remember that.

The trans-dimensional shift had begun. That was obvious.

Realization had come to the newcomers in Entropium almost simultaneously. There were pockets of silence in a hundred taverns throughout the city.

Renark forced himself to keep moving. Movement was something — movement proved he still had some control over his body if not over the insane environment he had entered. But, as the realization came, his legs slowed without his noticing. He had trained himself never to regret anything resulting from his conscious actions, but now he had to fight the emotion rising within him. The emotion came with the understanding that his chance of returning to his own universe before the Shifter's orbit brought it back again was low.

He could not afford to relax now until his mission was ended, could not afford to risk following up a wrong line of investigation, could not afford to think of anything but his ultimate reason for coming here.

The ground rose up like a tidal wave and as suddenly subsided again.

He pressed on. His intensity of thought was savage. He tore at his own mind, trying to force every extraneous thought, every piece of unnecessary information, out of it, to make himself into a calculating, acting machine with one object — to wrench the Shifter's secret from the chaotic turmoil of the trans-dimensional system.

He forgot the emotion momentarily engendered by the shift.

Light suddenly faded, bloomed again, faded. The buildings seemed to shimmer like a mirage, the very axis of the planet seeming to tilt once more, and Renark fell flat, clutching at ground which crawled beneath his hands.

He heard confused sounds of fright.

He looked up and, through the ghostly shapes that billowed ahead of him, saw the doorway of a tavern. He staggered up and moved towards it. Finally, he was inside, looking at the people there.

The newcomers were patently terrified, but the old residents seemed to be taking the planet's disordered behaviour with equanimity. They were evidently used to it. This must happen every time the system shifted into a new section of the multiverse.

Hoarsely, he said: "Where do I find Mary the Maze?"

He repeated the question until a swarthy man looked up from his girl and his drink and said: "Rupert House — two blocks that way." He pointed with his thumb.

The planet was still doing crazy things. It still flickered with alternate night and day; the ground seemed alive, liquid, crawling. But Renark pushed on through the nightmare until he saw the sign saying *Rupert House*.

He opened a door that made his hand itch, and went inside. "Mary the Maze?" he said thickly to the first man he saw.

The man, sharp-faced, small, dressed in black, said: "Who wants her?"

"Renark wants her — where is she?"

The man stayed silent.

Renark grasped him. "Where's Mary the Maze?"

"Let go — she's upstairs where she always is — room Red Seven."

Renark, his head thumping, half-blind with the strain which the Shifter's transition was putting on his mind and metabolism, forced himself up several escalators and found the room he wanted.

He knocked. Then he opened the door.

Mary the Maze was a miserable sight. Beautiful, blank — debased, in her mumbling insanity, to a travesty of ideal humanity.

Renark saw immediately that she had obviously been a highly intelligent woman. She was still physically beautiful, with a lean, clean face, large brown eyes, wide mouth, long black hair and full breasts. She had on only a dirty skirt and her fingers wandered across an intricate keyboard of the kind once used on the over-complicated sentient spaceships, popular a hundred years before, until scrapped for their tendency to have nervous breakdowns in emergencies. But there was only a keyboard — it was not connected to anything.

Renark's savage mood faded as he came softly into the little room, looked at its walls of bare plaster, the pilot's couch ripped from some ship and evidently used as a bed by the mad woman.

"Mary?" he said to the muttering wreck. "Mary?"

She stared at him and the look in her eyes repelled him.

"Adam? Ah, no. Come in, Castor, but leave Pollux outside. Or is it Ruben Kave, Hero of Space, come to visit me?" Her mouth broadened, the lips curving upwards. She made a vague, graceful gesture with her hand. "Do sit down," she said. "Are you Corum yet?"

There was nowhere to sit. He remained standing, disturbed, nonplussed.

"I'm Renark," he said. "I want information. It's important — can you help me?"

"Help .. .?" The voice was at first detached. Her fingers moved constantly over the keyboard. "Help ...?" Her face twisted. Then she screamed. *"Help!"*

He took a step forward.

The hands moved more swiftly, agitatedly over the board.

"Help!" She began to emit a kind of soft scream.

"Mary." he said urgently. He could not touch the smooth shoulders. He leaned over the drooling woman. "It's all right. They say you've explored the Shifter — is that true?"

"True? What's true, what's false?"

"What was it like, Mary? What did this to you?"

A groan, masculine and desperate, came from the woman. She stood up and walked unsteadily towards the couch, lay down on it, gripping the sides.

"What's the Shifter, Mary? What is it?" His face felt tight, as tight as his rigidly controlled emotions.

"Chaos ..." she mumbled, "madness — super-sanity, warmth. Oh, warmth... But I couldn't take it, no human being could — there's no anchor, nothing to recognize, nothing to cling to. It's a whirlpool of possibilities crowding around you, tossing you in all directions, tearing at you. I'm falling. I'm flying, I'm expanding, I'm contracting, I'm singing, I'm dumb — my body's gone, I can't reach it!"

Her eyes stared. Suddenly she looked at him with some sort of intelligence. "Renark you said your name was?"

"Yes." He was steeling himself to do something he didn't want to do.

"I saw you once, perhaps — there. Here. There." She dropped her head back and lay on the couch mumbling.

He sensed the chaos of the Shifter brawling about in the back of his mind. He thought he knew how it could have turned her mad — felt some sympathy with what she was talking about.

He gave all his attention to her, using his sensing ability to sort her out into her composite atoms, concentrated on her sensory nerves and her brain structure in an effort to get some clue to the effect which the Shifter had had on her.

But there was little physically wrong, although it was obvious that the quantity of adrenalin flooding her system was abnormally high and that this, perhaps, was the reason for her almost constant movement.

But her mind wasn't open to Renark. He was not a telepath and was almost glad at that moment that he couldn't see into her wrenched-apart mind. Neither was he telekinetic, but nonetheless he hated even this form of intrusion as he studied her muscle responses, her nervous system, in an effort to find some clue how to pull her together long enough to get some answers to his questions.

He felt her move.

"Asquiol!" she said. "Isn't that a name — something to do with you? Aren't you dead?"

How could she possibly know of Asquiol?

"Yes. Asquiol's the name of my friend. But I'm alive..."

He half-cursed the introduction of this new element of mystery in an already difficult situation. "What about Asquiol?"

But there was no response from the mad woman, who had now resumed her vacant staring at the ceiling.

He tried another tack. "Mary — where did you go? What did you discover?"

"The ragged planet," she muttered. "I go there — went there — last — the Lattice Planet. Stay away."

Now he wanted to shake the information out of her but he had to coax.

"Why?" he said more gently. "Why, Mary?"

"Doesn't travel with the Shifter — not all of it, some of it — exist in other dimensions, travelling independently? The Hole is there — the dwellers lurk in the Hole. They know everything — they mean no harm, but they are dangerous. They know the truth, and the truth is too much!"

"What truth?"

"I forget — I couldn't hold it. They told it to me. It wasn't fair." She stared at him again and once more intelligence was in her eyes. "Don't believe in justice, Renark — don't for an instant take its existence for granted. It doesn't exist. You learn that in the *gaps*, you can make it — but it breaks down in the real universe. You find that in the *gaps*."

"Gaps? What are they?" He wondered at the peculiar accent she put on the word.

"The ragged planet's *gaps*." She sighed and fidgeted on the couch. "That's where I finally forgot — where every theory, every scrap of information gathered on the other planets was meaningless. And I forgot — but it did me no good. I was curious ... I'm not now, but I want rest, peace, and I can't have it. It goes on. They know, though — they know, and their hate has kept them sane..."

"Who are 'they', Mary?"

"The Thron — the horrible Thron. And the Shaarn know, too, but they are weak — they couldn't help me. The beasts. Don't let them push you into the ... untime ... the unspace. Their weapons are cruel. They do not kill. You grow lost."

"Thank you, Mary," Renark said, at a loss to help her. "I will go to Thron."

She rose from the couch, screaming: "I said not, spiral, magenta, irri-bird, night. Not, sight of a droan — not: Oh, no..."

She began sobbing and Renark left the room.

He walked down the corridor, brooding, dissatisfied with the little he had learned, but now he had a definite plan of action. He must go to Thron and discover the truth of Mary's statement.

Whatever happened, the Thron would be of more help — assuming they could be encouraged to help — than the decadent inhabitants of Entropium, who refused to know anything. Though he could half-sympathize with anyone who didn't wonder or question. The boiling chaos of the Shifter as it moved through the dimensions of the multiverse was enough to disturb anyone.

He walked out of the hotel and found, to his relief, that the planet seemed to have quietened down and was presumably in normal space again, but in an alien universe.

As he walked swiftly towards the building, he allowed his mind to put out tendrils and was relieved when he sensed, beyond the insane perimeter of the Shifter, the solid, ordered planets and suns of a wide, spiral galaxy like his own in general components, although here and there he came across organic and chemical formations which he did not recognize.

When he got back to the control room in the skyscraper, Klein said: "Half the new Migaa-load are dead. As usual, they panicked and caused trouble while we were in transit, so we cleaned them up. The rest are settling down or running back to the launching pads... How did you get on with Mary?"

"She said that the Thron knew about the Shifter's nature — or that's what I believe she said."

Asquiol and Willow, both pale, walked in. He nodded to them.

"Were the Thron the race who initially attacked us?" he asked Klein.

Far away he heard ships blasting off. Klein cursed. "They were warned. That's another lot on their way to death."

"What do you mean?"

"Every time there are newcomers who try to use the Shifter as a transport from their own universe to another, we warn them that once they're here they're stuck. But they try. Maybe one or two make it — I don't know. But I think not. Something stops you leaving the Shifter once you're here."

"It's impossible to get off?" Willow said worriedly.

Renark glanced at Willow. It was funny, he thought, how crisis took different people in different ways. Willow sounded as if she was going to break down. Asquiol evidently hadn't noticed it. He was curious to see how Talfryn would look and act when he came back.

Klein was talking. "That's right, honey. It's harder to get out than in. You don't exist entirely in the space-time matrix of the universe which the Shifter is currently in. We kind of overflow into other dimensions. So when you try to leave, you hit the dimensions at a slight angle and — *whoof!* you break apart. Some of you goes one way, some of you goes another. No, you can't get out."

"Renark — you have more problems," Asquiol said, fiddling with his gloves.

"And more coming, from what I've learned," Renark said tiredly. "What did you find out?"

"Not much of anything definite. The eleven planets are called a variety of names by a variety of human and non-human people. There are a million theories about the Shifter's nature, mainly based on folklore and superstition. They say the Thron were here first and might be native to the system. This could explain some of their resentment of alien ships entering."

"Anything else?"

There's some race called, colloquially, the 'jellysmellies', who are supposed to know the history of the multiverse. There's a planet called Ragged Ruth which is supposed to be the epitome of Hell in this hellish system."

"That seems to confirm what Mary told me," he nodded.

Talfryn came in. His body was loose, worn out. He sat down on the couch.

Renark paused for a moment. "There are questions which we've got to answer. And we can't take our time getting those answers.

"Why does the Shifter follow this orbit? *How* does it do it? If we can discover the principle, there may be a chance of adapting it to build ships to evacuate our galaxy. The logic — if that's the word — is abhorrent to us, but it must be mastered. Are all the universes contracting at the same time, I wonder?"

He asked this last question almost hesitantly, bringing it into the open for the first time.

"If so, there is virtually no chance of evacuation. On the other hand, what we discover may enable us to…"

Klein laughed: "To stop a universe in its natural course of decay or reorganization? No, Renark!"

"Yes, Klein — if that has to be done!"

"What the hell are we all talking about?" Talfryn said tiredly from the couch. "We're only three men — against the natural universe. Not to mention the unnatural universe — this terrible place."

He shook his head. "Frankly, the little information I've picked up makes me feel helpless, useless, ineffectual in the face of what's happening. I feel ready to give up, not to fight against something that is, judging by all the facts, an immense and inescapable movement of the forces of nature which must logically result in the end of the human race — of all organic life both in our universe, and in others. The human race has had its day — we might as well face it. If you can answer that, Renark, I'd be grateful…"

Suddenly, Renark didn't want Talfryn with him anymore. "I doubt if I could give you an answer which would satisfy you," he said sadly. "You're fatalistic. And a fatalist, if you'll forgive me, is also a misanthropist.

"The quality which humanity has, unlike any other form of life in our universe, is its power to control nature. It is the mark of *homo sapiens* that he has, for millennia, refused to let his environment control him to any real extent. He has adapted to it, adapted it, conquered it. This imminent disaster facing the race is on a larger scale — but the rule still applies. In this case we may be forced to leave our environment and start to work adapting to, and controlling, a new one. If we can do that, we will have proved for ever our right and our reason for existence!"

Talfryn, taken aback by the force of Renark's reply, couldn't answer. He shook his head again and remained broodingly silent.

Renark had sensed the man's weakness as a mechanic senses that a piece of equipment, driven beyond its inherent endurance, is due to fail. So he said: "You'd better stay here."

Talfryn nodded. "I've failed you, Renark. But, honestly, it's too big — far too big. Some of us can be optimistic for just so long. But facts must be faced."

"Facts can be altered," Renark said, turning away.

"You're giving up?" Asquiol blinked. "Why?"

"I'm a creature of circumstance," said Talfryn with a bitter half-smile. He got up and left the room.

Asquiol turned to Renark. "Why has he done that? Is there something I don't know about?"

"Let's hope so," Renark said quietly.

He watched his friend who, disturbed and disorientated, turned to look for a long moment at Willow.

Her eyes began to fill with tears.

"I couldn't face it," she said. "Not anymore — not after what we just went through…"

"You've stopped loving me, is that it?"

"Oh, no, Asquiol — I'll always love you. You … you could stay here with me."

Asquiol looked sharply at Renark.

"We go to Thron," said Renark. "If you wish to come."

"Look after yourself, Willow," said Asquiol. "I may return — who knows?" And he walked away from her.

He and Renark left the room, left the building and the city and made for the pads, for their black ship, bound for horror and perhaps death.

"He was a fool," said Willow calmly to Klein. "There are many who refuse their responsibilities. Fooling themselves they search for a 'higher ideal'. He was a fool."

"What are responsibilities?" said Klein laconically. "He knows. Responsibility, my dear, is another word for self-interest. For survival."

She looked at Klein uncomprehendingly.

"I wish he had stayed," she said.

Renark spoke the ship's master-command, bringing the whole complicated vessel to life.

He could not be satisfied with thoughts and theories now. He wanted decisive and constant action — dynamic action which would bring him to a source that would answer the questions crowding his mind.

As he charted his course to Thron, he remembered something and turned to Asquiol who was sitting moodily in the gunnery seat, staring at his instruments.

"Did you ever know of Mary the Maze before you came here?" he asked.

Silently Asquiol shook his head.

Renark shrugged. He felt badly for his friend, but couldn't afford to let his personal emotions influence his chosen course of action.

From what he had gathered, fewer laws than ever applied in the interplanetary space of the Shifter than on the planets themselves. Therefore he was going to have difficulty in simply navigating the comparatively small area of space between them and Thron.

He said without turning, "Once in space I must not be disturbed, and am relying on you to perform all necessary functions other than the actual piloting of the spaceship. I have to anchor my mind to Thron, and must steer the ship through altering dimensions as well as space and time. Therefore, in the event of attack you must be ready, must meet it as best you can. But I will not be able to afford to know. Do you understand?"

"Let's get started, for God's sake," Asquiol said impatiently.

"And don't be too ready with that anti-neutron cannon," Renark said as he pressed the take-off button.

The ship throbbed spacewards.

And then they hit horror!

Chaos.

It had no business to exist. It defied every instinctively accepted law that Renark knew.

Turmoil.

It was fantastically beautiful. But it had to be ignored, mastered or destroyed, because it was wrong!

Agony.

The ship coursed through myriad, multi-dimensional currents that swirled and whirled and howled about it, that rent the sanity of the two brave men who battered at it, cursed it and, in controlling themselves, managed somehow to stave off the worst effects.

Terror.

They had no business to exist here. They knew it, but they refused to compromise. They made the disorder of the tiny universe bend to their courage, to their strength and their wills, creating a pocket of order in the screaming wrongness of unchained creation.

Temptation.

They had nothing but their pitiful knowledge that they were human beings — intelligent, reasoning beings capable of transcending the limits which the universe had striven to set upon them. They *refused*; they fought, they used their minds as they had never used them, found reserves of reason where none had previously been.

And, at last, because they were forced to, they used every resource of the human mind which had lain dormant since man had created "human nature" as an excuse to let his animal nature order his life.

Now they rejected this and Renark steered the ship through the malevolent currents of the unnatural area of space and howled his challenge to it. And the three words *"I am human!"* became his mental war-cry as he used his skill to control the metal vessel plunging on the random spatial and temporal currents — forcing its way through blazing horror towards the angry world of Thron!

All about him, Renark was aware of other dimensions which seemed to lie in wait for his ship, to trap it, to stop it from ever reaching its goal. But he avoided them and concentrated all his powers on keeping a course for Thron.

For hours the two men fought against insanity, fought the craziness that had turned Mary the Maze into an idiot.

Then, at last, Thron appeared on the V. Weak, trembling but exuberant, Renark coasted the spaceship into Thron's atmosphere and, although the brooding planet offered new dangers of a more tangible kind, it was with relief and hope that he arrived there.

They could not speak to one another just then. But both were conscious of the welding companionship which had come about during their journey.

They had been fused together, these two men, by mutually shared horror and victory.

Breathing deeply, Renark dropped the ship down and began a cautious reconnaissance of the planet.

Apart from one domed city at the northern pole, it appeared deserted. There were cities, certainly, but uninhabited. They picked up no signals, their scanners observed no obvious signs of life. Where were the ferocious Thron? Surely not all at the small city on the northern pole?

"The hell with it," Renark said. "Let's go right in and see what happens. I've staked everything so far on one throw, and haven't, as yet, lost by it. Are you willing?"

"I thought I was supposed to be reckless." Asquiol smiled. "Good. We can land in that big square we saw in the largest city."

Renark nodded agreement, adjusted the controls of the ship and flew in over the big city. He brought it flaming down on the hard, rocky substance of the city square.

They landed to find only silence.

"Shall we disembark?" Asquiol asked.

"Yes. There's a locker over there, beside you. Open it, will you?"

Asquiol swung the casing back and raised his eyebrows. There was a small armoury of handguns in the locker. Renark had never been known to carry or use any weapon designed to kill.

"Give me the anti-neutron beamer you see there," Renark said.

Asquiol didn't question Renark but took the holstered gun from its place and handed it over. Renark looked at it strangely.

"Desperate measures," he said softly. "I have little sympathy at the moment with the Thron, although they may have justifiable reasons for their seemingly unreasoning belligerence. But our mission transcends my moral code, much as I hate to admit such a thing possible, and our lives are, as far as the human race is concerned, important."

"Let's go," said Asquiol.

Renark sighed. They suited up and took the elevator to the airlock.

Although the buildings and machines were bizarre and obviously created by alien intelligence, Renark and Asquiol could generally decipher their functions as the pair padded through the streets of the apparently deserted city.

But they couldn't explain why the city was deserted or where the inhabitants had gone. Obviously they had not been gone for any length of time, for there were no signs of erosion or encroaching nature.

With his mind, Renark quested around, searching the buildings for life, but he could only sense peculiar disturbances in the temporal and spatial layers spreading out beyond the Shifter continuum.

Life hovered out there like a ghost, sometimes apparently close, sometimes farther away. It was disturbing.

They toured the city and were just returning to the square where the ship rested when something happened.

"God, I feel sick…" Asquiol screwed up his eyes.

Renark felt the same. He had momentary double vision. He saw faint shadows flickering at the edge of the structures about them, shadows of the same shape, size and appearance as the more solid buildings and machines. These shadows seemed to merge with the material structures — and all at once the city was alive, inhabited.

The place was suddenly full of doglike, six-legged beings using four legs for motion and two as hands.

The Thron!

Shocked, they pulled their pistols from their holsters and backed towards the ship as the Thron saw the humans in their midst.

All was consternation.

Thron soldiers levelled weirdly curled tubes at the two men and fired. The humans were flung to the ground as their suit-screens absorbed or repelled the worst of the charges.

"Shoot back or we've had it!" Renark yelled.

They raised themselves on their bellies, aiming their own dreadful weapons.

Beams of dancing anti-matter spread towards the Thron troops, met them, made contact and seethed into their bodies.

Those bodies imploded, crushing inwards and turning to minuscule specks of shattered matter before vanishing entirely. The backlash shivered against the humans' protective suits. And the beams waltzed on, fading slightly as they progressed, entered one group after another, destroying wherever they touched, whether organic or inanimate matter, until their power faded. Only a few Thron were left in the immediate area.

"They don't seem ready to talk," Asquiol said sardonically over the suit radio. "What now, Renark?"

"Back to the ship, for the meantime."

Inside the control cabin their communications equipment was making all sorts of noises. Asquiol attempted to tune it in and eventually succeeded in getting a regular series of high-frequency signals which he could not quite interpret as being coded signals or actual speech. He brought the pitch down lower and realized with astonishment that he was listening to stilted Terran. Renark was busy keeping the scanners trained on the Thron, who were coming out into the open around the square again. But he listened.

"Beware the Thron… Beware the Thron… Beware the Thron…"

Whether it was a warning or a threat, he couldn't tell. Asquiol said, careful to adjust his outgoing signal to the frequency involved: "Who are you? I am receiving you."

"We are enemies of the Thron. We are the Shaarn, whose ancestors consigned the Thron to this existence. But they have machines which you are not equipped against — forces which will hurl you out of this system altogether and into Limbo. Take off immediately and head for the northern pole. We saw you pass over us but have not, until now, been able to discover your means of communication and the form it takes. We apologize."

"How can we trust them?" Asquiol asked.

"The frying pan or the fire — it makes no difference," Renark replied. "I'm lifting off. Tell them we're coming."

Asquiol relayed the message.

"You must hurry," the Shaarn spokesman said, "for we are small and have few defensive devices against the Thron. You must reach our city before they do, since we will have but a short time to spare to let you in and close our barrier again."

"Have it ready — we're coming," said Asquiol.

The ship soared upwards again, levelled off and headed at high speed for the polar region.

They made it in under a minute. They saw the dome flicker and fade, entered its confines as it closed over them again, and came down gently on a small landing field within the city. It was more a town, with few buildings taller than three stories, encompassing a small area compared with the expanse of the Thron cities. Overhead they observed the Thron ships come rushing over the polar city and were half blinded by the bolts of energy which sprayed the force-dome above them.

They stayed where they were and waited to be contacted.

Eventually the communications equipment spoke: "I am pleased that we were successful. There is no point in waiting until the Thron have expended their rage. The force-shield will absorb their most ferocious attacks. We are sending out a vehicle for your assistance. Please take it to the city when you are ready to do so."

A few moments later a small air-carriage, open-topped and made of thin, golden metal, floated up to the ship and hovered by its airlock.

"Well, let's see how friendly the Shaarn really are!" said Renark.

They descended to the airlock, passed through it and entered the little airboat which spun on its axis and returned to the city at a more leisurely speed.

Renark felt fairly confident, from what Mary the Maze had said, that these people would be friendly.

They entered the city proper and the airboat cruised downwards, landing gently outside the entrance to a small, unornamented, unpretentious building.

Two figures came out. They were dog-like, having six appendages. Asquiol gasped and instinctively reached for his pistol in an unthinking response. Then he saw that these creatures, so like the Thron, were unarmed, and he calmed himself.

The Shaarn, like the Thron, were extremely pleasing to the human eye — perhaps because they resembled friendly dogs.

With peaceful gestures, the two figures beckoned Renark and Asquiol to leave the airboat. When they did so they passed through a series of simply furnished rooms containing no recognizable equipment, and out into a courtyard which, like the city, was covered with an iridescent force-dome.

Here was a transceiver not unlike their own. One of the Shaarn went up to it and spoke into the transmitter. It took them several moments to tune into the humans' suit wave-lengths and, for an instant, before they adjusted their own controls, they were blasted with the high-pitched noises they had heard before.

Then the Shaarn spokesman said: "We regret, sincerely, that our welcome could not have extended to the whole planet, but as you will have realized, we control little of it. I am Naro Nuis and this is my wife Zeni Ouis. You are von Bek and Asquiol of Pompeii, I believe."

"That's so, but how did you know?" Count Renark replied.

"We were forced — and you must forgive us — to intrude on your minds in order to discover the means to build the communications equipment. We are telepaths, I am afraid..."

"Then why the need for the laser?"

"We had no idea how you would take telepathic interference in your minds, and it is against our code to intrude except in the direst emergencies."

"I should have thought that's just what we were in," Asquiol said somewhat rudely.

"I see," said Renark. "Well, as far as I am concerned, telepathic communication would be preferable. We have telepaths among our own race."

"So be it," Naro Nuis said.

"You have obviously some important reason for braving the dangers of Thron," said a voice in Renark's skull, "but we avoided investigating it. Perhaps we can help?"

"Thank you," Count Renark said. "Firstly, I am curious to learn why the Thron are so belligerent; secondly, whether it is true that your race was the first to come to this system. Much hangs on what I learn from you." He told the Shaarn how his race faced annihilation.

The alien appeared to deliberate. At length he 'pathed:

"Would you object if we intruded still further on your minds for a while by means of a telepathic link? By this method you will see something of the history of the Shaarn and will discover how this system originally took this somewhat unusual orbit through the multidimensional universe."

"What do you say, Renark?" Asquiol's voice came over the suit-phone.

"I think the suggestion is excellent."

They were led into a semi-darkened room where food and drink were served to them. They felt relaxed for the first time in ages.

"This place is simply to aid your receptivity to what we are about to do."

"And what is that?"

"We are going to reconstruct for you the history of the war between the Shaarn and the Thron. The history began many millennia ago, when our ancestors were completing their explorations of our own space-time galaxy..."

At Naro Nuis's request they blanked their minds, and the history began...

S   I   X

They were the golden children of the galaxy. The Shaarn — the searchers, the wanderers, the inquirers. They were the magnificent bringers of gifts, bestowers of wisdom, dealers of justice. In their great star-travelling ships they brought the concept of mercy and law to the planets of their galaxy and formed order out of chaos, cut justice from the stuff of chance.

The Shaarn hurled their ships inwards to the Hub, outwards towards the Rim.

Proud, wise and merciful, self-confident and self-critical, they spread their seed to inhabit planets in many different systems. The laughing darlings of an ancient culture, they poured outwards, always searching.

The Shaarn ships sang and hurtled through the bewildering regions of chaos-space, avoiding war, recognizing privacy, but bringing their wisdom and knowledge to anyone requesting it. They had come, also, to accept that all intelligent races took roughly the same form as themselves.

The mighty Shaarn were cynics and idealists, innocent and ancient — and their ships coursed further towards the worlds of the Rim.

The starship *Vondel*, captained by Roas Rui, burst into normal space half a light-year from a binary star the Shaarn called Yito. Around Yito circled eleven worlds, each following a wider orbit than the next — eleven mysteries which Roas Rui and her crew of scientists and sorcerers regarded with excitement and curiosity. Eleven balls of chemicals and vegetation, organic and inorganic life. Would they find intelligence? New concepts, new knowledge? Roas Rui hoped that they would.

The Shaarn, in their early days of space-travel, had known fear when encountering foreign cultures, but those times were gone. In their power and their confidence, they were unable to conceive of a race greater than their own, a technology more highly developed. On some worlds near the Rim they had come across traces of a star-roving people; but the traces were incredibly ancient and pointed to a long-dead race — their ancestors, perhaps — who had travelled the stars and then degenerated. Thus, it was not with fear that Roas Rui regarded the fourth world nearest Yito when her ship, its reactor idling, went into orbit around it.

Roas Rui reared herself effortlessly onto her four hind limbs in order to see better the purple-clouded world which now filled the viewing-screen. Her shaggy, dog-like head craned towards the screen and her mouth curved downwards in an expression of pure pleasure. She turned her head and showed her long, slim teeth to emphasize her delight.

"It's a huge planet, Medwov Dei," she released to her lieutenant who stood by the screen control board, maneuvering dials in order to bring the world into closed perspective.

Medwov Dei thought, without moving his head, "The gravity is almost identical to that of Shaarn."

Rui thought, "Woui Nas was right in his hunch again. He always picks the planet which most closely approximates Shaarn in gravity and atmosphere. He's one of the best sorcerers we have in the Division."

Medwov made a clicking sound with his mouth to indicate agreement. He was very big, the largest member of the crew and every inch of five feet high. He was dedicated to the Exploratory Division, even more than the other members. With regard to his work, he was a fanatic, probably due to the fact that, because of his immense size, he had little success with the female Shaarn. At least he, personally, blamed his height, but it was well known that, as a young cadet, he had once killed a domestic beast in anger. Naturally, this had led to his near-ostracism and had precluded his ever rising above the rank of lieutenant. Medwov inhaled wetly and continued to work at the control panel, deliberately blocking his mind to any but the most urgent thoughts which might emanate from his commander.

Almost childishly, Roas Rui laughed the high-pitched whine of the Shaarn. Her excitement mounted as she directed her two pilots to prepare for descent on to the planet's surface.

"Prepare defense screens." She sent out the traditional commands as a matter of course. Some of her orders were obeyed by the control operators before she even thought of them. "Switch to gravity-resisters." Machines moaned delicately throughout the huge bulk of the starship. "Descend to two thousand feet."

The *Vondel* plunged through the atmosphere of the new planet and hovered two thousand feet above its surface. Now the screens showed a vast landscape of forest land composed predominantly of waving indigo fronds which stretched like a sea in all directions, broken occasionally by clumps of taller vegetation coloured in varying shades of blue. It was beautiful. Roas Rui's long body shook with emotion as she beheld it. To the Shaarn all new planets were beautiful.

"Begin testing," she said.

The computers began their intricate job of classifying all the components of the planet. At the same time, the sorcerers began to put themselves swiftly into trance-state, seeking to discover intelligent life of any kind, whether natural or supernatural, and also its attitude or potential attitude to the Exploratory Division.

The findings of computers and sorcerers were relayed instantly to Roas Rui, herself now in semi-trance. Both parts of her brain received the information and assembled it into an ever-increasing, detailed picture of the newly discovered planet.

Woui Nas:

I have found a mind. Bewildered. Uncertain. Passive. More minds. As before. New! Mind. High intelligence. Anger. Controlled. Urge to destroy very strong: directed at (possible) rulers or representatives. New! Mind. Low IQ. Misery. Bewildered. Passive. New! Something bad. Very bad. Evil here, but am finding resistance to probes.

Pause…

Power. Evil. Great resistance to probes. Am prepared to fight or retreat. Require orders!

Pause…

Repeat. Require orders!

Roas Rui beamed a message to the controllers to continue recording the data and concentrated all attention on making a full link with Woui Nas, who had 'pathed the urgent request.

"I am with you now, Woui Nas. Can you bring me in?"

"Unprecedented reaction, captain. Please absorb."

Roas Rui could sense the frightened amazement of Woui Nas as she submerged herself in the other's mind and allowed the old sorcerer to guide her outwards towards the source of the emanations. Almost instantaneously, she felt the aura of disgusting malevolence, coupled with an intelligence more powerful than her own. Roas Rui was one of the most intelligent members of her race — her capacity for absorbing and relating knowledge was tremendous — but she had found more than her match in the mind which now sensed the presence of her own.

Roas Rui, under the direction of Woui Nas, probed further into the mind which she had contacted. She probed while her senses shrieked with danger and urged her to retreat.

Suddenly her brain throbbed as a thought came savagely from the contacted entity: "*Get out! We intend to destroy you, intruders.*"

There was no attempt to ask questions of the explorers. No tinge of curiosity. An order — and a statement.

Roas Rui and Woui Nas retreated from the malevolence and separated minds.

"What now?" Woui Nas asked from his cabin, a quarter of a mile away from the control room where Roas Rui sat shaking.

"Incredible," the captain said. "Quite unprecedented, as you remarked. There is a force here to equal the Shaarn — even to better it. But the *evil!*"

"I must admit that, as we neared the planet, I sensed it," Woui Nas informed the captain. "But it was difficult then to define it. These entities are capable of blocking off our most powerful probes."

"Our ancestors would have been far more careful when making a new planet-fall," Roas Rui said grimly. "We are becoming too complacent, Brother Sorcerer."

"*Were,*" Woui Nas remarked dryly. "Perhaps this is the kind of shock our people need."

"Possibly," Roas Rui agreed. "But now we are in danger of turning our immediate peril into a philosophical problem. Since this contact is unprecedented, and since the regulations state categorically that we should obey any culture which demands that we leave its environs, I would suggest to you that a group make contact immediately with Headquarters on Shaarn and ask for instructions."

"And meanwhile?" Woui Nas inquired.

"I do not wish to be destroyed. And neither, I think, do any other members of the ship's complement." She beamed a quick order to her pilots. "We are returning to Shaarn. This is an emergency." She knew that her pilots would need no further orders.

Swiftly, the *Vondel* climbed into deep space and merged into chaos-space.

So the initial contact between the Shaarn and the Thron was made.

After millennia of ignorance of each other's existence, the exploratory team which had come to a Thron-dominated world brought the two mighty cultures into contact at last. It was inevitable.

And the war between Shaarn and Thron was also inevitable.

It was not a war like most wars. It did not hinge on economics. It only partially hinged on conflicting ideologies. It was simply that the Thron refused to tolerate the presence in the galaxy of another intelligent race, physically like themselves and almost as powerful.

They intended to destroy the Shaarn. To obliterate completely all traces of their civilization. The Thron had not concentrated so much on the building of starships, but it did not take them long to build ships which almost equalled those of the Shaarn.

Thron controlled an Empire comprising twenty-six systems. The Thron themselves were comparatively few in number — but they had total dominance over their subject planets.

The Federation of Shaarn comprised some fifty systems and three hundred planets upon which intelligent races, like themselves, existed. When Shaarn informed them of the impending war, one hundred and sixty-two of those planets elected to join with the Shaarn. The rest claimed neutrality.

The war progressed. It was vicious and dreadful. And a month after it had begun the first planet was destroyed by the Thron — a neutral planet. And all life was destroyed with the planet.

Realizing the danger was great, but unable to consider an alternative to continuing the struggle, the Shaarn directed their scientists to invent a way of stopping the war so that no more destruction of life should take place.

The scientists devised a means of removing the Thron from the galaxy, even from the very universe — a means, if it worked as they hoped, of forever exiling that malevolent and evil people.

They discovered the continuum-warp device which, they believed, would be capable of hurling the eleven Thron home-worlds out of their continuum and into another. This would efficiently halt the Thron's insensate aims of ruling the galaxy.

So a squadron of ships, each armed with the device, reached the Thron home-system of Yito and directed their beams onto the planets and their sun.

At first they succeeded only in shifting the planets through space, altering the position around the binary, resulting in the equidistant position they now occupied. The Thron retaliated and the Shaarn hurled the Thron warships effectively into another space-time continuum. Returning their attention to the system, they blasted it with warp rays time after time and, quite suddenly, it was gone — vanished from the Shaarn's space-time into another. The war was over.

But, as it happened, the Shaarn had not been entirely successful in their plan since the system kept right on travelling through the dimensions, eventually establishing an orbit which it still followed. Not only this, but most of the Shaarn ships were caught up in the vortex they had created and were drawn, by means of the force they had themselves released, after the Shifter.

They attempted, desperately, to return to their own space-time but, for some reason, it was now blocked, not only to them but to the Shifter itself. The system could never pass through the Shaarn's space-time again.

The Thron, demoralized and bewildered, did not offer a threat of immediate counter-attack for they were busily consolidating on their fortress world, abandoning their slaves to any fate that came.

The Shaarn were able to land their ships, establishing a small, well-protected city at the northern pole of a planet they called Glanii. Here they remained for ages, vainly attempting to devise a means of returning to their own system.

Later the Thron, too, came to Glanii, where they could be nearer their hated enemies.

The Thron eventually learned what had happened to them and also began work on the problem. They invented a machine which could fling them and all their artifacts through the multi-dimensional space-time streams to their home continuum and exact vengeance on the Shaarn. So far they had not been entirely unsuccessful.

This explained why Renark and Asquiol had found the planet apparently deserted of Thron, who at the time of their arrival had been attempting another jump through the dimensions.

The war between the Thron and the representatives of the Shaarn had become a stalemate, both races concentrating most of their energies on attempts to return to their home continuum. So it had been for millennia, with the Thron, resenting further encroachments on their sundered territory, attempting to destroy any newcomers who came, like vultures, opportunistically to the Shifter System.

And that, to the date of Renark's coming, was briefly the history of the Sundered Worlds...

Count Renark was in a calmer frame of mind when the experience was over. At last he was no longer working in the dark — he had definite, conclusive facts to relate to his questions and was confident that the Shaarn would supply him with further useful information.

Naro Nuis telepathed discreetly: "I hope the history was of some use to you, Renark von Bek."

"Of great use — but I gather you are unable to supply me with any detailed information of the dimension-warping device."

"Unfortunately, that is so. From what we can gather, the continua-warp, operating as it did by means of certain laws discovered in the Shaarn continuum, will not work in the same way from outside the continuum. I believe this was deliberately done by our scientists in order that the Thron would never be able to return."

"I'm surprised that by this time you haven't joined forces with the Thron, since you seem to have a common aim."

"Not so. In fact, this is our main point of contention these days. The Thron are determined to regain our original universe, whereas that is the last thing we want. We will be pleased to halt the progress of the Shifter in any continuum but our own, and this would destroy, for ever, their chance to continue the war." The alien sighed — a surprisingly human sound. "It may be that the Shifting mechanism is an irreversible process. In that case our efforts are hopeless. But we do not think so."

Renark was bitterly disappointed. If the beings who engendered the Shift no longer understood how it operated, this was logically the end of the trail. But he would not admit to himself that there was nothing more he could do. That was unthinkable.

He rose to his feet, his mind working intensely, busily forming the recent knowledge into the kind of pattern best suited to his present needs. Well, there was time yet. He had to be optimistic — there was no turning back. He refused to accept any factors other than those he could use objectively. Somewhere in this system…

They left the chamber and made for the ship. On the way, Renark noticed signs of animated work in a large, low-slung building with open-hangar-type doors. It struck him as out of tune with the millennia-long deadlock of which he had just learned.

He remarked on this to Naro Nuis. The alien immediately responded with interest.

"That is the result of a long period of research. We are now building equipment with which we hope to halt the Shifter System."

Renark stared in amazement. "*What?* After the story of gloom you have just told us?"

"I told you our experiments continued," Naro Nuis replied, puzzled. "Soon we will begin ferrying the equipment into space, to take it as near to the suns as possible."

"And yet you still claim to have no knowledge of the Shift principle!" Renark's excitement was mounting at the thought that the creature had been lying.

"That is so," Naro Nuis told him. "We have despaired of ever discovering the principle behind the phenomenon. But, with any luck, we think we might bring it to a stop, even though we don't understand it." He added: "This is the culmination of a very long series of experiments. Very long. If we succeed, we shall not need to know. The problem will have vanished."

Renark's sudden hope dissipated. "And what are your chances of succeeding?"

Naro Nuis paused before answering. "The expedition is fraught with dangers. Our long absence from space has lost us some of our skills in interplanetary flight."

"What of the Thron? Do they know of your plans?"

"They have some inkling, of course. They will try to stop us. There will be a great battle."

Renark continued the walk to his ship. "When do you plan to lift this equipment off?"

"In half a revolution of the planet."

He stopped abruptly. "Then I must ask one favour."

"What is that?"

"Delay your experiment. Give me time to find out what I must know."

"We cannot."

There was no arguing with the Shaarn. His tone was uncompromising. He explained: "How can we be sure that you will have even a chance of success in your endeavour? Every moment we delay means that our chances of stopping the Shifter and holding off the Thron are lessened."

"But the future of my entire race depends upon me!"

"Does it? Have you not taken it upon yourself presumptuously to save your fellows? Perhaps the process you described is natural — perhaps the members of your race will accept that they are to perish along with their universe. As for us, there is no need to delay and we must act quickly. The Thron — when they are not attempting to jump through the dimensions — patrol the planet in their ships. As soon as we begin ferrying the equipment there will be a battle. We will have to work speedily and hold off the Thron at the same time."

"I see," Renark said bitterly.

Later, Asquiol said: "But what if you did stop the Shifter? Supposing you stopped it in a universe like the one we have just left? You would be destroyed along with the rest."

"That is true — but the chances of that happening are not very great. We must risk it."

"Then you will not wait?"

"No," Naro Nuis said again, regretfully. "Your hopes of success are slim. Ours are better. You must understand our position. We have been trying to stop the Shifter for thousands of years. Would you call a halt to your progress on behalf of a race you never heard of — which, according to only two of its members, was in some kind of danger?"

"I might," Renark said.

"Not after thousands of years," said Asquiol. "Not that long."

Naro Nuis's thoughts came gently. "You are welcome to stay with us if you wish."

"Thanks," Renark said harshly, "but we don't have much time."

"I think your efforts will be wasted," the Shaarn 'pathed, "but since you are so anxious to find help you might go to the world of the Ekiversh."

"Ekiversh?"

"The Ekiversh are intelligent metazoa who have a fully developed race memory. They gave us some help in building the machine with which we intend to stop the Shifter. They have lived so long that their knowledge is very great. They are good-natured, friendly and, because of their structure and type, live on the only planet in the system which is not in some way torn by strife. The Thron could learn something from the Ekiversh but, in their arrogance, they would not deign to do so. We have not often visited them, for whenever we leave our city the wrath of the Thron is turned upon us. But we have made telepathic communication when certain favourable laws have applied, for short periods, in the system."

"Can you point out their planet on my chart?"

"With pleasure."

Naro Nuis accompanied them aboard their ship, looking around him with pleasure and curiosity. "A bizarre craft," he said.

"Not by our standards." Renark produced the chart.

The alien bent over it, studying the figures marked there. At last he pointed. "There."

"Thanks," said Renark.

"Let's get started, shall we?" Asquiol drummed his fingers.

"The Thron will be awaiting you when you leave here," Naro Nuis said. "Are you sure you want to risk it?"

"What else could we do?" Renark was close to anger.

The alien turned away from him.

Asquiol shouted at Naro Nuis: "Haven't you any idea what you will do if you stop the Shifter? You could strand us here with no means of saving our people — no means of going back, even if we did find the information we need. You *can't* begin your experiments yet!"

"We must."

Renark put his hand on Asquiol's arm. "We must get to Ekiversh as soon as possible and see what we can learn before the Shaarn succeed in stopping the Shifter in orbit."

"Then I had better leave," Naro Nuis said sadly.

With mixed emotions, Renark said goodbye to the alien, thanking him for his help.

In the control seat Renark tensed. Asquiol fidgeted in his own seat by the gunnery panel.

Suddenly the force-dome over the city flickered, flashed bright orange and boiled backwards, leaving a gap. Renark's finger smashed down on the firing switch. The ship trembled, screamed and lifted.

Then they were through the gap in the screen, whining up through the clouds towards the madness of the Shifter's space.

Thron ships spotted them instantly and came flashing in their direction.

Asquiol didn't wait for Renark's order this time. As they sped into deep space, he fired.

The Thron ships flickered away from the cold, searing stream of anti-neutrons which Asquiol, in his desperation, had dared again to employ, and which their instruments told them meant instant disruption. Even so, some vessels were caught for an instant in the periphery of the deadly flow, and must have suffered for it. Anti-neutrons, possessing no electrical charge, could not be stopped by any energy screen.

Asquiol could almost see the Thron licking their wounds.

He had hoped that this first exchange would frighten the attackers badly enough to give Renark time to make a clean getaway. But the Thron had the advantage of being able to maneuvre in Shifter space. Renark gritted his teeth as he piled on power and plunged into the billowy *twistiness* which this region presented to his mind. It was almost like piloting a boat through mad, storm-tossed seas.

But they were seas that intruded into the mind.

The Thron came after them, and Asquiol saw them somersault preparatory to firing. He hesitated, reluctant to use his weapon a second time. Then great slams of force hit them.

The ship skidded and bucked. "Don't pussyfoot, Asquiol," Renark roared uncharacteristically. "Let them have it!"

Asquiol clung to the firing arm of the anti-neutron gun. Blindly, he turned up the density to maximum and sprayed space. Phantasmal green flares showed, on the screen before him, where he scored hits.

Renark closed his eyes and concentrated hard on the piloting. The collapse of atomic structures on a large scale was not a pleasant experience for a Space Senser.

After that, the surviving Thron ships withdrew. There was silence in the cabin of Renark's ship for some time.

A few hours later Renark made a quick mental exploration. He found what he'd expected. The Shaarn had begun the first stages of the experiment. There was evidence of fierce fighting near the Thron planet, and somewhere sunward a sizeable installation was being set up.

He probed further. The Shaarn would not be unmolested for long. A large fleet was assembled an hour's journey away, and would soon no doubt do much to impede the progress of the Shaarn's labours. In spite of the friendliness shown him by his hosts, Renark began to regret the Thron warships destroyed by Asquiol.

Soon, Renark felt, he would be gaining a complete picture of the workings of the multiverse. There were other things he wished to know and he had a feeling that if he lived he would know them soon.

Once again they were experiencing the chaotic and bewildering currents of outer space. But this time there was little emotional reaction, for their self-confidence was strong.

But Renark still had to fight to keep the ship on course in the stormy, apparently lawless and random flowings of time and space, skimming the ship over them like a stone over water, through myriad sterechronia, through a thousand million twists of the spatial flow, to come finally to Ekiversh…

S   E   V   E   N

Immediately they landed on the peaceful oxygen planet, tiny, polite threads of thought touched their minds, asked questions.

Responding to the delicacy of the impressions, Renark and Asquiol made it clear that they wished to contact the Ekiversh as the Shaarn had suggested. They remained in the spaceship, pleased to see the light green chlorophyll-bearing plants which were not unlike Earth's.

At last there appeared outside the ship what at first appeared to be a heaving mass of semi-transparent jelly. Disgusted, Renark was repelled by the sight and Asquiol said: "The jellysmellies. Remember I told you they were some sort of legend on Entropium? Metazoa — ugh!"

A voice in Asquiol's head said humbly: "We are deeply sorry that our physical appearance should not appeal. Perhaps this will be a better form."

Then the whole mass reared up and slowly transformed itself into the shape of a giant man — a giant man composed of hundreds of gelatinous metazoa.

Renark could not decide which form was least unattractive, but he blocked the idea out of his mind and said instead: "We have come to converse with you on matters of philosophy and practical importance to us and our race. May we leave our ship? It would be good to breathe real air again."

But the metazoan giant replied regretfully: "It would be unwise, for though we absorb oxygen as you do, the waste gases we exhale are unpleasing to your sense of smell."

"The 'jellysmellies'," Renark said to Asquiol. "That explains their name."

"We were informed that you are equipped with race memory, that in effect you are immortal," Renark thought tentatively at the glutinous giant.

"That is so. Our great experience, as you may know, was to have witnessed, in the early days of our race, the Dance of a Galaxy."

"Forgive me, but I don't understand the implications of that," Renark said. "Could you perhaps explain what you mean?"

"It was believed," said the metazoa, "that those whom we call the Doomed Folk had passed away in a distant galaxy in our original universe, and that galaxy — which had known great strife — was quiet again in readiness for the Great Turn which would be the beginning of a new cycle in its long life. We and other watchers in nearby galaxies saw it shift like a smoky monster, saw it curl and writhe and its suns and planets pour in ordered patterns around the Hub and out around the Rim, reforming their ranks in preparation.

"The Dance of the Stars was a sight to destroy all but the noblest of watchers, for the weaving patterns depicted the Two Truths Which Bear the Third, so that while the galaxy reformed itself to begin a fresh cycle through its particular Time and Space, it also cleansed its sister galaxies of petty spirits and those who thought ignoble thoughts.

"For millions of years, the Dance of the Galaxy progressed — ordered creation, a sight so pleasing to intelligent beings. It gave us much in the way of sensory experiences and also enabled us to develop our philosophy. Please do not ask us to explain it further, for the sight of a galaxy dancing can be defined in no terms possessed by either of us.

"When at last the Dance was over, the Hub began to spin, setting the pattern for the new Cycle. And slowly, from the Hub outwards to the Rim, the suns and planets began to turn again in a course that would be unchanged for eons.

"So it began, and so — after time had passed — did its denizens begin to hammer out its marvellous history.

"They came, at length, to our galaxy and, because they were impatient of the philosophical conclusions we had drawn about the nature of the multiverse, set about destroying our ancient race. A few of us fled here, since we abhor violence."

"You witnessed a galaxy reorder itself by its own volition!" Renark sensed at last that his most important question was close to being answered.

"Not, we feel, by its own volition. Our logic has led us, inescapably, to believe that there is a greater force at work — one which created the multiverse for its own purposes. This is not a metaphysical conclusion — we are materialists. But the facts are such that they point to the existence of beings who are, in the true sense, supernatural."

"And the multiverse — what of that? Does it consist of an infinite number of layers, or...?"

"The multiverse is finite. Vast as it is, it has limitations. And beyond those limitations exist — other realities, perhaps."

Renark was silent. All his life he had accepted the concept of infinity, but even his rapidly developing mind could not quite contain the new concept hovering at the edge of his consciousness.

"We believe," said the metazoa gently, "that life as we know it is in an undeveloped, crude state — that you and we represent perhaps the first stage in the creation of entities designed, at length, to transcend the limitations of the multiverse. It has been our function, all of us, to have created some sort of order out of original chaos. There is no such thing, even now, as cause and effect — there is still only cause and coincidence; coincidence and effect. This, of course, is obvious to any intelligence. There is no such thing as free will. There is only limited choice. We are limited not only by our environment, but by our psychological condition, by our physical needs — everywhere we turn we are limited. The Ekiversh believe that, though this is true, we can conceive of a condition in which this is not so — and perhaps, in time, create that condition."

"I agree," Renark nodded. "It is possible to overcome all restrictions if the will is strong enough."

"That may be so. You have certainly come through more than any other entity — and it has been your spirit which has been the only thing to keep your mind and body coordinated for so long. But, if you wish to continue your quest for as far as you can go in a finite universe, you have the worst experience to come."

"What do you mean?"

"You must go to the Lattice Planet. There you will meet the dwellers in the Abyss of Reality. Perhaps you have heard of the place as the Hole."

Yes, Renark had heard the name. He remembered where. Mary had told him about it.

"What exactly is this planet?"

"It does not move through the multiverse in the same way as the rest of the planets in this system, yet in a sense it exists in *all* of them. Pieces of it move in different dimensions, all shifting independently. Sometimes the planet may be fairly complete on random occasions. At other times the planet is full of … *gaps* … where parts of it have ceased to exist according to the dimensional laws operating in whichever continuum the Shifter is in. It is believed that there exists somewhere in this planet a gateway through to a mythical race called the Originators.

"Since you have nowhere else to go. we would suggest that you risk a visit to this planet and attempt to find the gateway, if it exists."

"Yes, we shall try," said Renark softly. Then another thought came to him. "Why isn't this planet, Ekiversh, subject to the same chaotic conditions existing elsewhere?" he asked.

"That is because, before we fled our home universe, we prepared for the conditions which we expected to meet, and we used our skill and knowledge to create a very special organism."

The glutinous giant seemed to heave its shining body before the next thought came.

"We call it a conservator. The conservator is simply an object, but an object of a peculiar kind which can only exist under a certain set of laws. In order to maintain its own existence, it conserves these laws for a distance around it. These laws, of course, are those under which we exist and under which you, for the most part, exist also. With a conservator in your ship, you will not experience your earlier difficulties in traversing interplanetary space and, also, you will be less likely to lose your way on the Lattice Planet which, incidentally, you know of as Roth, or Ragged Ruth."

"I am grateful," Renark said. "The conservator will be of great assistance." Then another thought occurred to him. "You are aware of my reason for coming here — because the universe where I belong is contracting. Could not a number of these conservators be built in order to stop the course which my universe is taking?"

"Impossible. Your universe is not contravening any natural laws. The laws which apply to it are bringing about this change. You must discover why this is happening — for everything has a purpose — and discover what part your race is to play in this reorganization."

"Very well," said Renark humbly.

Several of the metazoa detached themselves from the main body and disappeared in the direction of a line of hills, travelling rapidly. "We go to fetch a conservator," the pseudo-giant told him.

Renark used the wait to explore his own state of mind. Strangely, without any great strain, he could now accept the enormity of the realization which had been dawning on him ever since he first came to the Shifter. And he knew now, unquestioningly, that his whole journey, his trials and endeavours, had had, from the beginning, a definite purpose — there was logic in the multiverse. The Ekiversh had convinced him. And that purpose, he thought with dawning clarity, transcended his original one — transcended it and yet was part of it!

But there was much more, he felt, to undergo before this new need in him would be consummated. For now he was to undergo the worst part of the journey — to the planet that had sent Mary the Maze insane. Roth — Ragged Ruth — the Lattice Planet.

The metazoa returned bearing a small globe of a dull ochre colouring. This they placed on the ground, near the airlock of the spaceship.

"We shall leave you now," the metazoa telepathed, "but let us wish you knowledge. You, Renark and Asquiol, are the messengers for the multiverse — you must represent us all if you succeed in reaching the Originators — presuming they exist. You go further towards reality than any other intelligent beings, apart from the dwellers of the Hole, have done before…"

Asquiol got into a suit and went outside to collect the conservator. Renark watched him, his gaze unblinking, his thoughts distant, as he returned and placed the globe on the chart desk beside Renark.

Automatically, Renark prepared himself for take-off, thanked the metazoa and pressed the drive control.

Then they were plunging upwards, cutting a pathway of law through the tumbling insanity of interplanetary space.

But this time there was no need to fight it. The conservator acted just as the Ekiversh had predicted, setting up a field all about itself where its own laws operated. Relieved, they had time to talk.

Asquiol had been taken aback by all the events and information he had received. He said: "Renark, I'm still bewildered. Why exactly are we going to Roth?"

Renark's mood was detached, his voice sounding far away even to his own ears. "To save the human race. I am realizing now that the means of salvation are of a subtler kind than I previously suspected. That is all."

"But surely we have lost sight of the original purpose for this mission? More — we are living in a fantasy world. This talk of reality is nonsense!"

Renark was not prepared to argue, only to explain. "The time has come for the dismantling of fantasies. That is already happening to our universe. Now that we have this one chance of survival we must finally rid ourselves of fantasies and seize that chance!

"For centuries our race has built on false assumptions. If you build a fantasy based on a false assumption and continue to build on such a fantasy, your whole existence becomes a lie which you implant in others who are too lazy or too busy to question its truth.

"In this manner you threaten the very existence of reality, because, by refusing to obey its laws, those laws engulf and destroy you. The human race has for too long been manufacturing convenient fantasies and calling them laws. For ages this was so. Take war, for instance. Politicians assume that something is true, assume that strife is inevitable, and by building on such false assumptions, lo and behold, they create further wars which they have, ostensibly, sought to prevent.

"We have, until now, accepted too many fantasies as being truths, too many truths as fantasies. And we have one last chance to discover the real nature of our existence. I am prepared to take it!"

"And I." Asquiol spoke softly, but with conviction. He paused and then added with a faint half-smile: "Though you must forgive me if I still do not fully comprehend your argument."

"You'll understand it soon enough if things go right." Renark smiled broadly. Roth now loomed huge on the V.

With a deliberate lack of reverence, Asquiol commented: "It looks like a great maggoty cheese, doesn't it?"

In the places seeming like glowing sores, they could see right through the planet. In other places there were *gaps* which jarred the eyes, numbed the mind.

Although they could see vaguely the circular outline, the planet was gashed as though some monstrous worm had chewed at it like a caterpillar on a leaf.

Refusing to let the sight overawe him — though it threatened to — Renark brought his skill as a Guide Senser to bear. Deliberately, yet warily, he probed the mass of the weird planet. Where the *gaps* were, he sensed occasionally the existence of parts of the planet which should, by all the laws he knew, be in the same space-time. But they were not — they existed outside in many other levels of the multiverse.

He continued to probe and at last found what he was searching for — sentient life. A warmth filled him momentarily.

Had he found the dwellers? These beings appeared not wholly solid, seemed to exist on all layers of the multiverse!

Could it be possible? he wondered. Did these beings exist on all planes and thus experience the full knowledge of reality, unlike the denizens who

THE ETERNAL CHAMPION

only saw their own particular universe and only experienced a fraction of the multiverse?

Though he could conceive the possibility. his mind could not imagine what these beings might be like, or what they saw. Perhaps he would find out?

He understood now why Mary the Maze played insanely with her lifeless keyboard on Entropium.

Another thought came to him and he felt about with his mind and learned, with a sinking regret, that the Shaarn had succeeded in beating back the Thron. He could not tell definitely, but it seemed that the Shifter's motion through the multiversal levels was slowing down.

Hastily he re-located the dwellers. There were not many and they were on a part of the planet he felt he could find — a part not having its whole existence in the area now occupied by the Shifter, but probably visible to the human eye. With the aid of the conservator he felt fairly certain of finding the mysterious Hole.

Speed was important, but so was caution. He did not wish to suffer an ironical end — perishing now that he was so close to his goal.

He brought the ship down over a gap in order to test the conservator's powers.

They were extremely strong. As he came closer, the planet seemed to form itself under him as the missing piece shifted into place like a section of a jig-saw puzzle. It worked.

Now Renark lifted the ship away again and saw the piece fade back, wrenched into its previous continuum. He could not afford to land his ship on such a dangerous location. So he moved on and came down slowly on a surface which, he hoped, would remain in this continuum until he was ready to return.

If he did return, he told himself. The ominous activity near the binary was increasing — perhaps, already, the Shifter had stopped!

Asquiol was silent. He clutched the conservator to him as he followed Renark out of the ship's airlock.

The planet seemed a formless mass of swirling gases and they received a distinct sense of weightlessness for a moment as they placed their feet on its unnatural surface.

Dominated by the dreamlike insecurity of the planet, striking, first, patches of weightlessness, and later patches where their feet seemed entrenched in dragging mud, they moved warily on, Renark in the lead.

Though it was dark, the planet seemed to possess its own luminous aura, so that they could see a fair distance around them. But there were places where, somehow, their vision could not penetrate — yet they could see beyond these Places! Even when they walked on rocky ground, it seemed impermanent.

As they moved, the area immediately around them would sometimes alter as the conservator exerted its strange power. But, as if to compensate for this, new *gaps* continued to form elsewhere.

Struggling to keep his objective clear, Renark felt ahead with his mind, awed by the remarkable fluxions taking place constantly.

The planet was perpetually *shifting*. It was impossible to tell which part of it would be in existence even for a few moments at a time. Sundered matter, as chaotic as the unformed stuff of the multiverse at the dawn of creation, wrenched, spread and flung itself about as if in agony.

But, remorselessly, Renark pushed onward, filled with a sense of purpose which dominated his whole being.

Stumbling on, drunk by their visions of Chaos, they did not lose their objective for a moment.

Sometimes near, sometimes distant, the Hole became their lode-star, beckoning them with a promise of truth — or destruction!

E I G H T

At last, after more than a weary day, they stood above the Hole, and as rock unformed itself and became gas, Renark said hollowly: "They are in there. This is where we'll find them, but I do not know what they are."

Though their tiredness made them inactive, Count Renark felt that he had never been more conscious, more receptive to what he saw. But his reception was passive. He could only look at the shifting, shining, dark and myriad-coloured Hole as it throbbed with power and energy.

They stared down at it, filled with knowledge and emotion.

After several hours' silence, Asquiol spoke. "What now?"

"This is the gateway of which we learned on Thron and Ekiversh," said Renark. "I can do nothing now but descend into it in the hope of achieving our aim." Now the human race seemed remote, a fantasy, unreal — and yet important. More important than it had ever been before.

He moved towards the very brink of the Hole and lowered himself into its pulsing embrace.

Asquiol paused for a moment behind him and then followed. They ceased to climb down, for they were now floating, going neither up nor down, nor in any definite direction, but yet floating — somewhere. The conservator had ceased to work — unless it still worked and, in some way, these laws applied more rigorously to it than any it had previously conserved.

Again they were on solid ground, on a small island in an ocean. They stepped forward and knew they were in the heart of a blazing sun; stepped back and were in the middle of a bleak mountain range. From the tops of the mountains an entity looked down and welcomed them.

They moved towards it and were suddenly in an artificial chamber which seemed, at first, to have dead, black walls. Then they realized they were looking out into a void — emptiness.

To their left a being appeared.

It seemed to be constantly fading and reappearing. Like a badly-tuned V-set, Renark thought, desperately looking for something to cling to. He felt cut off entirely from anything he knew.

The being began to speak. It was not Terran he spoke. He conversed in a combination of sonic and thoughtwaves which struck responses in Renark's mind and body. He realized that these entities may have once been like himself, but had lost the power of direct speech when they gained the power to dwell on all levels of the multiverse.

He found he could communicate with the entity by modulating his own speech and thinking as far as possible in pictures.

"*You wish* (complicated geometric patterns) *help...?*"

"Yes (picture of universe contracting)..."

"*You from* (picture of a pregnant woman which changed quickly to a womb — an embryo, not quite human, appeared in it)...?"

Renark deliberated the meaning of this, but did not take long to realize what the entity was trying to say. Already he had half realized the significance.

Logic, based on the evidence he had seen and heard in the rest of the Shifter, was leading Renark towards an inescapable conclusion.

"Yes," he said.

"*You must wait.*"

"For what?"

"(Picture of a vast universe, multi-planed, turning about a central point) *Until* (picture of the Shifter moving through time, space and other dimensions towards the Hub)..."

Renark realized what the picture meant. It could only mean one thing. He had only been shown it briefly, yet he understood clearly.

He had been shown the centre of the universe, the original place through which all the universal radii passed, from which all things had come. There were no alternate universes at the centre. When the Shifter passed through the centre — what...?

But what if the Shaarn succeeded in stopping the system's progress before it reached the Hub? He had to dismiss the idea. If the Shifter stopped too soon there would be no need for further speculation. No need for anything.

"What will happen there (misty picture of the multiverse)?" he asked.

"*Truth. You must wait here until* (Hub with Shifter) *then go* (the binary star — the Shifter's star)..."

He had to wait in Limbo until the Shifter reached the Hub and then they must journey towards — no, *into* — the sun!

He transmitted a horrified picture of himself and Asquiol burning.

The being said: "*No,*" and disappeared again.

When it reappeared, Renark said: "Why?"

"*You are expected.*" The being faded, then vanished.

Since time did not exist here they couldn't tell how long they had waited. There were none of the usual bodily indications that time was passing.

Quite simply, they were in Limbo.

Every so often the being, or one like it, would reappear. Sometimes he would impart information regarding the Shifter's slow progress, sometimes he would just be there. Once a number of his kind appeared but vanished immediately.

Then, finally, the dweller appeared and a picture of the Shifter entering the area of the Multiversal Centre manifested itself in Renark's mind.

With relief and a bounding sense of anticipation, he prepared to experience — *Truth.*

Soon, whether he lived or died, remained sane or went insane, he would know. He and Asquiol would be the first of their race to *know.*

And this, they both realized, was all that mattered.

Then they went outwards towards the flaring, agonizingly brilliant suns.

They felt they had no physical form as they had known it, and yet could sense the stuff of their bodies clinging about them.

They poured their massless bodies into the fiery heat, the heart of the star, and eventually came to the Place of the Originators — not their natural habitat, but a compromise between Renark's and theirs.

They saw, without using their eyes, the Originators.

They could hear the Originators communicating, but there was no sound. All was colour, light and formlessness. Yet everything had a quality of bright existence, true reality.

"You are here," said the Originators musingly, as one. "We have been awaiting you and grown somewhat impatient. Your rate of development was not what we had hoped."

On behalf of his race, in the knowledge of what the Originators meant, Renark said: "I am sorry."

"You were always a race to progress only when danger threatened."

"Do we still exist?" Renark asked.

"Yes."

"For how long?" Asquiol spoke for the first time.

The Originators did not answer his question directly. Instead, they said: "You wish us to make changes. We expected this. That is why we speeded up the metamorphosis of your universe. You understand that although your universe is contracting, it will still exist as individual galaxies, suns and planets, matter of most kinds in different formations?"

"But the human race — what of that?"

"We should have let it die. Intelligent organic life cannot undergo the strains of the change. If you had not come to us, we should have let it die — regretfully. But our judgement was correct. We let you know of the coming catastrophe and you used all your resources of will and judgement to come here as we hoped you would."

There was a pause, and then the Originators continued: "Like all other races in the multiverse, yours is capable of existing on all levels. Not just one. But, because of these links you have with the rest of the levels, you would have perished, being not fully natural to just one level. None of the intelligent forms could survive such a catastrophe. We were responsible for placing them all in their present environment. Each plane of the multiverse serves as a separate seeding bed for a multitude of races, one of which may survive and succeed us. Your plane serves, in your terms, as a womb. You are our children — our hope. But if you fail to overcome the special limitations we set upon you, you, like us, shall die. But you shall die... still-born."

"Then what is to become of us?"

"We made the changes in your universe in order to accelerate your rate of development, so that representatives of your race would find a way to us. To the greatest extent you have succeeded, but you must return rapidly and inform your race of their need to develop more rapidly. We shall afford you the means, this time, of evacuating your universe. But we are growing old, and you, of all the intelligent races in the multiverse, are needed to take our place. You cannot do that until you are ready. Either you succeed in achieving your birthright, or, like us, perish in chaos and agony.

"You have proved to us that we were justified in selecting you. You *can* overcome the boundaries we set around you. But hurry, we beg you — hurry..."

"What will happen if we succeed?"

"You will experience a stage of metamorphosis. Soon you will no longer need a universe of the kind you know now. Things are coming to an end. You have the choice of life — more than life or death!"

Renark accepted this. It was all he could do. "And us — what is our function now?"

"To perform what you set out to do."

There was a long, long pause.

Womb-warmth filled the two men and time stopped for them as the Originators exuded sympathy and understanding. But glowing like hard reality beneath this, Renark sensed — his own oblivion? His own death? Something lay there in the future. Something ominous was in store for him.

"You are right, Renark," said the Originators.

"I can't be right or wrong. I have no idea what my fate is."

"But you sense, perhaps, our foreknowledge of your termination as a physical entity — perhaps your end as a conscious entity. It is hard to tell. Your spirit is a great one, Renark — a mighty spirit that is too great for the flesh that chains it. It must be allowed to spread, to permeate the multiverse!"

"So be it," Renark said slowly.

Asquiol could neither understand nor believe what the Originators were saying. His form — golden, flashing red — bounced and flared before Renark as he said: "Are you to die, Renark?"

"No! No!" Renark's voice roared like a tower of flame. He addressed his friend. "When I am gone you must lead our race. You must direct them towards their destiny — or perish with them. Do you understand?"

"I accept what you say, but without understanding. This experience is driving us to madness!"

The cool tones of the Originators swept inwards like flowing ice to catch their attention and silence them. "Not yet, not yet. You must both retain something of your old forms and your old convictions. Your part is not played out yet. Now that you understand the nature of the multiverse, it will not be difficult to supply you with material means for escaping your shrinking universe. We will give you knowledge of a machine to produce a warp effect and enable your people to travel to another, safer universe where they will undergo further tests. Our plans have not fully worked themselves out yet. There are others of your race involved — and you must meet and react and harden one another before you can fulfill the destiny we offer you. You, Asquiol, will be entrusted with this part of the mission."

"Renark is the strongest," Asquiol said quietly.

"Therefore Renark's spirit must be sacrificed as a gift to the rest of you. This is necessary."

"How shall we accomplish this exodus to a new universe?" Renark asked hollowly.

"We will help. We shall instil in your fellow creatures a trust in the word of you both. It will necessarily be a temporary thing. Once you have left your universe, our workings must be of a subtler sort, and only the efforts of certain individuals will save you."

"We shall be on our own?" Asquiol questioned.

"Virtually, yes."

"What shall we find in this new universe?"

"We do not know, for it is likely that your jump will be a random one into any of the other multiversal planes. We cannot guarantee you a friendly reception. There are forces opposed to our purpose — meaner intellects who strive to prevent the evolution of our being."

"Our being?" Asquiol's shape flickered and reformed.

"Yours — ours — everyone's. We, the Originators, are intelligent optimists, since we see a purpose, of sorts, to existence. But there are pessimists in the universe. They prey upon us, seek to destroy us, since they themselves have given up hope of ever breaking the bonds which chain them to the half-real state in which they exist. They have their unknowing supporters among your own segment of the total race."

"I understand."

With those two words they became whole men. They saw, at last, the real universe — the myriad-planed universe comprising many, many dimensions so that there was no empty space at all, but a crowded, rich existence through which they had previously moved unknowing.

With an effort of his titanic will, Renark said urgently: "One thing. What is your purpose? What is our ultimate purpose?"

"To exist," was the simple reply. "You cannot have, as yet, real knowledge of what that means. Existence is the beginning and the end. Whatever significance you choose to put upon it is irrelevant. If we were to die before you were ready to take our place, then all our creation would die. The multiverse would die. Chaos would flood over everything and what to us would seem a formless, mindless, fluctuating shroud would mark our passing."

"We do not want that," said Asquiol and Renark together.

"Neither do we. That is why you are here. Now — the information you will need."

Their minds, it seemed, were taken by a gentle hand and sent along a certain course of logic until, at length, they had complete understanding of the principle involved in building dimension-travelling spaceships.

In what was, for them, normal space-time, it would have been virtually impossible to have formulated the principle in all its aspects. But now, dwelling in the whole multiverse, the logic seemed simple. They were confident that they could impart the information to their own race.

"Are you satisfied?" the Originators asked.

"Perfectly," Renark said. "We must hurry now, and return to our own universe. The exodus must begin as soon as possible."

"Farewell, Renark. It is unlikely that when we meet again you will remember us. Farewell, Asquiol. When we meet again let us hope that you have succeeded in this matter."

"Let us hope so," Asquiol said gravely.

Then their beings were spreading backwards and streaming through the multiverse towards the ship which still lay on Roth.

The traveller stopped at the sagging filling station, the last human artifact before the long, grey road began again.

A huge, shapeless haversack bulged on his stooping back, but he walked along effortlessly, smiling in the depths of his lean, black face, his hair and beard wild about him.

Kaal Yinsen whistled to himself and took the road north. It was several centuries since the Earth had been populated by more than the few thousand people living here now, and this was the way he liked it. Kaal Yinsen had never had a dream in his life, and when this one came it came with force.

The road faded, the whole surface of the planet reared up, whirled and bellowed. Suddenly he knew he must head south again. This he did and was joined, on the way, by hundreds of families going in the same direction.

Bossan Glinqvist, Elected of Orion, sat in an office which was part of an isolated metal city, hanging in space close to the heart of the galaxy. He picked up the file on Drenner Macneer and began to leaf through it, not sure that his duties as Moderator in the Galactic Council were sufficiently satisfying to make him live a third of his adult life in so unnatural an environment. Macneer's case was a difficult one, requiring all Glinqvist's concentration and intelligence to judge.

The man had instigated a breach-of-code suit against the Council — accusing it of failing to represent the interests of a minority group of traders who, because of a change in a tariff agreement between Lanring and Balesorn in the Clive System, had lost their initiative to survive by labour and were currently living off the citizen's grant on a remote outworld. It was a serious matter. Glinqvist looked up, frowning, and experienced a powerful hallucination.

Soon afterwards he was giving orders for the city to be set in motion — an unprecedented order — and directed towards the Kassim System.

These were but two examples of what was happening to every intelligent denizen of the galaxy.

Every human being, adult or child, was filled with the same compulsion to journey towards certain central planets where they gathered — and waited patiently.

On Earth, the few inhabitants of the planet felt that the very ground would give beneath the weight of so many newcomers. Normally, they would have been resentful of the appearance of outsiders on the recently healed globe, but now, with them, they waited.

And at last they were rewarded.

They saw its vague outlines in the sky. On PV screens all over the planet they watched it land on a tendril of fire. A spaceship — a Police Cruiser. It was scarred and battered. It looked old and scarcely spaceworthy.

There was silence everywhere as they watched the airlock open and two figures emerge.

Millions of pairs of eyes winced and failed to focus properly upon the figures. They strained to see all the figures, but it was impossible. The men who came out of the ship were like ghostly chameleons, their hazy bodies shifting with colour and energy and light.

The watchers seemed to see many images overlaid on the two they recognized as men, images which seemed to stretch out into other dimensions beyond their powers to see or to imagine.

These visitors were like angels. Their set faces glowed with knowledge; the matter of their bodies was iridescent; their words, when they began to speak, throbbed in tempo with the pulse of the planet so that it was as if they heard an earthquake speak, or an ocean or a volcano, or even the sun itself giving voice!

Yet they understood that these messengers were human. But humans so altered that it was almost impossible to regard them as such.

They listened in awe to the words and, in part at least, they understood what they must do.

Renark and Asquiol delivered the ultimate message. They told of the threat inherent in the contracting universe. They told how this had come about and why. And then they told how the destruction of the race could be avoided.

They spoke clearly, in careful terms, looking out at their listeners from the depths of their faraway minds. No longer existing wholly in any one plane of the multiverse, they needed to concentrate in order to keep this single level in complete focus.

The myriad dimensions of the multiverse coursed in ever-changing beauty as they spoke. But this experience they could not as yet convey, for it was beyond speech. And the stuff of their bodies changed with the multiverse in scintillating harmony so that the watchers could not always see them as men. But, none the less, they listened.

They listened and learned that the multiverse contained many levels and that their universe was but one level — a fragment of the great whole. That it was finite, yet beyond the power of their minds to comprehend. They learned that this structure had been created by beings called the Originators. They learned that the Originators, sensing they would die, had created this multiverse as a seeding ground for a race to take their place. They learned that they, the embryonic children of the Originators, were to be given their last chance to take over. They were given a choice: Understand and overcome the pseudo-real boundaries of time and space as they understood them, therefore claiming their birthright — or perish!

Then Renark and Asquiol left the planet Earth, passing on to another and then another to impart their news.

Wherever they passed they left behind them awed silence, and each human being that heard them was left with a feeling of *completeness* such as he knew he had been searching for all his life.

Then the two multi-faceted messengers called technicians and scientists and philosophers to them and told these men what they must do.

Soon after, the vehicles, which had been fitted with the Intercontinua-Travelling device, swarmed in the depths of space beyond the Rim, ready to carry the human race into another universe.

At the head of the tremendous space-caravan the small, battered Police Cruiser lay. In it, Renark and Asquiol took their final leave of one another.

Outside the Cruiser, a small space-car awaited Renark.

The two beings looked at one another's shifting forms, stared about them to absorb the pulsating sight of the total multiverse, clasped hands, but said nothing. It was pre-ordained that this must happen.

THE ETERNAL CHAMPION

Sorrowfully, Asquiol watched his friend board the space-car and vanish back towards the Hub of the galaxy.

Now he had to make ready the giant fleet. The Galactic Council had sworn him full powers of leadership until such a time as he would no longer be needed. The efficient administration which had run the galaxy for many years was admirably suited to organizing the vast fleet and they took Asquiol's orders and translated them into action.

"At precisely 1800 hours General Time, each ship will engage its I.T. drive." Asquiol's lonely voice echoed across the void through which the fleet drifted.

Somewhere, out of sight of Asquiol or the human race, a small figure halted its space-car, climbed into a suit, clambered from the car and hung in space as it drifted away.

Now they could observe the galaxies rushing down upon one another. They came together and joined in one blazing symphony of light as the human race plunged through the dimensions to the safety of another universe where another intelligent life-form waited to receive it — perhaps in friendship, perhaps in resentment.

Then the contraction was swifter, sudden.

Only Renark remained behind. Why, the race would never know — and even Renark was uncertain of his reasons. He only knew there had to be a sacrifice. Was it the ancient creed of his savage ancestors, translated into the terms of the Originators? Or did his action have some greater meaning? There would be no answer. There could be none.

Faster and faster, the universe contracted until all of it existed in an area that seemed little larger than Renark's hand. Still it shrank, as Renark watched it now as if from a distance. Then it vanished from his sight, though he could still sense it, was still aware of its rapidly decreasing size.

He knew that there was a point to which a thing can be reduced before it ceases to exist, and finally that point was reached. Now there was a gap, a real flaw in the fabric of the multiverse itself. His universe, the galaxy, the Earth, were no longer there — possibly absorbed into a larger universe beyond even Renark's marvellous senses. Perhaps, in this greater universe, his universe existed as a photon somewhere. Only Renark was left, his shifting, shimmering body moving in a void, the stuff of it beginning to dissipate and disappear.

"God!" he said as everything vanished.

His voice echoed and ached through the deserted gulf and Renark lived that moment for ever.

BOOK TWO:

THE BLOOD RED GAME

In his deep sorrow, Asquiol was resolved to carry on Renark's work and bring to finality the Originators' plans for the human race.

The fleet was dropping, dropping, dropping through layer after layer of the multiverse in a barely controlled escape dive.

Soon he must give the order to slow down and halt on one level. He had no idea which to choose. Though he was aware of the multiverse, his vision, unlike Renark's, could not extend beyond its previous limits. He had no inkling of what to expect in the universe in which they would finally stop.

In the great multiverse they were merely a scattering of seeds — seeds that must survive many elements if they were to grow.

Finite, yet containing the chaotic stuff of infinity, the multiverse wheeled in its gigantic movement through space.

To those who could observe it from beyond its boundaries — the Originators — it appeared as a solid construction, dense and huge. Yet within it there were many things, many intelligences who did not realize that they dwelt in the multiverse, since each layer was separated from another by dimensions. Dimensions that were like leaves between the layers.

Here and there the mighty structure was flawed — by fragments which moved *through* the dimensions, through the leaves, passing many universes; by a vacuum existing where one small part had vanished. But, on the whole, the universes remained unknown, one to another. They did not realize that they were part of a composite structure of fantastic complexity. They did not realize their purpose or the purpose for which the multiverse had been created.

Only the chosen knew — and of them only a few understood.

So, fleeing from their newly non-existent galaxy, the human race began its great exodus into a new space-time continuum — pierced the walls of the dimension-barrier and came, at last, into another universe.

By this action, humanity also entered a new period of its history.

But Asquiol of Pompeii was no longer an individual. He had become many individuals and was therefore complete. Now there was no better leader for the human fleet; no better mentor to guide it. For Asquiol existed in a multitude of dimensions, his vision extended beyond the limitations of his fellows, and saw all that humanity could one day become — if they could make the effort.

Asquiol of Pompeii, captain of destiny, destroyer of boundaries, becalmed in detachment, opened his eyes from a sad reverie and observed the fleet he led.

His screen showed him the vast caravan of vessels. There were space-liners and battleships, launches and factory ships, ships of all kinds and for all purposes, containing all the machinery of a complex society on the move. There were ships of many designs, some ornate, some plain, containing one part in common — the I.T. drive.

Asquiol deliberately ceased to wonder why Renark had elected to stay behind in the dying universe. But he still wished it had not happened. He missed the confidence which had come to him from Renark's presence, from Renark's will and spirit. But Renark and his will were in the past now. Asquiol had to find strength only from within himself — or perish.

And if he perished, ceased to be what he was, then the danger of the race itself perishing would be heightened considerably. Therefore, he reasoned, his survival and the survival of the race were linked.

Twenty-four hours of relative time had not passed since the fleet left the home universe. He decided that the next universe, irrespective of what it was, should be the one to remain in. Quickly he gave the order. "De-activate I.T. drive at 1800 hours."

At 1800 hours exactly, the fleet ceased to fall through the dimensions and found itself entering the fringes of a strange galaxy, not knowing what they might encounter or what danger might exist here.

On board the administration ships, men worked on data which was pouring in.

They charted the galaxy; they learned that, in construction, it was scarcely different from their own. Asquiol wasn't surprised — each layer of the multiverse differed only slightly from the next.

Guide Sensers investigated the nearer suns and planets, while telepaths explored the widespread systems for signs of intelligent life. If they discovered such life they would then have to assess, if possible, its attitude towards the refugee-invaders now entering the confines of its galaxy. This was a new technique, one which Asquiol had learned from the Shaarn.

Flanking the fleet were the great battlewagons of the Galactic Police, now entrusted with the guardianship of the mighty caravan as it plunged at fantastic speed through the scattering of suns that was the Rim of the spiral galaxy.

Hazy lights filled space for several miles in all directions, the ships of the fleet swimming darkly through it. Beyond the fleet was the sharper darkness and beyond that the faint sparks of the stars. The light emanated from the ships like a swirling, intangible nebula, moving constantly towards a destination it might never reach.

But Asquiol saw more than this, for Asquiol saw the multiverse.

It required, in fact, a certain effort now to devote his attention to only one plane, no matter how vast. As soon as he relaxed his attention, he felt the absolute pleasure of dwelling on all the planes simultaneously, of seeing around him all that there was in the area of the multiverse he now occupied.

It was like existing in a place where the very air was jewelled and faceted, glistening and alive with myriad colours, flashing, scintillating, swirling and beautiful.

This was a richer thing, the multiverse as a whole. In it Asquiol could see his own fleet and the faraway stars, but the space between everything was crammed full. The multiverse was packed thick with life and matter. There was not an inch which did not possess something of interest. Vacuum was, in a sense, that which separated one layer from another. When all the layers were experienced as a whole, there was no wasted vacuum, no dark nothingness. Here was everything at once, all possibilities, all experience.

He was suddenly forced to pull himself back from this individual experience. The special alarm over his screen was shrilling urgently.

A face appeared on the screen. It was pouched and puffy, heavily jowled like that of a bloodhound.

"Mordan," Asquiol addressed the Galactic Councillor who was Captain-in-chief of Police.

"Asquiol." Even now Asquiol's power was virtually absolute, Mordan couldn't bring himself to call him 'prince', for the Galactic Council had not agreed to restore the now meaningless title. Mordan spoke heavily: "Our Guide Sensers and Mind Sensers have come up with important information. We have located and contacted an intelligent species who appear to have noticed our entry into this space-time. They are evidently a star-travelling race."

"How have they reacted to our entry?"

"We aren't sure — the Sensers are finding it difficult to adjust to their minds..."

"Naturally, it will take time to understand a nonhuman species. Let me know if you have any further news."

Mordan had been screwing up his eyes while looking at Asquiol's image. There appeared to be several images, in fact, each containing a different combination of colours, overlapping one another. It was as if Asquiol looked out at Mordan through a series of tinted, opaque masks covering his body and interleaving on either side. The image that Mordan took to be the original lay slightly to one side of the multiple image and, for him, in better focus than the rest. He evidently could not equate this image with what he remembered — the cynical, moody, vital young man whom he had divested of title and power a few years before. Now he saw a lean, saturnine man, the face of a fallen archangel, stern with the weight of leadership, the eyes sharp yet staring into a distance containing little that Mordan felt he could observe.

With his usual feeling of relief, Mordan switched out and relayed Asquiol's message to the Senser team.

As he waited for further news, Asquiol didn't exert his mind by trying to contact the new species directly.

That would come later. He decided to allow the Sensers time to assemble as much general data as possible before he turned his full attention to the problem.

He kept in mind the Originators' warning that certain intelligences were quite likely to receive the human race with insensate hostility, but he hoped the universe they were in contained life that would welcome them and allow them to settle where they could. If the intelligences were hostile, the fleet was equipped to fight — and, in the last resort, run. He had already ordered the lifting of the ban on the anti-neutron cannon, and this devastating armament was virtually invincible. As far as he knew there was no known screen that could withstand it. The fleet was already alerted for battle. There was nothing to do at the moment but wait and see.

He returned his thoughts to problems of a different nature.

Landing on and settling new planets within this galaxy would only be a minor problem compared with the task of taking over from the Originators.

He thought of his race as a chicken in an egg. Within the shell it was alive, but aware of nothing beyond the shell. With the act of breaking through the barrier of dimensions separating its universe from others, it had broken from its enclosing and stifling shell to some awareness of the multiverse and the exact nature of things.

But a hatched chicken, thought Asquiol, may believe the breaking of the shell to be the ultimate action of its life — until the shell shattered and the whole world was visible in all its complexity. Then it discovered the farmyard and the countryside with all their many dangers. It discovered that it was only a chick and must learn and act to survive if it was to grow to adulthood.

And what, Asquiol considered ironically, was the eventual fate of the average chicken? He wondered how many other races had got this far in the ages of the multiverse's existence. Only one would survive, and now it had to be the human race, for if it did not attain its birthright before the Originators died, then none would take its place. The multiverse would return to the chaos from which the Originators had formed it.

Quasi-death and the stuff of death would engulf the cosmos. The tides of chance would roll over all existing things, and the multiverse, bereft of guidance and control, would collapse into its original components. All sentience, as the Originators and their creations understood it, would perish!

It was this knowledge that enabled him to keep his objective in the forefront. The race must not perish; it must survive and progress, must achieve the marvellous birthright that was its promised destiny. The race must replace the Originators while there was still a little time.

Was there sufficient time?

Asquiol didn't know. He had no way of knowing when the Originators would die. He had, in this case, to attempt to pack centuries of evolution into the shortest possible period. Whether, immediate danger averted, the race would allow him to continue with his mission he did not know. Now that the weird influence of the Originators had been removed, mankind could throw away its birthright, and consequently the life of all ordered creation, by one ill-judged or fear-inspired decision.

Even now there were elements in the fleet who questioned his leadership, questioned his vision and his motives. It was easy to understand this suspicious impulse which was at once man's salvation and doom. Without it he ceased to reason; with it he often ceased to act. To use the impulse objectively was the answer, Asquiol knew. But how?

Without the usual warning, Mordan's face appeared on the V. He stared into emptiness since he preferred not to have to see Asquiol's disturbing image.

"These intelligences are obviously preparing to attack us," he said urgently.

So the worst had happened. In which case the threat must be met. "What preparations are you making?" Asquiol said in a level voice.

"I have alerted our battle force and all essential craft are now protected by energy screens — administration ships, farm ships, factory ships. These I intend to reassemble at the centre of our formation since they are necessary for survival.

"Around these I will put all residential ships. The third section comprises all fighting craft, including privately owned vessels with worthwhile armament. The operation is working fairly smoothly, though there are a few recalcitrants I'm having difficulty with. We are forming totally to enclose your ship so that you are properly protected."

Asquiol drew a deep breath and said slowly: "Thank you, Mordan. That sounds most efficient." To Mordan, his voice seemed to produce — like his image — intrinsic, faraway echoes that carried past Mordan and beyond him. "How do you intend to deal with these recalcitrants?"

"I have conferred with the other members of the Galactic Council and we have come to a decision — subject to your approval."

"That decision is?"

"We will have to use more direct powers of action — make emergency laws only to be declared null and void after the danger has passed."

"The example of history should deter you from such a decision. Powers of dictatorship, which you give me and yourselves, once assumed are liable to last beyond the circumstances for which they were devised. We have not employed coercion, force, or anything like it, for two centuries!"

"Asquiol — there is no time for debate!"

Asquiol made up his mind immediately. Survival, for the moment, was of primary importance. "Very well. Take on these powers — force the recalcitrants to obey our orders, but be sure not to abuse the powers or we will find ourselves weakened rather than strengthened."

"This we know. Thank you."

Asquiol watched, his mood brooding and disquieted, as the fleet redeployed into a great oval shape with his own battered ship in the centre, the nut in an inordinately thick shell.

E L E V E N

Adam Roffrey was a loner, a rebel without a cause, a hater of state and organization.

He morosely watched the ships reforming about him, but remained where he was, refusing to answer the signal on his screen. His large head, made larger by the thick, black beard and hair covering it, had a dogged, insolent set. He was refusing to budge and knew he was within his rights.

The flexible laws of the galaxy had been bent by him many times, for the rights of the citizen were varied and complex. He could not be forced to take part in a war; without his permission the authorities could not even contact him. Therefore, he sat tight, ignoring the urgent signal.

When Councillor Mordan's bloodhound face appeared, unauthorized, on the V screen, Roffrey disguised his shock and smiled sardonically. He said lightly, as he always said things, whatever the gravity of the statement: "It's a lost cause, Mordan. We can't hope to win. We must be fantastically outnumbered. Asquiol's forcing the race to commit suicide. Are we voting?"

"No," said Mordan, "we're not. For the duration of the emergency all citizens' rights are liable to be waived if necessary. You have no choice but to comply with the decision of Asquiol and the Galactic Council. Asquiol knows what's best."

"He doesn't know what's best for me. I'm the only lost cause I've ever backed, and that's the way it's staying!"

Councillor Mordan regarded the black-bearded giant grinning out of the PV screen and he frowned. "Nobody leaves the fleet, Roffrey. For one thing, it's too dangerous, and for another, we've got to keep it tight and organized if we're to survive!"

He said the last words to a blank screen. He whirled round in his control chair and shouted to a passing captain. "Alert the perimeter guard. A ship may try to leave. Stop it!"

"How, Councillor Mordan?"

"Force — if there is no other alternative," said Mordan, shocking the captain, who had never received such an order in his whole career.

Adam Roffrey had been anti-social all his life.

His living had been made on the fringes of the law. He wasn't going to give in to the demands of society now. The chips were down for the fleet — that was his guess — and he had no reason for sticking around. He objected to the discipline required to fight complicated space-battles; he objected to the odds against the human race winning the battles; he objected to the fact that he was being personally involved. Personal involvement was not in his line.

So he broke the energy seals on his anti-neutron cannon and prepared to blast out. As he moved away from the rest of the fleet, several Geepee gunboats, alerted by Mordan, flitted towards him from nadir-north-west.

He rubbed his hairy chin, scratched his forehead and reached out a hairy hand to his drive control. At full power he retreated, away from the oncoming ships, away from the fleet, into the unknown space of the unknown universe.

He was prepared to take such chances to avoid curtailment of his personal liberty.

But his ship, a peculiar vessel, at first sight an impossible old hulk, a space launch got up to look like a merchantman and fitted like a battlewagon, could not hope to outdistance the Geepee craft in the long run. Already they were beginning to catch up.

Humming to himself, he debated his best course of action.

There was one sure method of evading immediate danger as well as the alien threat already visible as a huge fleet of spherical vessels, seen on his screens, approached the fleet from the depths of space.

But to take that way out, although he had considered it much earlier in another context, could be highly dangerous.

The odds were that, if he committed himself to it, he would never see another human being again.

The necessity to make a decision was increasing.

His ship, like all those in the great cosmic caravan, was fitted with the I.T. drive enabling him to travel through the dimensions. He had already taken the trouble to learn all he could about multi-dimensional space and certain things existing in it. He knew, suddenly, where he was going.

The idea had been in the back of his mind for years. Now he would be forced to go.

The Geepee ships were getting closer, their warning blaring on his communicator. He pressed a key on his chart-viewer, keeping a wary eye on the oncoming ships.

Though the Geepees were nearer, the two embattled fleets were far behind. He saw faint splashes of coloured light on his screen. He was tense and was surprised to note that he had a feeling half of relief, half of guilt that he had missed the battle. He wasn't a coward, but now he had something to do.

A quick glance at the slide of equations on the viewer and his hand was reaching for the crudely constructed controls of the I.T. drive. He pulled a lever, adjusted the controls, and quite suddenly the Geepee ships seemed to fade away. And fading into the place where they had been was a backdrop of great blazing suns that made his eyes ache.

Once again he experienced the unique sensation of falling through the layers of the multiverse.

Rapidly, as he operated the I.T. drive, the suns faded to be replaced by cold vacuum, which was replaced by an agitation of gases heaving about in an unformed state, scarlet and grey. He was phasing quickly through the layers, through universe after universe with only a slight feeling of nausea in his stomach and a fierce determination to reach his destination.

The Geepee ships hadn't followed him.

They had probably decided that their first priority was to aid the human fleet.

He travelled through space as well as time and the separating dimensions, and he was heading back in the direction where, in his home universe, the edge of the galaxy had been. He had all the bearings he needed and, as he moved on one level, he moved through others at reckless speed.

He knew where he was going — but whether he would make it was a question he couldn't answer.

Asquiol of Pompeii watched the battle on his screens with a feeling akin to helplessness. Mordan was conducting the war, needing only basic orders from him.

Am I doing as much as I could? he wondered. *Am I not accepting too complacently what I have discovered?*

It was easy for him to dominate the fleet, for his mind had become at once flexible and strong and his physical presence overawed his fellows. There was a part of him, too, which was not at ease, as if he were a jig-saw complete but for the last piece, and the section that would complete him was just — tantalizingly — out of reach.

Somewhere in the multiverse he felt the piece existed — perhaps another intelligence that he could share his thoughts and experiences with. He was almost certain it was out there, yet what it was and how he would find it he did not know. Without it, his picture of himself was incomplete. He felt that he functioned but could not progress. Had the Originators deliberately done this to him? Or had they made a mistake?

At first he had thought it was the loss of Renark which gave him the sense of incompleteness. But Renark's loss was still there, inside him, kept out of mind as much as possible. No, this was another lack. A lack of what, though?

He bent closer to observe the battle.

The fleet's formation was lost as yet another wave of attackers pounced out of space, their weapons lances of bright energy.

They were not impervious to anti-neutron cannon, but the two forces were fairly matched as far as technology went. There were more of the aliens and they had the double advantage of being in home territory and defending it. This was what primarily worried Asquiol.

But he could do nothing decisive at the moment. He would have to wait.

Again, while Mordan sweated to withstand and retaliate against this fresh attack, Asquiol let his mind and being drop through the layers of the multiverse and contact the alien commanders. If they would not accept peace terms, he strove to arrange a truce.

To his surprise, this suggestion seemed acceptable to them.

There *was* an alternative to open war — one which they would be delighted to negotiate.

That was?

The Game, they said. Play the Game with us — winner takes all.

After he had got some inkling of the Game's nature, Asquiol deliberated momentarily. There were pros and cons …

Finally, he agreed and was soon watching the enemy ships retreating away into the void.

With some trepidation, he informed Mordan of his decision and awaited its outcome. This new development in their struggle with the aliens disturbed Mordan. War he could understand. This, at first, he could not. All psychologists, psychiatrists, physiologists and kindred professionals had been ordered to the huge factory ship which engineers were already converting.

From now on, according to Asquiol, the battle was to be fought from this single ship — and it had no armaments!

Asquiol was unapproachable as he conferred with the alien commanders in his own peculiar way. Every so often he would break off to issue strange orders.

Something about a game. Yet what kind of game, wondered Mordan, required experts in psychology as its players? What was the complicated electronic equipment that technicians were installing in the great converted hold of the factory ship?

"This is our only chance of winning," Asquiol had told him. "A slim one — but if we learn how to play it properly, we have a chance."

Mordan sighed. At least the truce had allowed them time to regroup and assess damage. The damage had been great. Two-thirds of the fleet had been destroyed. Farm ships and factory ships were working at full capacity to supply the rest of the fleet with necessities. But tight rationing had been introduced. The race was subsisting on survival rations. The initial joy of escape was replaced by gloomy desperation.

Adam Roffrey could see his destination.

He slammed the I.T. activator to the "off" position and coasted towards the looming system ahead.

It hung in empty space, the outlines of its planets hazy, following a random progression around a magnificent binary sun.

The legendary system rose larger on his V-screen. The unnatural collection of worlds came closer.

The epic story of Count Renark and Prince Asquiol on their quest to the Sundered Worlds was common lore among the human race. But the story — or, at least, part of it — had had a special significance for Roffrey.

Renark and Asquiol had left two members of their party behind — Willow Kovacs and Paul Talfryn.

Roffrey knew their names. But dominant in his skull was another name — a woman's, the woman he had come to find.

If he did not find her this time, he told himself, then he would have to accept that she was dead. Then he would have to accept his own death also.

Such was the intensity of his obsession.

As he neared the Sundered Worlds he regarded them with curiosity. They had changed. The planets were spaced normally — not equidistantly, as he had thought. And, as far as he could tell, the system had stopped shifting.

Now he remembered part of the story which would fast become a myth among those who had fled their own galaxy. A dog-like race called the Shaarn had attempted to stop the system's course through the dimensions.

Evidently they'd succeeded.

His maps aided him to find Entropium and he cruised into the Shifter's area warily, for he knew enough to expect two kinds of danger — the Thron and the lawless nature of the Shifter itself.

Yet, wary as he was, it was impossible to observe either chaos or enemy as he swept down over Entropium, scanning the planet for the only city that had ever been built there.

He didn't find the city, either.

He found, instead, a place where a city had been. Now it was jagged rubble. He landed his ship on a scattered wasteland of twisted steel and smashed concrete.

Scanning the surrounding ruins, he saw shadowy shapes scuttling through the dark craters and between the shattered buildings. His experience told him nothing about the cause of this catastrophe.

At length, sick at heart, he climbed into space armour, strapped an anti-neutron pistol to his side, descended to the airlock and placed his booted feet on the planet's surface.

A bolt of energy flashed from a crater and spread itself over his force-screen. He staggered back to lean against one of his ship's landing fins, lugging the pistol from its holster.

He did not fire immediately for, like everyone else, he had a certain fear of the destructive effects of the a-n gun.

He saw an alien figure — a dazzling white skin like melted plastic covering a squat skeleton, long legs and short arms, but no head that he could see — appear over the edge of the crater, a long metal tube cradled in its arms and pointing at him.

He fired.

The thing's wailing shriek resounded in his helmet. It absorbed the buzzing stream of anti-neutrons, collapsed, melted and vanished.

"Over here!"

Roffrey turned to see a human figure, all rags and filth, waving to him. He ran towards it.

In a crater which had been turned into a crude fortress by the piles of wreckage surrounding its perimeter, Roffrey found a handful of wretches, the remnants of the human population of Entropium.

The man who had waved had a fleshless head and huge eyes. Dirty, scab-covered skin was drawn tight over his skull. He fingered his emaciated body and eyed Roffrey warily. He said: "We're starving here. Have you got any supplies?"

"What happened?" Roffrey said, feeling sick.

There was desolation everywhere. These human beings had evidently banded together for protection against similar bands of aliens. Evidently, also, only the fittest survived.

The ragged man pointed at the rubble behind him. "This? We don't know. It just hit us..."

"Why didn't you leave here?"

"No ships. Most of them were destroyed."

Roffrey grimaced and said: "Keep me covered while I return to my ship. I'll be back."

A short time later he came stumbling back over the rubble with a box in his hands, his boots slipping and sliding on the uneven ground. They clustered around him greedily as he handed out vitapacks.

Something terrible had happened to the planet — perhaps to the whole system. He had to know what — and why.

Now a woman separated herself from the group squatting over their food. The man with the fleshless head followed her.

She said to Roffrey: "You must be from the home galaxy. How did you get here? — Did they ... find how the Shifter worked?"

"You mean Renark and Asquiol?"

Roffrey looked hard at the woman, but he didn't know her. He noted that she had obviously been beautiful, probably still was under the filth and rags. "They got through. They discovered more than they bargained for here — but they got through. Our whole universe doesn't exist any more. But the race — or the part which left — is still going. Maybe it's wiped out by now. I don't know."

The man with the fleshless head put his arm around the woman. They looked like a pair of animated skeletons and the man's action enhanced the bizarre effect.

"He didn't want you then and he won't now," he said to her.

Roffrey saw tension between them, but couldn't understand why.

She said: "Shut up, Paul. Are Renark and Asquiol safe?"

Roffrey shook his head. "Renark's dead. Asquiol's okay — he's leading the fleet. The Council gave him complete leadership during the emergency." Roffrey felt he could name both of them now. He pointed at the man. "Are you Paul Talfryn?"

Talfryn nodded. He cocked his head towards the woman. She dropped her eyes. "This is Willow Kovacs — my wife. We sort of got married … Asquiol's mentioned us, eh? I suppose he sent you back for us?"

"No."

Willow Kovacs shuddered. Roffrey reflected that she didn't appear to like Talfryn very much: there was a kind of apathetic hatred in her eyes. Probably she regarded Talfryn merely as a protector, if that. But it was no business of his.

"What happened to the rest of the human population?" Roffrey said, concentrating on his own affairs and trying to ignore the sickening feeling of disgust at the sight of such degeneration. "Were they all killed?"

"Did you see anything when you came through the ruins?" Talfryn asked. "Little, scuttling animal shapes, maybe?"

Roffrey had seen them. They had been repulsive, though he didn't know why.

Talfryn said: "All those little creatures were intelligent once. For some reason, the Shifter stopped shifting. There was a long period of absolute madness before she seemed to settle down again. This happened — that happened.

"When the trouble started, the actual forms of human beings and aliens changed, devolving into these. Somebody said it was metabolic pressures combined with time-slips induced by the stop, but I didn't understand it. I'm a scientist — an astro-geographer. Unlicensed, you know …" He seemed to sink into an attitude of detachment and then looked up suddenly. "The city just crumbled. It was horrifying. A lot of people went mad. I suppose Asquiol told you…"

"I've never met Asquiol," Roffrey broke in. "All my information is second-hand. I came particularly to find another person. A woman — she helped Renark with information. Mary the Maze — a mad woman. Know her?"

Talfryn pointed upwards to the streaked sky.

"Dead?" said Roffrey.

"Gone," Talfryn said. "When the city started breaking apart, she took one of the only ships and just spun off into space. She probably killed herself. She was like a zombie, and quite crazy. It was as if some outside pressure moved her. I heard she wanted to get to Roth. That was a crazy thing to want to do, in itself! She took one of the best ships, damn her. A nice one — Mark Seven Hauser."

"She was heading for Roth? Isn't that the really strange planet?"

"As I said, she was crazy to go there. If she *did* get there."

"You think there'd be a chance of her still being alive if she made it?"

"Maybe. Asquiol and Renark obviously survived."

"Thanks for the information." Roffrey turned away.

"Hey!" The skeleton suddenly became animated. "You're not leaving us here! Take us with you — take us back to the fleet, for God's sake!"

Roffrey said: "I'm not going back to the fleet. I'm going to Roth."

"Then take us with you — anywhere's better than here!" Willow's voice was shrill and urgent.

Roffrey paused, deliberating. Then he said: "Okay."

As they neared the ship, something small and scaly scuttled across their path. It was like nothing Roffrey had seen before and he felt he never wanted to see it again. Entropium, when it flourished, had contained the seeds of corruption — and now corruption was dominant, a physical manifestation of a mental disease. It was an unhealthy place, with intelligent species scrabbling and fighting like animals to survive. It was rotten with the sickness that came from a state of mind as much as anything.

He was glad to reach the ship.

As Willow and Talfryn climbed into the airlock, he glanced back at the ruins. His face was rather grim. He helped them aboard and closed the lock.

Now he turned his thoughts to Mary the Maze.

T W E L V E

Roffrey debated his next move, sitting hunched at the controls while he checked the astrochart before him. It didn't tally with the Shifter as it now was, but it would do. He could recognize descriptions of planets even though they had changed their location.

Willow and Talfryn were cleaning up. They were both beginning to look better. The ship itself was hardly tidy. It was not even very clean and there was a smell of the workshop about it — of oil, burnt rubber, dirty plastic and old leather. Roffrey liked it that way.

He scowled then. He *didn't* like company. *I'm getting soft*, he told himself.

Now that he was going to Roth he began to feel nervous at what he might find there.

Talfryn said: "We're ready!"

He activated the ship's normal drive and lifted off. He was tempted to burn the city to rubble as he passed, but he didn't. He got into space with a feeling of relief, heading in a series of flickering hops used for short journeys towards Roth, now hanging the farthest away from the parent binary, as if deliberately set apart from the rest of the system.

Roth, more than any other planet in the Shifter, defied the very logic of the cosmos and existed contrary to all laws. Roth — nicknamed Ragged Ruth, he remembered — still contained the impossible *gaps*. There, two men had become supersane. But Mary, poor Mary who had helped them — she had found only madness there.

Had she gone back to try and lay the ghost that was her insanity? Or had her motives been induced by madness? Perhaps he would find out.

The planet was big now. The screens showed nothing but the monstrous globe with its speckled aura, its shifting light-mist, its black blotches and, worst of all, the *gaps*. The *gaps* which were not so much seen as unseen. Something should be there but human eyes couldn't see it.

Roffrey flung the ship down through Roth's erratically tugging gravisphere, swinging towards the unwelcoming surface which throbbed below like a sea of molten lava, changing and shifting. The seas of hell.

There seemed to be no consistent gravity. His instruments kept registering different findings. He fought to keep the descent as smooth as possible, concentrating on the operation, while Willow and Talfryn gasped and muttered, horrified by the vision.

He frowned, wondering what was familiar about the disturbing world. Then he remembered that the one time he had seen Renark and Asquiol they had possessed a similar quality, impossible to pin down, but as if their bodies had existed on different levels only just invisible to the human eye.

Yet this place was ominous. The men's images had been beautiful.

Ominous!

The word seethed around in his brain. Then, for one brief second, he passed through a warmth, a pleasure, a delight so exquisite yet so short-lived that it was as if he had lived and died in a moment.

He couldn't understand it. He had no time to try as the ship rocked in response to the weirdly unbalanced tug of Roth's gravity. Lasers scanned the unstable landscape as he navigated with desperate skill, gliding low over the flame-mist boiling on the surface, trying without success to peer into the *gaps*, all his instruments operating on full power but few giving him any sensible readings.

Had Mary tried, perhaps like Renark, to find the Originators? Had something driven her back to the world that had turned her mad?

Then he spotted a ship on his screens, a ship surrounded by achingly disturbing light-mist. It was the Mark Seven Hauser. Mary's ship. And his energraph told him that the drive was active. That meant it had only recently landed or else was about to take off. He had to land fast!

He made planet-fall in a hurry, cursing the sudden grip of gravity for which he only just succeeded in compensating as he brought his ship close to the other vessel. His gauntleted fingers stabbed at keys and he got into immediate contact with the Hauser on a tight PV beam.

"Anyone aboard?"

There was no reply.

Both Willow and Talfryn were peering at the screen now, bending over his shoulder.

"This ship seems to have arrived only recently," he said.

It meant nothing to them and he realized that it meant little to him, either. He was pinning his hopes on too thin a circumstance.

He operated the V, scanning as best he could the surrounding territory. Strange images jumped upon the screen, fading as rapidly as they approached. Harsh, craggy, crazy Roth, with its sickness of rock and the horror of the misty, intangible, unnatural *gaps*.

That men could survive here was astounding. Yet evidently they could. Asquiol and Mary had been living evidence. But it was easy to see how they went mad, hard to understand how they kept sane. It was a gaping, raw, boiling, dreadful world, exuding, it seemed, stark malevolence and baleful anger in its constant and turbulent motion.

Mary could easily have disappeared into one of the *gaps* or perished in some nameless way. His lips tightened as he left the screen and opened the spacesuit locker.

"If I need help I'll call you on my suit-phone," he said as he picked up his discarded helmet. "If you need them — suits are here." He went to the airlock's elevator. "I'll keep my suit-phone receiver on. If you see anything — any trace of Mary — let me know. Have the scanners working full-time."

"You're a fool to go out there!" Talfryn said heavily.

"You're a non-participant in this," Roffrey said savagely as he clamped his face-plate. "Don't interfere. If it's obvious that I'm dead, you've got the ship to do what you like with. I've got to see what's in the Hauser."

Now he was in the outer lock. Then he was lowering his body from the ship into a pool of yellow liquid that suddenly changed to shiny rock as he stepped on to it. Something slid and itched beneath his feet.

His lips were dry, the skin of his face seemed cracked and brittle. His eyes kept focusing and unfocusing. But the most disturbing thing of all was the silence. All his instincts told him that the ghastly changes taking place on the surface should make *noise*. But they didn't. This heightened the dreamlike quality of his motion over the shifting surface.

In a moment, his own ship could no longer be seen and he reached the Hauser, noting that the lock was wide open. Both locks were open when he got inside. Gas of some kind swirled through the ship. He went into the cabin and found traces of the pilot having been there recently. There were some figures scribbled on a pad beside the chart-viewer. The equations were incomprehensible — but they were in Mary's writing!

A quick search through the ship told him nothing more. Hastily he pulled himself through the cabin door and down the airlock shaft until he was again on the surface. He peered with difficulty through the shifting flame-mist. It was thoroughly unnerving. But he forced himself through it, blindly searching for a mad woman who could have gone anywhere.

Then two figures emerged out of the mist and, just as suddenly, merged back into it.

He was sure he recognized one of them. He called after them. They didn't reply. He began to follow but lost sight of them.

Then a piercing shout blasted into his suit-phone. "*Asquiol! Oh, Asquiol!*"

He whirled around. It was the voice of Willow Kovacs. Was Asquiol looking for him? Had the fleet been defeated? If so, why had the two men ignored his shout?

"*Asquiol! Come back! It's me, Willow!*"

But Roffrey wanted to find Mary the Maze; he wasn't interested in Asquiol. He began to run, plunging through hallucinations, through shapes that formed silently around him as if to engulf him, through turquoise tunnels, up mauve mountains. In places, gravity was low and he bounded along; in others it became almost impossible to drag his bulk.

Now he entered another low-gravity patch and bounded with bone-jarring suddenness into a heavy one. Painfully he lifted his booted feet, barely able to support his heavy body.

Then a voice — perhaps through his suit-phone, perhaps not. He recognized the voice. His heart leapt.

"*It's warm, warm, warm ... Where now? Here ... but ... Let me go back... Let me...*"

It was Mary's voice.

For a moment he didn't respond to the shock. His mouth was dry, his features petrified. His body froze as he strained to hear the voice again. "Mary — where are you?"

It was as if he were experiencing an awful dream where menace threatened but he was unable to escape, where every step seemed to take every ounce of energy and every scrap of time he possessed.

Again he croaked: "Mary!"

THE SUNDERED WORLDS

But it was not for some minutes that he heard the reply: *"Keep moving! Don't stop. Don't stop!"*

He didn't know whether the words were addressed to him or not, but he thought it best to obey them.

He began to sway and fall down, but he kept moving. It was as if the whole planet were above him and he was like Atlas, slowly crumpling beneath its weight.

He screamed.

Then Willow's voice blasted through: *"Asquiol! Asquiol!"*

What was happening? It was all too confusing. He couldn't grasp ... He felt faint. He looked up and saw several small figures scurrying across a planet he held in his hands. Then he was growing, growing, growing ... scale upon scale...

Again he screamed. A hollow, echoing roar in his ears.

His heart beat a frantic rhythm against his ribcage until his ears became filled with the noise. He panted and struggled, crawling up over the curved surface of the planet, hanging on to it as if by his fingernails.

He was a great giant, larger than the tiny planet — but at the same time he was a flea, crawling through syrup and cotton-wool.

He laughed then in his madness.

He laughed and stopped abruptly, grasping for the threads of sanity and pulling them together. He was standing in a light-gravity patch and things suddenly looked as normal as they could on Roth.

He glanced through a rent in the mist and saw Mary standing there. He ran towards her.

"Mary!"

"Asquiol!"

The woman was Willow Kovacs in a suit — Mary's old suit. He made as if to strike her down, but the look of disappointment on her face stopped him. He pushed past her, changed his mind, came back.

"Willow — Mary's here, I know ..." Suddenly he realized the possible truth. "My God, of course. Time's so twisted and warped we could be seeing anything that's happened at any time in the past — or the future!"

Another figure came stumbling out of the light-mist. It was Talfryn.

"I couldn't contact you from the ship. There's a woman there. She..."

"It's an illusion, man. Get back to the ship!"

"You come with me. It's no illusion. She entered the ship herself!"

"Lead the way back," Roffrey said. Willow remained where she was, refusing to budge. At length they had to lift her, squirming, and carry her back. The ship was only three yards away.

The woman wore a space suit. She was lying on the floor of the cabin. Roffrey bent over her, lifting the face-plate.

"Mary." he said, softly. "Mary — thank God!"

The eyes opened, the big soft eyes that had once held intelligence. For a short time intelligence was there — a look of incredible awareness. Then it faded and she formed her lips to say something, but they twisted downwards into an idiot grin and she subsided into a blankeyed daze.

He got up wearily, his body bowed. He made a gesture with his left hand. "Willow, help her out of the suit. We'll get her into a bunk."

Willow looked at him with hatred: "Asquiol's out there... You stopped me."

Talfryn said: "Even if he was he wouldn't want you. You keep pining for him, wishing you'd followed him earlier. Now it's too late. It's no good, Willow, you've lost him forever!"

"Once he sees me he'll take me back. He loved me!"

Roffrey said impatiently to Talfryn: "You'd better help me, then."

Talfryn nodded. They began getting Mary out of the suit.

"Willow," said Roffrey as they worked, "Asquiol wasn't there — not now. You saw something that probably happened months ago. The other man was Renark — and Renark's dead? You understand?"

"I saw him. He heard me call him!"

"Maybe. I don't know. Don't worry, Willow. We're going back to the fleet if we can — if it still exists. You'll see him then."

Talfryn wrenched off a piece of space-armour from Mary's body with a savage movement. His teeth were clenched but he said nothing.

"You're going back to the fleet? But you said ..." Willow was disconcerted. Roffrey noted a peculiar look, a mixture of eagerness and introspection.

"Mary needs treatment. The only place she'll get it is back there. So that's where I'm going. That should suit you."

"It does," she said. "Yes, it does."

He went over to the ports and closed their shutters so they couldn't see Roth's surface. It felt a little safer.

Talfryn said suddenly: "I get it, Willow. You've made it plain. I won't be bothering you from now on.

"You'd better not." She turned on Roffrey. "And that goes for you, too, for any man."

Roffrey smiled at Mary, who sat drooling and crooning in her bunk. He winked at her. "You're my type, Mary," he said genially.

"That's cruel," Willow said sharply.

"That's my wife." Roffrey smiled, and then Willow saw at least a trace of what the smiling eyes and grin hid.

She turned away.

"Let's get going," said Roffrey briskly. Now that he had made up his mind, he wanted to waste no time returning to the fleet.

He couldn't guess how long Mary had been on Roth. Maybe only a few minutes of real time. Maybe a hundred years of Roth's time. He did not let himself dwell on this, just as he refused to consider the extent of her mental derangement. The psychiatrists in the fleet might soon be supplying him with all the information they possibly could. He was prepared to wait and see.

He went over to her. She shrank away from him, muttering and crooning, her big eyes wider than ever. Very gently he made her lie down in the bunk and strapped her into its safety harness. It pained him that she didn't recognize him, but he was still smiling and humming a little tune to himself as he climbed into the pilot's seat, heaved back a lever, adjusted a couple of dials, flipped a series of switches and soon the drone of the drive was drowning his own humming.

Then, in a flicker, they were off into deep space and heading away from the Sundered Worlds into the depths of matterless void. It was such an easy lift-off, Roffrey felt, that it was almost as if a friendly hand had given them a push from behind...

It was with a sense of inevitability that he began the descent through the dimension layers, heading back to the space-time in which he'd left the fleet of mankind.

Meanwhile, human brains were jarred and jumbled as they strove to master the Game. Minds broke. Nerves snapped. But, while scarcely understanding what it was about, Mordan forced his team to continue, convinced that humanity's chance of survival depended on winning...

Whistling sounds were the first impressions Roffrey received as he phased the ship out of the Shifter's space-time and into the next level.

Space around them suddenly became bright with black and yellow stars, the not-quite-familiar whirl of a spiral galaxy soaring outwards in a wild sprawl of suns. The whistling was replaced by a dreadful moaning which pervaded the ship and made speech impossible.

Roffrey was intent on the new instruments. The little experience he had of the Intercontinua-Travelling device had shown him that the ship could easily slip back through the space-time layers and become totally lost.

The instruments hadn't been designed for wide travelling of this kind and Roffrey knew it, but each separate universe in the multiverse had its particular coordinates, and the instruments, crude as they were, could differentiate between them. On the main V-screen Roffrey had a chart which would recognize the universe into which the human race had fled. But the journey could be dangerous, perhaps impossible.

And then the noise increased to become painful, no longer a monotone but a pulsating, nerve-racking whine. Roffrey phased into the next layer.

The galaxy ahead was a seething inferno of unformed matter, hazy, bright, full of archetypal colour — reds, whites, blacks, yellows — pouring about in slow disorder. This was a universe in a state of either birth or dissolution.

There was near-silence as Roffrey phased out of this continuum and into the next. His whistling, which he had been doing all the while, was light and cheerful. Then he heard Mary's groans and he stopped.

Now they were in the centre of a galaxy.

Massed stars lay in all directions. He stared at them in wonder, noticing how, with every phase, the matter, filling the space around them, seemed to change its position as well as its nature.

Then the stars were gone and he was passing through a turbulent mass of dark gas forming into horrible half-recognizable shapes which sickened him so that he could no longer look but had to concentrate on his instruments.

What he read there depressed and shocked him!

He was off course.

He chewed at his moustache, debating what to do. He didn't mention it to the others. The co-ordinates corresponded to those on the chart above the screen.

As far as the ship's instruments were concerned, they were in the space-time occupied by Asquiol and the fleet!

Yet it was totally different from what he remembered. Gas swirled in it and he could not see the stars of the galaxy.

Had the fleet been completely wiped out?

There was no other explanation.

Then he cursed. The black gas suddenly became alive, a roaring and monstrous beast, many-tendrilled, dark blue, flame-eyed, malevolent. Willow and Talfryn gasped behind him as they saw it loom on the screen. Mary began shrieking, the sounds filled the cabin. The ship was heading straight towards the monster. But how could something like this exist in the near-vacuum of space?

Roffrey didn't have time for theories. He broke the energy seals of his anti-neutron cannon as an acrid smell filled the cabin and the beast rapidly changed from deep blue to startling yellow.

The guns swung on the beast and Roffrey stabbed the firing buttons, then backed the ship away savagely.

The ship shuddered as the guns sent a deadly stream of anti-neutrons towards the monster. Meanwhile, the beast seemed, impossibly, to be absorbing the beams and new heads had grown on its shoulders — disgusting, half-human faces gibbering and yelling, and they could *hear* the cries! Roffrey felt and tasted bile in his throat.

Talfryn was now bending over him, staring at the screen. "What is it?" he shouted above Mary's screams.

"How the hell should I know?" Roffrey said viciously. He righted the ship's backward velocity, stabbed the cannon buttons again. He heaved his big body round in the control seat and said: "Make yourself useful, Talfryn. See if the co-ordinates on that chart tally absolutely with those on this screen."

The monster lurched through the dark mist towards the little launch, its heads drooling and grinning. There wasn't time to wonder what it was, how it existed.

Roffrey aimed at its main head. He began to depress the firing button.

Then it had gone.

There were a few wisps of gas in the dark, sharp space of the galaxy Roffrey immediately recognized.

They were in the right galaxy!

But now a new danger threatened. Replacing the monster was a squadron of fast, spherical vessels — those he had glimpsed just before leaving the fleet. Were they the victors, cleaning up the last of the race? They were passing on the zenith-south flank of Roffrey's battered launch. He trailed the ship round on a tight swing so that he was now directly facing the oncoming alien ships.

The launch was responding well, but the cabin shook and rattled as he stood his vessel on a column of boiling black fire and glided away from the round ships, having shot a tremendous burst towards them. Something was disturbing him. He found it hard to concentrate properly. Talfryn was obviously having the same trouble. A quick look behind him showed Mary's gaping mouth as she screamed and screamed.

Talfryn clung instinctively to the hand-grip and shouted: "The co-ordinates tally perfectly."

"That's news?" Roffrey said lightly.

Willow had joined Mary and was attempting to comfort her. Mary was rigid, staring ahead of her with fixed, glazed eyes. It was as if she could see something that was invisible to the others. Her screams rang on, a horrible ululation in the confined cabin.

Willow peered through the bad light at the two men half-silhouetted up ahead, the one in the control seat, the other standing over him, their dark clothes picked out against the spluttering brightness of the screens and instruments, their faces in shadow, their hands white on the controls.

The lighting was very dim as all power-sources were drained to provide the ship with maximum power.

She looked out of the nearest port. Space was blank — suddenly colourless. She looked back at the men and her vision was engulfed by a horrible disharmony of colour and noise, sense impressions of all kinds — obscene, primeval, terrible — throwing her mind into disorder so that she found it almost impossible to differentiate between her five senses.

Then, when she had completely lost her ability to tell whether she was smelling or hearing a colour, her head was filled with a single impression that combined as one thing to her sense. Smell, sight, touch, sound and taste were all there, but the combination produced a unified sense that all were blood red.

She thought she was dead.

Roffrey shouted and the sound hung alone for a moment before he saw it merge into the blood red disharmony. He felt madness approach and then recede — approach and recede, like a horrible tide, for with each sweep it came a little closer. His body vibrated with the tension, sending out clouds of blood red trailers through the cabin which he saw — no, he heard it, as the note of a muted trumpet. It horrified him, for now something else was creeping through, something coming up from his oldest memories, something of which he hadn't even been aware.

He was immersed in self-loathing, self-pity, suddenly knowing what a debased thing he was...

But there was something — he didn't know what — aiding him in spite of his confusion, aiding him to cling to his personal being, to sweat out the tumble of disordered impressions and terrible thoughts, and to hit back.

He hit back!

Mary was still quivering in Willow's arms — taut, tense, no longer screaming.

The waves began to peter out.

Willow struck, too. Struck back at whatever it was that was doing this to them.

The waves faded and, slowly, their senses were restored to normal.

Suddenly Mary's body relaxed. She had passed out. Talfryn was slumped on the floor and Roffrey was hunched in the control seat, growling.

He peered through the rapidly fading pulsations and saw with satisfaction that the anti-neutrons had done their job, though he hadn't been able to direct them properly, nor had he been fully conscious of directing them.

Some of the ships were making off, others were warped lumps of metal spinning aimlessly in the void. He began whistling to himself as he adjusted the controls. The whistling died as he said: "You all right back there?"

Willow said: "What do you think, superman? Mary and Paul have passed out. Mary took it worse than any of us — she seemed to bear the brunt of it. What was it, do you think?"

"I don't know. Maybe we'll get our answers soon."

"Why?"

"I've sighted our fleet!"

"Thank God," said Willow, and she began to tremble. She dared not anticipate her reunion with Asquiol.

Roffrey headed for the fleet — going back as fast as he'd left.

T H I R T E E N

The fleet had been badly depleted since he left it. It was still big — a sprawling collection of ships, stretching mile upon mile in all directions and resembling nothing so much as a vast scrap-yard, guarded by the cruising Geepee battlewagons.

In the centre of the fleet, a little distance from Asquiol's battered cruiser (easily recognized by its slightly out-of-focus outline) was a huge factory ship with the letter "G" emblazoned on its side. This puzzled Roffrey.

Then the Geepee patrol contacted him.

To his astonishment, he had the pleasure of being received almost cordially. They began to guide him into a position fairly close to the factory ship with the "G" on its side.

While Roffrey was getting his ship into line, a man in the loose, unmilitary garb which was identical save for rank insignia with all other Geepee uniforms appeared on the PV screen, his stern, bloodhound face puzzled. The large band on his left sleeve also bore a letter "G".

"Hello, Mordan," Roffrey said with cheerful defiance.

Willow wondered at the vitality and control which Roffrey must possess in order to seem suddenly so relaxed and untroubled.

Mordan smiled ironically. "Good morning. So you decided to return and help us after all. Where have you been?"

"I've been on a mercy trip rescuing survivors from the Shifter," Roffrey said virtuously.

"I don't believe you," Mordan said candidly. "But I don't care — you've just done something nobody thought was possible. As soon as we assemble our data I'll be getting in touch with you again. We need all the help we can get in this business — even yours. We're up against it, Roffrey. We're damn near finished." He broke off as if to pull himself together. "Now, if you are carrying extra passengers, you'd better register them with the appropriate authorities." He switched out.

"What did all that mean?" said Talfryn.

"I don't know," Roffrey said, "but we may find out soon. Mordan obviously knows something. The fleet's evidently suffered from attacks such as we experienced. Yet there is more order now. The battle, or whatever it is, seems to have taken a different course."

Willow Kovacs cradled Mary Roffrey's head in her arm and gently wiped a trickle of saliva from the mad woman's mouth. Her own heart was beating swiftly and her stomach seemed contracted, her arms and legs weak. She was very frightened now at the prospect of reunion with Asquiol.

Roffrey locked the ship's controls and came aft, staring down at the two women with a light smile on his sensuous, bearded mouth. He began stripping off his suit and the overalls beneath, revealing a plain quilted jacket of maroon plastileather and grubby white trousers tucked into soft leather knee-boots. "How's Mary?"

"I don't know," Willow said. "She's obviously not sane ... Yet there's a different quality about her insanity. Something I can't pin down."

"A doctor maybe will help," Roffrey said. He patted Willow's shoulder. "Contact the admin ship will you, Talfryn? Send out a general call till you can get it."

"Okay," Talfryn said.

Worst of all, Roffrey thought as he stared down at his wife, had been the all-pervading red — blood red. It had been unmistakable as blood. Why had it affected him so badly? What had it done to Mary?

He scratched the back of his neck. He hadn't slept since he left the fleet. He was full of stimulants, but he felt the need for some natural sleep. Maybe later.

When Talfryn had contacted the Registration Ship, which had as its job the classification of all members of the fleet so that it would be easier to administer the survivors if they at last made planet-fall, they were told that an official would be sent over in a short while.

Roffrey said: "We need a psychiatrist of some sort, quickly. Can you help?"

"Try a hospital ship — though it's unlikely you'll be lucky."

He tried a hospital ship. The doctor in charge wasn't helpful.

"No, I'm afraid you won't get a psychiatrist for your wife. If you need medical treatment we'll put her on our list. We're overworked. It's impossible to deal with all the casualties…"

"But you've got to help her!" Roffrey bellowed.

The doctor didn't argue. He just switched out.

Roffrey, bewildered by this, swung round in his chair. Willow and Talfryn were discussing the earlier conflict with the alien ships.

"They must be hard pushed," Roffrey cursed. "But I'm going to get help for Mary."

"What about those hallucinations we had back there?" Talfryn said. "What caused them?"

"It's my guess we were experiencing the force of one of their weapons," Roffrey replied. "Maybe what happened to us on Roth made us more susceptible to hallucination."

"A weapon — yes, it could be."

The communicator buzzed. Talfryn went to it.

"Registration," said a jaunty voice. "Mind if I come aboard?"

He was a pale and perky midget with genial eyes and a very neat appearance. His gig clamped against Roffrey's airlock and he came bustling through with a case of papers under his arm.

"You would be Captain Adam Roffrey," he lisped, staring up at the black-bearded giant.

Roffrey stared down at him, half in wonder. "I would be."

"Good. And you embarked with the rest of the human race roughly two weeks ago — relative time, that is. I don't know how long it was in your time, since it is not always possible to leave and return from one dimension to another and keep the time flow the same — kindly remember that."

"I'll try," said Roffrey, wondering if there was a question there.

"And these three are…?"

"Miss Willow Kovacs, formerly of Migaa…"

The midget scribbled in his notebook, looking prim at the mention of the planet Migaa. It had possessed something of a reputation in the home galaxy.

Willow gave the rest of her data. Talfryn gave his.

"And the other lady?" the little official asked.

"My wife — Doctor Mary Roffrey, born on Earth, née Ishenko;

anthropologist; disappeared from Golund on the Rim in 457 Galactic General Time, reappeared from Shifter System a short while ago. The Geepees will have all her details prior to her disappearance. I gave them to the police when she disappeared. As usual, they did nothing."

The midget frowned, then darted a look at Mary. "State of health?"

"Insane," said Roffrey, quietly.

"Curable or otherwise?"

"Curable!" said Roffrey. The word was cold as flint.

The tiny official completed his notes, thanked them all and was about to leave when Roffrey said:

"Just a minute. Could you fill me in on what's happened to the fleet since I left?"

"As long as we keep it brief, I'd be pleased to. Remember, I'm a busy little man!" He giggled.

"Just before we got here we had a tussle with some alien ships, experienced hallucinations, and so on. Do you know what that was?"

"No wonder the lady is insane! For untrained people to withstand the pressure, it's amazing! Wait till I tell my colleagues! You're heroes! You survived a wild round!"

"Bully for us. What happened?"

"Well, I'm only a petty official — they don't come much pettier than me — but from what I've *gathered*, you had a "wild round." That is," he explained quickly, "anyone straying beyond the confines of the fleet is attacked by the aliens and has to play a wild round, as we call it — one that isn't scheduled to be played by the Gamblers. We're not really supposed to do that."

"But what *is* this Game?"

"I'm not sure. Ordinary people don't play the Game — only the Gamblers in the Game Ship. That's the one with the big "G" on it. It isn't the sort of game I'd like to play. We call it the Blood Red Game because of the habit they have of confusing our senses so that everything seems to be the colour of blood. Psychologists and other adepts play it and they are called Gamblers..."

"How often is it played?"

"All the time, really. No wonder I'm a bundle of nerves. We all are. Citizens' rights have been waived, food supplies reduced ... We're having a pause just at the moment, but it won't last long. Probably they're recovering from your little victory."

"Who'd know details about this Game?"

"Asquiol, of course, but it's almost impossible to see him. The nearest people ever get is to his airlock, and then only rarely. You might try Mordan, though he's not too approachable, either. Mr High and Mighty — he's worse than Asquiol in some ways."

"Mordan seems interested enough to tell us already," Roffrey nodded. "But I've got to speak to Asquiol on another matter, so I might as well try to combine them. Thanks."

"A pleasure," the midget enthused.

When he had gone, Roffrey went to the communicator and tried to contact Asquiol's ship. He had to get by nearly a dozen officials before he made contact.

"Adam Roffrey here, just in from the Shifter. Can I come to your ship?"

He received a curt acceptance. There had been no picture.

"Will you take me with you?" Willow asked. "He'll be surprised. I've been waiting a long, long time for this. He predicted we might meet again, and he was right."

"Of course," Roffrey agreed. He looked at Talfryn. "He was a friend of yours, too. Want to come?"

Talfryn shook his head. "I'll stay here and try to find out a bit more about what's going on here." He took a long, almost theatrical look at Willow and then turned away. "See you."

Roffrey said: "Just as you like." He went to the medical chest and took out a hypodermic and a bottle of sedative, filled the hypo and pumped the stuff into Mary's arm.

Then he and Willow left his launch and, by means of personal power units, made their way to Asquiol's ship.

The airlock was open, ready for them, and it closed behind them as they entered. The inner lock, however, did not open.

Instead, they saw the light of an internal viewer blink on as they waited and they heard a brooding voice — a polite, faraway voice that seemed to carry peculiar echoes which their ears could not quite catch.

"Asquiol speaking. How may I help you?"

Willow, masked in her space-suit, remained silent.

"I'm Adam Roffrey, just in from the Shifter System with three passengers."

"Yes?" Asquiol's acknowledgement bore no trace of interest.

"One of them is my wife — you know her as Mary the Maze. She helped Renark in the Shifter." Roffrey paused. "She sent you to Roth."

"I am grateful to her, though we didn't meet."

"I've tried to contact a psychiatrist in the fleet. I haven't succeeded." Roffrey kept his voice level. "I don't know where they all are, but my wife's condition is desperate. Can you help?"

"They are all playing the Game. I am sorry. Grateful as I am to your wife, the first priority is to the race. We cannot release a psychiatrist."

Roffrey was shocked. He had expected some response at least. "Not even to give me advice how to help her?"

"No. You must do what you can for her yourself. Perhaps a medical man will be able to give you certain kinds of help."

Roffrey turned disgustedly back towards the outer lock. He stopped as Asquiol's voice came again: "I suggest you contact Mordan as soon as you can."

The voice cut off.

Willow spoke. She felt as if she had died and the word was the last she would ever utter.

"*Asquiol!*"

At length, they returned to Roffrey's ship.

Mary was sleeping peacefully under the sedative but Talfryn had disappeared. They did not bother to wonder where he had gone. They sat by Mary's bunk, both of them depressed, their thoughts turned inward.

"He's changed," Willow said flatly.

Roffrey grunted.

"He doesn't sound human any longer," she said. "There's no way of appealing to him. He doesn't seem to care about the approval of the rest of us. His loyalty to these mysterious creatures he contacted seems greater than his loyalty to his friends — or the rest of mankind, for that matter."

Roffrey stared down at Mary. "He doesn't care about anything except this "mission" he has. Everything is being sacrificed and subordinated to that one aim. I don't even know how valid it is. If I did I might be able to argue with him!"

"Perhaps Paul could talk to him. I got scared. I meant to tell him who I was. I might be able to later."

"Save it. I'll see what Mordan wants with me first."

Roffrey moved over to his control panel and operated the screen. "Mordan?"

"Mordan here." The Gee-Councillor's face appeared on the screen. He seemed disconcerted when he saw Roffrey.

"I was just going to contact you. You and Talfryn have been enlisted as Gamblers — subject to preliminary tests."

"What the hell, Mordan? I'm not interested. Tell Talfryn about it. I've got a sick wife to think about."

"Talfryn's already here." Mordan's face was serious. "This is important — though it may not look like it to you. There's a war to the death on and we're up against it. I'm directly responsible to Asquiol for enlisting any men I think will help us win. You've given us a great deal of trouble already. I'm empowered to kill anyone liable to disrupt our security. Come over to the Game Ship — and come fast! If you refuse we'll bring you over forcibly. Clear?"

Roffrey switched out without answering.

Defiantly, he waited by Mary's bed. She was beginning to show signs of improving, physically, but how her mind would be when she came out of the drugged sleep he didn't know.

Later, two Geepees demanded entry. Their launch was clamped fast against his. They threatened to hole his ship and enter that way if they had to. He opened the airlocks and let them in.

"What can one extra hand do?" he said.

One of them replied: "Any man who can hold off an enemy attack virtually single-handed is needed in the Game Ship. That's all we know."

"But I didn't…" Roffrey stopped himself. He was losing his grip.

The Geepee said with false impatience: "You may not have realized it, Captain Roffrey, but you did something a while ago that was impossible. You held out under the combined attack, mental and physical, of ten enemy ships. Most people couldn't have taken an attack from even one!"

The other Geepee drawled: "That means something. Look at it this way. We're damn near beaten now. We took a hell of a lambasting during the initial alien attacks. We're the last survivors of the human race and we've got to stay together, work for the common good. That's the only way you'll look after your wife in the long run. Don't you see that?"

Roffrey was still not convinced. He was a stubborn man. There was an atavistic impulse in him which had always kept him away from the herd, and outside the law, relying entirely on his own initiative and wits. But he was also an intelligent man, so he nodded slightly and said: "Very well — I'll speak to Mordan anyway. Then he turned to Willow. "Willow, if Mary shows any sign of getting worse, let me know."

"Of course, Adam."

"You'll stay with her — make sure she's all right?"

She looked into his face. "Naturally. But when she's under the sedative there's something else I've got to do."

"Yes. I understand."

He shrugged at the Geepees, who turned and led him through the airlock.

F O U R T E E N

The Game Ship was bigger than an old battlewagon, even more functional-looking, a little barer of comforts. Yet it did not seem prepared for battle. There was an atmosphere of hushed silence aboard and their boots clanged loudly along the corridor which led to Mordan's cabin.

A sign on the door read: *Deputy Game Master Mordan. Strictly Private.* The letters were heavy black on the white door.

The Geepee accompanying Roffrey knocked on the door.

"Enter!"

They went through into a cabin cluttered with instruments.

There were some Roffrey recognized: an encephalograph, an optigraph-projector — machines for measuring the power of the brain, equipment for testing visualizing capacity, for measuring I.Q. potential, and so on.

Talfryn was sitting in a comfortable chair on the other side of Mordan's desk. Both men had their hands clenched before them — Talfryn's in his lap, Mordan's stretched out across the empty desk.

"Sit down, Roffrey," said Mordan. He made no reference to Roffrey's defiance of orders. He seemed perfectly controlled. Perhaps over-controlled, thought Roffrey. For a moment he sympathized — wasn't that his own condition?

He sat down as the Geepee guard left. "Okay," he said curtly. "Get on with it."

"I've been explaining to Talfryn how important you both are to this project," Mordan said crisply. "Are you prepared to go along with us on the first stage of our tests?"

"Yes." He was almost responding to the decisive mood.

"Good. We've got to find out exactly what qualities you possessed which made defeat of that alien fleet possible. There is a chance, of course, that you were lucky, or that being unprepared for the sense-impression attack on you and having no understanding of its origin, you were psychologically better prepared to meet the attack. We'll know the answers later. Let me recap on recent events first."

Mordan spoke rapidly: "As you know, we entered this universe several weeks ago and encountered its inhabitants shortly after entry. These people are non-human, as might be expected, and regard us as invaders. That's fair enough, since we should think the same in their position. But they made no attempt to assess our potential strength, to parley or order us away. They attacked. We have no idea even what they look like, these aliens. You saw how quickly they had mobilized an attack on our fleet, well before we had a chance to talk and tell them why we are here."

"What happened after the first battle — the one I saw?"

"There were several others. We lost a lot of ships of all kinds. Finally, Asquiol contacted them by his own methods, and intimated that we were quite prepared to settle on planets unsuitable for them and live in friendly co-operation with them. But they wouldn't accept this. However, they came up with an alternative to open warfare." He sighed and waved his hand to indicate the massed equipment.

"We did not reckon with the predominant society existing here. It is based on a Code of Behaviour which we find, in parts, very difficult to grasp.

"In our terms it means that the status of a particular individual or group is decided by its ability to play a warlike game which has been played in this galaxy for centuries. We call it the Blood Red Game, since one of their prime "weapons" is the ability to addle our sense-impressions so that we get a total sensory experience of the colour red. You already know this, I believe."

Roffrey agreed. "But what, apart from confusing us, is it meant to do? And how does it work?"

"We believe that the aliens have come to rely, when disputes break out among themselves, on more subtle weapons than energy-cannon or anything similar. If we wished, we might continue to use our familiar weapons to fight them, as we did at first. But we should have only a slight chance of winning.

Their weapons make you better than dead, in their view. They turn you insane. If you were dead you'd be out of the way. But since you're alive but useless as a fighter, you drain our resources and slow us down in many ways. But that's only part of it. There are rigid, complicated rules which we are having to learn as we go along."

"What are the stakes?" Roffrey asked.

"If we win so many rounds of the Game without relying on our ordinary armaments, the aliens will concede us the right to rule, as absolute monarchs, their galaxy! Big stakes, Captain Roffrey. We lose our lives, they lose their power."

"They must be confident of winning."

"Not according to Asquiol. The fact that they are winning at the moment is obvious, but their love of playing this Game is so ingrained that they welcome any new variety. You see, both sides have got to do more than simply play the Game, they have the added difficulty of not understanding the opponent's capabilities, susceptibilities, psychology and so forth. In that, we're even. In other things, such as experience of playing the Game, they have the advantage."

"Where do we come into this?"

"We're hoping that you are the aces we need in order to win. Your ship was the only human ship which has ever succeeded in beating the fantastic odds. Somehow, you have something we need to beat the aliens!"

"And you don't know what it is?"

"Right."

"Do we possess it jointly — or does only one of us possess this protective "shield-attack" quality, whatever it is?"

"We're going to find that out, Captain Roffrey. That's why we're testing you both. Although you were actually at the controls of your ship, Talfryn, I understand, was beside you."

Talfryn spoke slowly: "What we have to seek, I gather, is a *moral* advantage over the aliens. It is not a question of numbers but prestige. If we win, we gain sufficient status for them to accept our dominance. If we lose ... what?"

"If we lose, we'll be beyond caring. Our supplies are so short we can't risk phasing into a new universe at this late stage." Mordan turned his attention back to Roffrey. "Do you see that, captain? Your wife is only one of a few victims of insanity in the fleet at the moment. But if we don't win the Game, we'll all be mad — or dead."

Roffrey understood the logic. But he was still suspicious of it.

"Let's get these tests over with," he said. "Then maybe we'll know where we're going. I'll make up my mind afterwards."

Mordan tightened his lips, nodding a trifle. "As you like," he said. He spoke towards his desk. "Ask the testing team to come here."

Two men and a woman entered Mordan's cluttered cabin.

Mordan stood up to introduce them. "This is Professor Selinsky," he said.

The tallest of the group detached himself and walked over to Roffrey and Talfryn. He stretched out his fat hand and smiled warmly. "Glad you're here. It looks as if you and your friend may be able to help us out of our present difficulties." He shook hands with them and said: "These are my assistants. Doctor Zung" — a small, gloomy man of Mongolian appearance — "and Doctor Mann" — a young, blonde-headed woman who looked like an adventure-fiction heroine.

"I've heard of you, professor," said Talfryn. "You used to hold the Chair of Psychedelics at Earth."

"That's right," Selinsky nodded. Then he said: "We'll give you an ordinary test with the electro-encephalograph first. Then we'll put you to sleep and see if we can get at the subconscious. You're prepared to accept all our tests, I presume." He looked at Mordan, who made no reply.

Roffrey said: "Yes. As long as it doesn't involve brainwashing."

Selinsky said sternly: "This is the fifth century, you know — not the fifth century pre-war."

"I thought Asquiol's and Mordan's motto had become 'Needs Must When The Devil Drives'," Roffrey said as he sat in the seat which Doctor Zung had prepared for him.

But the reference made no impression on Mordan who had probably never heard it. Roffrey was given to obscure quotations — it was all part of his atavistic outlook. Mary had once accused him of being deliberately obscure in his references, of reading old books merely in order to pick up unfamiliar quotations to fling at people he despised or disliked. He had agreed. Part of her attraction, he had added, was that she, at least, knew what he was talking about.

A small, glass-alloy helmet was now being fitted over his scalp. He hated such devices. He hated it all. As soon as this is over, he promised himself, I'll show them what independence really means.

Such thoughts and emotions gave the scientists some interesting, if hardly usable, findings.

Professor Selinsky appeared calm as he checked over the material so far gained from the sleeping men. "All this will require careful analysis, of course," he said. Then he shrugged his shoulders.

"What have you found out?" Mordan said.

"Frankly, I can't find any clue at first sight as to what they've got that people we're using haven't already got. They're both intelligent — Roffrey quite superlatively so, but there's only a grain of something out of the ordinary. Naturally, this quality would be subtle — we expected that — but Roffrey isn't the only loner in the human race and he isn't the only one with a high I.Q." He sighed.

"But their memories for sensory-experiences are very good," Doctor Mann said eagerly. "In any event they will help swell the Gambling strength."

"A poor second," said Zung disgustedly as he uncoupled electrodes and neatly placed his personal equipment in its cases. "I'll agree that we need all the Gamblers we can recruit — but these men were going to give us the answer to the problem of defeating the aliens. That's what we hoped, didn't we, professor?"

Selinsky said: "This project is wearing us all down, Zung. There's not a scrap of reason for your defeatist tone. We have a lot of work to do before we can analyze our findings. Meanwhile" — he turned to Mordan who had been sitting in his chair with a look of studied indifference on his seamed, bloodhound's face — "I suggest we put these men on our regular strength. No need to waste them while we study their results. Let them be trained."

"You're sure they'll work all right with the rest?" Mordan said, getting up.

"Why shouldn't they?" Selinsky pointed his thumb towards the door. "You know what the atmosphere in there's like, with O'Hara and everything… None of them are what you would call 'normal'. Our Gamblers are all neurotics these days, by definition. Normal people couldn't stand the strain — normal people couldn't hit back. We count on unusual physiological and psychological patterns to play the Game."

"I trust Talfryn," Mordan said, "he's much more susceptible to persuasion. But Roffrey's a born troublemaker. I know — I've dealt with him more than once."

"Give him something important to handle, in that case." Selinsky swung the arm of the optigraph away from Roffrey's chair. The man stirred but didn't wake. "He's the kind who needs to be kept active — who needs to feel that every action he makes is personally inspired."

"There never was such a thing," said Mordan, walking over and staring down at his old enemy.

"Then don't tell him." Selinsky smiled faintly. "It's egocentricity of that order which has pushed humanity up the scale. Renark and Asquiol were the same — they may sometimes have the wrong information, but they get better results than we do."

"Of a kind," Mordan agreed reluctantly.

"It's the kind we need right now," Selinsky told him as he and his assistants bustled out of the cabin. "We'll send a couple of attendants to take care of them."

"You'll need the whole damn police force to take care of Roffrey once he starts getting stubborn," Mordan said fatalistically. He liked Roffrey, but he knew Roffrey didn't like him. He'd come to the somewhat comforting conclusion that Roffrey didn't really like anyone — apart from his wife. It was a great pity that he'd found her, Mordan reflected.

Selinsky and his assistants pored over their findings. Mann, although a good and clever scientist, was beginning to tire of the routine work. As they paused for coffee, she said to Selinsky: "Something occurred to me, professor, which may mean nothing, but it's worth throwing out for discussion, I think."

Selinsky, who disapproved of Mann's weakness for theorizing while on the job, said impatiently: "Which is?"

"Well, in the history we got from records, both Talfryn and Roffrey were on that planet they call Roth — in the Sundered Worlds — the Lattice Planet. Parts of it exist in different continua, rather like Asquiol is supposed to do. Could this planet have exerted some kind of influence on them? Or perhaps if they stood the test of staying sane on Roth — it turned Roffrey's wife mad, remember — they are therefore better fitted for fighting the aliens?"

Selinsky drained his coffee cup and ran a finger across his wet lips. "There may be something there," he said. "Look, I'll tell you what. Work something out properly, in your spare time, and show me your ideas in a report."

"Spare time!" Mann said explosively, though she was pleased at Selinsky's encouragement — a rare thing in itself.

"Well, you can't sleep *all* of those six hours," said Zung quietly, grinning to himself as he went back to his work.

Willow Kovacs felt more resigned now. Roffrey had been away too long for there to be much chance of his coming back soon. She filled the hypo and gave Mary another sedative, but she didn't, after all, take one herself. In this calmer frame of mind her thoughts had again turned to Asquiol. She must contact him, she felt. At least she would have a clearer idea of how to act after she had seen him — whatever happened.

She experienced some difficulty in getting Roffrey's communications equipment to work, but finally she contacted Mordan.

The Gee-Councillor's sagging face appeared on the screen. He was hunched over his desk apparently doing nothing. He looked incredibly tired. Willow decided he must be keeping himself awake with stimulants.

He gave her a nod of recognition and said: "Kovacs, if you re worried about Roffrey and Talfryn, there's no need. They have been recruited as Gamblers and will no doubt be getting in touch with you during a rest period."

"Thanks," she said, "but there was something else."

"How important is it, Kovacs? You understand that I'm very…"

"I wish to contact Asquiol directly."

"That's impossible now. And, anyway, you wouldn't find it desirable if you realized what he looks like. What do you want to say to him?"

"I can't deal through someone else — it's a purely personal matter."

"Personal? I remember — you had some emotional relationship…"

"We were very close on Migaa and on the Shifter worlds. I'm sure he would want to see me." She didn't sound as if she particularly believed her own words.

"Next time I report to him I'll pass your message on. That's all I can do, I'm afraid." Mordan stared curiously at her but said nothing more.

"Will he contact me if he gets your message?"

"If he wants to that's exactly what he will do. I'll tell him what you've said — I promise."

The screen shimmered and was empty again. Willow turned it off and walked slowly back to where Mary was sleeping.

"What's going to happen to you in all this?" she said.

There was in Willow a large capacity for sympathy with those in distress. Even now, with troubles of her own which she hadn't counted on before she'd reached the fleet, she could turn her attention to Mary.

But what had at first been a detached emotion of sympathy such as she could feel towards anyone in an unpleasant predicament was fast running into a less healthy feeling. She was beginning to sense a kinship with Mary. They were both very lonely women — the one lacking any contact with her fellows, trapped inside her disturbed and jumbled mind, veering between near-sanity and complete madness; the other with a growing conviction that, in her moment of need, she had been deserted — not only by Asquiol, but by Talfryn and Roffrey too.

She sat by the screen, waiting for Asquiol to contact her. She sat stiffly. The cabin was silent, as silent as the space through which the fleet moved. She shared with the rest of humanity a demoralized, disillusioned sense of loss, of unknowing, of confusion. And as in the rest of them, these feelings were crystallizing into fear.

Only the certain knowledge that loss of control at this time would bring utter destruction of mind or body allowed them to keep going.

Kept active by drugs, sent to sleep by sedatives, driven by the uncompromising will of Asquiol and his tool Mordan, the Gamblers prepared for another round of the Game.

F I F T E E N

They were seated in threes, each group before a large PV which mirrored the scene on the huge screen over their heads. The chamber was dark, illuminated solely by light from instruments and screens. Below the small screens were even smaller ones, in two rows of six. Mordan, who had brought Talfryn and Roffrey into the chamber, explained in a soft voice what purpose they served.

Roffrey looked about him.

Three sections of the circular chamber were occupied with the screens and seated before them each had its trio of operators — pale, thin men and women, for the most part, living off nervous energy and drugs. They had glass-alloy caps, similar to those he had worn while taking the tests. No one looked up as he entered.

"The screen above us is, as you can see, merely a wide-angle viewer which enables us to scan the space immediately around the fleet," Mordan was saying. "Each group of operators — Gamblers, we call them — is delegated a certain area of this space to watch for signs of alien expedition. So far as we can gather, it is part of their code to come close — within firing range — to our fleet before beginning the round. Apart from that, we are given no warning that a fresh round is about to commence. That's why we keep constant watch. Presumably among themselves the aliens have subtler ways of beginning, but this seems to be their compromise.

"When an alien expedition comes into view the team sighting it alerts the rest and they all concentrate on that area. The smaller rows of screens record the effect which we beam towards the aliens. They record hallucinatory impulses, and these are broken down into sections governed by the different senses, brain-waves of varying frequencies, emotional impulses such as fear, anger and so on, which we are capable of simulating. We have, of course, projectors, magnifiers and broadcasting equipment which is capable of responding to the commands of the Gamblers. But primarily, in the last resort, everything depends on the imagination, quick reactions, intelligence and ability to simulate emotions, thoughts and so on, which each individual Gambler possesses."

"I see." Roffrey nodded. In spite of himself, he was interested. "What happens then?"

"Just as many of our emotions and impulses are unfamiliar and incommunicable to the aliens, the same applies to them. Presumably half the impressions and mental impulses we have flung at us do not have the effect the aliens desire, or would get in their own kind. But we have the same difficulty.

"These men have been playing the Game long enough to recognize whether the effects they send are effective or not, and can guard against those effects which are most dangerous to us. Winning the Game, at this stage, anyway, depends largely upon the extent to which we can assimilate and analyze what works and what doesn't work. This also, of course, applies to the aliens. You, for instance, had the hallucination of a monster beast which shocked not only your instincts, triggering fear, panic, and so on, but shocked your logical qualities since you knew that it was impossible for such a beast to exist in the vacuum of space."

Roffrey and Talfryn agreed.

"This sort of effect is what the aliens are relying on — although in the general run of things these days they have learned to be much more subtle, working directly on the subconscious as they did to a large extent on you, after the beast-image didn't get the result they wanted. Therefore our psychologists and other researchers are gathering together every scrap of information which each round gives us, trying to get a clear picture of what effects will have the most devastating results on the aliens' subconscious. Here, as I mentioned, we are fairly well matched — our minds are as alien to them as theirs are to us.

"The prime object in playing the Blood Red Game, therefore, is to find the exact impulse necessary to destroy the qualities which we term self-respect, strength of character, intrinsic confidence, and so on."

Mordan exhaled heavily. "The number of losses we've had can be assessed when I tell you that we've got two hundred men and women alone who are curled up into foetal balls in the wards of our hospital ships."

Talfryn shuddered. "It sounds revolting."

"Forget that," Mordan said curtly. "You'll lose all sense of moral values after you've been playing the Game for a short time. The aliens are helping us to do what philosophers and mystics have been preaching for centuries. Remember it? *Know thyself*, eh?"

He shook his head, staring grimly around the chamber where the grey-faced Gamblers watched the screens concentratedly.

"You'll get to know yourself here all right. And I'm sure you won't like what you learn."

"Easier on the brooder, the introvert," Roffrey said.

"How deep can one man go in probing his innermost impulses before he pulls back — out of self-protection if nothing else?" Mordan said sharply. "Not far in comparison to what the aliens can do to you. But you'll find out."

"You're giving an attractive picture," Roffrey said.

"Damn you, Roffrey — I'll talk to you after your first round. This may, now I come to think of it, do you an awful lot of good!"

They were joined by a third individual. He had obviously been a Gambler for some time. They were beginning to recognize the type. He was tall, thin and nervous.

"Fiodor O'Hara," he said, not bothering to shake hands. They introduced themselves in the same curt manner.

"You will be in my charge until you become familiar with the Game," O'Hara said. "You will obey every order I give you. Try not to resist me. The sooner you are trained, the sooner you will be able to play the Game without any direction. I believe you are what they call an individualist, Roffrey. Well, you will have to conform here until you have mastered the Game — then your individualism will doubtless be of great use, since we depend on such qualities.

"Most of the people here are trained in some branch of psychology, but there are a few like yourselves — laymen — who have a sufficiently high I.Q. to be receptive, almost instinctively, to the needs of the Game. I wish you luck.

"You will find it a great strain to keep your ego free and functional — that is really all you have to learn to do as a beginner. You will carry out defensive strategy, as it were, until you are adept enough to begin attacking the enemy.

Remember, both of you, physical strength and daring mean absolutely nothing in this war. And you lose not your life, but your sanity — at first anyway."

Roffrey scratched the back of his neck. "For God's sake, let's get started," he said, impatiently.

"Don't fret," Mordan said as he left them. "You'll soon know when another round begins."

O'Hara took them to a row of empty seats. There were three seats, the usual screen and the miniature screens beneath it. Immediately in front of them were small sets of controls which were evidently used to operate the sense-projectors and other equipment.

"We have a short vocabulary which we shall use later for communication while the Game is in progress, O'Hara said, settling the skull-cap on his head. "Switch sound, for instance, means that if, at a certain moment, you are concentrating on taste sensations, I have decided that sounds would be more efficient against the enemy. If I say, "Switch taste," it means that you send taste impressions. That is simple — you understand?"

They showed their assent. Then they settled themselves to await their first — and perhaps last — round of the Blood Red Game.

The morality of what they were doing — invading this universe and attempting to wrest dominance of it from the native race — had bothered Asquiol little.

"Rights?" he had said to Mordan when the Councillor had relayed the doubts of some of the members of the fleet. "What rights have they? What rights have we? Because they exist here doesn't mean that they have any special *right* to exist here. Let them, or us, *establish* our rights. Let us see who wins the Game."

Asquiol had more on his mind than a squabble over property, dangerous as that squabble could be for the race.

This was humanity's last chance of attaining its birthright — something which Asquiol had almost attained in his ability to perceive simultaneously the entire multiverse — to take over from the Originators.

Somehow he had to teach his race to tap its own potential. Here, those Gamblers who might survive would be of use.

The race had to begin on the next stage of its evolution, yet the transition would have to be so sudden it would be a violent revolution.

And there was the personal matter of his *incompleteness*: the torturing frustration of knowing the missing piece that would make him whole was so close — he could sense it — as to be almost within his grasp. But what was it?

Dwelling in thought, Asquiol was grave.

Even he could not predict the eventual outcome if they won the Game. More able to encompass the scope of events than the rest of the race, in some ways he was as much in a temporal vacuum as they were — quite unable to relate past experience with present, or the present with whatever the future was likely to be.

He existed in all the many dimensions of the multiverse. Yet he, in common with all others, was bound by the dimension of Time. He had cast off the chains of space but was tied, as perhaps all denizens of the multiverse would always be, by the imperturbable prowl of Time, which brooked no halt, which condoned no tampering with its movement, whether to slow it or to speed it.

Time, the changer, could not be changed. Space, perhaps, the material environment, could be conquered. Time, never. It held the secret of the First Cause — a secret not known even to the Originators who had built the great, finite multiverse as a seeding bed — a womb — for their successors. But should the human race survive the birth pangs and succeed the Originators, Asquiol felt that it would not present a key to the secret.

Perhaps, in many generations — each generation measured as a stage in humanity's evolution — it would be found. But would the solution to the puzzle be welcomed? Not by his race — but maybe its great-grand-children would be capable of accepting and retaining such knowledge. For once they replaced the Originators they would have the task of creating *their* successors. And so it would continue, perhaps *ad infinitum* — to what greater purpose?

He stopped this reverie abruptly. In this respect he was a pragmatist. He could not concern himself with such pointless speculation.

There was a lull in the Game. The coming of Roffrey's ship and its defeat of the aliens had evidently nonplussed them for a while. But Roffrey, so far, had not experienced the real struggle, which was between trained minds capable of performing the most savage outrage there could be — destroying the id, the ego, the very qualities that set man above other beasts.

For a moment he wondered about Talfryn, but stopped the train of thoughts since it led to another question troubling him.

Asquiol allowed his concentration to cease for a moment as he enjoyed the rich nourishment that experience of dwelling on all planes of the multiverse gave him. He thought: *I am like a child in a womb, save that I know I am in the womb. Yet I am a child with a part missing; I sense it. What is it? What will complete me? It is as if the part would not only complete me, but complete itself at the same time.*

As was happening increasingly, he was interrupted by a sharp signal from the communicator.

He leaned forward in his chair, the strange shadows and curious half-seen images dancing about him. As he moved, the area of space between him and the communicator seemed to spray apart, flow and move spasmodically like water disturbed by the intrusion of an alien body. This happened whenever he moved, although he himself was only aware of his passing his arm through many objects which exerted a very faint pressure upon his limbs.

He could not only see the multiverse, he could also feel it, smell it, taste it. Yet this was little help in dealing with the aliens, for he found it almost as difficult as the rest of his race to understand the actual psychology of the non-human attackers.

The communicator came to life.

"Yes?" he said.

Again, Mordan had not turned on his own receiver, so that whereas Asquiol could see him, he need not subject himself to the eye-straining sight of Asquiol's scintillating body.

"A few messages," Mordan went through them quickly. "Hospital ship OP8 has disappeared. We heard that the I.T. field was becoming erratic. They were repairing it when they just... faded out of space. Any instructions?"

"I saw that happen. They're safe enough where they are. No instructions. If they're lucky and can adjust their field, they'll be able to rejoin the fleet."

"Roffrey and Talfryn, the two men who succeeded in withstanding the B.R. effect so successfully, have been subjected to all Professor Selinsky's tests and he is studying the results now. In the meantime they are being taught how to play the Game."

"What else?" Asquiol observed Mordan's worried expression.

"There were two others on Roffrey's ship. One of them was the mad woman — Mary Roffrey. The other calls herself Willow Kovacs. I have already forwarded this information, you remember."

"Yes. Is that all?"

"Kovacs asked me to pass a message on to you. She says that you were personally acquainted on Migaa and later in the Shifter. She would like it if you could spare the time to get in touch with her. The ship is on 050 L metres for tight contact."

"Thank you."

Asquiol switched out and sat back in his seat. There was in him still some part of the strong emotion he had felt for Willow. But he had had to rid himself of it twice. Once when she had declined to follow him to Roth, once after he met the Originators. His impression of her was, by now, a little vague — so much had happened.

He had had to dispense with many valuable emotions when he assumed control of the fleet. This was out of no spirit of ambition or will to dominate, simply that his position demanded maximum control of his mind. Therefore, emotions had to be sacrificed where they could not directly contribute to what he was doing. He had become, in so far as ordinary human relationships were included, a very lonely man. His perception of the multiverse had more than compensated for the breaks in human contact he had been forced to make, but he rather wished that he had not had to make those breaks.

Normally, he never acted on impulse, yet now he found himself turning his communicator dial to the wavelength 050 L metres. When it was done he waited. He felt almost nervous.

Willow saw her screen leap into life and she quickly adjusted her own controls with the information indicated above the screen. She acted hurriedly, excitedly, and then the sight she saw froze her for a moment.

After that, her movements were slower as she stared fascinatedly at the screen. "Asquiol?" she said in a faltering voice.

"Hello, Willow."

The man still bore the familiar facial characteristics of the Asquiol who had once raged through the galaxy spreading chaos and laughter in his wake.

She remembered the insouciant, moody youth she had loved. But this … this Satan incarnate sitting in its chair like some fallen archangel — this golden sight bore no relation to him as she remembered him.

"Asquiol?"

"I'm deeply sorry," he said, and smiled at her with a melancholy look for an archangel to wear.

Her face reflected the peculiar dancing effect which the image on the screen produced. She stepped back from it and stood with her shoulders drooping. And now she had only the memory of love.

"I should have taken my chance," she said.

"There was only one, I'm afraid. If I'd known, I perhaps could have convinced you to come with us. As it was I didn't want to endanger your life."

"I understand," she said. "Tough for me, eh?"

He didn't reply. Instead he was glancing behind him.

"I'll have to switch out — our opponents are starting another round of the Game. Goodbye, Willow. Perhaps, if we win, you and I can have another talk."

But she was silent as the golden, brilliant image faded from the screen.

S I X T E E N

O'Hara turned to his companions.

"This is your trial," he said. "Get ready."

There was a faint humming sensation in the huge, circular chamber.

O'Hara had adjusted his screen so that he could now see the alien ships swimming through space towards them. Only a few miles from the fleet they came to a stop and remained, in relation to the fleet, in a fixed position.

Roffrey suddenly found himself thinking of his childhood, his mother, what he had thought of his father and how he had envied his brother. Why should he suddenly decide to ...? Hastily he pulled himself out of this reverie, feeling slightly nauseated by a random thought that had begun to creep into his conscious mind. This was akin to what he'd experienced earlier, but not so intense.

"Careful, Roffrey — it's beginning," said O'Hara.

And it was only a mild beginning.

Whatever the aliens had learned of the human subconscious, they used. How they had gained such a store of information, Roffrey would never know — though the human psychiatrists had a similar store of "weapons" to turn back against their enemies.

Every dark thought, every unhealthy whim, every loathsome desire that they had ever experienced was dredged up by the alien machines and shoved before their conscious minds.

The trick, as O'Hara had said, was to forget values of good and evil, right and wrong, and to accept these impressions for what they were — desires and

THE SUNDERED WORLDS

thoughts shared by everyone to some degree.

But Roffrey found it hard going.

And this was not all. The alien means of triggering these thoughts was spectacular and mind-smashing in its clever intensity.

He found it difficult to define what was sight or smell, taste or sound. And pervading it all, in the aching background of everything, was the swirling, whirling, chattering, shrieking, odorous, clammy, painful colour — the Blood Red sense.

It was as if his mind had exploded. As if it were gouting its contents, awash with blood and the agony of naked thoughts, unclothed by prejudice and self-deception. There was no comfort in this world he had suddenly entered — no release, no rest or hope of salvation. The alien sensory-projectors were forcing him further and further into his own mind, jumbling what was there when it did not suit their purpose to show it to him as it really was. All his conscious thoughts and senses were scrambled and jellied and altered. All his subconscious feelings were paraded before him and he was forced to look.

In the back of his mind was a small spark of sanity repeating over and over again: "Keep sane — keep sane — hang on — it doesn't matter — it's all right." And at times he heard his own voice blended with dozens of others as he howled like a dog and cried like a child.

Yet in spite of all this that was flung against him and the rest, in spite of the loathing he began to feel for himself and his fellows, there was still the spark which kept him sane.

It was at this spark that the aliens aimed their main concentration, just as the more experienced Gamblers in the human ranks aimed to destroy the little sparks of sanity alive in their opponents.

Never in the history of the human race had such dreadful battles been fought. This was more like a war between depraved demons than between material creatures.

It was all Roffrey could do to keep that spark alive as he sweated and struggled against the columns of sound, the vast, booming waves of smells, in the groaning movement of colour.

And as if in keeping with this battleground, the Blood Red mingling of senses swam and ran and convulsed and heaved themselves through his racked being, hurled themselves along his neural tracts, hacked past his cortical cells, mauled his synapses and shook body and brain into a formless, useless jelly of garbled receptions.

Blood Red! There was nothing now save the Blood Red shrilling of a pervading, icy, stinking taste and a washed-out feeling of absolute self-loathing that crept in everywhere, in every cranny and corner of his mind and person so that he wanted nothing more than to shake it aside, to escape from it.

But it trapped him — the Blood Red trap from which he could only escape by retreating back down the corridors of his experience, to huddle comfortingly in the womb of...

The spark flared and sanity returned completely for a moment. He saw the sweating, concentrated faces of the other operators. He saw Talfryn's face writhing and heard the man groaning, saw O'Hara's thin hand on his shoulder and grunted an acknowledgement. He glanced at the tiny screen which was fluttering with dancing graphs and pulsating light.

Then he was reaching for the small control panel before him, and his bearded face bore a twisted half-smile as he shouted: "*Cats!*

"*And they crawl along your spines with their claws gripping your nerves.*

"*Tides of mud, oozing. Drown, creatures, drown!*"

The words themselves were of little effect, but they were not meant to be — they were triggering off emotions and impressions in his own mind.

He was attacking now! Using the very emotions and impressions which the aliens had released. And he had grasped some understanding of how they could react to these things, for there had been in their attack several impressions which had meant nothing to him, translated into his own terms. These he flung back with a will and his own screens began to lap to the horrid rhythms of his savagely working mind.

First he sent the Blood Red impressions back, since these were obviously a preliminary attack which formed the basis of the Game. He didn't understand why this should be, but he was learning quickly. And one of the things he had learned was that reason played little part while the Game was on. That instinct had to be turned into a fighting tool. Later the experts could analyze results.

But then he felt the hysteria leave him and there was silence in the chamber.

"Stop! Roffrey — stop! It's over — they won. Christ! We haven't got a hope now!"

"Won? I haven't finished..."

"Look—"

Several of the Gamblers were sprawled on the floor, mewling and drooling insanely. Others were curled into tight foetal balls. Attendants rushed in to tend to them.

"We've lost seven. That means the aliens won. We got perhaps five. Not bad. You nearly had your opponent, Roffrey, but they've pulled back now. You'll probably get another chance. For a first-timer you did exceptionally well."

Talfryn was insensible when they turned their attention to him.

O'Hara appeared unconcerned. "He's lucky — it looks as if he's only blacked out. I think he's tough enough to take another round or two now he's got used to the Game."

"It was — filthy…" Roffrey said. His whole body was tight with strain, his nerves were bunched, his head ached terribly, his heart pumped wildly. He even found it hard to focus on O'Hara.

Seeing his trouble, O'Hara took a hypodermic from a case in his pocket and gave Roffrey an injection before he could protest.

Roffrey began to feel better. He still felt tired, but his body started to relax and the headache was less intense.

"So that's the Blood Red Game," he said after a moment.

"That's it," said O'Hara.

Selinsky studied the papers Mann had prepared for him.

"You may well have something here," he said. "It is possible that the Shifter exerts a particular influence on the human mind that equips that mind for withstanding the attacks of the aliens."

He looked up and spoke to Zung, who was fiddling with some equipment in one corner of the room.

"You say that Roffrey stood up particularly well in his first round?"

"Yes," the little Mongolian nodded. "*And* he resumed the attack without direction. That's rare."

"He's valuable enough without having any special characteristics," Selinsky agreed.

"What do you think of my suggestions?" Mann said, almost impatiently, wanting to get back to her own line of inquiry.

"Interesting," Selinsky said, "but still nothing very definite to go on. I think we might ask to see Roffrey and Talfryn and find out what we can about their experiences in the Shifter."

"Shall I ask them to come here?" Zung suggested.

"Yes, will you?" Selinsky frowned as he studied Mann's notes.

Mary was emerging from the turmoil of her ruined brain. Half afraid, for the knowledge of her insanity preyed always on her sane mind, she was reassembling her reason.

Suddenly there was no more confusion. She lay there, eyes seeing nothing at all — no sights of disordered creation, no threatening creatures, no danger. All she heard was the slight scuffling sound of somebody moving about near her.

Very carefully, she thought back.

It was hard to distill a sense of time out of the chaos of memory. It had been as if she had spent most of her life in a whirlpool, performing such meaningless actions as piloting a ship, opening airlocks, making equations that flowed away from her and disappeared.

There had been periods when the turmoil of the whirlpool had abated — sane periods where she had hovered on the brink of insanity but never quite succumbed. There had been the first arrival at the Shifter, looking for the knowledge she had found on Golund. There had been a landing on Entropium, and then a chaotic journey among the planets through chaos-space that contained no perceivable laws, only a turbulent inconsistency; landing, finding nothing, keeping a hold on her sanity which kept threatening to crack; and finally to Roth where her mind had gone completely. Aware of warmth. Then away from Roth in a manner she could never remember, back to Entropium; a man who asked her questions — Count Renark — and the horror of half-sanity finally smashed by the cataclysm that had turned Entropium into rubble; the dash for the Hauser, crashing on a peaceful planet — Ekiversh, perhaps? — and resting, resting — then on to Roth... chaos... warmth... chaos...

Why?

What had kept pulling her back to Roth, so that every time she returned her sanity had given out a little more? Yet the last time there had been something extra — a turning point, as if she had gone full circle, on the road *back* to sanity. She had met entities there, things of formless light that had spoken to her. No, that was probably an hallucination...

With a healthy sigh she opened her eyes. Willow Kovacs stood over her. Mary recognized the woman who had comforted her and smiled.

"Where's my husband?" she said quietly, and composed her features.

"Feel better now?" Willow said. The smile she gave in reply was sorrowful, but Mary saw it was not her that Willow pitied.

"Much. Is Adam...?"

"He's been recruited to play this Game." Briefly Willow explained all she knew. "He should be getting in touch soon.

Mary nodded. She felt rested, at peace. The horror of her madness was a faint memory which she pushed further and further back. Never again, she thought. *That was it — I'm all right now. That was the last time.* She felt herself drifting into a deeper, more natural sleep.

Roffrey and Talfryn entered Selinsky's lab. Roffrey, huge and powerful, his black beard seeming to bristle with vitality, said: "More tests, professor?"

"No, captain. We wish merely to question you on one or two points which have cropped up. To tell you the truth, neither of you appears to possess any strong trait which can account for your besting so many opponents. We have discovered that the reason you were able to beat those ships with such apparent ease was that *every* one of their Gamblers was beaten — put out of action by some force so powerful that it crossed space without any sending equipment to aid it. Their receivers turned the emanations into a force which destroyed their minds completely. But you possess no qualities of sufficient strength which could account for this. It is as if you needed an … amplifier of some kind. Can you explain that?"

Roffrey shook his head.

But Talfryn was frowning and said nothing. He appeared thoughtful. "What about Mary?" he said slowly.

"Yes, that may be it!" Zung looked up from his notes.

"No, it isn't," Roffrey said grimly.

Talfryn broke in: "She's the one. Your wife, Roffrey. She was absolutely crazy on Entropium. She travelled between the Shifter's planets when space was wild and chaotic. She must have had a tremendous reserve of control somewhere in her if she could stand what she did. She could have picked up all kinds of strange impressions that worked on her brain. She did, in fact. She's our amplifier!"

"Well, what about it?" Roffrey turned round and looked at the three scientists standing there eagerly, like vultures who had spotted a dying traveller.

Selinsky sighed. "I think we're right," he said.

Mary stared out at the hazy light of the fleet dropping through darkness towards the far-off stars gleaming like lights at the end of a long, long tunnel.

"Adam Roffrey," she said aloud, and wondered what she would feel when she saw him.

"How did you get to the Shifter?" Willow asked from where she sat.

"I ran away from Adam. I got tired of his restless life, his constant hatred of civilization and ordered society. I even tired of his conversation and his jokes.

THE ETERNAL CHAMPION

"Yet I loved him. Still do. I'm an anthropologist by profession, and took advantage of Adam's trips to the remote outworlds to keep my hand in. One time, we landed on Golund — the planet with signs of having been visited by a race from another galaxy. I hunted around the planet but got no more than the scant information available. So I left Adam and went to the Shifter when it materialized in our space-time, hoping to find some clues there. I searched the Shifter System, I searched it and clung to my sanity by a thread. But Roth was the last straw; Roth finished me."

She turned back to look at Willow, smiling. "But now I feel saner than I've ever done — and I'm thinking of settling down if I can. What do you think of that, Willow?" Her eyes were serious.

"I think you're nuts," Willow said tactlessly. "Don't sell out for the easy life. Look at me…"

"It's been hard, though," said Mary, staring at the floor. "Far too hard, Willow."

"I know," she said.

The communicator whistled. Mary went to it, operated the control.

It was Roffrey.

"Hello, Adam," she said. Her throat felt constricted. She put her hand to it.

"Thank God," he said, his weary face impassive.

She knew she still loved him. That alone was comforting.

"You got a doctor, then?" he said.

"No," she said smiling. "Don't ask me how — just accept that I'm sane. Something happened — the fight with the aliens, something on Roth, maybe just Willow's nursing. I don't know. I feel a new woman."

His face softened as he relaxed. He grinned at her. "I can't wait," he said. "Can you and Willow come over to the Game Ship right away? That's why I contacted you — before I knew."

"Certainly," she said. "But why?"

"The people here think that all four of us, as a sort of team, managed to beat off the alien sense-impression attack. They want to give you a few routine tests along with Willow. Okay?"

"Fine," she said. "Send over a launch to collect us and we'll be with you."

She thought she saw him frown just before he switched out.

Much later, Selinsky screwed up his tired face and pushed his hand over it. He shook his head briskly as if to clear it, staring at the two women who, under sedatives, lay asleep in the testing chairs.

"There's certainly something there," he said, rolling a small light-tube between his palms. "Why couldn't we have tested all four of you together? A stupid oversight." He glanced at the chronometer on his right index finger.

"I've no idea why, but Asquiol is to broadcast to the entire fleet in a little while. About the Game, I think. I hope the news is good — we could do with some."

Roffrey was ill at ease, brooding, paying scant attention to the scientist. He stared down at Mary and he suddenly felt weak, ineffectual, as if he no longer played a part in her life, and could hardly control his own. An unusual feeling — connected, perhaps, with the shape that events seemed to be taking
...

Now she remembered. As she slept, physically, her mind was alert. She remembered landing on Roth, of stumbling over the surface, of falling down an abyss that took her upwards; of the strange, warm things that had entered her brain... She remembered all this because she could sense something similar quite close to her. She reached out to try and contact it, but failed — only just failed. She felt like a climber on a cliff-face who was reaching for the hand of the climber just above, the fingers stretching out carefully, desperately, but not quite touching.

There was somebody out there — somebody like her — but somehow more like her than she was! That was the impression she got. Who or what was it? Was it a person, such as she defined the word, or something else? Her original...?

Adam? No, it wasn't Adam. She realized she had spoken his name aloud.

"I'm here," he said, smiling down at her. She felt his big hand grasping her firmly, encouragingly.

"Adam... there's something ... I don't know..."

Selinsky appeared beside her husband. "How are you feeling?" he asked.

"Fine, physically. But I'm puzzled." She sat up in the chair, dangling her legs, trying to touch the floor. "What did you find out?"

"Quite a bit," he said. "And we'll be needing you. Are you willing to take a big risk and help us play the Game?"

Mary wondered why her husband was so quiet.

S E V E N T E E N

This time, Asquiol realized, he would have to visit the Game Ship personally, for the time he had feared had come.

The aliens had virtually won the Blood Red Game.

Jewelled, the multiverse spread around him, awash with life, rich with pulsating energy, but it could not compensate for his mood of near-despair. Coupled with the empty ache within him, the ache for the missing piece which seemed so close, it threatened to control him.

He still could not trace the source, but it was there. Something, like him but not so developed, was in touch with him, with the multiverse. He began to put mental feelers into the multiverse, searching.

But then his conscience made him withdraw from this and concentrate once more on the immediate problem. As had happened on past occasions, he had been in communication with the alien leaders. This time they had found it hard to disguise their jubilation, for the Game had taken firm shape.

They were winning. Even with the setback they had received from Roffrey's ship, their score had mounted enormously.

Asquiol still found it difficult to comprehend their method of scoring, but he trusted them. It was unthinkable for them to cheat.

His way of communicating with them was the way he and Renark had learned from the Originators. It wasn't telepathy. It relied on no exact human sense, but involved the use of waves of energy which only one in complete awareness of the multiverse might sense and harness. It did not involve words, but used pictures and symbols. It had been by analysis of some of these symbols which Asquiol had passed on to them that the psychiatrists had managed to devise "weapons" for use against the aliens.

Asquiol still had no idea of what the aliens called themselves and did not even have a clear impression of their physical appearance. But their messages were easy enough to interpret and the fact remained that the human race had reached a crisis point.

Only one more round of the Game would decide the issue!

Then, if the human race refused to accept the decision and began open war again, Asquiol knew they were doomed, for their fleet was too depleted to stand any chance at all.

News received recently did not alter this certainty. A number of farm ships had broken down, others had been lost completely or been destroyed in their early physical encounters with the aliens. Less than two thousand ships of all kinds remained in the fleet — a vast enough caravan by any ordinary standards, but nearly a quarter of a million ships had originally left the home universe.

It was in a mood bordering on hopelessness that he stretched out a scintillating arm and put his communicator on to a general broadcast wavelength to inform the race of what he had learned. It was rare for him to do this, since direct contact with members of his race was becoming increasingly less attractive. He began: "Asquiol here. Please listen attentively to my message. I have recently been in contact with our attackers and they have informed me that, as far as they are concerned, the game is virtually won. They are confident they will be the victors. This means our position is very nearly hopeless.

"We have, at most, enough supplies to last us for a month. Unless we make planet-fall on some habitable world soon, you will all be dead.

"The only way in which we can survive is to win, decisively, the last round of the Game. The aliens already have a considerable advantage over us and feel that they can, in the next round, sufficiently increase this to ensure victory.

"Our Gamblers are weary and we have no more recruits. We have drained our talent as we have drained our resources. Our scientists are still working to devise a new way of beating the aliens, but I must tell you that time is running very short. Those among you not directly involved in playing the Blood Red Game had best make what plans you can, bearing in mind what I have said.

"To the Gamblers and all those attached to the Game Ship I can only ask for greater effort, knowing you have worked at full capacity for many days.

Remember what we can win. *Everything!* Remember what we stand to lose. *Everything!*"

Asquiol sat back, his message still unfinished. He breathed in the exotic scents of the multiverse, saw the hull of his ship a stark outline against an overpoweringly beautiful background of living Chaos; sensed, again, that peculiar feeling of kinship with another entity. Where was it? In this universe — or another?

Then he continued: "I myself will not be directly affected by the outcome, as many of you have guessed. But this is not to say I am unaffected by my trust — to lead the race to safety in the first instance, and to something more in the second. There are those among you who ask what became of my companion Renark, our original leader. You wonder why he stayed behind in the contracting universe. My answer is vague, for neither of us got a clear idea from the Originators why this had to be. It is probably that the stuff of his great spirit was spread amongst us, to give all of us extra vitality — the vitality that we need. It may also have been that he sensed his role finished and mine only to have begun. Perhaps that is an arrogant thing to say.

"Renark was a brave man and a visionary. He was confident that our race, by its own efforts, could avoid, destroy or survive all danger. He was a believer in human will conquering all obstacles — physical, intellectual and metaphysical. In this, perhaps, he was naive. But without that idealism and naiveté, our race could not have survived.

"However, what saved us from one form of peril may not be able to save us from another. Different problems require different solutions. Will alone is not now sufficient to win the Blood Red Game. It must be remembered that the circumstances of our present predicament are much more complex than when Renark and I went on our quest.

"We must be totally ruthless, now. We must be strong and courageous. But we must also be devious, cautious and sacrifice any idealism which made us embark on this voyage. Sacrifice is for survival — and the survival of a greater ideal."

Asquiol wondered whether to continue. But he decided he had said sufficient for the moment.

Again he sat back, allowing himself to experience full unity with the multiverse.

"*Where are you...?*" he said, half-aloud. "*Who are you?*"

The need was tangible in him — disconcerting, distracting his attention from the matter he must give all his mind to.

He had already been in contact with the Game Ship and now waited impatiently for the signal which would tell him a vessel was ready to take him there.

He rose and paced the cluttered cabin, the light shivering and breaking apart into rays of shining blue, gold and silver; shadows quivered around him and at times there seemed to be several ghostly Asquiols in the cabin.

At length the launch clamped against the side of his ship and he passed through his airlock and into the cramped cabin of the launch. Quickly it cruised over to the Game Ship and eased sideways into a receiving bay. The great outer doors closed down swiftly and Asquiol stepped out to be greeted by Mordan.

"Perhaps," he said, "with your aid, Asquiol..."

But Asquiol shook his iridescent head. "I have little special power," he said. "I can only hope that my aid will help the Gamblers to hang on a little longer."

"There is something else. Selinsky wants to see you. It appears that all four of those people who came in from the Shifter have some kind of group-power..."

They were striding along the corridors, their boots clanging on metal.

Asquiol said, "I'll speak to Selinsky now."

He stopped as Mordan paused beside a door. "This is Selinsky's lab."

"Is he in?"

Mordan turned a stud and entered. Selinsky looked up, blinking as Asquiol followed Mordan in.

"An honour..." he said, half-cynically.

"Mordan tells me, professor, that you are on to some new development?"

"Yes, that's so. The woman — Mary Roffrey. She's not only sane now, she's ... what? Supersane! Something was done to her mind on Roth. The whole nature of it altered. It is very different from anyone else's — except, perhaps..."

"Mine?" Asquiol felt excitement creeping through him. "Is she, then, like me — as you see me?"

Selinsky shook his head. "She seems perfectly normal — until you analyze her brain structure. She's what we need, all right."

Asquiol was beginning to see the pattern now. Was this woman the missing piece in his existence? Had the Originators done something to her brain in order to form her into what she potentially was — a weapon? He could only guess.

Selinsky said: "She wasn't a product of the alien attack at all. She was a product of more than just a series of madness-inducing hallucinations on Roth. Something or somebody had actually tampered with her brain. It's the most delicately balanced thing I've ever seen!"

"What do you mean?" Asquiol asked.

"One way — utter madness; the other way — unguessable sanity." Selinsky frowned. "I'd hate to be in her position. We've got her doing a quick training course with O'Hara at the moment. But playing the Game could ruin her mind for good, tip the balance once and for all."

"You mean she'd be irredeemably insane?"

"Yes."

Asquiol pondered. "We must use her," he said finally. "Too much is at stake."

"Her husband is against the idea, but she seems to be taking it all right."

"He's the troublemaker — Roffrey," Mordan interposed.

"Will he give trouble in this business?"

"He seems resigned," Selinsky said. "A strange mood for him. Playing the Game seems to have wrought a change in him. Not surprising..."

"I must see her," Asquiol said with finality, turning to leave the laboratory.

They began the long walk down the corridor to the Game Chamber.

Now Asquiol wanted to see Mary Roffrey — wanted to see her desperately. As he strode along, his mind worked quickly.

Ever since he and Renark had gone to the Shifter, their paths had crossed indirectly. He had never met her — yet she had been the person to supply Renark with a lot of important information without which they might never have reached the Originators. What was she? Some puppet of the Originators which they were using to aid the race? Or was she something more than a puppet?

She must be the missing factor in his own existence. Yet obviously she had no direct contact with the multiverse. She had the power to strike devastatingly back at the aliens — and he had no comparable power. There were things that linked them, yet there were qualities that separated them also. It was as if they both represented certain abilities which humanity was capable of possessing. She had something he didn't have — he had something she didn't have. How similar were they?

This, perhaps, he would find out in a moment.

He went over in his mind the information he had. Mary's mind had been primarily responsible for disorientating the aliens in a wild round of the Game.

At that stage she had acted as a conductor for the rest. All of them having been on Roth, they were probably that much more capable of fighting the aliens than anyone else in the fleet. Therefore they would use the other three as well as Mary.

But uppermost in his mind was what Selinsky had just told him. Mary's mind could improve — or snap irreparably under the stress of this last round.

He knew what he would have to do now. But it was a heavy weight. As he contemplated it, the light around him seemed to fade, become colder and less frenetic in its movement. Sadness, such as he had never thought to experience again, filled him, and he fought it unsuccessfully.

He might, in essence, have to murder a woman — and cut himself off from the power she possessed. The power that was part of him as well as of her.

It was getting late — too late for anything but immediate action. The time of the last round was approaching.

They reached the door of the Game Chamber...

E I G H T E E N

In the main chamber, Mary was seated beside Willow and listening to the briefing. The other Gamblers were readying themselves for the last round. They were ill at ease and weary. Many of them did not look up even when Asquiol came in, flinging the door of the chamber open and striding quickly across the great room. The light flowed about the many facets of his body and streamed away behind him.

Mary turned round and saw him. "You!" she said.

A look of puzzlement crossed Asquiol's face. "We've met?" he said. "I don't remember."

"I saw you with Renark several times — on Roth."

"But we left Roth ages ago!"

"I know — but Roth is a strange planet. Time is non-existent there. Anyway, it wasn't only that."

"Then how else did you recognize me?"

"I've sensed you've been here all the time. Even before we reached the fleet, I think."

"But obviously you do not exist, as I do, in the entire multiverse. What could the link be, I wonder?" Then he smiled. "Perhaps our mutual friends the Originators could tell us."

"Probably it's simpler than that," Mary replied. The sense of empathy with Asquiol was like nothing she had ever experienced before. "Because we have seen them and gained from the contact, we recognize it in each other."

"Very likely." He nodded, then suddenly noticed that Willow was staring at him, her eyes full of tears. He took control of himself and said briskly: "Well, we had better get ready. I'm going to be in control of this project. You, Mary, will work under my direction using — as power, as it were — the other three: Roffrey, Talfryn and Willow. It's quite simple — a sort of gestalt link."

She looked at the others, who had crossed the room from where Selinsky and his team were working on a mechanism. "Did you hear that?" Adam had the look of a dumb beast in pain as he stared at her for a moment before dropping his eyes.

"We heard it," he said. "All of it."

She glanced at Asquiol as if seeking his advice, but he couldn't help her. Both of them were now in a similar position — Mary with Roffrey and Asquiol with Willow.

The time was nearing, Mary felt, when she would have to sever her ties with her husband.

The time had passed, Asquiol reflected, when he and Willow could have been united by the common bond which he and Mary possessed.

As they looked at one another, they seemed to convey this without need of speech.

O'Hara interrupted them: "Get ready, everyone! Remember, we need an overwhelming win in the round that is to follow. This round will be the last we have to play. Winning it must be decisive!"

The five people, Asquiol and Mary in the lead, went towards the specially prepared panel.

Selinsky and his team finished their work and stepped aside.

The five composed themselves to play.

Both Willow and Adam Roffrey had to force themselves to concentrate, but both were motivated by a different fear. Willow feared that Mary would become extra-sane through her ordeal. Roffrey feared she would become insane, while he hated the alternative which would break their relationship before it ever had a chance to resume.

Asquiol was his rival now, Roffrey saw. Yet Asquiol hardly knew it himself.

Only Talfryn was not afraid of the possible results. Either way, he felt, he stood to win — so long as Mary was effective in helping the Gamblers win the Game.

Asquiol bent close to Mary and whispered: "Remember I am in the closest possible touch with you, and you with me. However near you feel you are coming to insanity, don't panic. I'll keep you on the right course.

She smiled at him. "Thanks."

The tension rose as they waited.

It was so delicate, the first probe. As delicate as a slicing scalpel.

O'Hara shouted: "Don't wait for them. Attack! Attack!"

In contact with Mary now, Asquiol began to dredge up Mary's memories from the deepest recesses of her subconscious, doing to her what only a totally evil man might do.

Yet, even as she slipped into the giddy, sickening whirlpool of insanity, it was obvious to her that Asquiol was not evil. There was no malice in him at all. It was taking fantastic control for him to force himself to continue. But he did continue. He worked at her mind, slashing at it, tearing at it, working it apart in order to remould it, and he did it in the full knowledge that he might, in the final analysis, be committing a dreadful crime.

Beside him, the trio sweated, feeding power to Mary that was channelled by Asquiol and directed by him at the alien attackers.

"There they are, Mary — you see them!"

Mary turned glazed eyes towards the screen. Yes, she saw them.

It was suddenly like horrible darkness then rolling through her. Red-hot needles forced themselves into the grey mass of her brain. It was like being a tightened banjo string. Tighter and tighter until she must surely snap. She couldn't… She couldn't…

She laughed. It was a huge joke against her. They were all laughing at her.

She sobbed and mewled and lashed back at the pouring stream of demons and hobgoblins that came prancing and tumbling down the long corridors of her mind. They sniggered and simpered and fingered her brains and her body and pulled her nerves about, enjoying their sport, caressing the parts of her they captured.

She lashed back as the whole scene became pervaded with the Blood Red sense that had always been there. She knew it. She was familiar with it and she hated it more than anything else.

Gone were emotions — gone self-pity, gone love — gone yearning and jealousy and impotent sadness. The trio linked and locked and lent their strength to Mary. Everything that she felt, they felt. Everything she saw and did, they saw and did. And at times, also, so close were the five blended, they saw something of what Asquiol saw and it lent them strength to pass on to Mary.

On and on they went, driving at the aliens, hating them and sending back impression after impression from the multiple brain.

To the alien players of the Game, it was as if they had suddenly been attacked by an atomic cannon in a war that had previously been fought with swords. They reeled beneath the weight of the attack. They reeled, they marvelled and, in their strange way, they admired.

But they fought back even harder, playing, after the initial shock, coolly and efficiently.

Roffrey broke contact at the sound of a voice outside. It was O'Hara shouting: "We're winning; they were right. Somehow she has the key to the whole mastery of the Game. She does something with her mind that reflects back to them exactly the thing most loathsome to them. There's a twist there somewhere that no human experience could have made. She's doing it!"

Roffrey stared at him for a moment as if in panic, and then returned his attention to the Game. For a moment, O'Hara watched him before he returned his own attention. Their gains were slowly mounting — and Mary's inspiration seemed to be encouraging the rest of the Gamblers to give their best.

"This is our finest hour," O'Hara said thickly. "Our finest hour."

And as he passed her he saw Mary's twisted and distorted face with the sweat and saliva all over it, wreathed in the same flickering images that surrounded Asquiol's intent face.

Now she knew she was winning. *Now* she could see they were reeling back. *Now* she felt victory within her reach. Although the madness was frenzied and all-consuming, there was behind it all the confidence that Asquiol's presence gave her, and she kept sending, though her mind and body ached with searing agony.

Then, quite suddenly, she blacked out, hearing a voice call from a long way off: "*Mary! Mary!*"

Asquiol, knowing that he had aided her to reach this state, could hardly bear to continue. But he had to. He put a hand to her sweat-wet hair and dragged the head back to stare into the vacant eyes.

"Mary — you *can* send them away. You *can!*" He began to communicate with her. He forced her attention to the screens.

She threshed in her chair. For a second she stared at him. To his relief he saw sanity there.

"Asquiol," she said, "*what is it we were?*"

"*We can be the same, Mary — now!*"

And then she was bellowing in his face, her laughter seeming a physical weight battering around his head so that he wanted to fling up his hands to ward it off, to run and escape, to hide from what he had created. But again he forced control on himself and pushed her face towards the screens.

Roffrey, pain-drunk, glared at him, but did nothing.

Finally, she was roaring and tearing. Asquiol couldn't make contact with her. One of her hands flailed out, the nails slashing his face. Roffrey saw the blood come and was half-astonished. He had forgotten that Asquiol was in many ways as mortal as himself. Somehow it made the feelings in him worse.

Asquiol fought to control this rage, turn it against the aliens. He battled to resume empathetic contact with Mary.

She stirred; her name formed and curled and buzzed through the darkness. She reached out for it.

Elsewhere, many of the Gamblers had already succumbed to the force of the alien impressions. Tidal waves of garbled sense-impressions were being flung against them and even the strongest were finding it hard to resist, to keep the spark of sanity alive and to retaliate.

Asquiol used the communicating-sense that allowed him to contact the aliens and "converse" with them. He did this to Mary. He shoved impressions and pictures into her mind, things taken from his own memory. And so real did they become, in such close empathy was he with the woman, that he felt his own sanity slipping away. But he was the controlling part of the team — he had to keep aware. He held on for as long as he could, then straightened his back, gasping.

Those watching saw the light surrounding him skip erratically and dim suddenly. Then it became brighter, like a flaring explosion.

And then the light appeared to make contact with Mary. The same thing appeared to happen to her body. Her image split and became many images…

Asquiol! ASQUIOL! ASQUIOL!

Hello, Mary.

What is it?

Rebirth. You're whole now.

Is it over?

By no means!

Where are we, Asquiol?

On the ship.

But it's…

Different, I know. Look!

She saw, through facet after facet, her husband, the girl and the other man. They were staring at her in astonishment. Angled, opaque images surrounded every space they did not occupy.

"Adam," she said, "I'm sorry."

"It's all right, Mary. I'm not. Good luck — like I said." Roffrey was actually smiling.

A new image swam into focus — O'Hara gesticulating.

"I don't know what's happened to the woman and I don't care. Get your attention back to the Game, or it's lost!"

She turned, and the horrifying impressions came back, but it was as if they were pressed through a filter which took away their effect on her mind.

Carefully, she searched her being. She felt Asquiol beside her, felt the warmth of his encouragement. She lashed back, with deliberate and savage fury, searching out weaknesses, using them, splitting the alien minds to shreds. Asquiol guided her — she could feel it. Talfryn, Willow and Adam supplied power and extra impressions which she took and warped and sent out.

More of the Gamblers were dropping out and attendants were kept busy clearing them from the chamber. There were only five complete teams left.

But it was victory. Mary and Asquiol could feel it as they worked together — oblivious of everything else — to defeat the aliens. They felt at that moment as if they knew everything about their opponents, to such an extent that they were even in danger of giving up out of sympathy.

They fought on, riding a tide of conquest. Soon the entire alien complement was finished. They retreated back and stared around them.

"Asquiol — what happened?"

Asquiol and Mary saw Willow looking up at them. They smiled at her and said: *"This was the Originators' plan, Willow. They obviously did not allow sufficiently for human weakness — but they did not count on the strength of the human spirit, perhaps. Please don't suffer, Willow. You have done more today for humanity than you could ever have done for any single person."*

They turned to regard the others. *"You too, Roffrey — and you, Talfryn. Without you it is unlikely that we could have defeated the alien intelligences. Everything has suddenly become a clear pattern. There was, perhaps, a purpose for Willow and Talfryn when they stayed behind. There was a purpose, also, for Roffrey when he took it into his head to visit the Shifter. We nearly threw away our chance."*

"What exactly has happened?" Mordan interrupted. "Have you become one entity?"

"No." Asquiol spoke with a slight effort. "Existing on the multiversal level, we are capable of linking minds to form a more powerful single unity. That was how we finally defeated our opponents.

"Obviously this was part of the Originators' plan. But they never do anything for us directly. At best, they merely put certain aids in our path. If we can make use of them — assuming we realize what they are — so much to the good. If we can't, we suffer. We were near complete defeat there. If we had not got some hint of Mary's abilities when we did, the plan would have come to nothing. As it was, we were lucky."

Mary said: "I must have been watched by the Originators right from the start — even before I met you."

Asquiol continued: "The Originators make things especially difficult for people they think are ... material for the new, multiversal race. Simply, only the fittest survive."

Mordan said obsequiously, yet hastily: "But the aliens ... can we not discover what our peace terms are? We must hurry... the farm ships..."

"Of course," Asquiol nodded. "Mary and I will return to my ship and contact them from there."

Mary and Asquiol moved towards the exit, gave one last glance at the three others, and left.

"What the hell have you got to smile about, Roffrey?" Talfryn said accusingly.

Roffrey felt at peace. Maybe it was the mood induced by weariness, but he didn't think so. There was no more pain in him, no more jealousy, no more hatred. He moved over to the big blank screen and stared up at it. The place suddenly brightened as assistants switched on the central lights and began clearing up the mess the Gamblers had left...

"I give up." Talfryn shook his head, perplexed.

"That's the trouble," Willow said. "So many of us do, don't we?"

E P I L O G U E

Asquiol of Pompeii took Mary the Maze back to his ship. They felt more at ease there, since the ship was better suited to their own metabolic state.

Here, with Asquiol acting again as a guide for Mary, they pooled their resources together and contemplated the radiant multiverse around them.

Then they put out a tendril of multiversal thought-matter along the familiar layers, seeking the alien minds.

Then they were in contact!

When the alien leaders came to the ship, Mary gasped and said in normal speech: "God! They're beautiful."

They were beautiful, with delicate bones and translucent skins, great, golden eyes and graceful movements. Yet there was a look of decadence. Like depraved, wise children.

"The Originators warned me to beware of races they called pessimists," Asquiol said, "races who had despaired of ever attaining full awareness of the multiverse, who had so completely lost the urge to transcend their limitations that the tiny core of being had, over millennia, been almost completely eroded. Doubtless these are of that kind."

By use of their unique method, they once again conversed with the aliens and were astonished by the mood of total defeat, the unquestioning acceptance of the winners' rights to dictate any terms they wished.

They had lost their urge to transcend physical confines and in so doing had lost pride — real pride, also.

Absolute defeat — lost spirit — utter hopelessness — concede all rights you wish to take...

This mood was sufficient to add almost the last pressure on the victors' already weary minds. A great pity welled up in them as they communicated their terms to the conquered.

Accept terms — any terms acceptable — we have no status — you have all status — we are nothing but your tools to use...

So conditioned were the aliens to the code applying to the Game they had played for centuries, perhaps millennia, that they could let this unknown opponent do as it liked. They were conditioned to obeying the victor. They could not question the victor's right. Their shame was so intense that they threatened to die of it — yet there was no trace of bitterness, no trace of resentment or lingering pride...

Asquiol and Mary resolved to help them, if they could.

The aliens left.

Would they ever see them again? As the spherical ship moved away, Asquiol and Mary sent out a polite impression that congratulated them on their ingenuity and courage, but it met with no response. They were beaten — no praise could alter that. They gave them positions of planets suitable for human occupation — they were totally unsuited for themselves, anyway" — and then they fled.

They did not go to nurse grudges, for they had none. They did not plot retaliation, for such a thing was inconceivable. They went to hide — to reappear only if their conquerors demanded it.

They were a strange people whose artificial code had obviously completely superseded natural instincts.

As the alien ship disappeared, Asquiol and Mary broke their contact with the leaders.

"I'd better inform Mordan. He'll be delighted, anyway." Asquiol operated the V. He told the Gee-Councillor of his meeting.

"I'll start the fleet moving towards some habitable planets right away. Give me an hour." Mordan smiled tiredly. "We did it, Asquiol. I must admit I was close to accepting defeat."

"We all were," Asquiol smiled. "How are the other three?"

"They've gone back to Roffrey's ship. I think they're okay. Roffrey and the girl seem quite happy, strangely. Do you want me to keep tabs on them?"

"No." Asquiol shook his head, and as he did so the light broke and reformed around it, the images scattering and merging. Asquiol stared at Mordan's weary face for a moment. The Councillor shifted uncomfortably beneath the fixed stare.

"I could do with some natural sleep," he said at last, "but I've got to get the fleet moving first. Is there anything else?"

"Nothing," said Asquiol, and switched out.

There was a subdued mood of victory about the reformed fleet as he and Mary watched it from one of the ports.

"There's a lot more to do, Mary," he said. "This is really only the beginning. I once compared the human race to a chick smashing out of its shell. The comparison still applies. We've broken the shell. We've survived our first period in the multiverse — but will we survive the second and the third? Is there a huge, cosmic farmer with an axe somewhere thinking of serving us up for dinner when we're plump enough?"

She smiled. "You're worn out. So am I. Give yourself time to think properly. It's the reaction — you're depressed. That kind of emotion can harm a lot of the work we still have to do."

He looked at her in surprise. He was still unused to having company that he could appreciate, someone who could understand what he felt and saw.

"Where are we going?" he said. "We need to plan carefully. The degraded condition of the fleet can't be allowed to continue once we make planet-fall. Galactic Law will have to be firmly re-established. Men like Mordan, who have been more than useful in the past because of their pragmatic virtues which would have been hindered by possession of the kind of vision we need now, will have to be taken out of positions of power. We've become a grim race lately — out of necessity. If we let matters slide, Mary, the race could easily degenerate back into something worse than its pre-exodus state. If that happened, our destiny might be out of reach for good. There isn't much time. The Originators made that clear when Renark and I first met them."

He sighed.

"With me to help you," she said, "the hard work will be easier. I know it's going to be hard, but there are two of us now. You noticed how Adam and Willow were beginning to respond back in the Game Ship? There must be dozens like them in the fleet, potentially capable of joining us. Soon, perhaps in only a few generations, there will be a race of people like us, until there are enough to take the place of the Originators."

"Not that many," Asquiol said. "Most people are happy as they are. Who can blame them? It will be an uphill climb."

"That's the best way to climb hills." She smiled. "And remember — keep your impression of those aliens we saw firmly in your mind. We have an example now of how we could degenerate. Perhaps it was fated that we should meet that race. It will serve as a reminder — and a warning. And with a reminder like that, we are not likely to fail."

Around them, as they sat in contemplation, the multiverse flowed, thick and solid, so full. And this could be the heritage of their race.

He laughed lightly. "There's a scene in *Henry the Fourth* where Falstaff learns that Prince Hal, his old drinking companion, is now king. He gathers his friends about him and tells them good times have come, for he is 'Fortune's Steward,' and the king will honour them and allow them to behave as they like with impunity. But, instead, King Henry banishes Falstaff for a buffoon and troublemaker. Falstaff realizes then that instead of becoming better, things are going to be worse. I sometimes wonder if, perhaps, I'm not "Fortune's Steward" — leading the whole race towards a promise I can't keep ..."

Mary's multi-faceted face smiled encouragingly. "There are still the Originators. But even without them humanity has always had to act without being able to foresee the outcome of its actions — ever since we began the long climb upwards. We're stumblers; we have to convince ourselves of the results we will achieve without ever knowing if we can succeed. But we quite often do succeed. We have a long way to go, Asquiol, before we shall ever be able to know for certain the outcome of our actions. Meanwhile, we keep going. We have to keep trying to cut justice from the stuff of chaos."

"We're probably the most optimistic race in the multiverse!" said Asquiol, embracing her.

They laughed together. And the spirit of Renark, which had permeated humanity to give it a unified strength, seemed to share their joy.

The multiverse shifted, swirled and leapt, for ever changing and delighting them with its chaos, its colour, its variety. All possibilities existed there.

All promise, all faith, all hope.

P R O L O G U E

A bright plain without horizons. The plain is the colour of raw, red gold. The sky is a faded purple. Two figures stand on the plain: a man and a woman. The man, dressed in dented armour, is tall with weary angular features. The woman is beautiful — dark-haired and delicate, clad in a gown of blue silk. He is ISARDA OF TANELORN. THE WOMAN *is nameless.*

THE WOMAN

What are Time and Space but clay for the hand that holds the Cosmic Balance? This Age is moulded — that one squeezed from existence. All is flux. Lords of Law and Chaos struggle in eternal battle and neither ever completely wins or loses. The balance tilts this way and that. Time upon Time the Hand destroys its creations and begins anew. And the Earth is forever changing. The Eternal War is the only constant in Earth's many histories, taking a multitude of forms and names.

ISARDA OF TANELORN

And those who are involved in this struggle? Can they ever realise the true nature of their strivings?

WOMAN

Rarely.

And will the world at length be granted rest from this state of flux?

WOMAN

We shall never know, for we shall never come face to face with the One who guides the Hand.

ISARDA

(He spreads his arms.) But surely some things are constant...

WOMAN

Even the meandering river of Time can be dammed or rechannelled at the will of the Cosmic Hand. We are as uncertain of the shape of the future as we are of the validity of our reported history. Perhaps we only exist for this instant of Time? Perhaps we are immortal and will exist forever? Nothing is known for certain, Isarda. All knowledge is illusion — purpose is a meaningless word, a mere sound, a reassuring fragment of melody in a cacophony of clashing chords. All is flux — matter is like these jewels. *(She throws a handful of gleaming gems upon the golden surface; they scatter. When the last jewel has ceased to move, she looks up at him.)* Sometimes they fall into a rough pattern, usually they do not. So at this moment, a pattern has been formed — you and I stand here speaking. But at any moment that which constitutes our beings may be scattered again.

ISARDA

Not if we resist. Legends speak of those who forced Chaos into shape by effort of will. Aubec's hand formed your land and, indirectly, you.

WOMAN

(Wistfully.) Perhaps there are such people. But they go directly against the will of the One who formed them.

ISARDA

(After a pause.) And what if they do exist? What would become of them?

WOMAN

I do not know. But I do not envy them.

ISARDA

(He looks away across the golden plain. He speaks softly.) Nor I.

WOMAN

They say your city Tanelorn is eternal. They say that because of a Hero's will she has existed through every transformation of the Earth. They say that even the most haunted of folk find peace there.

ISARDA

It is also said that they must first have a will for peace before they can find Tanelorn.

WOMAN

(Bowing her head.) And few have that.

—The Chronicle of the Black Sword
(Vol. 1008 Scr. 14: *Isarda's Reckoning*)

BOOK ONE:
PREMONITIONS

But yesternight I pray'd aloud
In anguish and in agony,
Up-starting from the fiendish crowd
Of shapes and thoughts that tortured me:
A lurid light, a trampling throng,
Sense of intolerable wrong,
And whom I scorned, those only strong!
Thirst of revenge, the powerless will
Still baffled, and yet burning still!
Desire with loathing strangely mixed
On wild or hateful objects fixed.
Fantastic passions! Maddening brawl!
And shame and terror over all!
Deeds to be hid which were not hid,
Which all confused I could not know
Whether I suffered, or I did:
For all seem'd guilt, remorse or woe,
My own or others still the same
Life-stifling fear, soul-stifling shame.

S. T. Coleridge, "The Pains of Sleep"

O N E

OF AN EARTH REBORN

I know grief and I know love and I think I know what death may be, though it is said I am immortal. I have been told I have a destiny, but what that is, save forever to be moved by the tides of chance, to perform miserable deeds, I do not know.

I was called John Daker and perhaps many other names. Then I was called Erekosë, the Eternal Champion, and I slew the human race because it had betrayed what I considered to be my ideals, because I loved a woman of another race, a race I thought nobler and which was called the Eldren. The woman was called Ermizhad and she could never bear me children.

And, having slain my race, I was happy.

With Ermizhad and her brother Arjavh I ruled the Eldren, that graceful people which had existed on Earth well before mankind had come to disrupt its harmony.

The dreams, which had beset my sleeping hours when I had first come to this world, were now rare and hardly remembered at all on waking. Once they had terrified me, made me think that I must be insane. I had experienced fragments of a million incarnations, always as some sort of warrior; I had not known which identity was my "true" one. Torn by divided loyalties, by the stresses in my own brain, I had been mad for a while, of this I was now sure.

But I was mad no longer and I committed myself to restoring the beauty I had destroyed in my warrings — first as the Champion of one side, then of the other — over the Earth.

Where armies had marched we planted shrubs and flowers. Where cities had been we made forests grow. And the Earth became gentle, calm and beautiful.

And my love for Ermizhad did not wane.

It grew. It developed so that I loved each new facet I discovered in her character.

The Earth became harmonious. And Erekosë, the Eternal Champion, and Ermizhad, Paramount Princess of the Eldren, reflected that harmony.

The great, terrifying weapons which we had used to overcome mankind were sealed away, and we swore that we should never use them again.

The Eldren cities, razed by the Marshals of Humanity when I had led them, were restored, and soon Eldren children sang in their streets, flowering shrubs bloomed on their balconies and terraces. Green turf grew over the scars cut with the swords of mankind's paladins. And the Eldren forgot the men who had once sought to destroy their race.

Only I remembered, for mankind had called me to lead them against the Eldren. Instead I had betrayed mankind — every man, woman and child had died because of me. The Droonaa River had flowed with their blood. Now it flowed with sweet water. But the water could not wash away the guilt that would sometimes consume me.

And yet I was happy. It seemed to me that I had never known such peace of soul, such tranquillity of mind.

Ermizhad and I would wander about the walls and terraces of Loos Ptokai, the Eldren capital, and we never tired of each other's company. Sometimes we would discuss a fine point of philosophy, at other times we were content to sit in silence, breathing in the rich and delicate scents of a garden.

And when the mood took us, we would embark upon a slender Eldren ship and sail about the world to witness its wonders — the Plains of Melting Ice, the Mountains of Sorrow, the mighty forests and gentle hills, the rolling plains of the two continents once inhabited by mankind, Necralala and Zavara. But then, sometimes, a mood of melancholy would sweep over me and we would set sail again for the third continent, the Southern continent called Mernadin, where the Eldren had lived since ancient times.

It was at these times that Ermizhad would comfort me, soothing away my memories and my shame.

"You know that I believe all this was pre-ordained," she would say. Her cool, soft hands would stroke my brow. "Mankind's purpose was to destroy our race. This ambition destroyed them. You were merely the instrument of their destruction."

"And yet," I would reply, "have I no free will? Was the only solution the genocide I committed? I had hoped that mankind and the Eldren could live in peace."

"And you tried to bring such a thing to pass. But they would have none of it. They tried to destroy you as they tried to destroy the Eldren. They almost succeeded. Do not forget that, Erekosë. They almost succeeded."

"Sometimes," I would confide, "I wish that I were back in the world of John Daker. I once thought that world overly complicated and stifling. But now I realise that every world contains the same factors I hated, if in a different form. The Cycles of Time may change, Ermizhad, but the human condition does not. It was that condition I hoped to change. I failed. Perhaps that is my destiny — to strive to change the very nature of humanity and fail..."

But Ermizhad was not human and, while she could sympathise and guess at what I meant, she could not understand. It was the one thing she could not understand.

"Your kind had many virtues," she would say. Then she would pause and frown and be unable to complete her statement.

"Aye, but their very virtues became their vices. It was ever thus with mankind. A young man hating poverty and squalor would seek to change it by destroying something that was beautiful. Seeing people dying in misery, he would kill others. Seeing starvation, he would burn crops. Hating tyranny, he would give himself body and soul to that great tyrant War. Hating disorder, he would invent devices that brought further chaos. Loving peace, he would repress learning, outlaw art, cause conflict. The history of the human race was one prolonged tragedy, Ermizhad."

And Ermizhad would kiss me lightly. "And now the tragedy is ended."

"So it seems, for the Eldren know how to live in tranquillity and retain their vitality. Yet sometimes I feel that the tragedy is still being played — perhaps played a thousand times in different guises. And the tragedy requires its principal actors. Perhaps I am one such. Perhaps I shall be called again to play my role. Perhaps my life with you is merely a pause between scenes..."

And to this statement she could offer no reply, save to take me in her arms and bring me the comfort of her sweet lips.

Gaily coloured birds and graceful beasts played where mankind had once raised its cities and beaten its battle-drums, but within those new-born forests and on the grass of those fresh-healed hills there were ghosts. The ghosts of Iolinda, who had loved me, of her father, the weak king Rigenos, who had sought my help, of Count Roldero, kindly Grand Marshal of Humanity, of all the others who had died because of me.

Yet it had been no choice of my own to come to this world, to take up the sword of Erekosë, the Eternal Champion, to put on Erekosë's armour, to ride at the head of a bright army as mankind's chief paladin, to learn that the Eldren were not the Hounds of Evil which King Rigenos had described, that they were, in fact, the victims of mankind's insensate hatred...

No choice of my own...

At root, that was the phrase most often haunting my moods of melancholy.

Yet those moods came more rarely as the years rolled by and Ermizhad and I did not age and continued to feel the same passion we had felt at our first meeting.

They were years of laughter, fine conversation, ecstasy, beauty, affection. One year blended into another until a hundred or so had passed.

Then the Ghost Worlds — those strange worlds which shifted through Time and Space at an angle to the rest of the universe we knew — came again in conjunction with the Earth.

T W O

OF A GROWING DOOM

Ermizhad's brother was Prince Arjavh. Handsome, in the manner of the slender Eldren, with a pointed golden face and slanting eyes that were milky and blue-flecked, Arjavh had as much affection for me as I had for him. His wit and his wisdom had often inspired me and he was forever laughing.

So it was that I was surprised one day to visit him in his laboratory and find him frowning.

He looked up from his sheets of calculations and tried to alter his expression, but I could tell he was concerned — perhaps about some discovery he had made in his researches.

"What is it, Arjavh?" I asked lightly. "Those look to me like astronomical charts. Is a comet on course for Loos Ptokai? Must we all evacuate the city?"

He smiled and shook his head. "Nothing so simple. Perhaps not as dramatic, either. I am not sure there is anything to fear, but we would do well to be prepared, for it seems the Ghost Worlds are about to touch ours again."

"But the Ghost Worlds offer the Eldren no harm, surely. You have summoned allies from them in the past."

"True. Yet the last time the Ghost Worlds were in conjunction with Earth — that was the time you came here. Possibly it was coincidental. Possibly you are from one of the Ghost Worlds and that is how it was in Rigenos's power to call you."

I frowned. "I understand your concern. It is for me."

Arjavh nodded his head and said nothing.

"Some say Humanity came originally from the Ghost Worlds, do they not?" I gave him a direct look.

"Aye."

"Have you any specific fears on my behalf?" I asked him.

He sighed. "No. Though the Eldren invented a means of bridging the dimensions between our Earth and the Ghost Worlds, we never explored them. Our visits could, of necessity, only be brief and our contact was with those dwellers in the Ghost Worlds who were kin to the Eldren."

"Do you fear that I will be recalled to the world I left?" I became tense. I could not bear the thought of being parted from Ermizhad, from the tranquil world of the Eldren.

"I do not know, Erekosë."

Was I to become John Daker again?

Though I only dimly remembered my life in that era I for some reason called the Twentieth Century, I knew that I had not felt at ease there, that there had been within me an intense dissatisfaction with my life and circumstances. My naturally passionate and romantic disposition (which I did not regard as a virtue, for it had led me to commit the deeds I have already recounted) had been repressed by my surroundings, by my society and by the work I had done to make a living. I had felt more out of place there, among my own kind, than I did living here with an alien race. I felt that it might be better to kill myself, rather than return to John Daker's world, perhaps without even the memory of this one.

On the other hand, the Ghost Worlds might be nothing to do with me. They might belong to a universe which had never been inhabited by men (though the Eldren researches did not suggest this).

"Is there nothing else we can discover?" I asked Prince Arjavh.

"I am continuing my investigations. It is all I can do."

Gloomily, I left his laboratory and returned to the chambers where Ermizhad awaited me. We had planned to ride out over the familiar fields surrounding Loos Ptokai, but now I told her that I did not feel like riding.

Noting my mood, she said: "Are you remembering what passed a century ago, Erekosë?"

I shook my head. Then I told her what Arjavh had said.

She, too, became thoughtful. "It was probably a coincidence," she said. But there was little conviction in her tone. There was a trace of fear in her eyes when she looked up at me.

I took her in my arms.

"I should die, I think, if you were taken from me, Erekosë," she said.

My lips were dry, my throat tight. "If I were taken," I told her, "I would spend eternity in finding you again. And I would find you again, Ermizhad."

When she spoke next, it was almost in astonishment. "Is your love for me that strong, Erekosë?"

"It is stronger, Ermizhad."

She drew away from me, holding my hands in hers. Those hands, hers and mine, were trembling. She tried to smile, to banish the premonitions filling her, but she could not.

"Why, then," she said, "there is nothing at all to fear!"

But that night, as I slept beside her, the dreams which I had experienced as John Daker, which had plagued me in my first year on this new world, began to creep back into the caverns of my mind.

First there were no images. Only names. A long list of names chanted in a booming voice that seemed to have a trace of mockery in it.

Corum Jhaelen Irsei. Konrad Arflane. von Bek. Urlik Skarsol. Aubec of Kaneloon. Shaleen. Artos. Alerik. Erekosë…

I tried to stop the voice there. I tried to shout, to say that I was Erekosë — only Erekosë. But I could not speak.

The roll continued:

Ryan. Hawkmoon. Powys. Cornell. Brian. Umpata. Sojan. Klan. Clovis Marca. Pournachas. Oshbek-Uy. Ulysses. Ilanth. Renark…

My own voice came now:

"NO! I AM ONLY EREKOSË."

"Champion Eternal. Fate's Soldier."

"NO!"

Elric. Mejink-La-Kos. Cornelius.

"NO! NO! I AM WEARY. I CAN WAR NO MORE!"

The sword. The armour. The battle banners. Fire. Death. Ruin.

"NO!"

"Erekosë!"

"YES! YES!"

I was screaming. I was sweating. I was sitting upright in the bed.

And it was Ermizhad's voice that was calling my name now.

Panting, I fell back on to the pillows, into her arms.

PHOENIX IN OBSIDIAN

"The dreams have returned."

I lay my head upon her breast and I wept.

"This means nothing," she said. "It was only a nightmare. You fear that you will be recalled and your own mind gives substance to that fear. That is all."

"Is it, Ermizhad?"

She stroked my head.

I looked up and saw her face through the darkness. It was strained. There were tears in her blue-flecked eyes.

"Is it?"

"Yes, my love. Yes."

But I knew that the same sense of doom that lay upon my heart now lay upon hers.

We slept no more that night.

THE ETERNAL CHAMPION

T H R E E

OF A VISITATION

Next morning I went straight to Prince Arjavh's laboratory and told him of the voice that had come to me in my sleep.

It was plain that he was distressed and plain also that he felt impotent to help me.

"If the voice was a mere nightmare — and I agree that it might be — then I could give you a potion to ensure dreamless sleep," he said.

"And if not?"

"There is no way I can protect you."

"Then the voice could be calling from the Ghost Worlds?"

"Even that is not certain. It could be that the information I gave you yesterday merely triggered some empathetic impulse in your own brain — which allowed this "voice" to make contact with you again. Perhaps the tranquillity you have known here made it impossible for you to be reached. Now that your brain is again in torment, then whatever it is that seeks to speak to you might now be able to do so."

"These suppositions do not ease my mind," I said bitterly.

"I know they do not, Erekosë. Would that you had never come to my laboratory, and learned of the Ghost Worlds. I should have kept this from you."

"It would have made no difference, Arjavh."

"Who knows?"

I stretched out my hand. "Give me the potion of which you spoke. At least we'll be able to put the theory to the test — that my own brain conjures this mocking voice."

He went to a chest of glowing crystal and opened the lid, taking a small leather bag from it.

"Pour this powder into a goblet of wine tonight and drink all down."

"Thank you," I said as I took the bag.

He paused before he spoke again. "Erekosë, if you are called from us, we shall waste no time in trying to find you. You are loved by all the Eldren and we would not lose you. If, somewhere in those unimaginable regions of Time and Space, you can be found — we shall find you."

I was a little comforted by this assurance. Yet the speech was too much like a leave-taking for me to like it greatly. It was as if Arjavh had already accepted that I would be going.

Ermizhad and I spent the rest of that day walking hand in hand among the bowers of the palace garden. We spoke little, but gripped each other tightly and hardly dared look into each other's eyes for fear of the grief which would be mirrored there.

From hidden galleries came the intricate melodies of the great Eldren composers, played by musicians placed there by Prince Arjavh. The music was sweet, monumental, harmonious. To some degree it eased the dread that filled my brain.

A golden sun, huge and warm, hung in a pale blue sky. It shone its rays on delicately scented flowers in a multitude of hues, on vines and trees, on the white walls of the gardens.

We climbed the walls and looked out over the gentle hills and plains of the Southern continent. A herd of deer were grazing. Birds sailed lazily in the sky.

I could not leave all this beauty to return to the noise and the filth of the world I had left, to the sad existence of John Daker.

Evening came and the air was filled with bird song and the heavier perfume of the flowers. Slowly we walked back to the palace. Tightly we held each other's hands.

Like a condemned man, I mounted the steps that led to our chambers. Disrobing myself, I wondered if I should ever wear such clothes again. Lying down upon the bed while Ermizhad prepared the sleeping draught, I prayed that I should not rise next morning in the apartment in the city where John Daker had lived.

I stared up at the fluted ceiling of the chamber, looked around at the bright wall-hangings, the vases of flowers, the finely wrought furnishings, and I attempted to fix all this in my mind, just as I had already fixed Ermizhad's face.

She brought me the drink. I looked deep into her tear-filled eyes and drank. It was a parting. A parting we dare not admit.

Almost immediately I sank into a heavy slumber and it seemed to me at that moment that perhaps Ermizhad and Arjavh had been right and that the voice was simply a manifestation of my unease.

I do not know at what hour I was disturbed in that deep, drugged sleep. I was barely conscious. My brain seemed swaddled in fold upon fold of dark velvet, but muffled, and as if from far off, I faintly heard the voice again.

I could make out no words this time and I believe I smiled to myself, feeling relief that the drug was guarding me from that which sought to call me away. The voice became more urgent, but I could ignore it. I stirred and reached out for Ermizhad, throwing one arm across her slumbering body.

Still the voice called. Still I ignored it. Now I felt that if I could last this night, the voice would cease its attempt to recall me. I would know that I could not be drawn away so easily from the world where I had found love and tranquillity.

The voice faded and I slept on, with Ermizhad in my arms, with hope in my heart.

The voice returned some time later, but still I could ignore it.

Then the voice apparently ceased altogether and I sank again into my heavy sleep.

I think it must have been an hour or two before dawn that I heard a noise not within my head but in the room. Thinking that Ermizhad must have arisen, I opened my eyes. It was dark. I saw nothing. But Ermizhad was beside me. Then I heard the noise again. It was like the slap of a scabbarded sword against an armoured leg. I sat upright. My eyes were clogged with sleep, my head felt muzzy under the effects of the drug. I peered drowsily about the room.

And then I saw the figure who stood there.

"Who are you?" I asked, rather querulously. Maybe it was some servant? In Loos Ptokai there were no thieves, no threats of assassination.

The figure did not answer. It seemed to be staring at me. Gradually I distinguished more details and then I knew that this was no Eldren.

The figure had a barbaric appearance, though its apparel was rich and finely made. It wore a huge, grotesque helmet which completely framed a heavily bearded face. On its broad chest was a metal breastplate, as intricately ornamented as the helm. Over this was a thick, sleeveless coat of what appeared to be sheepskin. On his legs were breeches of lacquered hide, black and with sinuous designs picked out in gold and silver. Greaves on his legs matched the breastplate and his feet were encased in boots of the same shaggy, white pelt as his long coat. On his hip was a sword.

The figure did not move, but continued to regard me from the shadow cast by the peak of the grotesque helmet. The eyes were visible now. They burned. They were urgent.

This was no human of this world, no follower of King Rigenos who had somehow escaped the vengeance I had brought. A faint recollection came and went. But the garb was not that of any period of history I could remember from my life as John Daker.

Was this a visitor from the Ghost Worlds?

If so, his appearance was very different from that of the other Ghost Worlds dwellers who had once helped Ermizhad when she was a prisoner of King Rigenos.

I repeated my question.

"Who are you?"

The figure tried to speak but plainly could not.

He raised both hands to his head. He removed his helmet. He brushed back black, long hair from his face. He moved nearer to the window.

The face was familiar.

It was my own.

I shrank back in the bed. Never before had I felt such complete terror. I do not think I have felt it since.

"What do you want?" I screamed. "What do you want?"

In some other part of my churning brain I seem to remember wondering why Ermizhad did not awake but continued to sleep peacefully at my side.

The figure's mouth moved as if he was speaking, but I heard no words.

Was this a nightmare induced by the drug? If so, I think I should have preferred the voice.

"Get out of here! Begone!"

The visitation made several gestures which I could not interpret. Again its mouth moved, but no words reached me.

Screaming, I leapt from the bed and rushed at the figure which bore my face. But it moved away, a puzzled expression on its features.

There were no swords now in the Eldren palace, or I would have found one and used it against the figure. I think I had some mindless scheme to grasp his sword and use it against him.

"Begone! Begone!"

Then I tripped, fell scrabbling on the flagstones of the bedchamber, shaking still with terror, screaming at the apparition which continued to look down at me. I rose again, tottered and was falling, falling, falling...

And as I fell, the voice filled my ears once again. It was full of triumphant joy.

"URLIK," it cried. "URLIK SKARSOL! URLIK! URLIK! ICE-HERO, COME TO US!"

"I WILL NOT!"

But now I did not deny that the name was mine. I tried to refuse the one or ones who called it. As I whirled and tumbled through the corridors of eternity, I sought to fling myself back — back to Ermizhad and the world of the Eldren.

"URLIK SKARSOL! COUNT OF THE WHITE WASTES! LORD OF THE FROZEN KEEP! PRINCE OF THE SOUTHERN ICE! MASTER OF THE COLD SWORD! HE WILL COME IN FURS AND METAL, HIS CHARIOT DRAWN BY BEARS, HIS BLACK BEARD BRISTLING, TO CLAIM HIS BLADE, TO AID HIS FOLK!"

"I WILL GIVE YOU NO AID! I DESIRE NO BLADE! LET ME SLEEP! I BEG YOU — LET ME SLEEP!"

"AWAKE, URLIK SKARSOL. THE PROPHECY DEMANDS IT!"

Now fragments of a vision came to me. I saw cities carved from cliffs of volcanic rock — obsidian and moody, built on the shores of sluggish seas, beneath dark, livid skies. I saw a sea that was like grey marble veined with black and I realised it was a sea on which floated great ice-floes.

The vision filled me with grief — not because it was strange and unfamiliar, but because it was familiar.

I knew for certain then that, weary with war, I had been called to fight yet another fight...

BOOK TWO:
THE CHAMPION'S ROAD

The Warriors are in Silver,
The Citizens in Silk.
In Brazen Car the Champion rides,
A Hero clad in Grief.

—The Chronicle of the Black Sword

O N E

THE ICE WASTES

I was still travelling, but it was no longer as if I had been tugged down into a maelstrom. I was moving slowly forward, though I was not moving my legs.

My vision cleared. The scene before me was concrete enough, though scarcely reassuring. I clung to a wisp of hope that I was still dreaming, but everything in me told me that this was not so. Just as John Daker had been called against his will to the world of the Eldren, so had Erekosë been called to this world.

And I knew my name. It had been repeated often enough. But I knew it as if it had always been mine. I was Urlik Skarsol of the South Ice.

The scene before me confirmed it, for I stared across a world of ice. It came to me that I had seen other ice plains in other incarnations, but this one I recognised for what it was. I was travelling over a dying planet. And in the sky above me was a small, dim red sun — a dying sun. That the world was Earth, I was certain, but it was an Earth at the end of its cycle. John Daker would have seen it as being in his distant future, but I had long-since ceased to make easy definitions of 'past' and 'future'. If Time were my enemy, then she was an enemy without face or form; an enemy I could not see; an enemy I could not fight.

I was travelling in a chariot which seemed fashioned of silver and bronze, its heavy decoration reminiscent of the decoration I had seen on the armour of my voiceless visitor. Its four great iron-shod wheels had been bolted to skis apparently made of polished ebony. In the shafts at the front were the four creatures which dragged the chariot over the ice. The creatures were larger, longer-legged variations of the polar bears which had existed on John Daker's world. They loped at a regular and surprisingly rapid speed. I stood upright in the chariot, holding their reins. Before me was a chest designed to fit the space. It seemed made of some hard wood overlaid with silver, its corners strengthened with strips of iron. It had a great iron lock and handle at the centre of the lid and the whole chest was decorated in black, brown and blue enamel work depicting dragons, warriors, trees and flowers, all flowing and intertwining. There were strange, flowing runes picked out around the lock and I was surprised that I could read them easily: *This is the chest of Count Urlik Skarsol, Lord of the Frozen Keep.* On the right of the chest three heavy rings had been soldered to the side of the chariot and through the rings was placed the silver- and brass-shod haft of a lance which must have been at least seven feet long, ending in a huge, cruelly barbed head of gleaming iron. On the other side of the chest was a weapon whose haft was the twin to the spear's, but whose head was that of a great, broad-bladed axe, as beautifully decorated as the trunk, with delicately engraved designs. I felt at my belt. There was no sword there, only a pouch and, on my right hip, a key. I unhooked the key from my belt and looked at it curiously. I bent and inserted it with some difficulty (for the chariot had a tendency to lurch on the rough ice) and opened the trunk, expecting to find a sword there.

But there was no sword, only provisions, spare clothing and the like — the things a man would take with him if he were making a long journey.

I smiled despairingly. I had made a very long journey. I closed the chest and locked it, replacing the key on my belt.

And then I noticed what I was wearing. I had a heavily decorated iron breastplate, a huge coat of thick, coarse wool, a leather jerkin, breeks of lacquered leather, greaves of the same design as the breastplate, boots apparently of the same sheepskin-like stuff as the coat. I reached up to my head and touched metal. I ran my fingers over the serpentine designs which had been raised on the helmet.

With a growing sense of terror I moved my hands to my face. Its contours were familiar enough, but there was now a thick moustache on my upper lip, a great crop of black whiskers on my chin.

I had seen a hand-mirror in the chest. I seized the key, unlocked the bolt, flung back the lid, rummaged until I found the mirror which was of highly polished silver and not glass. I hesitated for a moment and then forced my hand to raise the mirror to my face.

I saw the face and helmet of my visitor — of the apparition which had come to me in the night.

I was now that apparition.

With a moan, with a sense of foreboding in my heart which I was unable to vocalize, I dropped the mirror back into the chest and slammed the lid shut. My hand went out to grip the haft of the tall lance and I clung to it. I squeezed it with such force I thought it would surely snap.

And here I was on the pale ice beneath a darkling sky, alone and in torment, cut off from the one woman who had brought me tranquillity of spirit, the one world where I had felt free and at peace. I felt as a man must feel who has been in the grip of uncontrollable madness, thinks he is cured and then finds himself once again seized by the horrible insanity of which he thought himself purged.

I opened my mouth and I cried out against the ice. The breath steamed from my lips and boiled in the air like ectoplasm, writhed as if imitating the agony of spirit that was within me. I shook my fist at the dim, red, far-away globe that was this world's sun.

And all the while the white bears loped on, dragging me and my chariot to an unknown destination.

"Ermizhad!" I cried. "Ermizhad!"

I wondered if somewhere she would hear me, call me as that other voice had called me.

"Ermizhad!"

But the dark sky was silent, the gloomy ice was still, the sun looked down like the eye of an old, old, senile man, uncomprehending.

On and on ran the tireless bears; on, across the perpetual ice; on, through perpetual twilight. On and on, while I wept and moaned and shrieked and at last was quiet, standing in my lurching chariot as if I, too, were made of ice.

I knew that, for the moment, I must accept my fate, discover where the bears were taking me, hope that when I reached my destination I would be able to discover a means of going back to the Eldren world, of finding my Ermizhad again.

I knew the hope was a faint one, but I clung to it as I had clung to the shaft of the spear. It was all I had. But where she was in the universe — in a host of alternate universes if the Eldren theories were right — I had no idea. Neither did I know where this world was. While it might be one of the Ghost Worlds and therefore possible for Eldren expeditions to reach, it could as easily be some other Earth, sundered by aeons from the world I had grown to love and to think of as my own.

But now I was again the Eternal Champion, summoned, no doubt, to fight in some cause with which I had scant sympathy, by a people who could easily be as wretched and self-deceiving as those who had been ruled by King Rigenos.

Why should I be singled out for this everlasting task? Why was I to be allowed no permanent peace?

Again my thoughts turned to the possibility that I had been responsible, in some incarnation, of a cosmic crime, so terrible that it was my fate to be swept back and forth across eternity. But what that crime could be that it deserved so frightful a punishment, I could not guess.

It seemed to grow colder. I reached into the chest and knew I should find gauntlets there. I drew the gloves on to my hands, wrapped the heavy coat more tightly about me, sat down on the chest, still holding the reins, and sank into a doze which I hoped would heal, at least a little, my wounded brain.

And still we drove over ice. Thousands of miles of ice. Had this world grown so old and cold that now there was nothing but ice from pole to pole?

Soon, I hoped, I would find out.

T W O

THE OBSIDIAN CITY

Across the timeless ice, beneath the waning sun, I moved in my chariot of bronze and silver. The long-limbed white bears only rarely slowed and never stopped. It was as if they, like me, were possessed of some force they could not control. Rusty clouds crossed the sky occasionally — slow ships on a livid sea — but there was nothing to mark the passing of the hours for the sun itself was frozen in the sky and the faint stars which gleamed behind it were arranged in constellations which were only vaguely familiar. It came to me then that the globe itself had apparently ceased to spin or, if it moved at all, moved so gradually as not to be apparent to a man without the necessary measuring instruments.

I reflected bitterly that the landscape certainly matched my mood, probably even exacerbated it.

Then, through the gloom, I thought I saw something which relieved the monotony of ice which hitherto had lain on all sides. Perhaps it was nothing more than a band of low cloud, but I kept my gaze fixed hopefully upon it and, as the bears drew closer, saw that these were the dark shapes of mountains apparently rising out of the ice plain. Were they mountains of ice and nothing more? Or were they of rock, indicating that not all the planet was covered by ice?

I had never seen such jagged crags. Despondently I concluded that they must be made of ice shaped by wind and time into such peculiar serrations.

But then, as we drew yet closer, I remembered the vision I had had when I was dragged away from Ermizhad's side. Now it seemed these were, indeed,

THE ETERNAL CHAMPION

rocks — volcanic rocks with a glassy lustre. Colours became apparent — deep greens and browns and blacks.

I shouted to the bears and jerked the reins to make them go faster.

And I discovered that I knew their names.

"Ho, Snarler! Ho, Render! Ho, Growler! Ho, Longclaw! Faster!"

They leaned in their harness and their speed increased. The chariot lurched and jogged and skipped over the rough ice.

"Faster!"

I had been right. Now I could see that the ice gave way to rock that was, if anything, smoother than glass. The ice thinned and then the chariot was bumping on to the rock that formed the foothills of the mountain range which now flung its spiky peaks into a mass of low, rust-coloured clouds, where they were lost to my view.

These were high and gloomy peaks. They dominated me, seemed to threaten me, and they were certainly no comfort to the eye. But they offered me some hope, particularly as I made out what could be a pass between two tall cliffs.

The range seemed principally a mixture of basalt and obsidian and on both sides of me now were huge boulders between which passed a natural causeway down which I drove my straining bears. I could see the strangely coloured clouds clinging to the upper slopes of the cliffs, almost as smoke clings to oil.

And now, as I discerned more detail, I could only gasp at the wonder of the cliffs. That they were volcanic in origin there was no doubt, for the spiky upper peaks were plainly of pumice, while the lower flanks were either of black, green or purple obsidian, smooth and shiny, or basalt which had formed into something not unlike the delicately fluted columns of fine Gothic architecture. They could almost have been built by some intelligence possessed of gigantic size. Elsewhere the basalt was red and deep blue and cellular in appearance, almost like coral. In other places the same rock was a more familiar coal black and dark grey. And at still more levels there were veins of iridescent rock that caught what little light there was and were as richly coloured as the feathers of a peacock.

I guessed that this region must have resisted the march of the ice because it had been the last volcanically active region on the planet.

Now I had entered the pass. It was narrow and the cliffs seemed as if they were about to crush me. Some parts of them were pitted with caves which my fancy saw as malicious eyes staring down at me. I kept a firm grip on my lance as I drove. For all my imaginings, there was always the chance that there were real dangers here from beasts which might inhabit the caves.

The pass wound around the bases of many mountains, all of the same strange formations and colours. The ground became less level and the bears had great difficulty pulling the chariot. At last, though I had no inclination to stop in that gloomy pass, I drew rein and dismounted from the chariot, inspecting the runners and the bolts attaching them to the wheels. I knew instinctively that I had the appropriate tools in my chest and I opened the lid and eventually discovered them in a box of the same design and manufacture as the chest itself.

With some effort I unbolted the runners and slid them into lugs along the side of the chariot.

Just as I had discovered, as Erekosë, that I had an instinctive skill with weapons and horses, that I knew every piece of armour as if I had always worn it, now I found that the workings of this chariot were completely familiar to me.

With the wheels free, the chariot moved much faster, though it was even more difficult to keep my balance than before.

Many hours must have passed before I rounded a curve in the pass and saw that I had come to the other side of the mountain range.

Smooth rock sloped down to a crystalline beach. And against the beach moved the sluggish tide of an almost viscous sea.

Elsewhere the mountains entered the sea itself and I could see jagged peaks jutting out of the water which must have contained a much greater quantity of salt than even the Dead Sea of John Daker's world. The low, brown clouds seemed to meet the sea only a short distance out. The dark crystals of the beach were devoid of plant life and here even the faint light from the small, red sun barely pierced the darkness.

It was as if I had come to the edge of the world at the end of time.

I could not believe that anything lived here — whether man, plant or beast.

But now the bears had reached the beach and the wheels crunched on the crystal and the creatures did not stop, but turned sharply towards the East, dragging me and the chariot along the shore of that dark and morbid ocean.

Though it was warmer here than it had been on the ice, I shuddered. Again my imagination took an unpleasant turn as I guessed at what kind of monsters might dwell beneath the surface of the twilit sea, what kind of people could bear to live beside it.

I was soon to have my answer — or, at least, part of it — when through the gloom I heard the sound of human voices and soon saw those who had uttered them.

They rode huge animals which moved not on legs but on strong, muscular flippers and whose bodies sloped sharply back to end in wide tails which balanced them. In some astonishment I realised that these riding beasts had been, at some earlier period of their evolution, sea-lions. They still had the dog-like, whiskered faces, the huge, staring eyes. The saddles on their backs had been built up so that the rider sat almost level. Each rider held a rod of some kind which issued a faint glow in the darkness.

But were the riders human? Their bodies, encased in ornate armour, were bulbous and, in comparison, their arms and legs were sticklike, their heads — also enclosed in helmets — tiny. They had swords, lances and axes at their hips or in sheaths attached to their saddles. From within their visors their voices boomed and were echoed by the lowering cliffs, but I could distinguish no words.

They rode their seal-beasts skilfully along the shores of the salt-thick sea until they were only a few yards from me. Then they stopped.

In turn, I stopped my chariot.

A silence fell. I placed my hand upon the shaft of my tall spear while my bears moved restlessly in their harness.

I inspected them more closely. They were somewhat froglike in appearance, if the armour actually displayed the basic shapes of their bodies. The accoutrements and armour was so ornate and, to my taste, over-worked, that it was almost impossible to pick out individual designs. Most of the suits were of a reddish gold in colour, though glowing greens and yellows became apparent in the light from their dim torches.

After some moments in which they made no further effort to communicate with me I decided to speak.

"Are you those who called me?" I asked.

Visors turned, gestures were made, but they did not reply.

"What people are you?" I said. "Do you recognise me?"

This time a few words passed between the riders but they still did not speak directly to me. They urged their beasts into a wide semicircle and then surrounded me. I kept my hand firmly on the shaft of my lance.

"I am Urlik Skarsol," I said. "Did you not summon me?"

Now one spoke, his voice muffled in his helm. "We did not summon you, Urlik Skarsol. But we know your name and bid you be our guest in Rowernarc." He gestured with his torch in the direction from which they had come. "We are Bishop Belphig's men. He would wish us to make you welcome."

"I accept your hospitality."

There had been respect in the speaker's voice after he had heard my name, but I was surprised that he had not been expecting me. Why had the bears brought me here? Where else was there to go, save beyond the sea? And it seemed to me that beyond the sea lay nothing but limbo. I could imagine those sluggish waters dripping over the edge of the world into the total blackness of the cosmic void.

I allowed them to escort me along the beach until it curved into a bay, at the end of which was a steep, high cliff up which climbed a number of paths, evidently cut by men. These paths led to the mouths of archways as heavily ornamented as the armour worn by the riders.

High above, the most distant archways were half hidden by the thick, brown clouds clinging to the rock.

This was not merely a village of cliff-dwellers. Judging by the sophistication of the ornament, it was a great city, carved from the gleaming obsidian.

"That is Rowernarc," said the rider nearest me. "Rowernarc — the Obsidian City."

T H R E E

THE LORD SPIRITUAL

The paths up to the yawning gateways in the cliff-face were wide enough to take my chariot. Somewhat reluctantly the bears began to climb.

The froglike riders led the way, ascending higher and higher along the obsidian causeways, passing several baroque arches festooned with gargoyles which, while being of exquisite workmanship, were the products of dark and morbid brains.

I looked towards the gloomy bay, at the low, brown clouds, at the heavy, unnatural sea, and it seemed for a moment that all this world was enclosed in one murky cave — in one cold hell.

And if the landscape reminded me of Hell, then subsequent events were soon to confirm my impression.

Eventually we reached an archway of particularly heavy decoration — all carved from the multicoloured living obsidian — and the strange seal-beasts turned and stopped and thwacked their forefins on the ground in a complicated rhythm.

Within the shadow of the arch I could now detect a barrier. It seemed to be a door — but a door that was made of solid porphyritic rock from which all kinds of strange beasts and half-human creatures had been carved. Whether these representations, too, were the inventions of near-crazed minds or whether they were taken from types actually to be found in this world, I could not tell. But some of the designs were loathsome and I avoided looking at them as much as possible.

In answer to the strange signal of the seals, this door began to scrape backwards — the whole block moving into the cavern behind it — to allow us passage around it. My chariot wheel caught on one edge and I was forced to manoeuvre for a moment before I could pass into the chamber.

This chamber was poorly lit by the same staffs of faint artificial light which the riders had carried. The staffs reminded me of battery-operated electric torches which needed recharging. Somehow I thought that these could not be recharged. I had the feeling that as the artificial brands died, so a little more light vanished from this world. It would not be long, I thought, before all the brands were extinguished.

The froglike riders were dismounting, handing their beasts over to grooms who, to my relief, looked ordinarily human, though pale and somewhat scrawny. These grooms were dressed in smocks bearing a complicated piece of embroidered insignia which again was so complex as to have no indication to me what it was meant to represent. I suddenly had an insight into the lives of these people. Living in their rock cities on a dying planet, surrounded by bleak ice and gloomy seas, they whiled away their days at various crafts, adding embellishment upon complicated embellishment, producing work which was so introverted that it doubtless lost its meaning even to them. It was the art of a decaying race and yet, ironically, it would outlast them by centuries, perhaps forever when the atmosphere eventually disappeared.

I felt a reluctance to deliver my chariot and its weapons over to the grooms, but there was little else I could do. Seal-beasts and chariot were led off down a dark, echoing passage and the armoured creatures once again turned to regard me.

One of them stretched, then lifted off his ornate helm to reveal a white, human face with pale, cold eyes — weary eyes, it seemed to me. He began to unbuckle the straps of his armour and it was drawn away to show the thick padding beneath. When the padding was pulled off, I saw that the body, also, was of perfectly normal proportions. The others stripped off their armour and handed it to those waiting to receive it. As a gesture, I took off my own helmet and held it crooked in my left arm.

The men were all pale, all with the same strange eyes which were not so much unfriendly as introspective. They wore loose tabards which had every inch covered in dark-hued embroidery, trousers of similar material which were baggy and tucked into boots of painted leather.

"Well," sighed the man who had first removed his armour, "here we are in Haradeik." He signed to a servant. "Seek our master. Tell him Morgeg is here with his patrol. Tell him we have brought a visitor — Urlik Skarsol of the

THE ETERNAL CHAMPION

Frozen Keep. Ask him if he would grant us an audience."

I frowned at Morgeg. "So you know of Urlik Skarsol. You know that I hail from the Frozen Keep."

A tiny, puzzled smile came to Morgeg's mouth. "All know of Urlik Skarsol. But I have heard of no man who has ever met him."

"And you called this city Rowernarc when we arrived, but now you call it Haradeik."

"Rowernarc is the city. Haradeik is the name of our particular warren — the province of our master, Bishop Belphig."

"And who is this bishop?"

"Why, he is one of our two rulers. He is Lord Spiritual of Rowernarc."

Morgeg spoke in a low, sad tone which I guessed was habitual rather than reflecting a particular mood of his at this moment. Everything he said sounded off-handed. Nothing seemed to matter to him. Nothing seemed to interest him. He seemed almost as dead as the murky, twilight world outside the cavern city.

Quite soon the messenger returned.

"Bishop Belphig grants an audience," he told Morgeg.

By this time the others had gone about their business and only Morgeg and I remained in the antechamber. Morgeg led me along a poorly lit passage, every inch of which was decorated — even the floor was of crystalline mosaic, and harpies, chimerae and musimonii glared down at me from the low ceiling. Another antechamber, another great door, slightly smaller than the outer one, which withdrew to allow us entrance. And we were in a large hall.

It was a hall with a high arched ceiling coming almost to a point at the top. At the end of it was a dais hung with draperies. On each side of the dais was a glowing brazier, tended by servants, which issued ruddy light and sent smoke curling towards the ceiling where, presumably, it found egress, for there was only a hint of smoke in the air I breathed. As if preserved in volcanic glass, stone monsters writhed and crouched on walls and ceiling, leering, baring unlikely fangs, laughing at some obscene joke, roaring, threatening, twisting in some secret agony. Many bore resemblances to the heraldic monsters of John Daker's world. Here were cockfish, opinicus, mantigoras, satyrs, man-lions, melusines, camelopards, wyverns, cockatrices, dragons, griffins, unicorns, amphisboenae, enfields, bagwyns, salamanders — every combination of man, beast, fish and fowl — all of huge size, rending each other, crawling over each other's backs, copulating, tangling tails, defecating, dying, being born…

This, surely, was a chamber of Hell.

I looked towards the dais. Behind draperies, in some sort of throne, a figure lounged. I approached the dais, half expecting the figure to be possessed of a spiked tail and a pair of horns.

A foot or two from the dais Morgeg stopped and bowed. I did likewise. The drapes were drawn back by servants and there sat a man very different from what I had expected — very different from the pale, sad-eyed Morgeg.

The voice was deep, sensuous, jovial. "Greetings, Count Urlik. We are honoured you should decide to pay a visit to this rat's nest we call Rowernarc, you who are of the free and open icelands."

Bishop Belphig was fat, dressed in rich robes, a circlet around his long, blond hair, keeping it from his eyes. His lips were very red and his eyebrows very black. With a sudden shock I realised that he was using cosmetics. Beneath them doubtless he, too, was as pale as Morgeg and the rest. Perhaps the hair was dyed. Certainly the cheeks were rouged, the eyelashes false, the lips painted.

"Greetings, Bishop Belphig," I replied. "I thank the Lord Spiritual of Rowernarc for his hospitality and would beg a word or two with him in private."

"Aha! You have some message for me, dear count! Of course. Morgeg — the rest of you — leave us for a while. But stay within earshot if I should want to call you suddenly."

I smiled slightly. Bishop Belphig did not want to risk the fact that I might be an assassin.

When they had gone Belphig waved a beringed hand in an expansive gesture. "Well, good count? What is your message?"

"I have no message," I said. "I have only a question. Perhaps several questions."

"Then ask them, sir! Please, ask them!"

"First, I would know why my name is familiar to you all. Secondly, I would ask if it was you, who must have certain mystical knowledge, who summoned me here. The other questions depend on your answers to the first two."

"Why, dear count, your name is known to all! You are a legend, you are a fabulous hero. You must know this!"

"Presume that I have awakened just recently from a deep sleep. Presume that most of my memories are gone. Tell me of the legend."

Bishop Belphig frowned and he put fat, jewelled fingers to fat, carmine lips. His voice was more subdued, more contemplative when next he spoke. "Very well, I will presume that. There are said to have been four Ice Lords — of North, South, East and West — but all died save the Lord of the South Ice, who was frozen in his great keep by a sorceress until he should be called for — summoned when his people were in great danger. All this took place in antiquity, only a century or two after the ice had destroyed the famous cities of the world — Barbart, Lanjis Liho, Korodune and the rest."

The names were faintly familiar but no memories were awakened within me by the remainder of the bishop's story.

"Is there any more of the legend?" I asked.

"That is the substance of it. I can probably find a book or two containing some sort of amplification."

"And it was not you who called me?"

"Why should I summon, you? To tell you the truth, Count Urlik, I did not believe the legend."

"And you believe it now? You do not think me an impostor ?"

"Why should you be an imposter? And if you are, why should I not humour you if it suits you to say you are Count Urlik." He smiled. "There is precious little that is new in Rowernarc. We welcome diversion."

I returned his smile. "A pleasantly sophisticated view, Bishop Belphig. However, I remain puzzled. Not long since, I found myself on the ice, travelling here. My accoutrements and my name were familiar, but all else was strange. I am a creature, my lord, with little volition of his own. I am a hero, you see, and am called whenever I am needed. I will not bore you with the details of my tragedy, save to say that I would not be here unless I was needed to take part in a struggle. If you did not call me, then perhaps you know who did."

Belphig drew his painted brows together in a frown. Then he raised them and gave me a quizzical look. "I fear I can offer no suggestion at present, Count Urlik. The only threat facing Rowernarc is the inevitable one. In a century or two the ice will creep over our mountain barrier and extinguish us. In the meantime, we while away the hours as best we can. You are welcome to join us here, if the Lord Temporal agrees, and you must promise to recount your whole story to us, no matter how incredible you think it is. In return, we can offer you such entertainments as we have. These may be stimulating if they are new to you."

"Has Rowernarc, then, no enemies?"

"None powerful enough to form a threat. There are a few bands of outlaws, some pirates — the kind of garbage that collects around any city — but they are all."

I shook my head in puzzlement. "Perhaps there are internal factions at Rowernarc — groups who wish, say, to overthrow you and the Lord Temporal?"

Bishop Belphig laughed. "Really, my dear count, you seem to desire strife above all else! I assure you that there are no issues in Rowernarc on which anyone would care to spend much time. Boredom is our only enemy and now that you are here that enemy has been put to flight!"

"Then I thank you for your offer of hospitality," I said. "I will accept it. Presumably you have libraries in Rowernarc — and scholars."

"We are all scholars in Rowernarc. Yes, we have libraries, many of which you may use."

At least, I thought, I would be able here to spend the best part of my time seeking to find a means of returning to Ermizhad and the lovely world of the Eldren (to which this world was in hateful contrast). Yet I could not believe that I had been called here for nothing, unless it was to a life of exile in which, as an immortal, I would be forced to witness the eventual death of the Earth.

"However," continued Bishop Belphig, "I cannot alone make this decision. We must also consult my fellow-ruler, the Lord Temporal. I am sure he will agree to your requests and make you welcome. Apartments must be found for you, and slaves and the like. These activities will also help relieve the ennui which besets Rowernarc."

"I desire no slaves," I said.

Bishop Belphig chuckled. "Wait until you see them before you make your decision." Then he paused and gave me an amused look from his made-up eyes. "But perhaps you are of a period where the holding of slaves is frowned upon, eh? I have read that history has had such periods. But in Rowernarc slaves are not held by force. Only those who wish to be slaves are such. If they choose to be something else, why, then, they can be whatever they desire. This is Rowernarc, Count Urlik, where all men and women are free to follow any inclination they choose."

"And you chose to be Lord Spiritual here?"

Again the bishop smiled. "In a sense. The title is an hereditary one, but many born to this rank have preferred other occupations. My brother, for instance, is a common sailor."

"You sail those salt-thick seas?" I was astonished.

"Again — in a sense. If you know not the customs of Rowernarc, I believe you will find many of them interesting."

"I am sure I will," I said. And I thought privately that some of those customs I should not find to my taste at all. Here, I thought, I had found the human race in its final stages of decadence — perverse, insouciant, without ambition. And I could not blame them. After all, they had no future.

And there was something, too, in me which reflected Bishop Belphig's cynicism. For had not I little to live for, also?

The bishop raised his voice. "Slaves! Morgeg! You may return."

They trooped back into the murky chamber, Morgeg at their head.

"Morgeg," said the bishop, "perhaps you will send a messenger to find the Lord Temporal. Ask him if he will grant an audience to Count Urlik Skarsol. Tell him I have offered the count our hospitality, if he should agree."

Morgeg bowed and left the chamber.

"And now, while we wait, you must dine with me, my lord," Bishop Belphig said to me. "We grow fruits and vegetables in our garden caverns and the sea provides us with meat. My cook is the best in all Rowernarc. Will you eat?"

"Gladly," I said, for I had realised that I was famished.

F O U R

THE LORD TEMPORAL

The meal, though somewhat rich and overspiced for my taste, was delicious. When it was over, Morgeg came back to say that the Lord Temporal had been given the message.

"It was some time before we could find him," Morgeg said, offering Belphig a significant look. "But he will give an audience to our guest now, if our guest desires." He looked at me with his pale, cold eyes.

"Have you had enough to eat and drink, Count Urlik?" Bishop Belphig asked. "Is there anything else you desire?" He wiped his red lips with a brocade napkin, removed a sauce stain from his jowl.

"I thank you for your generosity," I said rising. I had drunk more salty wine than I should have liked, but it helped dampen the morbid thoughts of Ermizhad which still plagued me — would plague me for ever, until I found her again.

I followed Morgeg from the grotesque chamber. As I reached the door I looked back, thinking to thank Bishop Belphig again.

He had smeared some of the sauce over the body of a young boy slave. As I watched, he bent to lick at the stuff he had put there.

I turned quickly and increased my stride as Morgeg led me back the way we had come.

"The Lord Temporal's province is called Dhotgard and lies above this one. We must go to the outer causeway again."

"Are there no passages connecting the various levels?" I asked.

Morgeg shrugged. "Aye, I believe so. But this way is easier than searching for the doors and then trying to get them open."

"You mean you do not use many of the passages?"

Morgeg nodded. "There are fewer of us now than there were even fifty years ago. Children are rare in Rowernarc these days." He spoke carelessly and once again I had the impression that I spoke to a corpse brought back from the dead.

Through the great main door of Haradeik we passed and into the cold air of the causeway that hung above the dark bay where the sluggish sea spread pale salt on the black crystals of the beach. It seemed an even gloomier landscape than it had seemed before, with the clouds bringing the horizon so close and the jagged crags on all other sides. I felt a sense of claustrophobia as we walked up the causeway until we came to an archway which was little different in style from the one we had just left.

Morgeg cupped his hands together and shouted through them. "Lord Urlik Skarsol comes to seek audience with the Lord Temporal!"

His voice found a muffled echo in the mountains. I looked up, trying to see the sky, trying to make out the sun behind the clouds, but I could not.

There was a grating noise as the door slid in just sufficiently for us to squeeze past and find ourselves in an antechamber with smooth walls and even less light than that which had barely illuminated Haradeik. A servant in a plain white tabard was waiting for us. He rang a silver handbell and the door moved back. The machinery operating these doors must have been very sophisticated, for I could see no evidence of pulleys and chains.

The passage we moved down was the twin to the one in Bishop Belphig's "province" save that here there were no bas-reliefs. Instead there were paintings, but the light was so poor and the paint so old that I could scarcely make out any details. We turned into a similar passage, our footsteps sounding loudly on the carpet-covered floor. Another passage and then we reached an archway which was not blocked by a door. Instead, a curtain of plain, soft leather had been hung across it. I felt that such simplicity was incongruous in Rowernarc, but I was even more surprised when the servant parted the curtain and led us into a chamber whose walls were completely bare, save that they had been covered with a surface of white paint. Huge lamps brightly lit the room. These lamps were probably oil-burning, for a faint smell issued from them. In the middle of the room was a desk and two benches. Save for ourselves, there were no other occupants.

Morgeg looked around at the room and his expression was one of discomfort.

"I will leave you here, Count Urlik. Doubtless the Lord Temporal will emerge soon."

When Morgeg had left, the servant indicated that I sit on one of the benches. I did so, placing my helm beside me. Like the room, the desk was bare, apart from two scrolls placed neatly near the end. There was nothing for me to do but look at the white walls, the silent servant who had taken up a position by the arch curtain, the almost bare desk.

I must have sat there for an hour before the curtain parted and a tall figure entered. I rose to my feet, hardly able to restrain the expression of astonishment which tried to come over my face. The figure signed for me to sit down again. He had an abstracted look as he walked to the desk and sat behind it.

"I am Shanosfane," he said.

His skin was a flat, coal black and his features were fine-boned and ascetic. I reflected, ironically, that somehow the roles of Shanosfane and Belphig had become muddled — that Belphig should have been the Temporal Lord and Shanosfane the Spiritual Lord.

Shanosfane wore loose, white robes. The only decoration was a fibula at his left shoulder which bore a device I took to be the sign of his rank. He rested his long-fingered hands on the desk and regarded me with a distant expression which none the less betrayed a great intelligence.

"I am Urlik," I replied, thinking it best to speak as simply.

He nodded, peering at the desk and tracing a triangle upon it with his finger. "Belphig said you wished to stay here." His voice was deep, resonant, far away.

"He told me there were books I might consult."

"There are many books here, though most are of a whimsical kind. The pursuit of true knowledge no longer interests the folk of Rowernarc, Lord Urlik. Did Bishop Belphig tell you that?"

"He merely said I should find books here. Also he told me that all men were scholars in Rowernarc."

A gleam of irony came into Shanosfane's dark eyes. "Scholars? Aye. Scholars in the art of the perverse."

"You seem to disapprove of your own people, my lord."

"How can I disapprove of the damned, Count Urlik? And we are all damned — they and I. It has been our misfortune to be born at the end of Time…"

I spoke feelingly. "It is no misfortune if death is all you have to face."

With curiosity he looked up. "You do not fear death, then?"

I shrugged. "I do not know death. I am immortal."

"Then you are really from the Frozen Keep?"

"I do not know my origins. I have been many heroes. I have seen many ages of the Earth."

"Indeed?" His interest grew and I could tell it was a purely intellectual interest. There was no empathy here, save possibly of minds. There was no emotion. "Then you are a traveller in Time?"

"I am, in a sense, though not, I think, the sense you mean."

"Some several centuries — or perhaps millennia — ago there was a race of folk lived on the Earth. I heard they learnt the art of time-travel and left this world, for they knew it was dying. But doubtless it is a legend. But then, so are you a legend, Count Urlik. And you exist."

"You believe that I am no impostor, then?"

"I think that is what I believe. In what sense do you travel in Time?"

"I am drawn wherever I am called. Past, present and future have no meaning for me. Ideas of cyclical time have little meaning, for I believe there are many universes, many alternative destinies. The history of this planet might never have included me, in any of my incarnations. And yet it might have included them all."

"Strange..." Shanosfane spoke musingly, raising a delicate black hand to his fine brow. "For our universe is so confined and clearly marked, while yours is vast, chaotic. If — forgive me — you are not insane, then some theories of mine are confirmed. Interesting..."

"It is my intention," I continued, "to seek the means of returning to one of these worlds, if it still exists, and using everything in my power to remain there."

"It does not excite you to move from world to world, from Time to Time?"

"Not for eternity, Lord Shanosfane. Not when, on one of those worlds, is a being for whom I have an abiding love and who shares that love."

"How found you that world?"

I began to speak. Soon I discovered that I was telling him my whole story, everything that had happened to me since John Daker had been called by King Rigenos to aid the forces of humanity against the Eldren, every fragment of my recollections of other incarnations, everything that had befallen me until the Rowernarc patrol had met me on the beach. He listened with great attention, staring up at the ceiling as I spoke, never interrupting me, until I had finished.

He said nothing for a while, but then signed to his patient servant. "Bring water and some rice." For a few moments more he considered my story. I thought he must surely believe me a madman now.

"You say you were called to come here," he said eventually. "Yet we did not call you. It is unlikely that, whatever the danger, we should place much faith in a legend of the sort that has existed throughout history if my reading is accurate on the matter."

"Are there any others who might have summoned me?"

"Yes."

"Bishop Belphig said this was unlikely."

"Belphig shapes his thoughts to fit his moods. There are communities beyond Rowernarc, there are cities beyond the sea. At least, there were, before the Silver Warriors came."

"Belphig mentioned nothing of the Silver Warriors."

"Perhaps he forgot. It has been some while since we last heard of them."

"Who are they?"

"Oh, ravagers of some description. Their motives are obscure."

"Where do they come from?"

"They come from Moon, I think."

"From the sky? Where is Moon?"

"On the other side of the world, they say. The few references I have seen do mention that it was once in the sky, but no longer."

"These Silver Warriors — are they human?"

"Not according to the accounts I received."

"And do they offer you harm, Lord Shanosfane? Will they try to invade Rowernarc?"

"Perhaps. I think they want the planet for themselves."

I looked at him feeling somewhat shocked by his lack of interest.

"You do not care if they destroy you?"

"Let them have the planet. What use is it to us? Our race will soon be overwhelmed by the ice that creeps a little closer each year as the sun fades. These people seem better adapted to live in the world than we are."

Though I could understand his argument, I had never encountered such complete disinterest before. I admired it, but I felt little true sympathy with it. It was my destiny to struggle — though for what cause I had no clear idea — and even while I hated the fact that I must do battle through eternity (or so it seemed) my instincts were still those of a warrior.

While I tried to think of an answer, the black Lord Temporal rose. "Well, we will talk again. You may live in Rowernarc until you desire to leave."

And with that he left the room.

As he left, the servant entered with the tray of rice and water. He turned and, holding the tray, followed behind his master.

Now that I had met both the Lord Spiritual and the Lord Temporal of Rowernarc I was even more confused than when I had first arrived here. Why had Belphig not told me of the alien Silver Warriors? Was I destined to fight them or — another thought came — were the folk of Rowernarc the enemy I had been called to war against?

F I V E

THE BLACK SWORD

And so, unhappy, torn by my longing for Ermizhad, by my great sense of loss, I settled in the Obsidian City of Rowernarc, there to brood, to pore over ancient books in strange scripts, to seek some solution to my tragic dilemma and yet feel my despair increasing with every day that passed.

To be accurate, there were no days and nights in the Obsidian City. People slept, awakened and ate when they felt like it and their other appetites were followed in the same spirit, for all that those appetites were jaded and novelty did not exist.

I had been given my own apartments on the level below Haradeik, Bishop Belphig's province. Though they were not quite as baroque as the bishop's apartments, I would have preferred the simplicity which Shanosfane's had. I learned, however, that Shanosfane himself had ordered most decoration removed from Dhotgard when he had assumed his position on the death of his father. The apartments were more than comfortable — the most committed sybarite would have found them luxurious — but for the first weeks of my stay I was plagued with visitors.

It was a seducer's dream, but for me, with my love for Ermizhad unwaning, it was a nightmare.

Woman after woman would present herself in my bedchamber, offering me more exotic delights than even Faust had known. As politely as I could — and much to their astonishment — I refused them all. Men, too, came with similar promises and, because the customs of Rowernarc were such that these advances were not considered shameful, I refused them with equal politeness.

And then Bishop Belphig would arrive with presents — young slaves as covered in cosmetics as he was — rich foodstuffs for which I had no appetite — books of erotic verse which did not interest me — suggestions of acts which might be committed upon my person which disgusted me. Since I owed my roof and the possibility of research to Belphig, I retained my patience with him and judged that he only meant well, though I found both his tastes and his appearance sinister.

On my visits to the various libraries situated on different levels of the Obsidian City I witnessed sights which I would not have believed existed outside the pages of Dante's *Inferno*. Orgies were unceasing. I would stumble upon them wherever I went. In some of the libraries I visited I found them. And they were never orgies of plain fornication.

Torture was common and witnessed by whoever chose to be a spectator. That the victims were willing did not make the sights any easier for me to bear. Even murder itself was not outlawed, for the murdered man or woman desired death as much as the murderer desired to kill.

These pale people with no future, no hope, nothing to prepare for save death, spent their days in experimenting with pain quite as much as they experimented with pleasure.

Rowernarc was a city gone mad. A dreadful neurosis had settled upon it and it seemed pitiful to me that these people, so sophisticated and talented, should waste their final years in such ultimately self-destructive pursuits.

The grotesque galleries and halls and passages would ring to the sound of screams — high-pitched screams of laughter, ululating screams of terror — with moans, with grunts and bellowings.

Through all this I would stride, sometimes tripping over a prone, drugged body in the gloom, sometimes having to disentangle myself from the arms of a naked girl barely out of puberty.

Even the books I found were frustrating. Lord Shanosfane had warned me in his own way. Most of the books were examples of completely decadent prose, so convoluted as to be nearly meaningless. Not only works of fiction, but all the works of fact, were written in this manner. My brain would spin as I attempted to make sense of it all — and failed.

At other times, when I had given up trying to interpret these decadent texts, I would pass through a gallery and see Lord Shanosfane wandering across a hall, his ascetic face frozen in abstracted thought, while all around him his subjects sported, sometimes leering and gesturing at him obscenely. Occasionally he would look up, put his head to one side, regard them with a slight frown and then walk on.

The first few times I saw him I hailed him, but he ignored me as he would have ignored anyone else. I wondered what ideas were forming and re-forming in that strange, cool brain. I felt sure that if he would grant me another audience I would learn much more from him than I had managed to learn from the texts I studied, but since the first day I had arrived at Rowernarc he had not agreed to see me.

My sojourn in Rowernarc was so much like a dream itself that perhaps that was the reason why my slumber was dreamless for the first fifty nights of my stay there. But on what I reckon to be the fifty-first night, those familiar visions returned.

They had terrified me as I lay in Ermizhad's arms. Now I almost welcomed them…

I stood on a hill and spoke with a faceless knight in black and yellow armour. A pale flag without insignia fluttered on a staff erected between us.

Below us, in the valley, towns and cities were burning. Red fires sprouted everywhere. Black smoke cruised above the scenes of carnage from time to time revealed.

It seemed to me that the whole human race fought in that valley — every human being who had ever drawn breath was there, save me.

I saw great armies marching back and forth. I saw ravens and vultures feasting on battlefields. I heard the distant sounds of drums and guns and trumpets.

"You are Count Urlik Skarsol of the Frozen Keep," said the faceless knight.

"I am Erekosë, adopted Prince of the Eldren," I replied firmly.

The faceless knight laughed. "No longer, warrior. No longer."

"Why am I made to suffer so, Sir Knight in Black and Yellow?"

"You need not suffer — not if you accept your fate. After all, you cannot die. True you may seem to perish, but your incarnations are infinite."

"That knowledge is what causes the suffering! If I could not remember previous incarnations, then I would believe each life to be my only one."

"Some people would give much for such knowledge."

"The knowledge is only partial. I know my fate, but I do not know how I earned it. I do not understand the structure of the universe through which I am flung, seemingly at random."

"It is a random universe. It has no permanent structure."

"At least you have told me that."

"I will answer any question you put to me. Why should I lie?"

THE ETERNAL CHAMPION

"Then that is my first question: Why should you lie?"

"You are over-cunning, Sir Champion. I should lie if I wished to deceive you."

"Do you lie?"

"The answer is..."

The knight in black and yellow faded. The armies were marching around and around the hills, up and down them, in all directions across the valley. They were singing many different songs, but one song reached my ears.

> "All Empires fall,
> All ages die,
> All strife shall be in vain.
> All kings go down,
> All hope must fail,
> But Tanelorn remains—
>
> > Our Tanelorn remains..."

A simple soldier's chant, but it meant something to me — something important. Had I once belonged to this place Tanelorn? Or had I sought to find it?

I could not distinguish which of the armies was singing the song. But it was already fading away.

> "All words must die,
> Fade into night,
> But Tanelorn remains—
>
> > Our Tanelorn remains..."

Tanelorn.

The sense of loss I had felt when parted from Ermizhad came to me then — and I associated it with Tanelorn.

It seemed to me that if I could find Tanelorn, I would find the key to my destiny, find a means of ending my misery and my doom...

Now another figure stood on the other side of the plain flag and still the armies marched below us, still the towns and cities burned.

I looked at the figure.

"Ermizhad!"

Ermizhad smiled sadly. "I am not Ermizhad! Just as you have one spirit and many forms, so has Ermizhad one form but many spirits!"

"There is only one Ermizhad!"

"Aye — but many who resemble her."

"Who are you?"

"I am myself."

I turned away. I knew that she spoke truth and was not Ermizhad, but I could not bear to look on Ermizhad's face; I was tired of riddles.

Then I said to her: "Do you know of Tanelorn?"

"Many know of Tanelorn. Many have sought her. She is an old city. She has lasted through eternity."

"How may I reach Tanelorn?"

"Only you may answer that question, Champion."

"Where lies Tanelorn? On Urlik's world?"

"Tanelorn exists in many Realms, on many Planes, in many Worlds, for Tanelorn is eternal. Sometimes hidden, sometimes there for all to visit — though most do not realise the nature of the city — Tanelorn shelters many Heroes."

"Will I find Ermizhad if I find Tanelorn?"

"You will find what you truly desire to find. But first you must take up the Black Sword again."

"Again? Have I borne a black sword before?"

"Many times."

"And where shall I find the sword?"

"You will know it. You will always know the Black Sword for to bear it is your destiny and your tragedy."

And then she, too, was gone.

But the armies continued to march and the valley continued to burn and over my head the standard without insignia still flew.

Then, where she had been, something inhuman materialised, turned into a smoky substance, formed itself in to a different shape.

And I did recognise that shape. It was the Black Sword. A huge, black broadsword carved with runes of terrifying import.

I backed away.

"NO! I WILL NEVER AGAIN WIELD THE BLACK SWORD!"

And a sardonic voice, full of evil and wisdom, seemed to issue from the blade itself.

"THEN YE SHALL NEVER KNOW PEACE!"

"BEGONE!"

"I AM THINE — ONLY THINE. THOU ART THE ONLY MORTAL WHO CAN BEAR ME!"

"I REFUSE YOU!"

"THEN CONTINUE TO SUFFER!"

I awoke shouting. I was sweating. My throat and mouth were parched.

The Black Sword. I knew the name now. I knew that it was somehow tied up with my destiny.

But the rest — had it been merely a nightmare? Or had it offered me information in a symbolic form? I had no means of telling.

In the darkness I flung out an arm and touched warm flesh.

I was back with Ermizhad again!

I took that naked body to me. I bent to kiss the lips.

Lips raised themselves to mine. Lascivious lips that were hot and coarse. The body writhed against me. A woman began to whisper obscenities into my ear.

I leapt back with an oath. Rage and disappointment consumed me. It was not Ermizhad. It was one of the women of Rowernarc who had slipped into my bed while I lay experiencing my dreadful dreams.

Despair swept through me, wave upon wave. I sobbed. The woman laughed.

And then something filled me — some emotion that seemed alien to me and yet which possessed me.

Fiercely I flung myself on the girl.

"Very well," I promised, "if you will have such pleasures — then have them all!"

And in the morning I lay in my disordered bed exhausted while the woman clambered from it and staggered away, a strange expression upon her features. I do not think pleasures were what she had experienced. I know that I had not. I felt only disgusted with myself for what I had done.

All the while one image remained in my brain. It was to rid myself of that image, I think, that I had taken the girl as I had. Perhaps the image had driven me to do what I had done. I do not know. I did know, however, that I would do it again if it would burn the image of the Black Sword from my mind for only a few moments.

There were no dreams the next night, but the old fear had returned. And when the girl I had ravaged the night before came to my room simpering I almost dismissed her before I learned that she came with a message from Bishop Belphig whose slave she apparently was.

"My master says that a change of scenery might improve your temper. Tomorrow he embarks on a great Sea Hunt and asks if you would care to join him."

I flung down the book I was trying to interpret. "Aye," I said. "I'll come. It sounds a healthier way of wasting time than puzzling over these damned books."

"Will you take me with you, Lord Urlik?"

The heated expression on her face, the moist lips, the way she held herself, all made me shudder.

But I shrugged my shoulders.

"Why not?"

She chuckled. "And shall I bring a tasty friend?"

"Do what you wish."

But when she had gone I flung myself down to my knees on that hard, obsidian floor and I buried my head in my arms and I wept.

"Ermizhad! Oh, Ermizhad!"

S   I   X

THE GREAT SALT SEA

I joined Bishop Belphig on the outer causeway the next morning. Even in the light of that perpetual dusk I could see better the face the cosmetics sought to hide. There were the jowls, the pouched eyes, the down-curved, self-indulgent mouth, the lines of depravity, all smeared about with colours and creams, serving only to make his appearance that much more hideous.

The Lord Spiritual's entourage was with him — painted boys and girls giggling and simpering, carrying pieces of luggage, shivering in the dull coolness of the outer air.

The bishop put a fat arm through one of mine and led me ahead of the crowd, down towards the bay where the strange ship waited.

I suffered this gesture and looked back to see if my weapons were being brought. They were. Slaves staggered along with my long, silver-shod spear and battle-axe. Why I had decided to bring these weapons I do not know, but the bishop plainly did not think my decision incongruous though I was not at all sure he was pleased about it, either.

For all its decadence and despair, I did not find Rowernarc itself menacing. The people offered me no harm and, once aware that I did not wish to join in their sports, tended for the most part to leave me to my own devices. They were neutral. Lord Shanosfane, too, had an air of neutrality. But I did not get this impression of Bishop Belphig. There was, indeed, something sinister about him and I was beginning to feel that he was perhaps the sole member of that peculiar community who possessed some sort of motive, however perverse; some ambition beyond the need to find new ways of whiling away the days.

Yet for all appearances Bishop Belphig was the most dedicated of all sybarites and it was my possibly puritanical eye that saw menace in him. I reminded myself that he was the sole inhabitant of Rowernarc who had displayed any sort of deviousness.

"Well, my dear Lord Urlik, what do you think of our craft?" Belphig gestured towards the ship with a fat, beringed finger. He was dressed in the bulbous armour I had originally seen worn by the riders on the beach, but his helm was being carried by a slave. A brocade cloak flowed from his shoulders.

"I have never seen an odder craft," I replied frankly.

We were approaching the shore and I could see the craft quite clearly. She was quite close to the beach on which stood a number of figures whom I guessed were part of her crew. She was about forty feet in length and very high. As ornately decorated as anything else of Rowernarc, plated with reliefs of silver, bronze and gold, she had a kind of pyramidal superstructure on which were situated various terraces — a succession of narrow decks. At the top was a square deck from which several banners flew. The hull was raised above the level of the ocean on struts connected to a broad, flat, slightly curved sheet of highly polished material resembling something very like fibreglass and resting on the water. She had no masts but on each side were arranged wheels of broad-bladed paddles. Unlike the blades of a paddle-steamer, these were not contained within an outer wheel but were naked. But even the large paddles did not seem strong enough to push the craft through the water.

"You must have very powerful engines," I commented.

"Engines?" Belphig chuckled. "She has no engines."

"Then..."

"Wait until we are aboard."

The group of people waiting on the beach had two litters ready. Plainly these were meant for us. Belphig and I crunched across the crystal until we reached them. Then the bishop entered one and, somewhat reluctantly, I climbed into the other. The alternative, I guessed, was to wade through that murky, viscous water and merely the sight of it filled me with distaste. A grey scum floated at the edges where it touched the beach and the smell of decay and ordure reached my nostrils. I guessed that this was the place into which Rowernarc's waste found its way.

The litters were lifted up and the slaves began to wade through the water that appeared to have the consistency of porridge and which had oily black weed growing on its surface.

A flight of collapsible steps had been lowered down the side of the ship and Belphig led the way up them, puffing and complaining until we were aboard and entering a doorway at the base of the pyramid.

Up we went again until we at last reached the top deck and stood on it, watching the rest of the crew and entourage assembling themselves on the various lower galleries. The prow of the ship was raised and curved and had a high gallery of its own which was protected by a rail of rococo iron. From this gallery what appeared to be long ropes went over the side and into the water. They were secured to stanchions and I took them to be anchor ropes.

Looking over the ship I had the peculiar impression that we were aboard a gigantic cart rather than a sea-going vessel, for the paddle-wheels were arranged on spokes, in pairs, with nothing, apparently, to drive them.

The slave arrived with my spear and axe and handed them to me. I thanked him and fixed them into lugs which were arranged for this purpose around the inside of the rail.

Belphig looked up at the sky, as an ordinary sailor might look to see the lie of the weather. I could see no change in the thick, brown cloud layers, the jagged mountain peaks or the sluggish sea. The sun was again invisible and its faint light was further diffused by the clouds. I drew my heavy coat about me and waited impatiently for Bishop Belphig to give the order to sail.

I was already regretting my decision to accompany the Lord Spiritual on this venture. I had no idea what we were to hunt or in what manner. My sense of discomfort was increasing as some instinct warned me that the bishop had invited me on this hunt for more specific reasons than the relief of my boredom.

Morgeg, the bishop's captain, climbed the central stairway to the top deck and presented himself to his master.

"We are ready to roll, Lord Bishop."

"Good." Belphig put a pale hand on my arm in a confiding gesture. "Now you will see our 'engines', Count Urlik." He smiled secretly at Morgeg. "Give the order, Sir Morgeg."

Morgeg leaned over the rail and addressed the armoured men who had now taken up positions in the prow gallery. They were strapped into seats and had the ropes that I thought anchor ropes around their arms. There were whips in their hands, long harpoons at their sides. "Prepare!" shouted Morgeg through cupped hands. The armoured men stiffened and drew back the arms holding the whips. "Begin!"

As one, the whips snapped out and cracked the surface of the water. Three times they did this and then I saw a disturbance just ahead of the prow and gasped as something began to emerge from below.

Then four huge, gnarled heads broke from the depths. The heads turned to glare at the whipmen in the prow. Strange, barking noises came from the sinuous throats. Monstrous, serpentine bodies threshed in the water. The beasts had flat heads from the mouths of which long, straight tusks protruded. A harness was attached to these heads and with tugs the whipmen forced them to turn until they were looking out to sea.

Again the whips cracked and the beasts began to move.

With a lurch the ship was off, its paddles not cutting *through* the water but supporting the ship *on* the water, as wheels support a chariot.

And that was what the ship was — a huge chariot designed to roll over the surface, pulled by these ugly monsters that seemed to me to be a cross between sea-serpents of legend, sea-lions of John Daker's world, with a trace of sabre-tooth tiger for good measure!

Out into that nightmare ocean swam the nightmare beasts, pulling our impossible craft behind them.

The whips cracked louder and the drivers sang out to the beasts who swam faster. The wheels rolled rapidly and soon Rowernarc's terrible shore disappeared in murky brown cloud.

We were alone on that nameless, hellish sea.

Bishop Belphig had become animated. He had placed his helm on his head and had opened the visor. In its nest of steel his face looked even more depraved.

"Well, Count Urlik. What do you think of our engines?"

"I have never seen such beasts. I could never have imagined them. How do you manage to train them?"

"Oh, they were bred for this work — they are domestic animals. Once Rowernarc had many scientists. They built our city, channelling our heat from the fires that still flickered in the bowels of the planet. They designed and built our ships. They bred our various beasts of burden. But that, of course, was a thousand years ago. We have no need of such scientists now..."

I thought it a slightly odd statement, though I said nothing. Instead, I asked: "And what do we hunt, my lord bishop?"

Belphig drew a deep, excited breath. "Nothing less than the sea-stag himself. It is dangerous work. We might all perish."

"The thought of dying in this dreadful ocean does not commend itself," I said.

He chuckled. "Aye, a foul death. Perhaps the worst death this world can offer. But that is where the thrill lies, does it not?"

"For you, perhaps."

"Ah, come now, Count Urlik. I thought you were beginning to enjoy our ways."

"You know that I am grateful for your hospitality. Without it I suppose I would have perished. But 'enjoy' is not the word I would have chosen."

He licked his lips, his pale eyes bright and lascivious. "But the slave girl I sent... ?"

I drew a heavy breath of that cold, salt-clogged air. "I had had a nightmare shortly before I discovered her in my bed. It seemed to me that she was merely part of that nightmare."

Belphig laughed and clapped me on the back. "Oho, you lusty dog! No need to be shy in Rowernarc. The girl told me all!"

I turned away and put my two hands on the rail, staring over the dark waters. A rime of salt had formed on my face and beard, scouring my flesh. I welcomed it.

The sea-beasts strained and threshed and barked, the wheels of the ship slapped the surface of the salt-thick water, Bishop Belphig chuckled and exchanged glances with the dead-faced Morgeg. Sometimes the brown clouds broke and I saw the contracted sphere of the dull, red sun like a jewel hanging from a cavern roof. Sometimes the clouds gathered so close that they blotted out all the light and we moved through pitch darkness broken only by the faint illumination of our artificial torches. A faint wind came and ruffled my coat, stirred the limp banners on their masts, but scarcely brought a ripple to the viscous ocean.

Within me my torment seethed. My lips formed the syllables of Ermizhad's name but then refused to move as if to utter that name, even under my breath, was to taint it.

Onward the ship rolled. Its crew, the slaves of despair, moved about upon its decks or sat listlessly against its rails.

And all the time Bishop Belphig's fat jowls shook as his obscene laughter bubbled through the air.

I began to think that I did not in the least care now if I perished in the waters of that great salt sea.

S E V E N

THE BELL AND THE CHALICE

Later Belphig retired to his cabin with his slaves and the girl who had brought me the message came on deck and put her warm hand on my cold one.

"Master? Do you not want me?"

"Give yourself to Morgeg or whoever else desires you," I said hollowly, "and I beg you forget that other time."

"But, master, you told me I could bring someone else, also… I thought you had learned to take pleasure in our ways…"

"I take no pleasure in your ways. Please go."

She left me alone on the deck. I rubbed at my weary eyes. They were encrusted with salt. After a few moments I, too, went below, sought my cabin, locked the door and ignored the shut-bunk with its profusion of furs and silks in favour of the hammock, doubtless slung there for a servant's use.

Rocked in the hammock, I was soon asleep.

Dreams came, but they were faint dreams. A few scenes. A few words. But the only words that made me shiver were the words which forced me to wake myself:

BLACK SWORD
BLACK SWORD
BLACK SWORD
THE BLACK SWORD IS THE CHAMPION'S SWORD
THE WORD OF THE SWORD IS THE CHAMPION'S LAW

BLACK SWORD
BLACK SWORD
BLACK SWORD
THE BLADE OF THE SWORD HAS THE BLOOD OF THE SUN
THE HILT OF THE SWORD AND THE HAND ARE AS ONE
BLACK SWORD
BLACK SWORD
BLACK SWORD
THE RUNES ON THE SWORD ARE THE WORMS THAT ARE WISE
THE NAME OF THE SWORD IS THE SAME AS THE SCYTHE
BLACK SWORD
BLACK SWORD
BLACK...

The rhythm continued to drum in my skull. I shook my head and half fell from my hammock. Outside the cabin I heard hasty footsteps. Now they sounded above my head. I went to a washstand, splashed water over my hands and face, opened the door and climbed the intricately carved companionway to the top deck.

Morgeg and another man stood there. They were leaning over the rail, their ears cocked to the wind. Below, in the prow, the drivers continued to lash the sea-beasts on.

Morgeg stepped back from the rail when he saw me. There was a trace of concern in his pale eyes.

"What is it?" I asked.

He shrugged his shoulders. "We thought we heard something. A sound we have not heard before in these waters."

I listened for a while with some concentration but all I could hear was the crack of the drivers' whips, the slap of the wheels on the water.

Then I heard it. A faint booming ahead of us. I peered into the murky brown fog. The booming came more strongly now.

"It's a bell!" I said.

Morgeg frowned.

"A bell! Perhaps there are rocks ahead and they are warning us off."

Morgeg jerked his thumb at the sea-beasts. "The *slevahs* would sense rocks if they were near and turn aside."

The sound of the tolling bell increased. It must have come from a huge bell, for it was deep and the ship vibrated with the noise.

Even the sea-beasts were disturbed by it. They tried to turn away, but the drivers' whips kept them on course.

Still the tolling grew in intensity until it seemed to surround us. Bishop Belphig appeared on deck. He was not wearing his armour, but some kind of nightshirt by the look of it. Over this he had thrown a huge fur. His cosmetics were smeared and only half applied. Doubtless the bell had disturbed him in the middle of his revels. There was fear on his face.

"Do you know what that bell is?" I asked him.

"No. No."

But I thought that he did know — or that he guessed what it was. And he was afraid of the bell.

Morgeg said: "Bladrak's—"

"Silence!" Belphig snapped. "How could it be?"

"What is Bladrak?" I said.

"Nothing," Morgeg murmured, his eyes on the bishop.

I did not pursue the subject, but the sense of menace I had felt when first boarding the craft now increased.

The tolling was so loud now that it hurt my ears to hear it.

"Turn the ship about," Belphig said. "Give the order, Morgeg. Hurry!"

His evident fear I found almost amusing after the bland impression of self-assurance he had given me earlier.

"Are we going back to Rowernarc?" I asked him.

"Yes, we'll…" He frowned, his eyes flashing first to me, then to Morgeg, then to the rail. He tried to smile. "No, I think not."

"Why have you changed your mind?" I asked.

"Be quiet, curse you!" Immediately he controlled himself. "Forgive me, Count Urlik. This dreadful noise. My nerves…" And he disappeared down the companionway.

Still the bell boomed, but the drivers were turning the *slevahs* now. They reared and threshed in the water, dragging the ship full about.

The drivers lashed them again and their speed increased.

The booming continued, but it was just a little fainter now.

Spray rose with the speed and force with which the wheels slapped the sea's surface. The huge sea-chariot rocked and jolted and I clung hard to the rail.

The tolling of the bell subsided.

Soon silence sat upon the sea once again.

Bishop Belphig re-emerged, clad in his armour, wearing his cloak. His cosmetics had been properly applied, but I saw that the face beneath them was paler than usual. He bowed to me, nodded to Morgeg. He tried to smile.

"I am sorry that I lost my head for a moment, Count Urlik. I had but recently awakened. I was disorientated. That sound was terrifying, was it not?"

"More terrifying, I suspect, to you than to me, Bishop Belphig. I thought you recognised it."

"No."

"And so did Morgeg — he uttered a name — Bladrak..."

"A legend of the sea." Belphig waved his fat hand dismissively, "Um — concerning a monster, Bladrak, with a voice like a huge bell. Naturally Morgeg, who is of a superstitious turn of mind, thought that Bladrak had come to... er, gobble us up." His titter was high-pitched, his tone completely unconvincing.

However, as the man's guest I could scarcely push my questioning any farther. I had to accept what was, to me, evidently a hastily invented lie. I returned to my cabin as Belphig instructed Morgeg in a fresh course. And in my cabin I again found the girl I had dismissed. She was lying in the bed, smiling at me, completely naked.

I returned her smile and climbed into my hammock.

But I was soon to be disturbed again.

Almost as soon as I had closed my eyes I heard a shout from above. Again I leapt from the hammock and rushed up on to the top-deck. This time I heard no bells, but Morgeg and Belphig were calling down to a sailor on a lower deck. I heard the sailor's voice.

"I swear I saw it! A light to port!"

"We are miles from the nearest land," Morgeg argued.

"Then perhaps, sir, it was a ship."

"Is this another legend coming true?" I asked Belphig. He started when he heard me and straightened up.

"I really cannot understand it all, Count Urlik. I think the sailor is imagining things. Once you get one unexplained event at sea, others quickly follow, eh?"

I nodded. There was truth in that. But then I saw a light. I pointed. "It must be another ship."

"The light is too bright for a ship."

I then found an opportunity to put a question to him which had been on my mind since my meeting with Lord Shanosfane. "What if it is the Silver Warriors?"

Belphig darted me a penetrating look. "What do you know of the Silver Warriors?"

"Very little. Their race is not the same as yours. They have conquered most of the farther shore of this sea. They are thought to come from a land called Moon on the other side of the world."

He relaxed. "And who told you all this?"

"My Lord Shanosfane of Dhotgard — the Lord Temporal."

"He knows little of the events in the world," Bishop Belphig said. "He is more interested in abstracted speculation. The Silver Warriors are not a great threat. They have harried one or two cities of the farther shore, that is true, but I believe they have disappeared again now."

"Why did you not tell me of them when I asked if you had any enemies or potential enemies?"

"What? Enemies?" Belphig laughed. "I do not consider warriors from the other side of the world, who have never offered us threat, *enemies!*"

"Not even potential enemies?"

"Not even that. How could they attack us? Rowernarc is impregnable."

The hoarse voice of the sailor came again. "There! There it is!"

He was right.

And also I seemed to hear a voice calling over the ocean. A lost voice, an ethereal voice.

"Some mariner in trouble perhaps?" I suggested.

Bishop Belphig assumed an impatient expression. "Most unlikely."

Both light and voice were coming closer. I made out a word. It was a very definite word.

"BEWARE!" cried the voice. "BEWARE!"

Belphig sniffed. "A pirate's trick, maybe. Best ready the warriors, Morgeg."

Morgeg went below.

And then the source of the light was much closer and a peculiar screaming began. A wail.

It was a huge golden cup, suspended against the darkness. A great chalice. Both the bright light and the wailing came from it.

Belphig staggered back, shielding his eyes. Doubtless he had never seen such brightness in his whole life.

A voice spoke once again.

"URLIK SKARSOL, IF YOU WOULD RID THIS WORLD OF ITS TROUBLES AND FIND A SOLUTION TO YOUR OWN – YOU MUST TAKE UP THE BLACK SWORD AGAIN."

The voice of my dreams had entered the realm of reality. Now it was my turn to be terrified.

"No!" I shouted. "I will never wield the Black Sword. I swore I would not!"

Though I spoke the words, they did not come from my conscious brain, for I still had no idea what the Black Sword was and why I refused to use it. These words were spoken by all the warriors I had been and all the warriors I was to become.

"YOU MUST!"

"I will not!"

"IF YOU DO NOT THIS WORLD WILL PERISH."

"It is already doomed!"

"NOT SO!"

"Who are you?" I could not believe that this was a supernatural manifestation. Everything I had experienced so far had had some kind of understandable explanation — but not this screaming chalice — not this voice that boomed from the heavens like the voice of God. I tried to peer at the great golden cup, see what held it, but apparently nothing did hold it.

"Who are you?" I shouted again.

Bishop Belphig's unhealthy face was wreathed in light. It writhed in terror.

"I AM THE VOICE OF THE CHALICE. YOU MUST TAKE UP THE BLACK SWORD."

"I will not!"

"BECAUSE YOU WOULD NOT LISTEN FROM WITHIN, I HAVE COME TO YOU IN THIS FORM TO IMPRESS UPON YOU THAT YOU MUST TAKE UP THE BLACK SWORD—"

"I will not! I swore I would not!"

"—AND WHEN YOU HAVE TAKEN UP THE SWORD, THEN YOU MAY FILL THE CHALICE! ANOTHER CHANCE WILL NOT COME, ETERNAL CHAMPION"

I clapped my hands to my ears, closing my eyes tight shut.

I felt the light fade.

I opened my eyes.

The screaming chalice had disappeared. There was only gloom again.

Belphig was shaking with fear. It was plain, when he looked at me, that he associated me with the source of his terror.

I said grimly: "That was no doing of mine, I assure you."

Belphig cleared his throat several times before he spoke. "I have heard of men able to create illusions, Count Urlik, but never illusions so powerful. I am impressed, but I hope you will not see fit to use your power again on this voyage.   Merely because I could not answer your questions concerning that bell does not mean that you can—"

"If that were an illusion, Bishop Belphig, it was no creation of mine."

Belphig began to speak, then changed his mind. Shuddering, he went below.

E I G H T

THE SEA STAG'S LAIR

I stayed on the deck for a long time, peering into the twilight, wondering if I would see something that would give me a clue as to the origin of that strange visitation. Save for the experience in my bedroom on the Eldren Earth, when I had seen myself as I now was, this was the first time that my dreams had come in waking hours.

And it had been no dream, of course, because Bishop Belphig had witnessed it — as had many members of his crew and entourage. On the lower terraces they were murmuring among themselves, looking up at me in some trepidation, doubtless hoping I would bring no further manifestations of that sort upon them.

But if the screaming chalice had been connected with me, the unseen bell had been connected in some way with Bishop Belphig.

And why was Belphig continuing with the hunt, when any sensible person would have returned to the safety of the Obsidian City? Perhaps he had arranged a rendezvous with someone in these waters? But with whom? One of the pirates he had mentioned? Perhaps even the Silver Warriors?

But these were minor matters of speculation compared with the latest event. What was the Black Sword? Why did something within me refuse it, even though I did not know what it was. Certainly the name had a peculiar sort of familiarity and it was also plain that I did not wish to think about it — that was why I had taken the girl that night. It seemed I was ready to do anything to forget the sword, to escape from it.

At length, weary and full of confusion, I returned to my quarters and fell into my hammock.

But I could not sleep. I did not want to sleep, for fear the dreams would return.

I remembered the words: *If you would rid this world of its troubles and find a solution to your own, you must take up the Black Sword again.*

And the monotonous chant came back to me: *Black Sword. Black Sword. Black Sword. The Black Sword is the Champion's Sword — the Word of the Sword is the Champion's Law...*

In some previous incarnation — whether in the past or the future, for Time in my own context was a meaningless word — I must have rid myself of the Black Sword. And in parting with it I had, say, committed a crime (or at least had offended someone or something which desired that I retain the sword) for which I was now being punished by being moved hither and yon through Time and Space. Or perhaps, as my dream had suggested, the punishment was that I be aware of my incarnations and thus know my true tragedy. A subtle punishment if that were so.

Although I desired nothing more than rest and a chance to be reunited with Ermizhad, something in me still refused to pay the price, which was my agreement that I would take up the Black Sword again.

The Blade of the Sword has the Blood of the Sun — The Hilt of the Sword and the Hand are as One...

A rather more cryptic statement. I had no idea what the first part meant. Presumably the second part simply meant that my own fate and that of the sword were intertwined.

The Runes on the Sword are the Worms that are wise — The Name of the Sword is the same as the Scythe.

Here the first part was easier to understand than the second. It merely meant that some kind of wisdom was written on the blade. And it was just possible that the Scythe referred to was nothing more than the same scythe that Death was said to wield.

But I still knew no more than I had known before. It seemed that I must decide to take up the sword again without being told why I had originally decided to put it down...

There was a knock on the cabin door. Thinking it was the girl again, I cried out: "I do not wish to be disturbed."

"It is Morgeg," replied the one who had knocked. "Bishop Belphig instructed me to tell you that the sea-stag has been sighted. The hunt is about to begin."

"I will come in a moment."

I heard Morgeg's footfalls fade. I put my helm on my head, took up my axe and my spear and went to the door.

Perhaps the excitement of the hunt would drive some of my confusion away.

Belphig seemed to have regained all his old bland confidence. He was in full armour, his visor raised, and Morgeg now wore armour, too.

"Well, Count Urlik, we shall soon have the diversion we actually sought when we originally set out, eh?" He slapped the rail with his gauntleted hand.

The wheels of the ship were moving comparatively slowly over the viscous ocean and the sea-beasts pulling the gigantic sea-chariot were swimming at an almost leisurely rate.

"The sea-stag's horns broke the surface a while ago," Morgeg said. "The beast must be quite near. It has no gills and must eventually surface again. That is when we must be ready to strike." He indicated the warriors lining the rails above the ship's hull. They all held long, heavy harpoons, each with up to ten cruel barbs.

"Is the beast likely to attack?" I asked.

"Have no fear," Bishop Belphig said. "We are safe enough up here."

"I came for the excitement," I told him. "I would experience It."

He shrugged. "Very well. Morgeg, will you escort Count Urlik to the lower deck?"

Spear and axe in hand I followed Morgeg down the several companionways to the lower deck and emerged to discover that the sea-chariot's wheels had stopped almost completely.

Morgeg craned his neck and peered into the gloom. "Ah," he said. And he pointed.

I had the impression of antlers very much like those of the stags I had seen on John Daker's world. I had no means, however, of judging their size.

I wondered if this were some land beast that had taken to the sea just as the seals had returned to the land. Or perhaps it was another hybrid, bred centuries before by Rowernarc's scientists.

The atmosphere on the great chariot was tense. The antlers seemed to be coming closer, as if to inspect the strangers who had intruded into its province.

I moved nearer to the rail, a warrior making room for me.

Morgeg murmured, "I will return to my master's side." And he left me.

I heard a snort — a gigantic snort. This beast was plainly larger than an ordinary stag!

Now I could see red eyes glaring at us. A huge, bovine face emerged from the twilight, its nostrils dilating and contracting. It snorted again and this time I felt its breath strike my face.

In silence, the harpooners prepared for its charge.

I looked up at the prow, noticing that the *slevahs* had submerged, as if they wanted no part of this madness…

The sea-stag bellowed, raising its massive body from the viscous waters. The thick, saline liquid ran in streamers down its coarse, oily pelt and I saw that its muscular forelegs were, in fact, flippers terminating in a clublike appendage that only barely recalled the hoof of a true stag. These flippers it now thrashed in the air, then sank down into the sea again, re-emerging a moment later with lowered head to charge our chariot.

From the top deck Morgeg's voice came:

"Let fly with the first harpoons!"

A third of the warriors flung back their arms and hurled their heavy lances at the advancing beast. The horns were almost fifteen feet long, with an even longer span.

Some of the harpoons flew past the sea-stag and lay for a moment on the surface of the water before sinking, others buried themselves in the body of the stag. But none struck the head and while it screamed with pain, it paused only for a moment before continuing its charge.

"Let fly with the second harpoons!"

The second wave of lances flew out. Two struck the horns and clattered harmlessly off them. Two struck the body but were shaken out by a twist of the animal's shoulders. The horns struck the chariot and sharp bone met metal with an awful clangour. The ship rocked, threatened to topple, righted itself on its flat, lower hull. One of the horns swept along the rail and, shrieking, several harpooners were hurled overboard, their armour gashed. I leaned over to see if they could be helped, but they were already sinking, as a man sinks in quicksand, some holding up their arms pleadingly, though their eyes spoke of the hopelessness of help.

This was a brutal, disgusting business, particularly since the instigator of the hunt was at the top of the ship in a relatively safe position.

Now the dripping head loomed over us and we staggered back as it opened its mouth to show teeth half the size of a large man's height, a red, curling tongue.

Dwarfed by the monster, I took up my stance on the swaying deck, drew back the arm holding my own spear and flung it into that open mouth. Its point entered the flesh of the gullet and the mouth instantly closed as, in agony, the beast backed off, moving its jaw from side to side as it tried to rid itself of the thing inside it.

One of the harpooners clapped me on the back as we saw dark blood begin to run from the sea-stag's snout.

From far above came the bland voice of Bishop Belphig. "Well done, Sir Champion!"

At that moment I would rather the spear had entered Belphig's heart than the gullet of the monster whose territory we had invaded.

I grabbed up a harpoon from where it had been dropped by one of the men who had been swept overboard. I aimed again for the head, but the point struck the base of the left horn and dropped harmlessly into the sea.

The monster coughed and bits of the shaft of my spear were spewed out, some of them striking the ship's superstructure.

Then it charged again.

This time, as if encouraged by my partial success, one of the harpooners managed to drive his weapon into the sea-stag's flesh just below the right eye. A terrible scream came from the injured throat and, admitting defeat, the beast turned and began to swim away.

I drew a sigh of relief, but I had not reckoned with Bishop Belphig's bloodlust.

"Pursue it — quickly. It is making for its lair!" he cried.

The drivers lashed the sea-beasts to the surface, jerked on the ropes that were their reins and, using the long goads, turned them in pursuit of the disappearing stag.

"This is insanity! Let the thing go!" I shouted.

"What — and return to Rowernarc without a trophy!" screamed back the bishop. "Give chase, whipmen. Give chase!"

The wheels began to whirl over the water again as we pursued our wounded quarry.

One of the harpooners gave me a sardonic look. "They say our Lord Spiritual prefers slaughter to fornication." He rubbed at his face. Blood spat by the stag had covered him.

"I do not know if he understands the difference any longer," I said. "Where is the monster heading?"

"Sea-stags make their lairs in caves. There is probably a small island nearby. Our friend will head for that."

"Have they no herds?"

"At certain times. But this is not their herding season. That is why it is relatively safe to hunt them. A herd, even mainly of cows, would quickly finish us."

Two of the wheels on our side of the ship had been badly battered and the sea-chariot lurched unevenly as it sped over the ocean. The *slevahs* must have been even more powerful than the sea-stag to be able to cut through those thick waters and draw the heavy craft behind them.

The horns of the stag were still in sight through the gloom and, just ahead of that, the outline of a spike of obsidian rock, doubtless of the same range as the mountain from which Rowernarc had been carved.

"There!" The harpooner pointed. Grimly he hefted his barbed lance.

I bent and took the remaining harpoon off the deck.

Morgeg's distant voice shouted: "Prepare!"

The stag had disappeared, but the tiny island of glassy rock could clearly be seen. The sea-chariot slewed round as the sea-beasts avoided dashing themselves on to the rock. We saw the black mouth of a cave.

We had found the monster's lair.

From within the cave came an almost pathetic snort of pain.

And then came the astonishing order from above.

"Prepare to disembark!"

Belphig meant his men to enter the cave armed only with their harpoons!

N I N E

THE SLAUGHTERING IN THE CAVE

And so we disembarked.

All save Belphig, his entourage and the whipmen in the prow, began to wade through the clinging shallows and gain a slippery foothold on the rock. I had my battle-axe crooked in one arm, the barbed harpoon held at my side in the other hand. Belphig watched and waved from the top deck.

"Good luck, Count Urlik. If you kill the stag it will be another great deed to add to your long list…"

I thought the whole nature of the hunt was useless and cruel, but I felt I must go with the others to finish what we had begun — either to kill the monster or be killed by it.

With some difficulty we clambered around the rock until we had reached the mouth of the cave. A terrible stench was issuing from it, as if the beast had already begun to rot.

The man who had spoken earlier now said: "That's the stink of its dung. The sea-stag is not a clean beast."

Now I felt even more reluctant to enter the cave.

Another bellow came, as the stag scented us.

The harpooners hung back nervously. No man wished to be the first into the lair.

At last, dry-mouthed but desperate, I elbowed my way forward, took a good grip on my harpoon and stepped into the black maw.

The stench was nauseating and I felt I would choke on it. There was a heavy movement and I thought I saw the outline of one of the stag's great antlers. A rapid snorting came from the thing's nostrils then. I heard its gigantic flippers thud on the floor. I had the impression of a long, sinuous body ending in a wide, flat tail.

The rest of the men were following me. From one of them I took a brand and touched the stud in its handle. Faint light illuminated the cavern.

The shadow of the sea-stag was what I saw first and then I saw the beast himself, on my right, pressed against the wall, blood pouring from its wounds, its massive body looking even larger on land than it had in the sea.

It hauled itself about on its giant flippers. It lowered its head menacingly but it did not charge. It was warning us away. It was giving us the chance to leave without a fight.

I was tempted to recall the men — lead them from the cave — but I had no authority over them. Bishop Belphig was their master and he would punish them if they did not obey him.

So, knowing that this would incense the beast, I hurled my harpoon at its left eye.

It turned its head just as the lance left my hand and the weapon grazed its snout.

It charged.

There was confusion then. Men screamed, tried to dodge, tried to get a clear cast at it, backed away, were impaled on its antlers.

When it raised its head three men hung on its horns, their bodies completely pierced. Two were dead. One was dying. Small moans came from his lips.

There was nothing I could do to save him. The stag shook its great head, trying to dislodge the corpses, but they remained where they were.

An idea began to form in my mind.

But then the stag lowered its head and charged again. I jumped aside, striking out with my long-hafted battle-axe and cutting a deep groove in its left shoulder. It turned towards me, its teeth snapping, its red eyes glaring in a mixture of anguish and surprise. I struck it another blow and it withdrew its bleeding snout. Again it shook its horns and now one of the torn bodies fell limply to the filthy floor of the cave. The stag nudged at it awkwardly with a flipper.

I looked for the remaining harpooners. They were huddled near the cave entrance.

The stag was now between me and the others. The cave was lit still by two brands which had fallen to the floor. I retreated into the shadows. The stag saw the others, lowered its head again and charged.

THE ETERNAL CHAMPION

I was knocked flat by its huge fish tail as it moved past.

The beast bellowed as the harpooners scattered. I heard their cries as they were caught on its horns, as they plunged into the thick waters, seeking to escape.

And now I was alone in the cave.

The sea-stag began to scrape its horns on the edges of the cave mouth, scraping off human flesh.

I decided that I was as good as dead. How could I defeat such a monster alone? Its body blocked the entrance — my only chance of escape. Sooner or later it would remember I was there, or possibly scent me.

I kept as still as possible. The stink of ordure clogged my mouth and nostrils. I had no harpoon with which to defend myself, only the axe — an unsuitable weapon for dealing with a giant sea-stag...

Once again the beast opened its bovine snout and sent up a huge bellowing. Then the noise dropped as it moaned to itself.

Would it decide to enter the sea again? To heal its wounds in the salt?

I waited tensely for it to decide. But then there was another rattle of harpoons against rock and antlers and the monster screamed and backed into the cave.

Again I was forced to dodge its tail.

I prayed that the harpooners would return — at least long enough to give me the chance to get past the stag to a safer position.

The stag snorted, dragging its whale-like body first one way and then another across the floor of the cave, as it, too, expected the arrival of the warriors.

But nothing happened.

Did they think me dead?

Were they abandoning the chase?

I listened for shouts, but heard nothing.

Another bellow. Another movement of the unnatural body.

I began to edge along the wall of the cave, moving as softly as possible.

I was half-way to the cave-mouth when my foot struck a yielding object. It was the corpse of one of the harpooners. I lifted my leg to step over the thing but my foot then caught on a piece of loose armour and sent it clattering across the obsidian floor.

The beast snorted and turned its baleful eyes to regard me.

I stood stock still, hoping it would not realise that I lived.

It shook its horns again and dragged its body round. My mouth and throat were dry.

It raised its muzzle and bellowed, its lips curling back from its huge teeth. Blood now encrusted those lips and it was plainly half blind in one eye.

Then, horrifyingly, it raised its body up and its strange flippers with their club-like appendages, thrashed at the air, fell back to the ground, shook the floor of the cavern.

The antlers were lowered.

The stag charged.

I saw the huge horns bearing down on me and I had seen how they could impale a man. I flung my body flat against the wall and to one side. The antlers crashed within inches of my right shoulder and the stag's massive forehead — as wide as my body was long — was a foot from my face.

The idea I had had earlier came back to me. I believed there was only one chance of defeating the monster.

I jumped.

I leapt towards that forehead, grabbed the oily pelt, literally ran up its snout and then wrapped my legs and one arm around the branches of the left antler.

The beast was puzzled. I do not think it realised I was there.

I raised the axe.

The stag looked about the cavern for me, still snorting.

I brought the axe down.

It bit deep into his skull. He roared and screamed and shook his head rapidly from side to side. But I had expected this and I clung to the branches as tenaciously as was possible, striking again at the exact place I had struck before.

I split the bone. A little blood came. But all this served to do was to make the stag's movements more frantic. Its body sliding behind it, it waddled on its flippers, moving rapidly about the cave, scraping its antlers on roof and walls, trying to dislodge me.

But I hung on.

And I struck again.

This time pieces of bone flew into the air and a stream of blood poured from the skull.

Another fearsome bellow which became a scream of rage and terror.

THE ETERNAL CHAMPION

Another blow.

The axe haft snapped with the force of my striking and I was left holding nothing but a piece of broken pole.

But the blade had buried itself in the brain.

The bulk of the stag crashed to the floor as the strength went out of the flippers.

It moaned pathetically. It tried to rise.

With a spluttering noise the last mixture of breath and blood left its body.

The head fell to one side and I fell with it, leaping free just as the antlers reached the floor.

The sea-stag was dead. I had killed it single-handed.

I tried to tug the broken haft of the axe out of the beast's head, but it was buried too deep. I left my axe there and stumbled, half dazed, from the mouth of the cave.

"It is over," I said. "Your quarry is vanquished."

I felt no pride in my accomplishment. I looked towards the ship.

But no ship was there.

Bishop Belphig's sea-chariot had rolled away, presumably back to Rowernarc — doubtless because they thought me dead.

"Belphig!" I shouted, hoping my voice would carry over the waters where my eye could not see. "Morgeg! I am alive! I have killed the stag!"

But there was no reply.

I looked at the low, brown clouds. At the murky, moody ocean.

I had been abandoned in the middle of a nightmare sea through which, as Belphig had said, no ships passed. I was alone save for the corpses of the harpooners, the carcass of the sea-stag.

Panic seized me.

"BELPHIG! COME BACK!"

A slight echo. Nothing more.

"I AM ALIVE!"

And the echo seemed stronger this time and it seemed sardonic.

I could not stay alive for long on that bleak sliver of rock which was less than fifty yards across. I stumbled up the sides, climbing as high as I could. But what point was there in that when the twilight sea had no horizon that was not obscured on all sides by the brown cloudbanks?

I sat down on a small ledge, the only reasonably flat surface on the entire rock.

I was trembling. I was afraid.

The air seemed to grow colder and I drew my coat about me but it would not keep out the chill that grasped my bones, my liver, my heart.

An immortal I might be. A phoenix for ever reborn. A wanderer in eternity.

But if I was to die here, that dying would seem to take an eternity. If I were a phoenix, then I was a phoenix trapped in obsidian as a fly is trapped in amber.

At that thought all my courage went out of me and I contemplated my fate with nothing but despair.

BOOK THREE: VISIONS AND REVELATIONS

Destiny's Champion,
Fate's fool.
Eternity's Soldier,
Time's Tool.
　　　　　—The Chronicle of the Black Sword

O N E

THE LAUGHING DWARF

The fight with the sea-stag had so exhausted me that, after a while, I fell asleep with my back against the rock and my legs stretched before me on the ledge.

When I awoke it was with some of my courage returned, though I could see no easy solution to my plight.

From the mouth of the cave below the stench had increased as the stag's flesh began to rot. There was also an unpleasant slithering sound. Peering over the edge I saw that small snakelike creatures were wriggling into the cave in their thousands. Doubtless these were the carrion eaters of the sea. Hundreds of black bodies were tangled together as they moved up the rock to where the sea-stag lay.

Any thought I might have entertained of using the stag's carcass as meat to sustain me disappeared completely. I hoped the disgusting creatures would finish their meal quickly and leave. At least there were harpoons in the cave. As soon as I could reach them I would gather them up. They would be useful for defence against any other monster that might lurk in these waters and there might also be fish of some kind in the shallows, though I rather doubted It.

It occurred to me that Bishop Belphig might have planned to maroon me all along, simply because my questions were embarrassing him.

Had he planned the hunt with that in mind? If so, by going with the men into the sea-stag's lair, I had played completely into his hands.

For want of anything else to do, I made a circuit of the island. It did not take long. My first impression had been the right one. Nothing grew here.

There was no drinkable water. The people of Rowernarc got their water from melting ice, but there was no ice on that jagged spur of obsidian.

The writhing carrion creatures were still entering the cavern which was now filled with a slithering and hissing as they fought over the carcass.

Momentarily a rent appeared in the bank of clouds overhead and the faint rays of the dying sun were reflected on the black waters.

I returned to my ledge. There was nothing to do until the carrion had finished their meal.

Hope of finding Ermizhad had waned, for it was unlikely I could ever return to Rowernarc. And if I died I might find myself in an incarnation worse than this one. I might not even remember Ermizhad, just as I could now not remember why the Black Sword was such an important factor in my destiny.

I remembered Ermizhad's lovely face. I recalled the beauty of the planet to which I had brought tranquillity at the cost of genocide.

I began to doze again and soon I was no longer alone, for the familiar visions and voices returned. I fought to drive them from my brain, keeping my eyes open and staring into the gloom. But soon the visions imposed themselves against the clouds and the sea, the words seemed to come from all sides.

"Leave me in peace," I begged. "Let me die in peace!"

The slithering and hissing from the cavern of death mingled with the whispers and the echoes of the ghostly voices.

"Leave me alone!"

I was like a child, frightened by the things it imagines in the dark. My voice was the impotent pleading of a child.

"Please leave me alone!"

I heard laughter. It was low, sardonic laughter and it seemed to come from above. I looked up.

Once again a dream seemed to have assumed physical reality, for I saw the figure quite clearly. It was climbing down the rock towards me.

It was a dwarf with bandy legs and a light beard. Its face was young and its eyes bright with humour.

"Greetings," it said.

"Greetings," I replied. "Now vanish, I beg you."

"But I have come to pass the time with you."

"You are a creature of my imagination."

"I resent that. Besides, you must have an unpleasant imagination if you can create so poor a thing as myself. I am Jermays the Crooked. Do you not remember me?"

"Why should I remember you?"

"Oh, we have met once or twice before. Like you, I have no existence in time as most people understand it — as you once understood it, if my memory serves. I have been of assistance to you in the past."

"Mock me not, phantom."

"Sir Champion, I am not a phantom. At least, not much of one. True I live for the most part in the shadow worlds, the worlds which have little true substance. A trick played on me by the gods that made me the crooked thing I am."

"Gods?"

Jermays winked. "Those who claim to be gods. Though they're as much slaves of fate as we are. Gods — powers — superior entities — they are called many things. And we, I suppose, are demi-gods — the tools of the gods."

"I have no time for mystical speculation of that kind."

"My dear Champion, at this moment you have time for anything. Are you hungry?"

"You know that I am."

The dwarf reached into his green jerkin and pulled out half a loaf of bread. He handed it to me. It seemed substantial enough. I bit it. It seemed quite real. I ate it and I felt my stomach filled.

"I thank you," I said. "If I am to go mad, then this seems the best way."

Jermays sat beside me on the ledge, resting the spear he carried against the rock. He smiled. "You are certain my face is not familiar?"

"I have never seen you before."

"Strange. But then perhaps our temporal identities are in different phases and you have not yet met me, though I have met you."

"Quite possible."

Jermays had a wine-skin hanging on his belt. He unhooked it, took a swig and handed it to me.

The wine was good. I drank sparely and gave him back the skin.

"I see you do not have your sword with you," he commented.

I gave him a searching look, but there seemed no irony in his voice. "I have lost it," I said.

He laughed heartily. "Lost it! Lost that black blade! Oh! ho! ho! ho! You are making fun of me, Sir Champion."

I frowned impatiently. "It is true. What do you know of the Black Sword?"

"What all know. It is a sword that has possessed many names, as you have possessed many names. It has appeared in different guises, just as your physical appearance is not always the same. They say it was forged by the Forces of Darkness for the one destined to be their champion, but that is a rather unsophisticated view, wouldn't you agree?"

"I would."

"The Black Sword is said to exist on many planes and it is also said to have a twin. Once when I knew you you were called Elric and the blade was called *Stormbringer* — its twin *Mournblade*. However, some say that the duality is an illusion, that there is only one Black Sword and that it existed before the gods, before Creation."

"These are legends," I said. "They do not explain the nature of the thing at all. I have been told it is my destiny to bear it, yet I refuse. Does that mean ought to you?"

"It means that you must be an unhappy man. The Champion and the Sword are One. If man betrays blade or blade betrays man, then a great crime is committed."

"Why is this so?"

Jermays shrugged and smiled. "I know not. The gods know not. It has always been. Believe me, Sir Champion, it is the same as asking what created the universes through which you and I move so freely."

"Is there any means of staying on one plane, on one world?"

Jermays pursed his lips. "I have never considered the problem. It suits me to travel as I do." He grinned. "But, then, I am not a Hero."

"Have you heard of a place called Tanelorn?"

"Aye. You might call it a veteran's town." He rubbed his long nose and winked. "It's said to be in the domain of the Grey Lords, those who serve neither Law nor Chaos..."

A faint memory stirred. "What do you mean by Law and Chaos?"

"Some call them Light and Darkness. Again there are disputes among philosophers and the like as to what defines them. Others believe that they are one — part of the same force. On different worlds, in different times, they believe different things. And what they believe, I suppose, is true."

"But where is Tanelorn?"

"Where? A strange question for you to ask. Tanelorn is always there."

I rose impatiently. "Are you part of my torment, Master Jermays? You further complicate the riddles."

"Untrue, Sir Champion. But you ask impossible questions of me. Perhaps a wiser being could tell you more, but I cannot. I am not a philosopher or a hero — I am just Jermays the Crooked." His smile wavered and I saw sadness in his eyes.

"I am sorry," I said. I sighed. "But I feel there is no solution to my dilemma. How did you get to this place?"

"A gap in the fabric of another world. I do not know how I go from plane to plane, but I do and there it is."

"Can you leave?"

"I will, when it is time to leave. But I do not know when that will be."

"I see." I peered out at the gloomy sea.

Jermays wrinkled his nose. "I have seen few places as unpleasant as this. I can see why you should want to leave. Perhaps if you took up the Black Sword again...?"

"No!"

He was startled. "Forgive me. I did not comprehend that you were so adamant about the matter."

I spread my hands. "Something spoke from within me. Something that refuses — at all costs — to accept the Black Sword."

"Then you..."

Jermays was gone.

Again I was alone. Again I wondered if he had been an illusion, if my whole experience here was an illusion, if this entire thing were not some event taking place in the sleeping or insane brain of John Daker...

The air before me suddenly shivered and became bright. It was as if I looked through a window into another world. I moved towards the window but it always remained the same distance from me.

I peered through the window and I saw Ermizhad. She looked back at me. "Erekosë?"

"Ermizhad. I will return to you."

"You cannot, Erekosë, until you have taken up the Black Sword again..."

And the window closed and I saw only the dark sea again.

I roared my rage to the lowering sky.

"Whoever you are who has done this thing to me — I will have my vengeance on you!"

My words were absorbed by stark silence.

I knelt upon the ledge and sobbed.

"CHAMPION!"
A bell tolled. The voice called.
"CHAMPION!"
I stared about and saw nothing.
"CHAMPION!"

Now a whisper: "*Black Sword. Black Sword. Black Sword.*"
"No!"
"*You avoid the destiny for which you were created. Take up the Black Sword again, Champion. Take it up and know glory!*"
"*I know only misery and guilt. I will not wield the Sword.*"
"*You will.*"

The statement was a positive one. It had no threat in it, only certainty.

The slithering carrion had retreated to the sea. I made my way down to the cave and discovered the bones of the mighty sea-stag, the skeletons of my companions. The huge skull with its proud antlers regarded me as if in accusation. Quickly I found the harpoons, wrenched my broken axe from the skull and retreated back to my ledge.

I frowned, remembering the sword of Erekosë. That strange, poisoned blade had seemed powerful enough. I had had little reluctance to wield it. But perhaps that sword had been, as Jermays had hinted, merely an aspect of the Black Sword. I shrugged the thought off.

On my ledge, I arranged my weapons about me and waited for another vision.

Sure enough, it came.

It was a large raft, fashioned rather like a huge sleigh and reminiscent, in ornament, of the sea-chariot that had brought me here. But this was not drawn by sea-beasts. Instead it was pulled over the waters by birds that were like overgrown herons covered not by feathers but with dull, gleaming scales.

There was a group of men aboard the sleigh, dressed in heavy furs and mail armour, carrying swords and spears.

"Go away!" I shouted. "Leave me in peace!"

THE ETERNAL CHAMPION

They did not heed me, but turned their weird craft towards the rock.

I picked up the battle-axe by its broken haft. This time, I decided, hallucination or not, I would drive my tormentors away or perish in the attempt.

Now someone was calling to me and the voice seemed familiar. I knew I had heard it in one of my dreams.

"Count Urlik! Count Urlik — is that you?"

The speaker had thrown back his fur hood to reveal a shock of red hair, a young, handsome face.

"Begone!" I cried. "I will listen to no more riddles!"

The face seemed puzzled.

The scaly herons turned in the sky and the baroque sleigh bounced closer. I stood on my ledge, my battle-axe held threateningly in my hand.

"Begone!"

But the herons were over my head. They settled on the top of the crag and folded their leathery wings. From the sleigh the red-haired man jumped, the others following. His arms were spread wide. His face held a grin of relief.

"Count Urlik. We have found you at last. We expected you at the Scarlet Fjord many days since!"

I did not lower my guard.

"Who are you?" I said.

"Why I am Bladrak Morningspear. I am the Hound of the Scarlet Fjord!"

Still I was wary.

"And why are you here?"

He put his hands on his hips and laughed uncertainly. His fur robe fell away to reveal muscular arms on which barbaric golden bracelets were twined.

"We have been seeking you, my lord. Did you not hear the bell?"

"I heard a bell, aye."

"It was the Bell of Urlik. The Lady of the Chalice told us it would bring you to us to help in our war against the Silver Warriors."

I slightly relaxed my grip on the broken haft. Then these people really were of this world. But why had Belphig feared them? Now, at least, it seemed, I would find an answer to some of the mysteries.

"Will you return with us, my lord, to the Scarlet Fjord? Will you come aboard our boat?"

Warily, I left the ledge and approached him.

I do not know how many days or hours I had been on the sea-stag's island, but I suppose I made a peculiar appearance. My eyes were wild and wary, like those of a madman, and I clung to a broken axe as if it were the only thing in the world I trusted.

Bladrak was puzzled but he kept his good humour. He spread one hand out to indicate the boat. "We are relieved to see you, Count Urlik of the Frozen Keep. It is almost too late. We hear the Silver Warriors plan a massive attack on the southern shore."

"Rowernarc?"

"Aye, Rowernarc and the other settlements."

"Are you enemies of Rowernarc?"

He smiled. "Well, we are not allies. But let us make haste to return. I will tell you more when we are safe in port. These are dangerous waters."

I nodded. "I have discovered that."

Some of the men had been inspecting the cave. They came out, lugging the massive skull of the slain sea-stag.

"Look, Bladrak," one called. "It has been killed by an axe.

Bladrak raised his eyebrows and looked at me. "Your axe?"

I nodded. "I had nothing against the poor beast. It was really Belphig's quarry."

Bladrak threw back his head and laughed. "Look, friends," he called, pointing at me, "there is proof we have our Hero!"

Still somewhat dazed I entered the boat and took my place on one of the benches bolted to the bottom. Bladrak sat beside me. "Let's be away," he said.

The men who had found the sea-stag's skull hastily dumped it in the back of the boat and clambered aboard. Some of them jerked on the herons' reins and they took to the air again.

Suddenly the boat lunged forward and was flying across the dark sea.

Bladrak looked back. The giant skull had been placed so that it covered a long, slender box which was, in contrast to everything else aboard, completely without ornament. "Be careful of the box," he said.

"The bell you sounded," I said. "Did it toll just recently?"

"Aye — we tried again, since you had not come. Then the Lady of the Chalice said that you were somewhere on the Great Salt Sea and so we went looking for you."

"When did you first summon me?"

"Some sixty days ago."

"I went to Rowernarc," I said.

"And Belphig captured you?"

"Perhaps. Yes, I suspect that is what he did. Though I did not know it at the time. What do you know of Belphig, Sir Bladrak?"

"Little enough. He has always been an enemy of the free sailors."

"Are you those whom he called pirates?"

"Oh, doubtless, aye. Traditionally we have lived by raiding the ships and cities of the softer folk along the coast. But now we give our full attention to the Silver Warriors. With you to aid us we stand some chance of beating them, though time is very short."

"I hope you do not rely too much on me, Bladrak Morningspear. I have no supernatural powers, I assure you."

He laughed. "You are very modest for a hero. But I know what you mean — you are without weapons. All that has been dealt with by the Lady of the Chalice." He flung his hand backward to indicate the slender box in the stern. "See, my lord, we have brought your sword for you!"

THE SCARLET FJORD

At Bladrak's words a great sense of dread filled me. I stared at him in horror, hardly able to comprehend what had happened.

I had been manipulated into this situation and Bladrak had been an unknowing agent of this trick.

Bladrak was taken aback. "What is it, my lord? Have we done wrong? Have we done something that will bring doom upon you?"

My voice was hoarse and I hardly knew the words I spoke for, consciously, I still had no idea of the Black Sword's nature. "Doom on us all, Bladrak Morningspear, in some form or other. Aye, and perhaps the accomplishment of what you desire. Do you know the price?"

"Price?"

My face twisted. I flung my hands to cover it.

"What price is that, Count Urlik?"

I cleared my throat but still did not look at him. "I do not know, Bladrak. That, in time, we shall both discover. As for now, I wish that sword kept away from me. I do not want the box opened."

"We will do all you desire, Count Urlik. But you will lead us, will you not, against the Silver Warriors?"

I nodded. "If that was why I was called, that is what I will do."

"Without the sword?"

"Without the sword."

I said nothing further on our journey to Bladrak's home, but sometimes, involuntarily, my eyes strayed to the black box which lay beneath the staring skull of the slain sea-stag. Then I would twist my head away and my melancholy would suffuse my brain.

Then, at last, tall cliffs loomed out of the clouds. Massive, black, they were even more unwelcoming than the obsidian crags of Rowernarc.

Hanging over a part of this range I detected a rosy glow and I stared at it in curiosity.

"What is that?" I asked Bladrak.

He smiled. "The Scarlet Fjord. We are about to enter it."

We were very close to the cliffs, but we did not alter course. The herons flew directly towards them. Then I saw why. There was a gap between two and deep water filled it. This must be the entrance to the fjord. One of Bladrak's men raised a huge, curling horn to his lips and blew a wild blast upon it. From above came an answering blast and, looking up, I saw that there were battlements carved on both sides of the narrow opening and at the battlements stood warriors.

It was so dark between the cliffs that I thought we must surely be dashed to pieces, but the herons guided us around a bend and then I blinked in wonder. The water was scarlet. The air was scarlet. The rock shone with a deep, ruby colour, and the fjord was full of warmth.

The warm, red light issued from the mouths of a thousand caves which honeycombed the eastern wall of the fjord.

"What are those fires?" I asked.

Bladrak shook his head. "None know. They have been there forever. Some believe them to be volcanic, others say that ancient scientists invented a peculiar kind of fire which fed on rock and air alone, but when they had invented it they had no use for it. They could not put it out, so they buried it. And the Scarlet Fjord was born."

I could not keep my gaze off the wonder of those burning cliffs. Everything was bathed in the same red light. I felt truly warmed for the first time since I had arrived.

Bladrak indicated the western and southern walls of the fjord. "That is where we live."

Carved where the cliffs met the water were long quays. At these quays were tied many boats of a similar design to that in which we sailed. Above the quays were ramps and steps and terraces. Plain, square doorways had been cut from the rock and outside them now stood hosts of men, women and children, all dressed in simple, plain-coloured smocks, tabards and dresses.

When they saw us head for the southern quay they began to cheer. Then they began to chant.

It was one word they chanted.

"Urlik! Urlik! Urlik!"

Bladrak raised his arms to them, begging for silence, his grin widening as they only reluctantly subsided.

"Friends of the Scarlet Fjord! Free folk of the South! Bladrak has returned with Count Urlik who will save us. Look! He pointed dramatically first at the sea-stag's skull and then at my broken axe. "With that axe alone he killed the Bellyripper. Thus will we destroy the Silver Warriors who enslave our brothers of the North!"

And this time the cheer, to my embarrassment, was even louder. I resolved to tell Bladrak as soon as possible that I had not been solely responsible for slaying the stag.

The boat was berthed and we stepped on to the quay. Rosy-cheeked women approached us and embraced Bladrak, curtsied to me.

I could not help but notice the contrast between these folk and the neurasthenic people of Rowernarc, with their pale skins and their unhealthy appetites. Perhaps it was that the folk of Rowernarc were over-civilised and could only think of the future, while the dwellers of the Scarlet Fjord lived in the present, concerning themselves with immediate problems.

And the immediate problem of these people was plainly the threat of the Silver Warriors.

At least, I told myself, I would not now be dealing with the evasions of a Bishop Belphig. Bladrak would tell me everything he knew.

The so-called Hound of the Scarlet Fjord led me into his apartments. They were comfortably furnished and lit by lamps that also shone with a rosy glow. The decoration of the furniture and wall-hangings more closely resembled those that I had seen on my chariot and my weapons when I had found myself on the frozen plain.

I sat down thankfully in a chair carved from solid amber and surprisingly comfortable. Many of the furnishings were in amber and the table itself was carved from a solid block of quartz.

I could not help reflecting on the irony that if Man's history had begun with the Stone Age it was about to end with a Stone Age, also.

The food was simple but tasty and I learned from Bladrak that this, like that of Rowernarc, was grown in special gardens in the deepest caves.

When we had eaten, we sat with our wine-cups and said nothing for a while.

Then I spoke.

"Bladrak. You must assume that my memory is poor and answer even the simplest questions I ask you. I have endured much of late and it has made me forgetful."

"I understand," he said. "What do you wish to know?"

"First, exactly how I was summoned."

"You know that you slept in the Frozen Keep, far away on the South Ice?"

"I know that I found myself on the South Ice, riding in a chariot towards the coast."

"Aye — heading for the Scarlet Fjord. But as you came along the coast you were diverted at Rowernarc."

"That explains much," I said, "for I could find no one there who admitted to summoning me. Indeed, some, like Belphig, seemed to resent me."

"Aye, and they held you there until they could maroon you on the island we found you on."

"Perhaps that was their intention. I am not sure. But why Belphig should wish to do such a thing is hard to say."

"The brains of the folk of Rowernarc are" — Bladrak gestured at his head with his finger — "addled — askew — I know not — something..."

"But Belphig must have known of the bell, for when it sounded a second time he turned the ship about and your name was mentioned. That means that he knew you were summoning me. And they did not tell me. Why did the bell sound over the sea? And why did I not hear a bell the first time, only a voice."

Bladrak looked at his beaker. "They say the bell speaks with a human voice across the planes of the universe, but only sounds like a bell on this plane. I do not know if that is true, for I have only heard it ring in the ordinary way."

"Where is the bell?"

"I know not. We pray, the bell rings. The Lady of the Chalice told us that."

"Who is the Lady of the Chalice? Does she appear with a gigantic golden cup which screams?"

"Nay..." Bladrak gave me a sideways look. "That is just her name. She came to us when the danger of the Silver Warriors grew great. She said there was a hero who would help us. She said he was Urlik Skarsol, Count of the White Wastes, Lord of the Frozen Keep, Prince of the Southern Ice, Master of the Cold Sword...

"The *Cold* Sword? Not the Black Sword?"

"The Cold Sword."

"Continue."

"The Lady of the Chalice said that if we called the hero urgently enough it would sound Urlik's Bell which would summon him. He would come to our aid, he would take up the Cold Sword and the blood of the Silver Warriors would fill the Chalice and feed the Sun."

I sighed. I supposed that the Cold Sword was the local name for the Black Sword. Jermays had said the sword had many names on many worlds. But something within me was still resolute.

"We shall have to manage against the Silver Warriors without the sword," I said firmly. "Now tell me who these warriors are."

"They came from nowhere a year or so since. It is believed that they are Moonites whose own home grew too cold to support them. They have a cruel queen it is said, but none has ever seen her. They are virtually invulnerable to ordinary weapons and therefore well-nigh invincible in battle. They easily took the cities of the Northern coast, one after the other. Most of the people there, like those of Rowernarc, are too self-absorbed to know what happens to them. But the Silver Warriors have enslaved them and put them to death and made them brainless, inhuman creatures. We are the free sailors, we lived off the soft citizens, but now we rescue those we can and bring them here. For some while that is what we have been doing. But now all the signs show that the Silver Warriors are planning to attack the Southern coasts. In a direct fight we could not possibly defeat them. Soon the whole race will be enslaved."

"Are these warriors of flesh and blood?" I asked, for I had the notion that they might be robots or androids of some kind.

"Aye, they are of flesh and blood. They are tall and thin and arrogant and speak rarely and wear that strange silver armour. Their faces, too, are silver, as are their hands. We have seen no other parts of their bodies."

"You have never captured one?"

"Never. Their armour burns us when we touch it."

I frowned.

"And what do you want me to do?" I asked.

"Lead us. Be our Hero."

"But you seem well equipped to lead your folk."

"I am. But we are dealing here with something beyond our usual experience. You are a Hero — you can anticipate more things than can we."

"I hope you are right," I said. "I hope you are right, Sir Bladrak of the Scarlet Fjord."

T H R E E

THE RAID ON NALANARC

Bladrak informed me that an expedition against the Silver Warriors was already planned for the next day. The ships had been prepared for it and he had been awaiting my arrival before setting off against the island of Nalanarc which lay a few miles distant from the Northwestern coast. The object of the raid was not to kill the Silver Warriors, but to rescue the prisoners they had on the island. Bladrak was not sure what the prisoners were being used for, but he suspected they were engaged in making ships and weapons for the attack the Silver Warriors planned on the Southern coast shortly.

"How do you know they plan this attack?" I asked.

"We got the news from some of the slaves we rescued. Besides, it's been obvious to anyone who's been near 'em that they're planning the attack on the South. What would you do if you were a conqueror and were constantly raided from one particular area?"

"Set out to eliminate the source of my irritation," I said.

When the great fleet sailed I sailed with it.

We left the waving, cheering women behind in the Scarlet Fjord, passed between the cliffs and were soon on the open sea.

Initially there was some confusion as the herons crossed some of their lines and had to be untangled, but this did not last long and soon we were heading north.

Bladrak was singing some obscure, symbolic chant that I doubt even he knew the meaning of. He seemed full of high spirits though I discovered he had made no specific plans for the raid, save to get there somehow and get the slaves off somehow.

I outlined a plan to him and he listened with keen interest. "Very well," he said, "we'll try it."

It was a simple enough plan and, not knowing the Silver Warriors, I had no idea if it would work or not.

We sped over the waters for some time, the runners of the sleds skipping over the thick surface.

Through the murk we passed until a large island could be seen ahead.

Now Bladrak shouted to his leading craft. "Go in quickly, loose your weapons and then retreat. Wait for their own boats to follow and then lead them a dance while we get the slaves aboard in the confusion."

That was my plan. I prayed it was a good one.

The leading craft acknowledged Bladrak's orders and sped ahead while the others slowed and waited in a bank of brown cloud.

Soon we heard a distant commotion, then we saw the ships of the Scarlet Fjord scudding away from the island. They were pursued by larger, heavier craft which seemed to be the first ships that actually moved through the waters, but I could not see, from that distance, what powered them.

Now we moved in.

The island of Nalanarc grew larger and larger and I could see through the twilight that there were buildings actually raised on parts of the place. Perhaps the Silver Warriors did not build habitually in the living stone as did Bladrak's and Rowernarc's people.

The buildings were square, squat, dimly lit from within. They were built down a hill with a large building centrally placed at the top. At the bottom of the hill were the familiar openings to caverns.

"That is where the slaves are," Bladrak told me. "They are worked in those caverns building ships and weapons until they die, then a new batch replaces them. Men and women of all ages are there. They are hardly fed anything. There are always plenty more, you see. I do not think the Silver Warriors mean our folk to live once the world is theirs."

While I was prepared to believe Bladrak, I had once before been told by those who had summoned me that the people they fought were unremittingly evil. I had discovered that the Eldren were in fact the victims. I wanted to see for myself what the Silver Warriors were doing.

The herons drew our boats up on to the island's beach and we piled out, heading for the caverns at the base of the hill.

It was plain that almost all the Silver Warriors had gone in pursuit of the few ships we had sent in ahead. I guessed it would not be a tactic we could use twice.

Into the caves we ran and I had my first sight of the warriors.

THE ETERNAL CHAMPION

They were on average a good seven feet high, but extremely thin, with long arms and legs and narrow heads. Their skin was actually white, but with a faint silver sheen. Their armour covered their bodies, apparently without joins, and their heads were encased in tight-fitting helmets.

They were armed with long, double-bladed halberds. When they saw us, they came rushing at us with them. But they seemed somewhat clumsy with the halberds and I guessed they might be used to some other kind of weapon.

We had armed ourselves with what Bladrak had assured me were the only useful tools against the Silver Warriors whose armour could not be pierced and would burn whoever tried to handle it.

These weapons were wide-meshed nets which we flung at them as they approached. The nets clung to their bodies and tripped them and they could not free themselves.

I looked about the cavern workshops and was horrified by the condition of the naked men, women and children who had been set to labouring here.

"Get these people out as quickly as you can," I said.

One Silver Warrior had not been entangled by a net. He came running at me with his halberd. I knocked it aside with my restored battle-axe and, heedless of the warning Bladrak had given me, chopped at his body.

A horrible jolt ran up my arms and sent me staggering. But the Silver Warrior had been toppled too.

I was incredulous. I knew I had received nothing less than an electric shock.

Now Bladrak and his men were herding the dazed slaves out of the caves towards the ships.

I looked up at the larger building on the top of the hill. I saw a glint of silver and I saw a shape that was familiar framed against a window.

It was someone wearing the bulbous armour of Rowernarc.

Filled with curiosity and careless of the potential danger, I dodged behind one of the square, featureless buildings and then began to creep closer up the hill.

The figure was probably unaware that he could be seen so easily from below. He was gesturing angrily as he watched Bladrak's men helping the wretched slaves aboard their ships.

I heard a voice.

I could not make out the words, but the tone was more than familiar to me.

I crept closer, anxious to have confirmed by my eyes what had already been confirmed by my ears.

I saw the face now.

It was Bishop Belphig, of course. Every suspicion I had had about him was proved right.

"Have you no understanding?" he was crying. "That pirate Bladrak will not only make off with most of your labour force — he will turn half of those into soldiers to fight against you."

I heard a murmured reply, then a group of Silver Warriors came running down the hill, saw me — and charged with their halberds.

I turned and fled, just as Bladrak's boat was leaving.

"We thought we had lost you, Sir Champion," he grinned. "What were you doing up there?"

"I was listening to a conversation."

Halberds fell into the water on either side of us but we were soon out of range.

Bladrak said: "It will take them time to bring up their heavier weapons. We did well. Not a man wounded, even — and a satisfactory cargo." He gestured towards the boats crammed with rescued slaves. Then what I had said registered with him.

"Conversation? What did you learn?"

"I learned that Rowernarc has a leader who would bring about her ruin," I said.

"Belphig?"

"Aye. He's up there, doubtless with the leader of the Silver Warriors on the island. Now I know his main reason for his "hunt". He wished to rid himself of me, for fear I should aid you against his allies — and he needed to make a secret rendezvous with the Silver Warriors."

Bladrak shrugged. "I always suspected him of something of the sort. They have no values, those folk in Rowernarc."

"Save, perhaps, their Lord Temporal — Shanosfane. And no human being deserves the fate of these wretches." I jerked my thumb at the thin, dirty bodies of the Silver Warriors' ex-slaves.

"What would you do about it, Count Urlik?"

"I must think, Sir Bladrak."

He gave me a long, hard look and said softly: "Are you sure it is not yet time to use your sword?"

I avoided his eye and stared out to sea. "I have not said I intend to use the sword at any time."

"Then I do not think we shall live long," he said.

F   O   U   R

THE LADY OF THE CHALICE

And thus we came back to the Scarlet Fjord. The freed slaves looked around them in wonder as our boats tied up at quays bathed in rosy light from the honeycombed cliff on the far side of the fjord.

"Best mount extra guards from now on," Bladrak told one of his lieutenants. Absently, he twisted one of the golden bracelets on his arm. "Belphig knows us and he knows the Scarlet Fjord. They'll try reprisals."

Weary from our expedition we went inside and pleasant women brought us meat and wine. There was plenty of extra room in the city of the Scarlet Fjord and the freed slaves would find themselves well provided for. Bladrak was frowning, though, as he sat opposite me and looked across the quartz table.

"Are you still thinking of the Black Sword?" I asked him.

He shook his head. "No. That's for you to think about. I was considering the implications of Belphig's perfidy. From time to time we have the odd man or woman in the Scarlet Fjord who decides that Rowernarc offers pursuits more to their taste. We allow them to leave, of course, and — they go…"

"You mean that Belphig may be aware of many of your plans?" I said.

"You mentioned that he was unnerved by the sound of Urlik's Bell. Plainly he knows everything about you, about the Lady of the Chalice and so on. Equally plainly, he sought to soften you up in Rowernarc — in the hope he could bring you over to his side. When that failed…"

"He marooned me. But now he must know I sail with you."

"Aye. And he will pass on all his information to his alien masters. What do you think they will do then?"

"They will try to strike before we grow any stronger."

"Aye. But will they strike at the Scarlet Fjord first — or will they take Rowernarc and the cities further up the coast?"

"It will be easier for them to take the cities, I suspect," I replied. "Then they can concentrate their full power upon the Scarlet Fjord."

"That's my guess, also."

"The question now is — do we remain here, building up our strength for a siege, or do we go to the aid of Rowernarc and the rest?"

"It's a difficult problem." Bladrak stood up, running his fingers through his red hair. "I would like to consult one who could offer us wisdom on the matter."

"You have philosophers here? Or strategists?"

"Not exactly. We have the Lady of the Chalice."

"She dwells in the Scarlet Fjord? I did not realize…"

He smiled and shook his head. "She may come to the Scarlet Fjord, however."

"I should like to meet this woman. After all, she seems responsible for my fate."

"Then come with me," Bladrak said, and he led me through an inner door and into a long passage which sloped sharply downward.

Soon a strong saline smell reached my nostrils and I noticed that the walls were damp. I guessed that we were actually under the fjord itself.

The passage widened into a chamber. From the roof grew long stalactites in milky blues, yellows and greens. A soft radiance issued from the stalactites themselves and cast our gigantic shadows on the rough igneous rock of the cavern's walls. In the centre of the chamber an area of basalt had been smoothed and levelled and into it had been placed a small staff of about half a man's height. The staff was a deep, lustreless black with mottlings of dark blue. The cavern contained no other artifact.

"What is the staff for?" I asked.

Bladrak shook his head. "I do not know. It has always been here. It was here long before my ancestors came to the Scarlet Fjord."

"Has it any connection with the Lady of the Chalice?"

"I think it might have, for it is here that she appears to us." He looked about him, half nervously I thought. "Lady?"

It was all he said. Then a distant, high-pitched, oscillating whine came from all around us in the air. The stalactites vibrated and I prayed they would not be brought down on our heads by the sound. The short staff imbedded in the basalt seemed to change colour slightly, but that might have been something cast by one of the vibrating stalactites. The whine increased until it began to sound like a human scream and I recognised it with some trepidation. I blinked my eyes. I thought I saw the outline of the huge golden chalice again. I turned to say something to Bladrak and then looked back in astonishment.

A woman stood there. She was wreathed in golden light. Her dress and her hair were of gold and on her hands she wore gloves.

Her face was covered by a golden veil.

Bladrak kneeled. "Lady, we need your help again."

"My help?" came a sweet voice. "When your great hero Urlik has joined you at last?"

"I have no power of prophecy, my lady," I replied. "Bladrak believes that you might have."

"My own powers are limited and I am not permitted to reveal all I see, even then. What do you wish to know, Sir Champion?"

"Let Bladrak tell you."

Bladrak climbed to his feet. Quickly he outlined the problem. Should we go to the aid of Rowernarc and the other cities? Or should we wait until the Silver Warriors attacked us?

The Lady of the Chalice seemed to deliberate. "The fewer killed in this struggle the better I shall like it," she said. "It would seem to me that the sooner it is over the more folk will be saved."

Bladrak gestured with his hands. "But Rowernarc has brought this on herself. Who is to say how many warriors are on Belphig's side? Perhaps the city will fall without bloodshed…"

"There would be bloodshed soon enough," said the Lady of the Chalice. "Belphig would destroy all he did not trust."

"Likely, aye…" mused Bladrak Morningspear. He glanced at me.

"Is there a way of killing the Silver Warriors?" I asked the mysterious woman. "At the moment we are badly handicapped."

"They cannot be killed," she said. "Not by your weapons, at least."

Bladrak shrugged. "Then I will risk many men in trying to save the worthless citizens of Rowernarc. I am not sure they would like to die for that cause, Lady."

"Surely some are not worthless," said she. "What of Lord Shanosfane? He would be in great danger if Belphig gained complete power over Rowernarc."

I admitted that Shanosfane was in danger and I agreed that the strange, abstracted Lord Temporal was worth saving from Belphig.

Then she asked, rather strangely: "Would you say that Lord Shanosfane was a good man?"

"Aye," I replied. "Eminently good."

"I think, then, that you will need him in the near future," she said.

"Perhaps we can get to Rowernarc before Belphig finishes his business on Nalanarc?" I suggested. "We could get the populace away before the Silver Warriors attacked."

"Belphig's business on Nalanarc was finished for him," Bladrak pointed out. "And now that he knows he is allied to the Silver Warriors, he will waste no time in attacking."

"True."

"But only the Black Sword will defeat Belphig," said the veiled woman, "and now you possess it, Lord Urlik."

"I will not use it," I said.

"You will use it." The air pulsed. She vanished.

I recognised the statement. It had no threat in it, only certainty. I had heard it before while marooned on the sea-stag's island.

I rubbed my face with my hands. "I would be grateful if I was allowed to work out my own destiny for once," I said. "For good or ill."

"Come." Bladrak began to leave the cavern.

I followed him, lost in my own thoughts. Everything was conspiring to force me into a pattern of behaviour which all my instincts rejected. But perhaps my instincts were wrong...

We returned to Bladrak's apartments in time to receive a messenger who had just arrived.

"My lords, the Silver Warriors' fleet has left harbour and is sailing directly south."

"Bound for...?" Bladrak queried.

"For Rowernarc, I think."

Bladrak snorted. "We've been wasting time, I see. We'll never reach Rowernarc before they do. Also it could be a trick to divert us. For all I know their real ambition is to draw us off while another fleet attacks the Scarlet Fjord." He looked sardonically at me. "We are still in a quandary, Count Urlik."

"The Lady of the Chalice seemed to indicate that it would be to our advantage if Shanosfane were saved," I said. "We must think of him, at least."

"Risk a fleet for one man of Rowernarc?" Bladrak laughed. "No, Sir Champion!"

"Then I must go alone," I said.

"You'll achieve nothing — save to lose us our Hero."

"Your Hero, Sir Bladrak," I pointed out, "has done precious little for you so far."

"Your role will be clear soon."

"It is clear now. I have a great respect for Lord Shanosfane. I cannot bear to think of him being butchered by Belphig."

"I understand — but you cannot risk so much, Count Urlik."

"I could afford to," I said, "if I had an ally."

"An ally? I could not desert my folk to embark upon an—"

"I speak not of you, Bladrak. I appreciate that you must stay with your people. I did not mean a human ally."

He looked at me in astonishment. "Supernatural? What?"

In me now was a mixture of melancholy and relief. There was but one course open to me. I took it. I at once felt that I was giving in and making a courageous decision.

"The Black Sword," I said.

Bladrak, too, looked as if he had had a weight removed from his shoulders. He grinned and clapped me on the back. "Aye. It would seem a shame not to blood it now that you have it."

"Bring it to me," I told him.

.

F   I   V   E

THE WAKING OF THE SWORD

They brought the ebony case and they laid it on the table carved from quartz while conflicting emotions fought within me until I was so dizzy I could scarcely see the thing.

I put my hands upon the case. It felt warm. There seemed to be a faint pulse coming from within it, like the beating of a heart.

I looked at Bladrak who was staring at me, grim-faced. I took hold of the clasp and tried to raise it.

It was tightly locked.

"It will not open," I said. I was almost glad. "I cannot move it. Perhaps, after all, it was not meant..."

And then, inside my head, loudly came the chant again:

BLACK SWORD
BLACK SWORD
BLACK SWORD
THE BLACK SWORD IS THE CHAMPION'S SWORD
THE WORD OF THE SWORD IS THE CHAMPION'S LAW
BLACK SWORD
BLACK SWORD
BLACK SWORD
THE BLADE OF THE SWORD HAS THE BLOOD OF THE SUN
THE HILT OF THE SWORD AND THE HAND ARE AS ONE

BLACK SWORD
BLACK SWORD
BLACK SWORD
THE RUNES ON THE SWORD ARE THE WORMS THAT ARE WISE
THE NAME OF THE SWORD IS THE SAME AS THE SCYTHE
BLACK SWORD
BLACK SWORD
BLACK SWORD
THE DEATH OF THE SWORD IS THE DEATH OF ALL LIFE
    IF THE BLACK SWORD IS WAKENED IT MUST TAKE ITS BLACK FIEF
BLACK SWORD
BLACK SWORD
BLACK SWORD

Now I wavered in my resolve at the last phrase. A huge sense of doom pressed upon me. I staggered back, my lips writhing, my whole soul in agony.

"No..."

Bladrak leapt forward and supported me.

My voice was strangled. "Bladrak — you must leave here."

"Why, Lord Urlik, you seem to need

"Leave here!"

"But I would help you..."

"You will perish if you stay."

"How do you know that?"

"I am not sure — but I do know it. I speak truly, Bladrak. *Leave — for pity's sake!*"

Bladrak hesitated for another moment and then ran from the room, locking the door behind him.

I was alone with the case that held the Black Sword and the voice continued to chant in my head

BLACK SWORD
BLACK SWORD
BLACK SWORD
AROUSE THE BLACK BLADE AND THE PATTERN IS MADE
THE DEED WILL BE DONE AND THE PRICE WILL BE PAID

BLACK SWORD
BLACK SWORD
BLACK SWORD

'Very well!" I screamed. "I will do it. I will take up the Black Sword again. I will pay the price!"

The chanting ceased.

There was a terrible stillness in the room.

I heard my own breath rasping as my eyes fixed on the case on the table and were held by it.

In a low voice I said at last:

"Come to me, Black Sword. We shall be as one again."

The lid of the case sprang open. A wild, triumphant howling filled the air — an almost human voice which awakened a thousand memories within me.

I was Elric of Melniboné and I defied the Lords of Chaos with my runesword Stormbringer in my hands and a wild joy in my heart...

I was Dorian Hawkmoon and I fought against the Beast Lords of the Dark Empire and my sword was called The Sword of the Dawn...

I was Roland dying at Roncesvalles with the magic blade Durandana slaying half a hundred Saracens...

I was Jeremiah Cornelius. No sword now but a needle-gun shooting darts as I was chased through a city by a surging, insane mob...

I was Prince Corum in the Scarlet Robe, seeking vengeance at the Court of the Gods...

I was Artos the Celt, riding with my burning blade uplifted against the invaders of my kingdom's shores...

And I was all of these and more than these and sometimes my weapon was a sword, at others it was a spear, at others a gun... But always I bore a weapon that was the Black Sword or a part of that strange blade.

Always a weapon — always the warrior.

I was the Eternal Champion and that was my glory and my doom...

And a strange mood of reconciliation came over me then and I was proud of my destiny.

Yet why had I denied it?

I recalled a billowing cloud of brightness. I remembered grief, I remembered sealing the sword in its case and swearing I would not bear it again. I remembered a voice and a prophecy...

"In refusing one doom, ye shall know another — a greater..."

"No doom can be greater," I shouted.

Then I was John Daker — unhappy, unfulfilled, before the voice called across the aeons for him to become Erekose:

The crime I had committed was in refusing the Black Sword.

But why had I refused it? Why had I tried to rid myself of it?

It seemed to me that that had not been the first time I had tried to part my own destiny from that of the Black Sword...

"Why?" I murmured. "Why?"

"Why?"

Then from the case a strange, black radiance spilled and I was drawn towards it until I stared down upon that familiar sight.

It was a heavy, black broadsword. Carved into its blade and hilt were runes which I could not read. Its pommel was a sphere of gleaming black metal. It was more than five feet long in its blade and its hilt was more than large enough to accommodate two hands.

My own hands reached involuntarily towards it now.

They touched the hilt and the sword seemed to rise and settle comfortably in my grip, purring as a cat might purr.

I shuddered and yet I was filled with joy.

But now I understood what was meant by the term "unholy joy'.

With this sword in my hands I ceased to be a man and became a demon.

I laughed. My laughter was gigantic and shook the room. I swung the sword about and it shrieked its wild music. I raised it and I brought it down upon the table of quartz.

The table split completely in twain. Chips of quartz flew everywhere.

"This is the Whole Sword!" I cried. "This is the Cold Sword! This is the Black Sword and soon it must feed!"

In the recesses of my brain I understood that it was rare for me to hold the actual blade. Usually I had a weapon which drew its power from the Black Sword, which was a manifestation of the Black Sword.

Because I had sought to challenge Destiny, Destiny had taken vengeance. What followed could only be accomplished with the whole power of the Black

Sword, but I still did not know what it was to be.

One of Bladrak's girls entered the room through another door. Her face was horrified as she saw me.

"My master sent me to ask if—" She screamed.

The Black Sword twisted in my hand and plunged towards her, almost dragging me with it. It buried itself in her body, passing completely through to the other side. She danced in a dreadful jig of death as, with her remaining life, she sought to drag herself off the blade.

"It is cold — aaah, how it is cold!" she sighed.

And then she died.

The sword was wrenched from her. Blood seemed to increase its dark radiance. It howled again.

"No!" I shouted. "That should not have been! Only my enemies are to be slain!"

And I thought something like a chuckle escaped the sated sword as Bladrak rushed in to see what had happened, looked at me, looked at the sword, looked at the dead girl and groaned in terror.

He rushed to the case. There was a sheath in there and he flung it at me. "Sheath the thing, Urlik! Sheath it, I beg you!"

Silently I accepted the sheath. Almost without my raising it the Black Sword slid into the scabbard.

Bladrak looked at the poor, dead woman, at the shattered table.

Then he looked at my face and an expression of anguish covered his features.

"Now I know why you did not wish to wield the blade," he said softly.

I could not speak. I attached the great scabbard to my belt and the Black Sword hung at my side at an angle.

Then I said: "You all wished me to arouse the blade and use it. Now, I think, we begin to understand the consequences. The Black Sword must be fed. It will feed on friends if it cannot feed on enemies…"

Bladrak turned his eyes away.

"Is a boat ready?" I asked him.

He nodded.

I left that ruined room of death.

S I X

THE BLACK BLADE'S FIEF

They had given me a boat and a steersman.

The boat was a small one, with high, curving sides, plated with red gold and bronze. The steersman sat in front of me, controlling the leather-winged herons which flew low through the twilight air.

The Scarlet Fjord was soon no more than a glow hanging above the distant cliffs, then that vanished and brown clouds enclosed our gloomy world.

For a long while we sped over the black and sluggish sea until the jagged obsidian cliffs came in sight. Then we saw the bay overlooked by Rowernarc — and in the bay were crammed the besieging ships of the Silver Warriors.

Belphig had not wasted time. It was possible that I had arrived too late.

The craft of the invaders were very large and similar in design to Belphig's sea-chariot, but apparently with no *slevahs* to tow them.

We stayed out of sight and the steersman brought the boat to a halt on the crystalline beach quite close to the spot where Belphig's men had first encountered me.

Telling the steersman to await my return, I began to move cautiously along the shore in the direction of the Obsidian City.

Keeping to the cover of the rocks, I was able to round the corner of the bay and see exactly what I faced.

Plainly Rowernarc had capitulated without a battle. Prisoners were being herded down the ramps towards the ships.

Handling their halberds as awkwardly as ever, the slim Silver Warriors were dotted everywhere on the causeways.

Belphig himself was not in sight, but half-way up the cliff I saw my chariot, its bears in their harness, being trundled down to the beach. Doubtless this was part of their booty.

Shanosfane was not among the prisoners. I guessed that Belphig had had him confined to his "province" of Dhotgard for the moment — if the Lord Spiritual had not already killed the Lord Temporal.

But how was I to reach Dhotgard when every level was crowded with the alien invaders?

Even with the aid of the Black Sword I would surely be swamped by weight of numbers if I tried to cut my way up to Dhotgard. And if I reached the place, how would I return?

Then a thought came to me as I watched my bears being urged towards the sea where a series of planks had been placed between the shallows and the nearest ship.

Deliberating no further I leapt up, drew my sword and ran for the chariot.

I had almost reached it before I was seen. A Silver Warrior shouted in a high, fluting voice, flinging his halberd at me. I knocked it aside with the sword, which, for all its weight, handled as easily as a fencing foil. I sprang into the chariot and gathered up the reins, turning the bears back towards the Obsidian City.

"Ho, Render! Ho, Growler!"

As if their spirits had risen at my sudden appearance, the bears reared in their harness and wheeled about.

"Ho, Longclaw! Ho, Snarler!"

The wheels of the chariot scraped round in the crystal rock and then we were driving straight for the causeway.

I ducked as more halberds were thrown, but they were poor throwing weapons at the best of times and the Silver Warriors' lack of skill with them did not help. Slaves and soldiers scattered and we had reached the first level in no time.

Now the Black Sword was crooning again. An evil song, a mocking song.

As I raced past them, I slashed at warriors who tried to stick me with their weapons and now when I struck their armour it was they who yelled, not me...

Up and up we charged and I felt an old, familiar battle-joy returning. The Black Sword cut off heads and limbs and bright blood streamed the length of its blade, dappling the sides of the chariots and the white pelts of the bears.

THE ETERNAL CHAMPION

"On, Render! On, Longclaw!"

We were almost at the level of Dhotgard. Everywhere men were shouting and running in all directions.

"On, Snarler! On, Growler!"

Even faster ran my mighty bears until we came to the great door which protected Dhotgard. It had been drawn right back. I guessed that some spy in Shanosfane's household had been paid to do this. But it suited me now for I was able to drive the chariot right into the palace and continue at breakneck speed through the very passages themselves.

At last I reached the plain chamber where I had first met Shanosfane. I brushed aside the curtain and there he was.

He looked a little thinner, there was some hurt in his eyes, but he looked up from a manuscript as if he had been disturbed only for a moment when the Silver Warriors had arrived in Rowernarc.

"My Lord Urlik?"

"I have come to rescue you, Lord Shanosfane."

His black features showed mild surprise.

"Belphig will kill you now that he has helped betray Rowernarc."

"Why should Belphig kill me?"

"You threaten his rule."

"Rule?"

"Lord Shanosfane, if you remain here you are doomed. There will be no more reading. No more study."

"I do it only to pass the time…"

"Do you not fear death?"

"No.

"Well, then…" I sheathed my sword, ran forward and knocked him sharply on the back of the neck. He slumped on to the desk. I flung him over my shoulder and ran for the exit. My bears were snarling as Silver Warriors rushed towards us. I dumped Shanosfane in the chariot and leapt at the warriors.

Plainly they were used to weapons that could not harm them. The Black Sword whined and howled and it sheered through their strange armour to reveal that they were, indeed, very much like men. Their blood spilled as easily. Their innards spewed from the cuts the blade made. Their silver-flecked faces showed their pain.

I got back into the chariot, flicked the reins, turning it in the narrow passage and then gathering speed as we made for the main door.

Then I saw Belphig. He yelped as he saw our headlong approach and he flattened himself against the wall. I leaned out, trying to reach him with the sword, but he was too far distant.

We went around the door block and out on to the causeway again, going down much faster than we had come up.

This time our path was not blocked by Silver Warriors. They had learned to be wary. But they still flung their halberds at a safe distance and two nicked slight wounds in my left arm and my right cheek.

I was laughing at them again, holding my huge sword aloft. More powerful than the sword of Erekosë (which had been one of its partial manifestations) it thrummed out its evil song of death as my bears bore us towards the beach.

There was cheering now, from some quarters, as the prisoners saw me re-emerge. I shouted to them.

"Fight, men of Rowernarc! Fight! Turn on the Silver Warriors! Slay them if you can!"

Downward the chariot rumbled.

"Kill them or you will die!"

Some of the prisoners picked up halberds and began to fling them at their vanquishers. The Silver Warriors were again startled, not knowing how to react.

"Now flee!" I cried. "Make for the depths of the mountains and then head along the coast for the Scarlet Fjord. You will be welcome there — and safe. The Black Sword will defend you!"

I hardly knew what I was shouting, but it had a surprising effect on the spiritless people of Rowernarc. While the Silver Warriors were confused, they began to run. They still had time to be soldiers, I thought. And soldiers the survivors would become — for now they knew what their fate would be if they did not fight.

Laughing in my crazy battle-joy I drove the chariot down the cliff and its wheels bounced over the crystal.

"Shanosfane is safe!" I called to those who listened. "Your leader is with me." As best I could I raised his prone body. "He is alive but unconscious!" I saw one of his eyelids flutter. He would not be unconscious for long.

Belphig and a party of Silver Warriors were still in pursuit. From one of the entrances now came Morgeg and his men on their seal-beasts and I knew I had to fear these more than the clumsy aliens.

Across the beach they crashed in pursuit. A spear grazed the shoulder of one of my bears. The powerful animals were labouring somewhat now, for I had driven them hard.

And then, half-way to where I had left the boat, the chariot wheel hit a rock and Shanosfane and I were flung on to the ground as the bears raced on, dragging the chariot behind them. It bounced, hit another rock, righted itself and, riderless, disappeared into the gloom.

I put Shanosfane over my shoulder again and began to run; but the thump of the seal-beasts' fins came close behind. I saw the boat ahead. I turned to look at Morgeg and the others. They would reach me before I could get to the boat.

Shanosfane was moaning, rubbing his head. I put him down.

"See that boat, Lord Shanosfane. It will take you to safety. Get to it as quickly as you can."

I took the Black Sword in both hands as the dazed Shanosfane staggered away.

Then I prepared to stand my ground.

Morgeg and six other riders, all armed with axes, charged at me. I whirled the huge sword around my head and sheered half through the necks of two of the seals. They bellowed as the blood pumped from their veins. They tried to come on, but collapsed and threw their riders from their saddles. I killed one of the riders at once, lunging the Black Sword through steel and padding straight into his heart. I brought the blade round and killed a man who was still mounted. He jerked in his saddle and then toppled out.

The other man on foot came at me crablike with his battle-axe circling his head. I chopped at the haft of the axe and the blade went spinning through the air to strike a rider directly in the face and knock him from his saddle. I drove my sword through the weaponless warrior's gorget.

Now Morgeg fought to control his frightened mount. He glared at me in hatred.

"You are tenacious, Count Urlik," he said.

"It seems so." I feinted at him.

There was only one rider left alive save Morgeg. I lowered my sword and spoke to the man. "Would you leave while I kill Morgeg? Or will you stay and be slain with him?"

The man's pale face twitched, his mouth dropped open, he tried to say something, failed and wheeled his seal-beast about, heading back to Rowernarc.

Morgeg said quietly, "I think I should like to return, also."

"You cannot," I said simply. "I have to repay you for marooning me on that island."

"I thought you were dead."

"You did not check."

"I thought the sea-stag killed you."

"I killed the sea-stag."

He licked his lips. "In that case, I should definitely like to return to Rowernarc."

I lowered the Black Sword. "You may do so if you tell me one thing. Who leads you?"

"Why, Belphig leads us!"

"No. I mean who is the leader of the Silver Warr—"

Morgeg thought he had seen a chance. He swung his axe down on me.

But I blocked the blow with the flat of the sword. I turned my own weapon and the axe flew from his hand. The sword could not be stopped as it went to his groin and the point drove deeply in.

"Cold…" murmured Morgeg as his eyes closed. "So cold…"

The corpse fell backwards in the saddle and the seal-beast reared and turned, charging towards the bay.

I saw Belphig at the head of a group of Silver Warriors. There were a score of them and I wondered if even the Black Sword could deal with so many.

I heard a shout from seaward. I heard the noise of wings beating overhead.

"Lord Urlik! Now!"

It was the steersman's voice. He had bundled Shanosfane aboard and had come along the coast to find me.

I sheathed the Black Sword and plunged knee-deep into the water. The stuff clung to my legs, hampering me. Belphig and his men were almost upon us. Behind him, in the way, everything was still in confusion.

I grasped the smooth side of the boat and hauled myself in, gasping. Immediately the steersman turned the herons and we were heading out to sea.

Belphig and the Silver Warriors came to a stop at the edge of the water and were soon swallowed in the gloom.

We raced back for the Scarlet Fjord.

Bladrak Morningspear had an unusually grim expression on his face as he sat in an amber chair and looked across the room at Shanosfane and myself.

We were in another room of his apartments, as far away from the chamber of death as possible. I had taken off the scabbarded Black Sword and leaned the thing against the wall.

"Well," said Bladrak quietly, "the Black Sword has earned its price, it seems. You must have killed many Silver Warriors as well as those riders of Belphig's — and perhaps you showed the folk of Rowernarc that there was some point in defending themselves."

I nodded.

"And you, my Lord Shanosfane, are you pleased that you have avoided death?"

Bladrak spoke almost sardonically.

Shanosfane looked at him from those deep, detached eyes. "I am not sure what difference there is between life and death, Sir Bladrak."

Bladrak's expression seemed to indicate that he had made a point. He got up and began to pace about.

I said to Shanosfane: "Do you know who rules the Silver Warriors?"

Shanosfane looked slightly surprised. "Why, Belphig, of course..."

"He means that he wants to know who commands Belphig," Bladrak said. "Who is supreme ruler of the Silver Warriors?"

"Why, Belphig. Bishop Belphig. He is their supreme ruler."

"But he is not of their race!" I exclaimed.

"He has their queen prisoner." Shanosfane's gaze wandered around the room and then fixed curiously on the Black Sword. "They are not really warriors, those people. They are peaceful. They have never known war. But Belphig makes them do his will — for if they do not, he will destroy their queen, whom they love above life."

I was astonished and I could see that Bladrak was equally surprised. "So that is why they are such poor halberdiers," I murmured.

"They know how to build engines to make ships move through the water," Shanosfane said. "They have several such mechanical skills. Belphig told me all this."

"But why is he enslaving our people?" Bladrak demanded. "What use is there in it?"

Shanosfane looked calmly at Bladrak. "I do not know. What use is there in any activity? Perhaps Belphig's plan is as good as any other."

"You have no idea of his ultimate ambitions?" I said.

"I told you. None at all. I did not think to enquire."

"Do you not care that your people are being enslaved — killed!" Bladrak shouted. "Does not that touch you anywhere in that cold soul of yours?"

"They were slaves already," Shanosfane said reasonably. "And they were dying. How much longer do you think our race could have lived like that?"

Bladrak turned his back on the Lord Temporal.

"Lord Urlik, you wasted your time," he said.

"Because Lord Shanosfane does not think as we do," I replied, "it does not follow that he was not worth saving."

"I was not worth saving." A peculiar look came into Shanosfane's eyes. "I do not think I have been saved. Who told you to rescue me?"

"We decided to do it ourselves," I replied. And then I paused. "No, perhaps not — perhaps it was the Lady of the Chalice who suggested it."

Shanosfane returned his attention to the Black Sword.

"I think I would like it if you could leave me alone," he said. "I would meditate."

Bladrak and I went to the door and walked out into the corridor.

"Well, perhaps he was worth saving after all," Bladrak admitted reluctantly. "He gave us information we should not have had otherwise. But I have no liking for the fellow and cannot see why you admire him. He is nothing but a —"

We stopped in our tracks as a blood curdling scream came from the room we had just left. We looked at each other, sharing a certain knowledge.

We ran back towards the door.

But the Black Sword had done its work. Shanosfane lay spread-eagled on the floor with the blade waving from the middle of his chest like an obscene plant. Whether the sword had attacked him or whether he had managed to kill himself with it we would never know.

Shanosfane was not dead. His lips were moving.

I bent to listen to the words he whispered. "I had not realised it would be so — so chill..."

Those incredibly intelligent eyes closed and he spoke no more.

I tugged the Black Sword from his body and put it back in its sheath.

Bladrak was pale. "Was that why the Lady of the Chalice made you bring him here?" he said.

I did not understand him at first. "What do you mean?"

"Did the sword need the life of a good man — an especially good man — as its price for helping us? The Black Sword's reward — the soul of the Black King?"

I remembered the words of the chant: *If the Black Sword is wakened, it must take its Black ...*

I clenched my hands together as I looked down at the corpse of the scholar king.

"Oh, Bladrak," I said, "I am afraid of our future."

And a coldness, colder than the coldest ice, filled the room.

BOOK FOUR:

THE BLOOD OF THE SUN

THE ETERNAL CHAMPION

A knife, a cup and a man shall be
The means by which the world's set free.

—The Chronicle of the Black Sword

O N E

SIEGE OF THE SCARLET FJORD

Depression settled over us and even the fires of the Scarlet Fjord seemed to fade.

We lived in the shadow of the Black Sword and now I had an inkling of the reasons why I had wanted to rid myself of it.

One could not master the sword. It demanded lives as some greedy Moloch — some fierce, barbaric god of ancient times — demanded sacrifice. And, what was worse, it often chose its own sacrifices from among the friends of the man who bore it.

A jealous sword, indeed.

I know that Bladrak did not blame me for what had taken place. In fact he claimed that the fault was shared between himself and the Lady of the Chalice — for they had encouraged me, against my will, to awaken the Black Sword and use it.

"It has already aided us," I pointed out. "Without it, I should not have survived in Rowernarc and we should not have learned from Shanosfane the truth of Belphig's status and the nature of his hold over the Silver Warriors."

"It has been well paid for its work…" Bladrak growled.

"If we knew where Belphig hid this queen," I said, "then we could free her. The Silver Warriors would refuse to serve Belphig and the threat would be over."

"But we know not where, in the whole world, she is!"

"If the Lady of the Chalice were to be asked…" I began, but Bladrak silenced me.

"I am not sure that the Lady works entirely in our interest," he said. "I think she uses us in some larger scheme of her own."

"Aye — you could be right."

Now we walked along the quays, staring down at the red-stained water, at the many boats we were preparing for our war against the Silver Warriors. The knowledge that the slender, awkward aliens fought us only because they had been forced to do so by Belphig took some of the savagery out of our feelings and our work had slowed accordingly.

Unable to hate the Silver Warriors, it was harder for us to contemplate killing them. But we should have to kill them or see the whole of humanity slain or enslaved.

I looked across the fjord to the mysterious source of its heat and light — the honeycomb cliff from which the scarlet radiance issued.

There was a power there but I could not begin to guess at its nature. Something created millennia before which continued to burn at the same constant temperature while the rest of the world grew cold. Once, I thought, the Scarlet Fjord had been something other than a camp for the outlaws who chose not to live in the soft decadence of cities like Rowernarc. Was the Lady of the Chalice the last descendant of the scientists who had dwelt here? Perhaps Shanosfane could have told us. Perhaps that was why the Black Sword had killed him, because we were meant to remain in ignorance…

Suddenly Bladrak put a hand on my shoulder. He cocked his head and listened.

I heard it then. The sound of a horn. It blew louder.

"The guards," said Bladrak. "Come, Lord Urlik, let's see why they sound the alarm." He leapt into a boat which had already been harnessed to a pair of the heron-like flying creatures. They were asleep on the perches built along the quayside. He shook their reins and awakened them as I joined him. The birds squawked and took to the air. We headed towards the narrow opening of the fjord.

Between the tall, black cliffs we moved until the open sea was in sight. And then we saw the reason for the guards' alarum.

It was Belphig's fleet.

There were between five hundred and a thousand great ships massing there and the air was full of the drone of their engines. Low, sluggish waves rocked our craft as their wash reached us.

"Belphig brings all his strength against us!" Bladrak rasped. "Our boats could never hope to beat those huge craft…"

"But in one thing their size is against them," I pointed out. "They can only enter the fjord one at a time. If we mass our warriors on the cliffs above the opening, we might be able to attack them when they try to enter the approach to the Scarlet Fjord."

He brightened a little. "Aye. It might work. Let's get back."

We were waiting in the heights when the first of the great craft, with its strange pyramidal arrangement of decks, nosed its way between the cliffs. We had arranged boulders on the ledges in readiness.

The ship came directly beneath us and I drew the Black Sword and shouted: "Now!"

The boulders were levered over the ledges and crashed into the decks. Several crunched straight through, while others smashed down the terraces, taking timbers and warriors with them.

A mighty cheer went up from the warriors of the Scarlet Fjord as the ship keeled over and the soldiers in their silver armour were toppled into the viscous sea which sucked them down as they struggled and screamed in their strange high-pitched voices.

As I watched them die, I thought that these poor creatures were as much victims of Belphig's perfidy as were we. Yet what else could we do but kill them? They fought so that a queen they loved more than life would not perish. We fought for our freedom. What Belphig himself fought for I was yet to learn.

Another ship tried to enter the gulf and again we showered down our boulders. This ship split in twain, both ends rising steeply out of the water like the slowly closing snout of some sea monster, sandwiching those who had survived and crushing them before there was a burst of white hotness from the centre and the waters bubbled and steam struck our faces. I realised that we had destroyed one of the engines. They seemed unstable things. Perhaps we had found another weakness of the Silver Warriors.

After two more attempts, the ships withdrew, surrounding the entrance to the fjord in a semicircle many craft deep.

The siege of the Scarlet Fjord had begun in earnest.

Bladrak and I conferred in his apartments again. His spirits had lifted with our victories but now, as the implications dawned on him, he began to frown.

"You are afraid that we cannot sustain a long siege," I said.

He nodded. "We grow much of what we need in our cavern gardens, but the slaves we have rescued have tripled our numbers and the gardens cannot support so many. Our raids brought us the extra food we needed, but with Belphig's ships blocking the fjord we can do no more raiding."

"How long do you think we can last?"

He shrugged his shoulders. "Twenty days or so. We have no stores. They all went to feed the newcomers. Crops continue to grow, but not fast enough. Belphig probably knows this."

"I am sure he does and is counting on it."

"What are we to do, Lord Urlik? Go and do battle? At least we will die swiftly…"

"That is the last resort. Is there no other way out of the fjord?"

"Not by sea. And the path across the mountains leads only to the ice wastes. We should perish there as quickly as we'd perish here."

"How long does it take to reach the ice?"

"On foot? Eight days, I think. I have never made the journey."

"So even if a foraging party was sent out it could not expect to find food and return in time."

"Exactly."

I rubbed at my beard, thinking deeply. Eventually I said: "Then there is only one thing to do at this point."

"What is that?"

"We must seek the advice of the Lady of the Chalice. Whatever her motives, she seems to want Belphig defeated. She must aid us, if she can."

"Very well," said Bladrak. "Let us go now to the cavern where the dark staff is."

'Lady?"

Bladrak looked around him, his face shadowed in the soft, weird glow from the stalactites.

The strong smell of salt was in my nostrils. While Bladrak called the Lady of the Chalice, I inspected the short staff that was imbedded in the basalt of the floor. I touched it and withdrew my fingers with a gasp, for it had burned them. Then I realised that it was not extreme heat that had caused the pain — but extreme cold.

"Lady?"

The thin whine came and it grew to an oscillating shriek. I turned, caught a glimpse of an outline of a great chalice, saw it fade as the shriek died, and then the Lady of the Chalice, clad in golden radiance, her face, as before, completely veiled, stood before us.

"Belphig has almost vanquished you," she said. "You should have used the Black Sword sooner."

"And slain more friends?" I asked.

"You are too sentimental for a great Champion," she said. "The issues for which you fight are vast in scope and implication."

"I am tired of great issues, madam."

"Then why did Bladrak summon me?"

"Because there was nothing else to do. We are boxed up and will eventually die. The only solution I can see is to rescue the Queen of the Silver Warriors whom Belphig has captured. If she is freed, then Belphig will lose his main strength."

"That is true."

"But we know not where to seek this queen," Bladrak said.

"Ask me a direct question," the Lady of the Chalice told him.

"Where is the Queen of the Silver Warriors?" I asked. "Do you know?"

"Aye — I know. She is at Moon, a thousand miles from here across the ice. She is guarded both by Belphig's men and by enchantments of Belphig's arrangement. She cannot leave her apartments and neither can she be visited, save by Belphig himself."

"So she cannot be rescued."

"She can be by one man — by you, Urlik, with the aid of the Black Sword."

I looked at her sharply. "This is why you helped Bladrak summon me. This is why you brought the sword here and made me use it. For reasons of your own you wish the Silver Queen freed."

"A simple judgement, Count Urlik. But it will benefit us all if she is freed, I agree."

"I could not cross a thousand miles of ice on foot. Even if I had not lost my bear chariot, I would not be able to get there in time to free the queen and save the Scarlet Fjord."

"There is one way," said the Lady of the Chalice. "A dangerous way."

"By using a boat as a sled and having the herons drag it?" I said. "They would not last that long and I suspect that the boats are not sturdy enough to —"

"I do not mean that."

"Then explain quickly, Lady," I said grimly.

"The people who created the Scarlet Fjord were engineers who experimented with many devices. Many were unsuccessful. Many were partially successful. When they went away from here having found a means of travelling through time, they left some of their inventions behind them. One of these was sealed in a cave in a mountain on the far side of this range, near the ice wastes. It was an air chariot, flying under its own power, but it was abandoned because of one defect. The engine used radiated a substance which enfeebled the pilot, blinded him and eventually killed him."

"And you want me to use such a craft to go to Moon?" I laughed. "And die before I reach the place? What would be accomplished by that?"

"Nothing. I do not know how long the radiation takes to kill. It could be that you would get to Moon before that happened."

"Are there any permanent effects of these rays should I survive?"

"None that I know of."

"Where exactly is this craft hidden?"

"There is a pass that leads through the mountains to the ice. At the end of the pass is a mountain that stands alone. Steps are carved into the mountain and at the top of the steps is a sealed door. You must break the door and enter. There you will find the air chariot."

I frowned. I still distrusted the Lady of the Chalice. She, after all, had been the immediate cause of my separation from Ermizhad and my subsequent agony of mind.

"I will do this thing, Lady," I said, "if you will promise me something."

"What is that?"

"That you will reveal all that you know of my fate and my place in this universe."

"If you are successful I promise I shall tell you all I know."

"Then I leave at once for Moon."

T W O

THE CITY CALLED MOON

And so I left the Scarlet Fjord, climbing up into the black, igneous cliffs that brooded eternally beneath the dark, twilight sky. I had a map with me, some provisions and my sword. My bulky furs keeping out the worst of the cold, I moved through the mountains as rapidly as was possible.

I slept little, with the result that I could barely keep my eyes open and the whorls of obsidian, the frozen cascades of basalt, the oddly shaped pumice visible in all directions took on the appearance of leering faces, of menacing figures of giants and monsters, until I felt surrounded by the creatures of nightmare and I gripped my sword tighter but continued, doggedly, to move on. And at last I saw the ice plains ahead and the clouds thinned out to reveal the red sphere of the sun, the faint stars gleaming behind it.

I welcomed that sight. If I had thought the ice gloomy and bleak when I first found myself in this world, it had been nothing compared with the mood of the mountains which surrounded Earth's last, dark sea. I trudged over the smooth, glassy rock of the pass and I saw the mountain ahead of me.

As the Lady of the Chalice had said, it stood alone, directly before me, on the edge of the ice plain.

I staggered as sleep tried to overcome me. I forced my feet to plod the last half-mile to the base of the mountain where ancient steps had been carved. And on the first of those steps I succumbed to sleep, not knowing for what new task my energies would be needed.

I awoke only barely refreshed and began to climb the steps until I came at length to what had evidently once been the mouth of a natural cave. But that cave mouth had been sealed with molten rock. The length and breadth was filled with a flow of red and yellow obsidian.

I had expected to find a door which I should be able to force, but there was no means of opening this!

I turned and looked back over the mountains. The brown clouds clung to them, increasing their enigmatic appearance. They seemed to share the joke which the Lady of the Chalice had played upon me.

"Damn you!" I yelled.

"Damn you," they replied. "Damn you." And those echoes damned me a hundred times before they died.

Snarling with frustrated anger I drew the Black Sword. Its black radiance spilled out against the obsidian flow. Fiercely I attacked that which sealed the cavern's entrance. The blade bit deep into the rock and pieces of it flew in all directions.

Astonished, I struck again. And again a huge piece of the glassy stone fell away as if blasted.

Again the Black Sword crashed against the rock. And this time, with a rumble, it collapsed completely, revealing a dark chamber. I stepped over the rubble, sheathing the sword. I peered about me, but could see nothing. From my belt I took the torch Bladrak had given me just before I left. I depressed the stud in the handle and a faint light blossomed.

There was the machine the Lady of the Chalice had told me I should find...

But she had not told me I should also find the pilot.

He sat in the air chariot and he stared at me in silence, grinning as if in anticipation of my fate. He was long and thin and dressed in the silver armour of those who now served Belphig. He lounged awkwardly in the seat and I guessed he had lounged in the same attitude for centuries, for it was a fleshless skull that grinned at me and fleshless hands that gripped the side of the chariot. I guessed that he had been left there as a warning, perhaps, of the lethal rays of the chariot's engine. With an oath I knocked the skull from the neck and dragged the bones out of the car, hurling them across the cavern floor.

The Lady of the Chalice had told me that I should find the controls simple enough. She had been right. There were no instruments as such that I recognised, merely a crystal rod rising from the floor. By squeezing the rod in my hand I could activate the engine. By pushing the rod forward I could move ahead, by pushing it back I could slow my speed and stop, by pulling it back at an angle I could gain height and by pushing it forward at an angle I could lose height. Similarly the crystal rod could be moved from side to side.

I was anxious to leave the former pilot behind. I got into the chariot and squeezed the rod. Immediately the whole chariot began to glow with a pink luminosity so that it resembled flesh. A throb came from below my feet and I guessed that the engine was there. I licked my dry lips and pushed the lever very slightly forward. The air chariot began to move towards the entrance of the cave. I took it into the air a few feet to avoid the rubble and then we were in the open air again and I discovered that quite small movements of my hand would control the craft. I inspected my map and took a bearing from the compass imbedded in the top of the lever, then I increased speed and headed for the city called Moon.

The obsidian mountains had disappeared and now there was only ice — seemingly infinite ice that streamed past me as I flew. Occasionally the flat plain was broken by frozen drifts and spires but for the most part nothing relieved that cold, desolate landscape.

I began to doubt that the Lady of the Chalice had been right when she had mentioned the engine's poisonous radiations, but soon I realised that my vision had dimmed slightly, that I felt lethargic and my bones ached.

I was driving the air chariot at its maximum speed, but there was no clear means of judging how fast that was. The cold air bit at my flesh and frost rimed my beard and my thick coat was blown about as the white breath was whipped from my mouth.

The discomfort increased. It also seemed to me that I was leaving the sun far behind, that the world was growing darker.

Soon the sun was close to the horizon and the stars blazed more brightly in the sky. But by this time I had fallen back against the support of my seat and nausea shook my body.

I was dying, I was sure. At one stage I was forced to slow my speed and vomit over the side of the craft. I wanted to stop altogether, to get away from the source of my discomfort, but I knew that to leave the aircraft would be to ensure my death. I increased speed again.

And then I saw it ahead. It was a huge white mountain, pitted with great craters, rising out of the ice. I recognised it, of course, for it was the moon itself. How many thousands of years had passed since it had crashed into the

Earth? A dim memory came back to me. I was sure I had witnessed this sight before. A name, an impression of despair. What was the name?

It had gone.

With the last of my strength I brought the air chariot to a skidding halt on the ice and pulled my aching body from it.

Then I began to crawl across the ice towards the towering mountain that had once been Earth's satellite.

The farther from the air chariot I crawled the more my strength began to return. By the time I had reached the curved side of the mountain I felt greatly recovered. I could see now that even the mountain was covered with a thin layer of ice in some parts, but not enough to obscure its outlines. Above me I could see a light gleaming and wondered if this was an entrance to the city the Silver Warriors had been forced to desert when they joined Belphig in his war against us. There was nothing for it but to begin to climb. The ice and the rock were rough enough to make climbing fairly easy but I was forced to rest several times and had by no means regained my full strength when I neared the top and saw fierce light suddenly burst out from the centre of a crater and a dozen riders, mounted on seal-beasts, framed against It.

I had been seen. Perhaps Belphig had even been prepared for my coming.

I slid down the walls of the crater, put my back against the rock, drew out the Black Sword in both hands and awaited the riders.

They charged me with the long, barbed harpoons I had last seen when we had hunted the sea-stag. One of them would rip me from chin to stomach if it pierced my armour.

But the Black Sword itself seemed to be lending me energy. With a single movement I swung it so that I sheared through the head of every harpoon. They clattered to the rock and the useless shafts thudded into the stone as the astonished riders pulled their beasts up short. I plunged the blade into the throat of the nearest seal-beast and it coughed and collapsed, tumbling its rider forward so that I could bring the sword crashing down to shear into his back as he fell.

The laughter began to bubble from my lips now.

I jeered at them as I slew them. They milled in confusion, drawing axes and swords from their scabbards, shouting to each other. An axe struck my mailed shoulder but did not cut through the links. I killed my antagonist with a stroke that cut his face in half and the impetus of my swing clove the body of the man beside him.

They tried to press in, to hamper my movements so that they could cut me down. But the Black Sword would not let them. It moved so rapidly that it opened their ranks every time they managed to close them. A hand, still clutching a sword, flew away into the shadows. A head dropped to the ground. A body spilled entrails over the high saddle. Everywhere the Black Sword swept it left red ruin in its wake.

And at last they were all dead, save for a few seal-beasts that lumbered back towards the source of the bright light.

I followed them, still laughing.

Instead of exhausting me, the slaughter seemed to have filled me with extra power. I felt light-headed and light-footed, too. I raced after the seal-beasts, blinking in the light, and saw them moving down a long metal ramp which curved into the bowels of the fallen sphere.

More cautiously now I began to move down the ramp. I was just in time, for two doors began to move across the opening and met. I prayed that I had not entered a trap.

Down and down I went until I could see a floor below me. It seemed made of molten silver and it rippled like water, but as I reached it and set a wary foot upon it it felt solid enough.

From out of a doorway in the far wall three more men came running. They, too, were dressed in the bulbous armour of Rowernarc, but they carried the double-bladed halberds I had until now only seen in the hands of the Silver Warriors.

These men were more skilled with the weapons. They spread out and began to swing the things around their heads. I watched them all warily, seeking an opening.

Then one released his and it whistled through the air at me. I flung up my sword to block it and just managed to hurl it aside as the next halberd flew — and then the next. I dodged one and was caught a glancing blow by the other. I was flung to the ground, the Black Sword leaving my hand and skidding across that floor of rippling silver.

Weaponless I rose to my feet as Belphig's men drew their swords. They were grinning. They knew I was doomed.

I looked for the sword but it was too far away to reach in time. I backed away from the warriors and my foot struck something. I glanced down. It was the haft of one of the fallen halberds. They saw it at the same time and began to run towards me. I picked up the halberd, knocked one swordsman in the face with the butt and rammed the spike into another's throat. Then I burst through them and ran for the sword.

But they closed with me before I could reach it. I turned again, blocking a thrust with the shaft and then reversing the movement to bring the axe-blade down on to the helm of the second man. He staggered, dazed, and I skidded across the floor to the sword.

It settled into my hands and began to moan like a savage hound that needs to kill.

I let it kill. I split my first assailant from skull to midriff and I chopped the body of the second man in two.

Then I shuddered as the battle-fever began to leave me. Sheathing the sword again I ran towards the entrance through which the warriors had come.

I was in a long, twisting corridor. It was more like a tube, for it was completely round and the floor curved steeply upwards on both sides. Down this I ran and emerged at length into a spherical chamber. I had a feeling that these passages had not originally been used by human beings but had possibly carried traffic or liquids of some kind. Steps led up to the domed roof of the chamber. I climbed them and emerged in a circular room which had a roof like frosted glass. I peered through the glass and realised that it formed the floor of the chamber above me. But I could see no means of reaching that chamber. Then I thought I saw something move in the room above. I drew my sword.

An opening suddenly appeared in the smooth ceiling. A perfectly round opening in the exact centre of the circle. Then a kind of clear tube descended until it was only a few feet above the floor of the lower chamber. There were handholds on the inside of the tube.

Still wary, I approached the tube and began to climb, the Black Sword balanced in my right hand. I poked my head over the top and there was a sparsely furnished room of great size. Walls and floor were of the same rippling silver. A white bed was there and various chairs and objects whose use I could not guess. And standing near the bed was a woman whose skin was silver, whose eyes were deep black and whose dress was blood red. Her hair was nearly white and her beauty was ethereal. She smiled at me and she moved her lips, but I could not hear her.

I advanced across the transparent floor towards her and suddenly my face struck something cold and hard and I recoiled. I put out my hand and felt smoothness. I was separated from the Silver Queen by an invisible wall.

She gestured, trying to tell me something, but I could not understand her.

What kind of enchantment had Belphig put upon her? His scientific powers were either much greater than he had led me to suspect or else, more likely, he had borrowed them from the Silver Warriors whose ancestors, I now guessed, were the same scientists who had originally occupied the place I knew as the Scarlet Fjord.

Desperation now consumed me. I took the Black Sword and I struck a mighty blow against the invisible wall.

A dreadful shrieking filled the air. A shock ran the length of my body and I was hurled backward. My senses swam. I had grown to rely too much on the power of the Black Sword, I thought, as I collapsed into oblivion.

The Eternal Champion

T H R E E

THE PHOENIX AND THE QUEEN

There was a chanting in my ears:

BLACK SWORD
BLACK SWORD
BLACK SWORD
THE BLADE OF THE SWORD HAS THE BLOOD OF THE SUN...

I opened my eyes and saw the stars in the dark sky. I turned my head, realising that I was in the air chariot again.

At the wheel sat a man in silver armour.

This must be a dream. I was dreaming that the skeleton was piloting the chariot.

If not, then I was a prisoner of the Silver Warriors. I straightened my back and felt the pommel of my sword. I was not tied and I had not been disarmed.

The pilot in silver armour turned his head — and I saw that it was no man at all but the woman I had seen just before I lost consciousness. She had a sardonic look in her black eyes.

"I thank you for your valour in saving me," she said.

I knew the voice.

"Your sword shattered the barrier. Now we return to the Scarlet Fjord so that I may tell my warriors I am free and they need do Belphig's work no longer."

"You are the Lady of the Chalice," I said incredulously.

"That is what Bladrak's people called me."

"Then all my fighting was in vain. You were already free!"

She smiled. "No. What you saw was only a manifestation. I could not have appeared anywhere else but in that chamber — the chamber of the staff. Belphig did not realise that I had a means of communicating with his enemies."

"But I saw the chalice at sea!"

"The image of the chalice could be projected to a few other places, true, but I could not transfer my own image there."

I looked at her with deep suspicion. "And how came you by the Black Sword?"

"The folk of Moon have much wisdom, Sir Champion. We were great once. There was a prophecy that you would come again, awakening from your Frozen Keep. It seemed nothing but a legend, but I studied it for I needed to hope. I discovered a great deal."

"And you promised to tell me everything you learned."

"Aye, I did."

"First, you could inform me what Belphig's ambition is."

"Belphig is a fool — though cunning. He knew of Moon and he found it eventually, having trekked for weeks across the ice with his men. Having forgotten that war existed, we trusted him. He learned many of our secrets and then, one day, imprisoned me as you found me. He then forced the Silver Warriors to serve him, as you know."

"But why?"

The Silver Queen swayed in her seat and I realised that the rays from the craft's engine were affecting us both.

"He — he had a scheme but it needed more labour than the warriors themselves could supply. Ultimately he desired to build a vessel that would travel through space. He wished to find a new sun that had not grown old. It was a stupid scheme. We have the knowledge for building such a ship, but we do not know how to power it or how long it would take to travel to another sun. Belphig would believe none of this. He felt that if he tortured me and my people long enough we would eventually reveal everything to him. He is insane."

"Aye," I said, "and his insanity has caused much grief on this already grieving planet."

She moaned. "My eyes — I cannot see..."

I hauled her out of the seat and climbed in myself, grasping the crystal rod and keeping the craft on course.

"So you conjured up the Black Sword," I said. "And the chalice of gold. And did you send those dreams to plague me?"

"I — I sent no — dreams . . . ,

"I thought not. I do not believe you understand everything you have been doing, my lady. You used the legend and you used me. But I believe that the Black Sword — or whatever power controls it — has used us both. Do you know of Tanelorn?"

"I know where it is said to be."

"Where is that?"

"At the centre of what we call the "multiverse" — the infinite matrices — universe upon universe, each divided from the other. But there is a centre, it is said — a hub about which these universes revolve. The hub is a planet, some think, and that planet is mirrored in many of the other worlds. This Earth is one version. The Earth you came from is another — and so on. And Tanelorn is mirrored elsewhere — but with one difference, it does not change. It does not decay as the other worlds decay. Tanelorn, like you, Sir Hero, is eternal."

"And how may I find Tanelorn and the powers who rule there?"

"I know not. You must seek that information elsewhere."

"I may never find it."

The conversation had exhausted her and I, too, was seriously feeling the effects of the poison radiation. I was bitterly disappointed for, though I had discovered something more, I still had not all the information I had hoped for.

"Tell me what the chalice is," I said weakly. But she had fainted. Unless we reached the Scarlet Fjord soon, there would be little point in seeking more information.

Then, at last, I saw the mountains ahead and I pulled back the lever to increase the aircraft's height for I intended to fly all the way to the Scarlet Fjord and that was still a good distance away on the other side of the range.

We passed into a bank of thick, brown cloud and I felt salty moisture on my face. I could see only a short distance ahead and I prayed I had taken the vessel up high enough to avoid the highest crags. If not, then we should crash and be killed instantly.

I fought to keep my vision clear and rid my head of dizziness, my body of its ache. If I lost control of the craft we were bound to go into the side of a mountain.

Then came a break in the cloud.

I saw the dark, brooding sea below me.

We had overshot the fjord.

Quickly I turned the craft and decreased height.

Within moments I saw the bishop's great fleet below.

I fought against the nausea and the dizziness engulfing me. I circled down and saw that Belphig stood on the top deck of the largest ship. He was talking to two tall Silver Warriors but looked up in astonishment when he saw my craft.

"Urlik!" he screamed. Then he laughed. "Do you think you can save your friends with that little flying boat? A third of them are dead of starvation already. The rest are too weak to resist us. We are just about to sail into the fjord. Bladrak was the last to resist. Now the world is mine."

I turned and tried to revive the Silver Queen. She moaned and stirred but I could not arouse her. I lifted her upright as best I could in my own weakened condition and I showed her to Belphig.

Then the air chariot began to lose height as I could control it no longer.

In a moment, I knew, I would be swallowed by that salt-thick sea.

But now a new sound came to my ears and I forced my head around to see Bladrak's boats emerging from the gap between the cliffs.

Despairing of my help, Bladrak had decided to die fighting.

I tried to call out, to tell him there was no need, but the boat had hit the water and was skidding over the surface towards the looming shape of one of the ships of Belphig's fleet.

I managed to turn the craft a little, but we smashed into a paddle with a mighty crash, the air chariot overturned and the Silver Queen and myself were plunged into the thick water.

There were other sounds of confusion. I heard a shout and saw something drop from the side of the ship. Then the water entered my mouth and I knew I was drowning.

A moment later something seized me and dragged me from the ocean. I gasped. I was in the hands of one of the Silver Warriors. But he was smiling at me — he was virtually grinning. He pointed. Nearby the Silver Queen was reviving. He knew I had rescued her.

We were on a raft that must have been flung overboard the moment we struck. And now they were hauling the raft up the side of the ship. From high

THE ETERNAL CHAMPION

above a querulous voice was screaming.

We had crashed into Belphig's flagship.

I let the Silver Warriors help me to my feet when we reached the deck.

I looked up.

Belphig looked down.

He knew he was beaten, that the men from Moon would no longer follow him.

And he laughed.

I found myself laughing back.

I drew my Black Sword, still laughing. He drew his own sword and chuckled. I ducked my head and entered the door and began to climb the staircase that wound through the levels of the deck until I emerged on the top one and faced him.

He knew he was going to die. The thought had turned him quite mad.

I could not kill him then. I had killed too much. He was harmless now. I would spare him.

But the Black Sword thought otherwise. As I made to sheath the blade it turned in my hand, flung my arm back.

Belphig screamed and raised his sword to defend himself from the imminent blow. I tried to stop the Black Sword from falling.

But fall it did.

It was inevitable.

It sheared through Belphig's sword, then it paused as the bishop wept and stared at it. Then, my hands still round its hilt, it drew itself back and plunged itself deep into his fat, painted body.

Belphig shivered and his carmined lips fluttered. A strange intelligence entered his eyes. He screwed up his decorated eyes and tears fell down his rouged cheeks.

I think he died then. I hoped that he had.

Aboard the big ships the Silver Warriors were handing out food to the men who had sailed from the Scarlet Fjord expecting to be killed.

From below the Silver Queen called to me and I saw that she had Bladrak aboard. He was thin, but he still had his swagger as he hailed me.

"You have saved us all, Sir Champion."

I smiled bitterly. "All but myself," I said. I climbed back down the staircase until I stood on the lowest deck. The Silver Queen was talking with her men whose faces were full of joy now that she was safe.

She turned to me. "You have earned the undying loyalty of my people," she said.

I was unimpressed. I was weary. And, oh, how I needed my Ermizhad.

I had thought that if I followed my fate, if I took up the Black Sword, then at least I would have a chance of being reunited with her.

But it seemed this was not to be.

And still I did not understand all of the prophecy concerning the Black Sword.

The Blade of the Sword has the Blood of the Sun…

Bladrak clapped me on the back. "We are going to feast, Count Urlik. We are going to celebrate. The Silver Warriors and their lovely Queen are to be our guests in the Scarlet Fjord!"

I looked hard at the Silver Queen. "What has the chalice to do with me?" I said firmly, not replying to Bladrak.

"I am not sure…"

"You must tell me what you do know," I said, "or I will kill you with the Black Sword. You have unleashed forces you do not understand. You have tampered with destinies. You have brought great grief upon me, O Queen in Silver. And still, I think, you do not understand. You sought to save a few lives on a dying planet by scheming to call the Eternal Champion. It suited those forces of destiny which control me to help you in your scheme. But I do not thank you for it — not with this hell-sword hanging from me — this thing I thought myself rid of!"

She stepped back, the smile fading, and Bladrak looked grim.

"You have used me," I said, "and now you celebrate. But what of me? What have I to celebrate? Where am I to go now?"

And then I stopped, angered at my own self-pity. I turned away, for I was weeping.

The Scarlet Fjord rang with merriment. Women danced along the quays, men roared out songs. Even the Silver Warriors seemed lusty in comparison with their former demeanour.

But I stood on the deck of the great sea-chariot and I talked with the Silver Queen.

We were alone. Bladrak and the rest were joining in the merrymaking.

"What is the golden chalice?" I said. "What do you mean by using it to such a petty end?"

"I do not think the end petty."

"How did you gain the power to use the chalice?"

"There were dreams," she said, "and voices in the dreams. Much of what I did was in a trance."

I looked at her with sympathy then. I had known the kind of dreams she described.

"You were told to call the chalice as you were told to call the Black Sword?"

"Aye."

"And you do not know what the chalice is or why it makes that sound?"

"The legend said that the chalice is meant to hold the blood of the sun. When that blood is poured into it, the chalice will take it to the sun and the sun will come to life again."

"Superstition," I said. "A folk tale."

"Possibly." She was subdued. I had shamed her. Now I felt sorry for my outburst.

"Why does the chalice scream?"

"It calls for the blood," she murmured.

"And where is that blood?" Suddenly I looked down at my sword and grasped the hilt. "The Blade of the Sword has the Blood of the Sun!" I frowned. "Can you summon the chalice again?"

"Aye — but not here."

"Where?"

"Out there," she said, pointing beyond the mountains.

"On the ice. Will you come with me to the ice — now?"

"I owe you that," she said.

F O U R

THE KNIFE AND THE CUP

The Silver Queen and the Eternal Champion were two weeks departed from the Scarlet Fjord. They had gone in a boat which had taken them to deserted Rowernarc. They had sought the chariot in which the Eternal Champion had come to Rowernarc. They found it. They fed the beasts that pulled the chariot and then they climbed into it and were borne through the mountains, out to the plains of the South Ice.

Now the Silver Queen and the Eternal Champion stood surrounded on all sides by ice and a wind came up. It blew our cloaks about our bodies as we stared up at the small red sun.

"You affected many destinies when you chose to summon me," I said.

She shivered. "I know," she said.

"And now we must fulfil the whole prophecy," I said. "The whole of it."

"If that will free you, Champion."

"It might bring me an inch nearer to that which I desire," I told her. "No more. We deal in cosmic matters, Silver Queen."

"Are we only pawns, Sir Champion? Can we control nothing of that destiny?"

"Precious little, Queen."

She sighed and spread her arms, turning her face to the brooding sky. "I summon the Screaming Chalice!" she cried.

I unsheathed the Black Sword and I stood with it point first in the ice, my two hands gripping the two halves of the crosspiece.

The Black Sword began to tremble and it began to sing.

"I summon the Screaming Chalice!" the Queen of Moon cried again.

The Black Sword shuddered in my grasp.

Now tears fell down the Silver Queen's silver cheeks and she fell to her knees on the ice.

The wind blew stronger. It came from nowhere. It was not a natural wind.

For the third time she called: "I summon the Screaming Chalice!"

I raised the Black Sword — or it dragged my hands behind it — and almost tenderly I plunged the blade into her back as she lay spread-eagled on the ice. I had slain her in this manner so that I should not see her face.

Her body writhed. She groaned and then she screamed and her voice blended with the moan of the wind, with the howling of the sword, with my cries of anguish and then, at last, with the shrill whine that grew so that it drowned all other sound.

And the Screaming Chalice stood upon the ice, blinding me with its radiance. I flung one hand over my eyes and felt the Black Sword leave my grasp.

When I looked again I saw that the huge sword was hovering over the chalice.

And from it poured blood.

Blood ran down the black blade and flooded into the chalice, and when the chalice was full the Black Sword fell to the ice.

And it seemed to me then — although I could not swear this happened — that a huge hand reached down from the faded sky and picked up the chalice and drew it higher and higher into the air until it vanished.

And then I saw a crimson aura spring around the sun. It flickered and was hardly visible at first, but then it grew brighter and the twilight turned into late afternoon and I knew that soon it would be morning again.

Do not ask me how this came to pass — how time itself was turned back. I have been many heroes on many worlds, but I do not believe I have ever witnessed another event as strange and terrifying as that which took place on the South Ice after the Black Sword slew the Silver Queen.

The prophecy was complete. It had been my fate to bring death to this dying world — and now life.

I thought of the Black Sword differently then. It had done much that was evil in my eyes, but perhaps the evil had been to accomplish a greater good.

I walked to where it had fallen. I stooped to pick it up.

But the sword had gone. Only its shadow was left on the ice.

I removed the scabbard from my belt and put it near that shadow. I walked back to where I had left my chariot and I climbed into it.

I looked at the corpse of the Silver Queen, stretched where I had slain her. To save her people she had conjured up cosmic forces of indescribable power. And those forces had brought about her death.

"Would that they had brought about mine," I murmured as the chariot's wheels began to roll.

I did not expect to be much longer on the South Ice. Soon, I knew, I would be called again. And when I was called I would try once more to find my way back to Ermizhad, my Eldren princess. I would look for Tanelorn — eternal Tanelorn — and one day, perhaps, I would know peace again.

TO RESCUE
TANELORN

All know the road to Tanalorn
  The map lies in their hearts...
    —Wheldrake.

TO RESCUE TANELORN. . .

Beyond the tall and ominous glass-green forest of Troos, well to the North and unheard of in Bakshaan, Elwher or any other city of the Young Kingdoms, on the shifting shores of the Sighing Desert lay Tanelorn, a lonely, long-ago city, loved by those it sheltered. Tanelorn had a peculiar nature in that it welcomed and held the wanderer. To its peaceful streets and low houses came the gaunt, the savage, the brutalized, the tormented, and in Tanelorn they found rest.

Now, most of these troubled travellers who dwelt in peaceful Tanelorn had thrown off earlier allegiances to the Lords of Chaos who, as gods, took more than a mild interest in the affairs of men. It happened, therefore, that these same Lords grew to resent the unlikely city of Tanelorn and, not for the first time, decided to act against it.

They instructed one of their number (more they could not, then, send) Lord Narjhan, to journey to Nadsokor, the City of Beggars, which had an old grudge against Tanelorn and raise an army that would attack undefended Tanelorn and destroy it and its inhabitants. So he did this, arming his ragged army and promising them many things.

Then, like a ferocious tide, did the beggar rabble set off to tear down Tanelorn and slay its residents. A great torrent of men and women in rags, on crutches, blind, maimed, but moving steadily, ominously, implacably Northwards towards the Sighing Desert.

In Tanelorn dwelt the Red Archer, Rackhir, from the Eastlands beyond the Sighing Desert, beyond the Weeping Waste. Rackhir had been born a Warrior Priest, a servant of the Lords of Chaos, but had forsaken this life for the quieter pursuits of thievery and learning. A man with harsh features slashed from the bone of his skull, strong, fleshless nose, deep eye-cavities, a thin mouth and a thin beard. He wore a red skull-cap, decorated with a hawk's feather, a red jerkin, tight-fitting and belted at the waist, red breeches, and red boots. It was as if all the blood in him had transferred itself to his gear and left him drained. He was happy, however, in Tanelorn, the city which made all such men happy, and felt he would die there if men died there. He did not know if they did.

One day he saw Brut of Lashmar, a great, blond-headed noble of shamed name, ride wearily, yet urgently, through the low wall-gate of the city of peace. Brut's silver harness and trappings were begrimed, his yellow cloak torn and his broad-brimmed hat battered. A small crowd collected around him as he rode into the city square and halted. Then he gave his news.

"Beggars from Nadsokor, many thousands, move against our Tanelorn," he said, "and they are led by Narjhan of Chaos."

Now, all the men in there were soldiers of some kind, good ones for the most part, and they were confident warriors, but few in number. A horde of beggars, led by such a being as Narjhan, could destroy Tanelorn, they knew.

"Should we, then, leave Tanelorn?" said Uroch of Nieva, a young, wasted man who had been a drunkard.

"We owe this city too much to desert her," Rackhir said. "We should defend her — for her sake and ours. There will never be such a city again."

Brut leaned forward in his saddle and said: "In principle, Red Archer, I am in agreement with you. But principle is not enough without deeds. How would you suggest we defend this low-walled city against siege and the powers of Chaos?"

"We should need help," Rackhir replied, "supernatural help if need be."

"Would the Grey Lords help us?" Zas the One-handed asked the question. He was an old, torn wanderer who had once gained a throne and lost it again.

"Aye — the Grey Lords!" Several voices chorused this hopefully.

"Who are the Grey Lords?" said Uroch, but no one heard him.

"They are not inclined to aid anyone at all," Zas the One-handed pointed out, "but surely Tanelorn, coming as it does under neither the Forces of Law nor the Lords of Chaos, would be worth their while preserving. After all, they have no loyalties either."

"I'm for seeking the Grey Lords' aid," Brut nodded. "What of the rest of us?" There was general agreement, then silence when they realized that they knew of no means of contacting the mysterious and insouciant beings. At last Zas pointed this out.

Rackhir said: "I know a seer — a hermit who lives in the Sighing Desert. Perhaps he can help?"

"I think that, after all, we should not waste time looking for supernatural assistance against this beggar rabble," Uroch said. "Let us prepare, instead, to meet the attack with physical means."

"You forget," Brut said wearily, "that they are led by Narjhan of Chaos. He is not human and has the whole strength of Chaos behind him. We know that the Grey Lords are pledged neither to Law nor to Chaos but will sometimes help either side if the whim takes them. They are our only chance."

"Why not seek the aid of the Forces of Law, sworn enemies of Chaos and mightier than the Grey Lords?" Uroch said.

"Because Tanelorn is a city owing allegiance to neither side. We are all of us men and women who have broken our pledge to Chaos but have made no new one to Law. The Forces of Law, in matters of this kind, will help only those sworn to them. The Grey Lords only may protect us, if they would." So said Zas.

"I will go to find my seer," Rackhir the Red Archer said, "and if he knows how I may reach the Domain of the Grey Lords, then I'll continue straight on, for there is so little time. If I reach them and solicit their help you will soon know I have done so. If not, you must die in Tanelorn's defense and, if I live, I will join you in that last battle."

"Very well," Brut agreed, "go quickly, Red Archer. Let one of your own arrows be the measure of your speed."

And taking little with him save his bone bow and quiver of scarlet-fletched arrows, Rackhir set off for the Sighing Desert. From Nadsokor, South West through the land of Vilmir, even through the squalid country of Org which has in it the dreadful forest of Troos, there was flame and black horror in the wake of the beggar horde, and insolent, disdainful of them though he led them, rode a being completely clad in black armour with a voice that rang hollow in the helm. People fled away at their approach and the land was made barren by their passing. Most knew what had happened, that the beggar citizens of Nadsokor had, contrary to their traditions of centuries, vomited from their city in a wild, menacing horde. Someone had armed them — someone had made them go Northwards and Westwards towards the Sighing Desert. But who was the one who led them? Ordinary folk did not know. And why did they head for the Sighing Desert? There was no city beyond Karlaak, which

THE ETERNAL CHAMPION

they had skirted, only the Sighing Desert — and beyond that the edge of the world. Was that their destination? Were they heading, lemming-like, to their destruction? Everyone hoped so, in their hate for the horrible horde. Rackhir rode through the mournful wind of the Sighing Desert, his face and eyes protected against the particles of sand which flew about. He was thirsty and had been riding a day. Ahead of him at last were the rocks he sought.

He reached the rocks and called above the wind.

"Lamsar!"

The hermit came out in answer to Rackhir's shout. He was dressed in oiled leather to which sand clung. His beard, too, was encrusted with sand and his skin seemed to have taken on the colour and texture of the desert. He recognized Rackhir immediately, by his dress, beckoned him into the cave, and disappeared back inside. Rackhir dismounted and led his horse to the cave entrance and went in.

Lamsar was seated on a smooth rock. "You are welcome, Red Archer," he said, "and I perceive by your manner that you wish information from me and that your mission is urgent."

"I seek the help of the Grey Lords, Lamsar," said Rackhir. The old hermit smiled. It was as if a fissure had suddenly appeared in a rock. "To risk the journey through the Five Gates, your mission must be important. I will tell you how to reach the Grey Lords, but the road is a difficult one."

"I'm willing to take it," Rackhir replied, "for Tanelorn is threatened and the Grey Lords could help her."

"Then you must pass through the First Gate, which lies in our own dimension. I will help you find it."

"And what must I do then?"

"You must pass through all five gates. Each gateway leads to a realm which lies beyond and within our own dimension. In each realm you must speak with the dwellers there. Some are friendly to men, some are not, but all must answer your question; "Where lies the next Gate?" though some may seek to stop you passing. The last gate leads to the Grey Lords' Domain."

"And the first gate?"

"That lies anywhere in this realm. I will find it for you now." Lamsar composed himself to meditate and Rackhir, who had expected some sort of gaudy miracle-working from the old man, was disappointed. Several hours went by until Lamsar said: "The gate is outside. Memorize the following: If X is equal to the spirit of humanity, then the combination of the two must be of double power, therefore the spirit of humanity always contains the power to dominate itself."

"A strange equation," said Rackhir.

"Aye — but memorize it, meditate upon it and then we will leave."

"We — you as well?"

"I think so."

The hermit was old. Rackhir did not want him on the journey. But then he realized that the hermit's knowledge could be of use to him, so did not object. He thought upon the equation and, as he thought, his mind seemed to glitter and become diffused until he was in a strange trance and all his powers felt greater, both those of mind and body. The hermit got up and Rackhir followed him. They went out of the cave-mouth but, instead of the Sighing Desert, there was a hazy cloud of blue shimmering light ahead and when they had passed through this, in a second, they found themselves in the foothills of a low mountain-range and below them, in a valley, were villages. The villages were strangely laid out, all the houses in a wide circle about a huge amphitheatre containing, at its center, a circular dais.

"It will be interesting to learn the reason why these villages are so arranged," Lamsar said, and they began to move down into the valley.

As they reached the bottom and drew close to one of the villages, people came gaily out and danced joyfully towards them. They stopped in front of Rackhir and Lamsar and, jumping from foot to foot as he greeted them, the leader spoke.

"You are strangers, we can tell — and you are welcome to all we have, food, accommodation, and entertainment."

The two men thanked them graciously and accompanied them back to the circular village. The amphitheater was made of mud and seemed to have been stamped out, hollowed into, the ground encompassed by the houses. The leader of the villagers took them to his house and offered them food.

"You have come to us at a Rest Time," he said, "but do not worry, things will soon commence again. My name is Yerleroo."

"We seek the next Gate," Lamsar said politely, "and our mission is urgent. You will forgive us if we do not stay long?"

"Come," said Yerleroo, "things are about to commence. You will see us at our best, and must join us."

All the villagers had assembled in the amphitheater, surrounding the platform in the center. Most of them were light-skinned and light-haired, gay and smiling, excited — but a few were evidently of a different race, dark, black-haired, and these were sullen.

Sensing something ominous in what he saw, Rackhir asked the question directly: "Where is the next Gate?"

Yerleroo hesitated, his mouth worked and then he smiled. "Where the winds meet," he said.

Rackhir declared angrily: "That's no answer."

"Yes it is," said Lamsar softly behind him. "A fair answer."

"Now we shall dance," Yerleroo said. "First you shall watch our dance and then you shall join in."

"Dance?" said Rackhir, wishing he had brought a sword, or at least a dagger.

"Yes — you will like it. Everyone likes it. You will find it will do you good."

"What if we do not wish to dance?"

"You must — it is for your own good, be assured."

"And he —" Rackhir pointed at one of the sullen men. "Does he enjoy it?"

"It is for his own good."

Yerleroo clapped his hands and at once the fair-haired people leapt into a frenetic, senseless dance. Some of them sang. The sullen people did not sing. After a little hesitation, they began to prance dully about, their frowning features contrasting with their jerking bodies. Soon the whole village was dancing, whirling, singing a monotonous song.

Yerleroo flashed by, whirling. "Come, join in now."

"We had better leave," Lamsar said with a faint smile. They backed away.

Yerleroo saw them. "No — you must not leave — you must dance."

They turned and ran as fast as the old man could go. The dancing villagers changed the direction of their dance and began to whirl menacingly towards them in a horrible semblance of gaiety.

"There's nothing for it," Lamsar said and stood his ground, observing them through ironic eyes. "The mountain gods must be invoked. A pity, for sorcery wearies me. Let us hope their magic extends to this plane. Gordar!"

Words in an unusually harsh language issued from Lamsar's old mouth. The whirling villagers came on.

Lamsar pointed at them.

The villagers became suddenly petrified and slowly, disturbingly, their bodies caught in a hundred positions, turned to smooth, black basalt.

"It was for their own good," Lamsar smiled grimly. "Come, to the place where the winds meet," and he took Rackhir there quite swiftly.

At the place where the winds met they found the second gateway, a column of amber-coloured flame, shot through with streaks of green. They entered it and, instantly they were in a world of dark seething colour. Above them was a

TO RESCUE TANELORN . . .

sky of murky red in which other colours shifted, agitated, changing. Ahead of them lay a forest, dark, blue, black, heavy, mottled green, the tops of its trees moving like a wild tide. It was a howling land of unnatural phenomena.

Lamsar pursed his lips. "On this plane Chaos rules, we must get to the next gate swiftly for obviously the Lords of Chaos will seek to stop us."

"Is it always like this?" Rackhir gasped.

"It is always boiling midnight — but the rest, it changes with the moods of the Lords. There are no rules at all."

They pressed on through the bounding, blossoming scenery as it erupted and changed around them. Once they saw a huge winged figure in the sky, smoky yellow, and roughly man-shaped.

"Vezhan," Lamsar said, "let's hope he did not see us."

"Vezhan!" Rackhir whispered the name — for it was to Vezhan that he had once been loyal.

They crept on, uncertain of their direction or even of their speed in that disturbing land.

At length, they came to the shores of a peculiar ocean.

It was a grey, heaving, timeless sea, a mysterious sea which stretched into infinity. There could be no other shores beyond this rolling plain of water. No other lands or rivers or dark, cool woods, no other men or women or ships. It was a sea which led to nowhere. It was complete to itself — a sea.

Over this timeless ocean hovered a brooding ochre sun which cast moody shadows of black and green across the water, giving the whole scene something of the look of being enclosed in a vast cavern, for the sky above was gnarled and black with ancient clouds. And all the while the doom-carried crash of breakers, the lonely, fated monotony of the ever-rearing white-topped waves; the sound which portended neither death nor life nor war nor peace — simply existence and shifting inharmony. They could go no further.

"This has the air of our death about it," Rackhir said shivering.

The sea roared and tumbled, the sound of it increasing to a fury, daring them to go on towards it, welcoming them with wild temptation — offering them nothing but achievement — the achievement of death.

Lamsar said: "It is not my fate wholly to perish." But then they were running back toward the forest, feeling that the strange sea was pouring up the beach towards them. They looked back and saw that it had gone no further, that the breakers were less wild, the sea more calm. Lamsar was a little way behind Rackhir.

The Red Archer gripped his hand and hauled him towards him as if he had rescued the old man from a whirlpool. They remained there, mesmerized, for a long time, while the sea called to them and the wind was a cold caress on their flesh.

In the bleak brightness of the alien shore, under a sun which gave no heat, their bodies shone like stars in the night and they turned towards the forest, quietly.

"Are we trapped, then, in this Realm of Chaos?" Rackhir said at length. "If we meet someone, they will offer us harm — how can we ask our question?"

Then there emerged from the huge forest a great figure, naked and gnarled like the trunk of a tree, green as lime, but the face was jovial.

"Greetings, unhappy renegades," it said.

"Where is the next gate?" said Lamsar quickly.

"You almost entered it, but turned away," laughed the giant. "That sea does not exist — it is there to stop travellers from passing through the gate."

"It exists here, in the Realm of Chaos," Rackhir said thickly.

"You could say so — but what exists in Chaos save the disorders of the minds of gods gone mad?"

Rackhir had strung his bone bow and fitted an arrow to the string, but he did it in the knowledge of his own hopelessness.

"Do not shoot the arrow," said Lamsar softly. "Not yet." And he stared at the arrow and muttered.

The giant advanced carelessly towards them, unhurried. "It will please me to exact the price of your crimes from you," it said, "for I am Hionhurn the Executioner. You will find your death pleasant — but your fate unbearable." And he came closer, his clawed hands outstretched.

"Shoot!" croaked Lamsar and Rackhir brought the bow-string to his cheek, pulled it back with might and released the arrow at the giant's heart. "Run!" cried Lamsar, and in spite of their forebodings they ran back down the shore towards the frightful sea. They heard the giant groan behind them as they reached the edge of the sea and, instead of running into water, found themselves in a range of stark mountains.

"No mortal arrow could have delayed him," Rackhir said. "How did you stop him?"

"I used an old charm — the Charm of Justice, which, when applied to any weapon, makes it strike at the unjust."

"But why did it hurt Hionhurn, an immortal?" Rackhir asked.

"There is no justice in the world of Chaos — something constant and inflexible, whatever its nature, must harm any servant of the Lords of Chaos."

"We have passed through the third gate," Rackhir said, unstringing his bow, "and have the fourth and fifth to find. Two dangers have been avoided — but what new ones will we encounter now?"

"Who knows?" said Lamsar, and they walked on through the rocky mountain pass and entered a forest that was cool, even though the sun had reached its zenith and was glaring down through parts of the thick foliage. There was an air of ancient calm about the place. They heard unfamiliar bird-calls and saw tiny golden birds which were also new to them.

"There is something calm and peaceful about this place — I almost distrust it," Rackhir said, but Lamsar pointed ahead silently.

Rackhir saw a large domed building, magnificent in marble and blue mosaic. It stood in a clearing of yellow grass and the marble caught the sun, flashing like fire.

They neared the domed construction and saw that it was supported by big marble columns set into a platform of milky jade. In the center of the platform a stairway of blue-stone curved upwards and disappeared into a circular aperture. There were wide windows set into the sides of the raised building but they could not see inside. There were no inhabitants visible and it would have seemed strange to the pair if there had been. They crossed the yellow glade and stepped on to the jade platform. It was warm, as if it had been exposed to the sun. They almost slipped on the smooth stone.

They reached the blue steps and mounted them, staring upwards, but they could still see nothing. They did not attempt to ask themselves why they were so assuredly invading the building; it seemed quite natural that they should do what they were doing. There was no alternative. There was an air of familiarity about the place. Rackhir felt it but did not know why. Inside was a cool, shadowy hall, a blend of soft darkness and bright sunlight which entered by the windows. The floor was pearl-pink and the ceiling deep scarlet. The hall reminded Rackhir of a womb.

Partially hidden by deep shadow was a small doorway and beyond it, steps. Rackhir looked questioningly at Lamsar. "Do we proceed in our exploration?"

"We must — to have our question answered, if possible."

They climbed the steps and found themselves in a smaller hall similar to the one beneath them. This hall, however, was furnished with twelve wide thrones placed in a semicircle in the center. Against the wall, near the door, were several chairs, upholstered in purple fabric. The thrones were of gold, decorated with fine silver, padded with white cloth.

A door behind the throne opened and a tall, fragile-looking man appeared, followed by others whose faces were almost identical. Only their robes were noticeably different. Their faces were pale, almost white, their noses straight, their lips thin but not cruel. Their eyes were unhuman — green-flecked eyes which stared outwards with sad composure. The leader of the tall men looked at Rackhir and Lamsar. He nodded and waved a pale, long-fingered hand gracefully.

"Welcome," he said. His voice was high and frail, like a girl's, but beautiful in its modulation. The other eleven men seated themselves in the thrones but the first man who had spoken, remained standing. "Sit down, please," he said.

Rackhir and Lamsar sat down on two of the purple chairs.

"How did you come here?" inquired the man.

"Through the gates from Chaos," Lamsar replied.

"And were you seeking our realm?"

"No — we travel towards the Domain of the Grey Lords."

"I thought so, for your people rarely visit us save by accident."

"Where are we?" asked Rackhir as the man seated himself in the remaining throne.

"In a place beyond time. Once our land was part of the earth you know, but in the dim past it became separated from it. Our bodies, unlike yours, are immortal. We choose this, but we are not bound to our flesh, as you are."

"I don't understand," frowned Rackhir. "What are you saying?"

"I have said what I can in the simplest terms understandable to you. If you do not know what I say then I can explain no further. We are called the Guardians — though we guard nothing. We are warriors, but we fight nothing."

"What else do you do?" inquired Rackhir.

"We exist. You will want to know where the next gateway lies?"

"Yes."

"Refresh yourselves here, and then we shall show you the gateway."

"What is your function," asked Rackhir.

"To function," said the man.

"You are unhuman!"

"We are human. You spend your lives chasing that which is within you and that which you can find in any other human being — but you will not look for it there — you must follow more glamorous paths — to waste your time in order to discover that you wasted your time. I am glad that we are no longer like you — but I wish that it were lawful to help you further. This, however, we may not do."

"Ours is no meaningless quest," said Lamsar quietly, with respect. "We go to rescue Tanelorn."

"Tanelorn?" the man said softly. "Does Tanelorn still remain?"

"Aye," said Rackhir, "and shelters tired folk who are grateful for the rest she offers." Now he realized why the building had been familiar — it had the same quality, but intensified, as Tanelorn.

"Tanelorn was the last of our cities," said the Guardian. "Forgive us for judging you — most of the travellers who pass through this plane are searchers, restless, with no real purpose, only excuses, imaginary reasons for journeying on. you must love Tanelorn to brave the dangers of the gateways?"

"We do," said Rackhir, "and I am grateful that you built her."

"We built her for ourselves, but it is good that others have used her well — and she them."

"Will you help us?" Rackhir said. "For Tanelorn?"

"We cannot — it is not lawful. Now, refresh yourselves and be welcome."

The two travellers were given foods, both soft and brittle, sweet and sour, and drink which seemed to enter the pores of their skin as they quaffed it, and then the Guardian said: "We have caused a road to be made. Follow it and enter the next realm. But we warn you, it is the most dangerous of all."

And they set off down the road that the Guardians had caused to be made and passed through the fourth gateway into a dreadful realm — the Realm of Law.

Nothing shone in the grey-lit sky, nothing moved, nothing marred the grey.

Nothing interrupted the bleak grey plain stretching on all sides of them, forever. There was no horizon. it was a bright, clean wasteland. But there was a sense about the air, a presence of something past, something which had gone but left a faint aura of its passing.

"What dangers could be here?" said Rackhir shuddering, "here where there is nothing?"

"The danger of the loneliest madness," Lamsar replied. Their voices were swallowed in the grey expanse.

"When the Earth was very young," Lamsar continued, his words trailing away across the wilderness, "things were like this — but there were seas, there were seas. Here there is nothing."

"You are wrong," Rackhir said with a faint smile. "I have thought — here there is Law."

"That is true — but what is Law without something to decide between? Here is Law — bereft of justice."

They walked on, all about them an air of something intangible that had once been tangible. On they walked through this barren world of Absolute Law.

Eventually, Rackhir spied something. Something that flickered, faded, appeared again until, as they neared it, they saw that it was a man. His great head was noble, firm, and his body was massively built, but the face was twisted in a tortured frown and he did not see them as they approached him.

They stopped before him and Lamsar coughed to attract his attention. The man turned that great head and regarded them abstractedly, the frown clearing at length, to be replaced by a calmer, thoughtful expression.

"Who are you?" asked Rackhir.

The man sighed. "Not yet," he said, "not yet, it seems. More phantoms."

"Are *we* the phantoms?" Rackhir smiled. "That seems to be more your own nature." He watched as the man began slowly to fade again, his form less definite, melting. The body seemed to make a great heave, like a salmon attempting to leap a dam, then it was back again in a more solid form.

"I had thought myself rid of all that was superfluous, save my own obstinate shape," the man said tiredly, "but here is something, back again. Is my reason failing — is my logic no longer what it was?"

"Do not fear," said Rackhir, "we are material beings."

"That is what I feared. For an eternity I have been stripping away the layers of unreality which obscure the truth. I have almost succeeded in the final act, and now you begin to creep back. My mind is not what it was, I think."

"Perhaps you worry lest we do not exist?" Lamsar said slowly, with a clever smile.

"You know that is not so — you do not exist, just as I do not exist." The frown returned, the features twisted, the body began again to fade, only to resume once more its earlier nature. The man sighed. "Even to reply to you is betraying myself, but I suppose a little relaxation will serve to rest my powers and equip me for the final effort of will which will bring me to the ultimate truth — the truth of non-being."

"But non-being involves non-thought, non-will, non-action," Lamsar said.

"Surely you would not submit yourself to such a fate?"

"There is no such thing as self. I am the only reasoning thing in creation — I am almost pure reason. A little more effort and I shall be what I desire to be — the one truth in this non-existent universe. That requires first ridding myself of anything extraneous around me — such as yourselves — and then making the final plunge into the only reality."

"What is that?"

"The state of absolute nothingness where there is nothing to disturb the order of things because there is no order of things."

"Scarcely a constructive ambition," Rackhir said.

"Construction is a meaningless word — like all words, like all so-called existence. Everything means nothing — that is the only truth."

"But what of this realm? Barren as it is, it still has light and firm rock. You have not succeeded in reasoning that out of existence," Lamsar said.

"That will cease when I cease," the man said slowly, "Just as you will cease to be. Then there can be nothing but nothing and Law will reign unchallenged."

"But Law cannot reign — it will not exist either, according to your logic."

"You are wrong — nothingness is the Law. Nothingness is the object of Law. Law is the way to its ultimate state, the state of non-being."

"Well," said Lamsar musingly, "then you had better tell us where we may find the next gate."

"There is no gate."

"If there were, where would we find it?" Rackhir said.

"If a gate existed, and it does not, it would have been inside the mountain, close to what was once called the Sea of Peace."

"And where was that?" Rackhir asked, conscious, now of their terrible predicament. There were no landmarks, no sun, no stars — nothing by which they could determine direction.

"Close to the Mountain of Severity."

"Which way do you go?" Lamsar inquired of the man.

"Out — beyond — to nowhere."

"And where, if you succeed in your object, will we be consigned?"

"To some other nowhere. I cannot truthfully answer. But since you have never existed in reality, therefore you can go on to no non-reality. Only I am real — and I do not exist."

"We are getting nowhere," said Rackhir with a smirk which changed to a frown.

THE ETERNAL CHAMPION

"It is only my mind which holds the non-reality at bay," the man said, "and I must concentrate or else it will all come flooding back and I shall have to start from the beginning again. In the beginning, there was everything — Chaos. I *created* nothing."

With resignation, Rackhir strung his bow, fitted an arrow to the string and aimed at the frowning man.

"You wish for non-being?" he said.

"I have told you so."

Rackhir's arrow pierced his heart, his body faded, became solid and slumped to the grass as mountains, forests, and rivers appeared around them. It was still a peaceful, well-ordered realm and Rackhir and Lamsar, as they strode on in search of the Mountain of Severity, savored it. There seemed to be no animal life here and they talked, in puzzled terms, about the man they had been forced to kill, until, at length, they reached a great smooth pyramid which seemed, though it was of natural origin, to have been carved into this form. They walked around its base until they discovered an opening.

There could be no doubt that this was the Mountain of Severity, and a calm ocean lay some distance away. They went into the opening and emerged into a delicate landscape.

They were now through the last gateway and in the Domain of the Grey Lords. There were trees like stiffened spider-webs.

Here and there were blue pools, shallow, with shining water and graceful rocks balanced in them and around their shores. Above them and beyond them the light hills swept away towards a pastel yellow horizon which was tinted with red, orange, and blue, deep blue.

They felt overlarge, clumsy, like crude, gross giants treading on the fine, short grass. They felt as if they were destroying the sanctity of the place.

Then they saw a girl come walking towards them.

She stopped as they came closer to her. She was dressed in loose black robes which flowed about her as if in a wind, but there was no wind. Her face was pale and pointed, her black eyes large and enigmatic. At her long throat was a jewel.

"Sorana," said Rackhir thickly, "you died."

"I disappeared," said she, "and this is where I came. I was told that you would come to this place and decided that I would meet you."

"But this is the Domain of the Grey Lords — and you serve Chaos."

"I do — but many are welcome at the Grey Lords' Court, whether they be of Law, Chaos, or neither. Come, I will escort you there."

Bewildered, now, Rackhir let her lead the way across the strange terrain and Lamsar followed him.

Sorana and Rackhir had been lovers once, in Yeshpotoom-Kahlai, the Unholy Fortress, where evil blossomed and was beautiful. Sorana, sorceress, adventures, was without conscience but had high regard for the Red Archer since he had come to Yeshpotoom-Kahlai one evening, covered in his own blood, survivor of a bizarre battle between the Knights of Tumbru and Loheb Bakra's brigand-engineers. Seven years ago, that had been, and he had heard her scream when the Blue Assassins had crept into the Unholy Fortress, pledged to murder evil-makers. Even then he had been in the process of hurriedly leaving Yeshpotoom-Kahlai and had considered it unwise to investigate what was obviously a death-scream. Now she was here — and if she was here, then it was for a strong reason and for her own convenience. On the other hand, it was in her interests to serve Chaos and he must be suspicious of her.

Ahead of them now they saw many great tents of shimmering grey which, in the light, seemed composed of all colours. People moved slowly among the tents and there was an air of leisure about the place.

"Here," Sorana said, smiling at him and taking his hand, "the Grey Lords hold impermanent court. They wander through their land and have few artifacts and only temporary houses which you see. They'll make you welcome if you interest them."

"But will they help us?"

"You must ask them."

"You are pledged to Eequor of Chaos," Rackhir observed, "and must aid her against us. Is that not so?"

"Here," she smiled, "is a truce. I can only inform Chaos of what I learn of your plans and, if the Grey Lords aid you, must tell them how, if I can find out."

"You are frank, Sorana."

"Here there are subtler hypocrisies — and the subtlest lie of all is the full truth," she said, as they entered the area of tall tents and made their way towards a certain one.

In a different realm of the Earth, the huge horde careered across the grasslands of the North, screaming and singing behind the black-armoured horseman, their leader. Nearer and nearer they came to lonely Tanelorn, their motley weapons shining through the evening mists. Like a boiling tidal wave of insensate flesh, the mob drove on, hysterical with the hate for Tanelorn which Narjhan had placed in their thin hearts. Thieves, murderers, jackals, scavengers — a scrawny horde, but huge...

And in Tanelorn the warriors were grim-faced as their out-riders and scouts flowed into the city with messages and estimates of the beggar army's strength.

Brut, in the silver armour of his rank, knew that two full days had passed since Rackhir had left for the Sighing Desert. Three more days and the city would be engulfed by Narjhan's mighty rabble — and they knew there was no chance of halting their advance. They might have left Tanelorn to its fate, but they would not. Even weak Uroch would not. For Tanelorn the Mysterious had given them all a secret power which each believed to be his only, a strength which filled them where before they had been hollow men. Selfishly, they stayed — for to leave Tanelorn to her fate would be to become hollow again, and that they all dreaded.

Brut was the leader and he prepared the defense of Tanelorn — a defense which might just have held against the beggar army — but not against it and Chaos. Brut shuddered when he thought that if Chaos had directed its full force against Tanelorn, they would be sobbing in Hell at that moment.

Dust rose high above Tanelorn, sent flying by the hooves of the scouts' and messengers' horses. One came through the gate as Brut watched. He pulled his mount to a stop before the nobleman. He was the messenger from Kaarlak, by the Weeping Waste, one of the nearest major cities to Tanelorn.

The messenger gasped: "I asked Kaarlak for aid but, as we supposed, they had never heard of Tanelorn and suspected that I was an emissary from the beggar army sent to lead their few forces into a trap. I pleaded with the Senators, but they would do nothing."

"Was not Elric there — he knows Tanelorn?"

"No, he was not there. There is a rumour which says that he himself fights Chaos now, for the minions of Chaos captured his wife Zarozinia and he rides in pursuit of them. Chaos, it seems, gains strength everywhere in our realm."

Brut was pale.

"What of Jadmar — will Jadmar send warriors?" The messenger spoke urgently, for many had been sent to the nearer cities to solicit aid.

"I do not know," replied Brut, "and it does not matter now — for the beggar army is not three days march from Tanelorn and it would take two weeks for a Jadmarian force to reach us."

"And Rackhir?"

"I have heard nothing and he has not returned. I have the feeling he'll not return. Tanelorn is doomed."

Rackhir and Lamsar bowed before the three small men who sat in the tent, but one of them said impatiently: "Do not humble yourselves before us, friends — we who are humbler than any." So they straightened their backs and waited to be further addressed.

The Grey Lords assumed humility, but this, it seemed, was their greatest ostentation, for it was a pride that they had. Rackhir realized that he would need to use subtle flattery and was not sure that he could, for he was a warrior, not a courtier or a diplomat. Lamsar, too, realized the situation and he said:

"In our pride, Lords, we have come to learn the simpler truths which are only truths — the truths which you can teach us."

The speaker gave a self-deprecating smile and replied: "Truth is not for us to define, guest, we can but offer our incomplete thoughts. They might interest you or help you to find your own truths."

"Indeed, that is so," Rackhir said, not wholly sure with what he was agreeing, but judging it best to agree. "And we wondered if you had any suggestions on a matter which concerns us — the protection of our Tanelorn."

"We would not be so prideful as to interfere with our own comments. We are not mighty intellects," the speaker replied blandly, "and we have no confidence in our own decisions, for who knows that they may be wrong and based on wrongly assessed information?"

"Indeed," said Lamsar, judging that he must flatter them with their own assumed humility, "and it is lucky for us, Lords, that we do not confuse pride with learning — for it is the quiet man who observes and says little who sees the most. Therefore, though we realize that you are not confident that your suggestions or help would be useful, none the less we, taking example from your own demeanor, humbly ask if you know of any way in which we might rescue Tanelorn?"

Rackhir had hardly been able to follow the complexities of Lamsar's seemingly unsophisticated argument, but he saw that the Grey Lords were pleased. Out of the corner of his eye he observed Sorana. She was smiling to herself and it seemed evident, by the characteristics of that smile, that they had behaved in the right way. Now Sorana was listening intently and Rackhir cursed to himself that the Lords of Chaos would know of everything and might, even if they did gain the Grey Lords' aid, still be able to anticipate and stop any action they took to save Tanelorn.

The speaker conferred in a liquid speech with his fellows and said finally: "Rarely do we have the privilege to entertain such brave and intelligent men. How may our insignificant minds be put to your advantage?"

Rackhir realized quite suddenly, and almost laughed, that the Grey Lords were not very clever after all. Their flattery had got them the help they required. He said:

"Narjhan of Chaos heads a huge army of human scum — a beggar army — and is sworn to tear down Tanelorn and kill her inhabitants. We need magical aid of some kind to combat one so powerful as Narjhan *and* defeat the beggars."

"But Tanelorn cannot be destroyed . . ." said a Grey Lord. "She is Eternal . . ." said another. "But this manifestation . . ." murmured the third, "Ah, yes . . ."

"There are beetles in Kaleef," said a Grey Lord, "which emit a peculiar venom."

"Beetles, Lord?" said Rackhir.

"They are the size of mammoths," said the third Lord, "but can change their size — and change the size of their prey if it is too large for their gullets."

"As for that matter," the first speaker said, "there is a chimera which dwells in the mountains south of here — it can change its shape and contains hate for Chaos since Chaos bred it and abandoned it with no real shape of its own."

"Then there are four brothers of Himerscahl who are endowed with sorcerous power," said the second Lord, but the first interrupted him:

"Their magic is no good outside our own dimension," he said. "I had thought, however, of reviving the Blue Wizard."

"Too dangerous and, anyway, beyond our powers," said his companion.

They continued to debate for a while, and Rackhir and Lamsar said nothing, but waited.

Eventually the first speaker said:

"The Boatmen of Xerlerenes, we have decided, will probably be best equipped to aid you in defense of Tanelorn. You must go to the mountains of Xerlerenes and find their lake."

"A lake," said Lamsar, "in a range of mountains, I see."

"No," the Lord said, "their lake lies above the mountains. We will find someone to take you there. Perhaps they will aid you."

"You can guarantee nothing else?"

"Nothing — it is not our business to interfere. It is up to them to decide whether they will aid you or not."

"I see," said Rackhir, "thank you."

How much time had passed since he had left Tanelorn? How much time before Narjhan's beggar army reached the city? Or had it already done so?

Suddenly he thought of something, looked for Sorana, but she had left the tent.

"Where lies Xerlerenes?" Lamsar was asking.

"Not in our realm," one of the Grey Lords replied. "Come we will find you a guide."

Sorana spoke the necessary word which took her immediately into the blue half-world with which she was so familiar. There were no other colours in it, but many, many shades of blue. Here she waited until Eequor noticed her presence. In the timelessness, she could not tell how long she had waited.

The beggar horde came to an undisciplined and slow halt at a sign from its leader. A voice rang hollowly from the helm that was always closed.

"Tomorrow, we march against Tanelorn — the time we have anticipated is almost upon us. Make camp now. Tomorrow shall Tanelorn be punished and the stones of her little houses will be dust on the wind."

The million beggars cackled their glee and wetted their scrawny lips. Not one of them asked why they had marched so far, and this was because of Narjhan's power.

In Tanelorn, Brut and Zas the One-handed discussed the nature of death in quiet, over-controlled tones. Both were filled with sadness, less for themselves than for Tanelorn, soon to perish. Outside, a pitiful army tried to place a cordon around the town but failed to fill the gaps between men, there were so few of them. Lights in the houses burned as if for the last time, and candles guttered moodily.

Sorana, sweating as she always did after such an episode, returned to the plane occupied by the Grey Lords and discovered that Rackhir, Lamsar, and their guide were preparing to leave. Eequor had told her what to do — it was for her to contact Narjhan. The rest the Lords of Chaos would accomplish. She blew her ex-lover a kiss as he rode from the camp into the night. He grinned at her defiantly, but when his face was turned from her he frowned and they went in silence into the Valley of the Currents where they entered the realm where lay the Mountains of Xerlerenes. Almost as soon as they arrived, danger presented itself.

Their guide, a wanderer called Timeras, pointed into the night sky which was spiked by the outlines of crags.

"This is a world where the air elementals are dominant," he said. "Look!"

Flowing downwards in an ominous sweep they saw a flight of owls, great eyes gleaming. Only as they came nearer did the men realize that these owls were huge, almost as large as a man. In the saddle Rackhir strung his bow. Timeras said:

"How could they have learned of our presence so soon?"

"Sorana," Rackhir said, busy with the bow. "She must have warned the Lords of Chaos and they have sent these dreadful birds." As the first one homed in, great claws grasping, great beak gaping, he shot it in its feathery throat and it shrieked and swept upwards. Many arrows fled from his humming bow-string to find a mark while Timeras drew his sword and slashed at them, ducking as they whistled downwards.

Lamsar watched the battle but took no part. He seemed thoughtful at a time when action was desired of him.

He mused: "If the spirits of air are dominant in this realm, then they will resent a stronger force of other elementals," and he racked his brain to remember a spell.

Rackhir had but two arrows left in his quiver by the time they had driven the owls off. The birds had not been used, evidently, to a prey which fought back and had put up a poor fight considering their superiority.

"We can expect more danger," said Rackhir somewhat shakily, "for the Lords of Chaos will use other means to try and stop us. How far to Xerlerenes?"

"Not far," said Timeras, "but it's a hard road."

They rode on, and Lamsar rode behind them, lost in his own thoughts.

Now they urged their horses up a steep mountain path and a chasm lay below them, dropping, dropping, dropping. Rackhir, who had no love for heights, kept as close to the mountainside as was possible. If he had had gods to whom he could pray, he would have prayed for their help then.

The huge fish came flying — or swimming — at them as they rounded a bend. They were semi-luminous, big as sharks but with enlarged fins on which they planed through the air like rays. They were quite evidently fish. Timeras drew his sword, but Rackhir had only two arrows left and it would have been useless against the airfish to have shot them, for there were many of them.

But Lamsar laughed and spoke in a high-pitched, staccato speech.

"*Crackhor — pishtasta salaflar!*"

Huge balls of flame materialized against the black sky — flaring balls of multicoloured fire which shaped themselves into strange, war-like forms and streamed towards the unnatural fish.

The flame-shapes seared into the big fish and they shrieked, struck at the fire-balls, burned, and fell flaming down the deep gorge.

"Fire elementals!" Rackhir exclaimed.

"The spirits of the air fear such beings," Lamsar said calmly.

The flame-beings accompanied them the rest of the way to Xerlerenes and were with them when dawn came, having frightened away many other dangers which the Lords of Chaos had evidently sent against them.

They saw the boats of Xerlerenes in the dawn, at anchor on a calm sky, fluffy clouds playing around their slender keels, their huge sails furled.

"The boatmen live aboard their vessels," Timeras said, "for it is only their ships which deny the laws of nature, not they."

Timeras cupped his hands about his mouth and called through the still mountain air: "Boatmen of Xerlerenes, freemen of the air, guests come with a request for aid!"

A black and bearded face appeared over the side of one of the red-gold vessels. The man shielded his eyes against the rising sun and stared down at them. Then he disappeared again.

At length a ladder of slim thongs came snaking down to where they sat their horses on the tops of the mountains. Timeras grasped it, tested it and began to climb. Rackhir reached out and steadied the ladder for him. It seemed too thin to support a man but when he had it in his hands he knew that it was the strongest he had ever known.

Lamsar grumbled as Rackhir signaled for him to climb, but he did so and quite nimbly. Rackhir was the last, following his companions, climbing up through the sky high above the crags, towards the ship that sailed on the air.

The fleet comprised some twenty or thirty ships and Rackhir felt that with these to aid him, there was good chance to rescue Tanelorn — if Tanelorn survived. Narjhan would, anyway, be aware of the nature of the aid he sought.

Starved dogs barked the morning in and the beggar horde, waking from where they had sprawled on the ground, saw Narjhan already mounted, but talking to a newcomer, a girl in black robes that moved as if in a wind — but there was no wind. There was a jewel at her long throat.

When he had finished conversing with the newcomer, Narjhan ordered a horse be brought for her and she rode slightly behind him when the beggar army moved on — the last stage of their hateful journey to Tanelorn.

When they saw lovely Tanelorn and how it was so poorly guarded, the beggars laughed, but Narjhan and his new companion looked up into the sky.

"There may be time," said the hollow voice, and gave the order to attack.

Howling, the beggars broke into a run towards Tanelorn. The attack had started.

Brut rose in his saddle and there were tears flowing down his face and glistening in his beard. His huge war-axe was in one gauntleted hand and the other held a spiked mace across the saddle before him.

Zas the One-handed gripped the long and heavy broadsword with its pommel of a rampant golden lion pointed downwards. This blade had won him a crown in Andlermaigne, but he doubted whether it would successfully defend his peace in Tanelorn. Beside him stood Uroch of Nieva, pale-faced but angry as he watched the ragged horde's implacable approach.

Then, yelling, the beggars met with the warriors of Tanelorn and, although greatly outnumbered, the warriors fought desperately, for they were defending more than life or love — they were defending that which had told them of a reason for living.

Narjhan sat his horse aside from the battle, Sorana next to him, for Narjhan could take no active part in the battle, could only watch and, if necessary, use magic to aid his human pawns or defend his person.

The warriors of Tanelorn, incredibly, held back the roaring beggar horde, their weapons drenched with blood, rising and falling in that sea of moving flesh, flashing in the light of the red dawn.

Sweat now mingled with the salt tears in Brut's bristling beard and with agility he leapt clear of his black horse as the screaming beast was cut from under him. The noble war-cry of his forefathers sang on his breath and, although in his shame he had no business to use it, he let it roar from him as he slashed about him with biting war-axe and rending mace. But he fought hopelessly, for Rackhir had not come and Tanelorn was soon to die. His one fierce consolation was that he would die with the city, his blood mingling with its ashes.

Zas, also, acquitted himself very well before he died of a smashed skull. His old body twitched as trampling feet stumbled over it as the beggars made for Uroch of Nieva. The gold-pommelled sword was still gripped in his single hand and his soul was fleeing for Limbo as Uroch, too, was slain fighting.

Then the Ships of Xerlerenes suddenly materialized in the sky and Brut, looking upward for an instant, knew that Rackhir had come at last — though it might be too late.

Narjhan, also, saw the Ships and was prepared for them.

They skimmed through the sky, the fire elementals which Lamsar had summoned, flying with them. The spirits of air and flame had been called to rescue weakening Tanelorn ...

The Boatmen prepared their lines and made themselves ready for war. Their black faces had a concentrated look and they grinned in their bushy beards. War-harness clothed them and they bristled with weapons — long, barbed tridents, nets of steel mesh, curved swords, long harpoons. Rackhir stood in the prow of the leading ship, his quiver packed with slim arrows loaned him by the Boatmen. Below him he saw Tanelorn and was relieved that the city still stood.

He could see the milling warriors below, but it was hard to tell, from the air, which were friends and which were foes. Lamsar called to the frisking fire elementals, instructing them. Timeras grinned and held his sword ready as the ships rocked on the wind and dropped lower.

Now Rackhir observed Narjhan with Sorana beside him.

"The bitch has warned him — he is ready for us," Rackhir said, wetting his lips and drawing an arrow from his quiver.

Down the Ships of Xerlerenes dropped, coursing on the currents of air, their golden sails billowing, the warrior crews straining over the side and keen for battle.

Then Narjhan summoned the *Kyrenee*.

Huge as a storm-cloud, black as its native Hell, the *Kyrenee* grew from the surrounding air and moved its shapeless bulk forward towards the Ships of Xerlerenes, sending out flowing tendrils of poison towards them. Boatmen groaned as the coils curled around their naked bodies and crushed them.

Lamsar called urgently to his fire elementals and they rose again from where they had been devouring beggars, came together in one great blossoming of flame which moved to do battle with the *Kyrenee*.

The two masses met and there was an explosion which blinded the Red Archer with multi-coloured light and sent the Ships rocking and shaking so that several capsized and sent their crews hurtling downwards to death.

THE ETERNAL CHAMPION

Blotches of flame flew everywhere and patches of poison blackness from the body of the *Kyrenee* were flung about, slaying those they touched before disappearing.

There was a terrible stink in the air — a smell of burning, a smell of outraged elements which had never been meant to meet.

The *Kyrenee* died, lashing about a-wailing, while the flame elementals, dying or returning to their own sphere, faded and vanished. The remaining bulk of the great *Kyrenee* billowed slowly down to the earth where it fell upon the scrabbling beggars and killed them, leaving nothing but a wet patch on the ground for yards around, a patch glistening with the bones of beggars.

Now Rackhir cried: "Quickly — finish the fight before Narjhan summons more horrors!"

And the boats sailed downwards while the Boatmen cast their steel nets, pulling large catches of beggars aboard their Ships and finishing the wriggling starvelings with their tridents or spears.

Rackhir shot arrow after arrow and had the satisfaction of seeing each one take a beggar just where he had aimed it. The remaining warriors of Tanelorn, led by Brut who was covered in sticky blood but grinning in his victory, charged towards the unnerved beggars.

Narjhan stood his ground, while the beggars, fleeing, streamed past him and the girl. Sorana, frightened, looked up and her eyes met Rackhir's. The Red Archer aimed an arrow at her, thought better of it and shot instead at Narjhan. The arrow went into the black armour but had no effect upon the Lord of Chaos.

Then the Boatmen of Xerlerenes flung down their largest net from the vessel in which Rackhir sailed and they caught Lord Narjhan in its coils and caught Sorana, too.

Shouting their exhilaration, they pulled the struggling bodies aboard and Rackhir ran forward to inspect their catch. Sorana had received a scratch across her face from the net's wire, but the body of Narjhan lay still and dreadful in the mesh.

Rackhir grabbed an axe from a Boatman and knocked back the helm, his foot upon the chest.

"Yield, Narjhan of Chaos!" he cried in mindless merriment. He was near hysterical with victory, for this was the first time a mortal had ever bested a Lord of Chaos.

But the armour was empty, if it had ever been occupied by flesh, and

Narjhan was gone.

Calm settled aboard the Ships of Xerlerenes and over the city of Tanelorn. The remnants of the warriors had gathered in the city's square and were cheering their victory.

Friagho, the Captain of Xerlerenes, came up to Rackhir and shrugged. "We did not get the catch we came for — but these will do. Thanks for the fishing, friend."

Rackhir smiled and gripped Friagho's black shoulder. "Thanks for the aid — you have done us all a great service." Friagho shrugged again and turned back to his nets, his trident poised. Suddenly Rackhir shouted: "No, Friagho — let that one be. Let me have the contents of that net."

Sorana, the contents to which he'd referred, looked anxious as if she had rather been transfixed on the prongs of Friagho's trident. Friagho said: "Very well, Red Archer — there are plenty more people on the land." He pulled at the net to release her.

She stood up shakily, looking at Rackhir apprehensively.

Rackhir smiled quite softly and said: "Come here, Sorana." She went to him and stood staring up at his bony hawk's face, her eyes wide. With a laugh he picked her up and flung her over his shoulder.

"Tanelorn is safe!" he shouted. "You shall learn to love its peace with me!" And he began to clamber down the trailing ladders that the Boatmen had dropped over the side.

Lamsar waited for him below. "I go now, to my hermitage again."

"I thank you for your aid," said Rackhir. "Without it Tanelorn would no longer exist."

"Tanelorn will always exist while men exist," said the hermit. "It was not a city you defended today. It was an ideal. That is Tanelorn."

And Lamsar smiled.

THE END

OF THE FIRST VOLUME

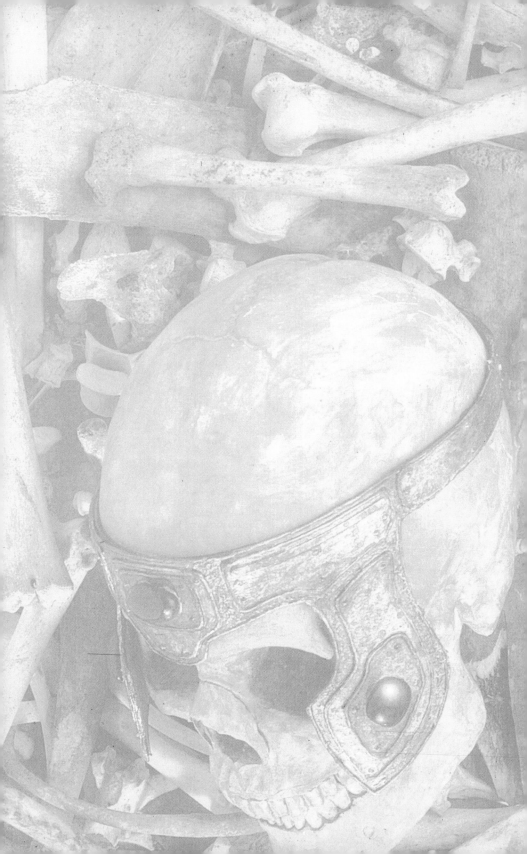